CRITICS' PRAISE

SNOW

"A captivating story of three friends on opposing sides of a
betrayal ... a well-paced tale with intricate storylines."
– *Kirkus*

"An action-packed adventure, but also a morality tale of
what happens when two men who should know better
get entangled in a crime from which they can't escape."
– *Denver Post*

"More than just a thriller, *Snow* lights up the complexities
of American culture, the tensions of morality and
obligation and the human search for love and freedom, all
of which makes it clear Bond is a masterful storyteller."
– *Sacramento Bee*

"A complex interplay of fascinating characters." – *Culture Buzz*

"Exploring the psyche and the depths of human reasoning and
drive, *Snow* is a captivating story." – *BookTrib*

"An action-packed thriller that wouldn't let go. The heart-
pounding scenes kept me on the edge of my seat."
– *Goodreads*

"A simple story at its heart that warps into a splendid morality
tale." – *Providence Sunday Journal*

"An epic spy story ... Bond often writes with a staccato beat, in sentence fragments with the effect of bullet fire. His dialogue is sharp and his description of combat is tactical and detached, professional as a soldier's debriefing. Yet this terseness is rife with tension and feeling ... A cohesive and compelling story of political intrigue, religious fanaticism, love, brotherhood and the ultimate pursuit of peace."
– *Honolulu Star-Advertiser*

"An exhilarating spy novel that offers equal amounts of ingenuity and intrigue." – *Kirkus*

"Packs one thrilling punch after the other ... A first-rate thriller." – *Book Chase*

"Powerful, true to life, and explosive ... The energy is palpable and the danger is real ... A story that could be ripped right out of the headlines." – *Just Reviews*

"Bond is one of America's best thriller writers ... You need to get this book ... It's an eye-opener, a page-turner ... very strongly based in reality." – *Culture Buzz*

"Riveting, thrilling ... so realistic and fast-paced that the reader felt as if they were actually there." – *NetGalley*

"The action is outstanding and realistic. The suspense flows from page to page ... The background is provided by recent events we have all lived through. The flow of the writing is almost musical as romance and horrors share equal billing ... I wish everyone could read and understand this book."
– *Goodreads*

KILLING MAINE
(A PONO HAWKINS THRILLER)

FIRST PRIZE FOR FICTION, 2016, *New England Book Festival*:
"A gripping tale of murders, manhunts and other crimes
set amidst today's dirty politics and corporate graft, an
unforgettable hero facing enormous dangers as he tries to
save a friend, protect the women he loves, and defend a
beautiful, endangered place."

"Another terrifically entertaining read from a master of the
storytelling craft ... A work of compelling fiction ... Very
highly recommended." – *Midwest Book Review*

"Quite a ride for those who love good crime thrillers ... I can't
recommend this one strongly enough." – *Book Chase*

"Bond returns with another winner in *Killing Maine*. Bond's
ability to infuse his real-world experiences into a fast-paced
story is unequaled." – *Culture Buzz*

"The suspense, mystery, and intrigue will keep you on the edge
of your seat." – *Goodreads*

"Bond tackles many important social and environmental
issues in a fast-paced, politically charged plot with a
passionate main character. *Killing Maine* is a twisting
mystery with enough suspicious characters and red
herrings to keep you guessing. It's also a dire warning
about the power of big industry and a commentary on our
modern ecological responsibilities. A great read for the
socially and environmentally conscious mystery lover."
– *Honolulu Star-Advertiser*

"Sucks in the reader and makes it difficult to put the book
down until the very last page ... A winner of a thriller."
– *Mystery Maven*

"Another stellar ride from Bond; checking out Pono's first
adventure isn't a prerequisite, but this will make readers
want to." – *Kirkus*

SAVING PARADISE
(A PONO HAWKINS THRILLER)

"Bond is one of the 21st century's most exciting authors …
An action-packed, must read novel … taking readers behind
the alluring façade of Hawaii's pristine beaches and tourist
traps into a festering underworld of murder, intrigue and
corruption." – *Washington Times*

"A complex, entertaining … lusciously convoluted story."
– *Kirkus*

"Highly recommended." – *Midwest Book Review*

"A rousing crime thriller – but it is so much more … a highly
atmospheric thriller focusing on a side of Hawaiian life that
tourists seldom see." – *Book Chase*

"An intersection of fiction and real life." – *Hawaii Public Radio*

"An absolute page-turner." – *Ecotopia Radio*

"An unusual thriller and a must-read." – *Fresh Fiction*

"A complex murder mystery about political and corporate greed
and corruption … Bond's vivid descriptions of Hawaii bring
Saving Paradise vibrantly to life." – *Book Reviews and More*

"*Saving Paradise* will change you … It will call into question
what little you really know, what people want you to believe
you know and then hit you with a deep wave of dangerous
truths." – *Where Truth Meets Fiction*

HOLY WAR

"An action-filled thriller." – *Manchester Evening News (UK)*

"This suspense-laden novel has a never-ending sense of impending doom ... An unyielding tension leaves a lasting impression." – *Kirkus*

"A profound tale of war ... Impossible to stop reading."
– *British Armed Forces Broadcasting*

"A terrific book ... The smells, taste, noise, dust, and fear are communicated so clearly." – *Great Book Escapes*

"A supercharged thriller ... A story to chill and haunt you."
– *Peterborough Evening Telegraph (UK)*

"A tale of fear, hatred, revenge, and desire, flicking between bloody Beirut and the lesser battles of London and Paris."
– *Evening Herald (UK)*

"If you are looking to get a driver's seat look at the landscape of modern conflict, holy wars, and the Middle East then this is the perfect book to do so." – *Masterful Book Reviews*

"A stunning novel of love and loss, good and evil, of real people who live in our hearts after the last page is done ...Unusual and profound." – *Greater London Radio*

HOUSE OF JAGUAR

"A riveting thriller of murder, politics, and lies."
– *London Broadcasting*

"Tough and tense thriller." – *Manchester Evening News (UK)*

"A high-octane story rife with action, from U.S. streets to Guatemalan jungles." – *Kirkus*

"A terrifying depiction of one man's battle against the CIA and Latin American death squads." – *BBC*

"Vicious thriller of drugs and revolution in the wilds of Guatemala." – *Liverpool Daily Post (UK)*

"With detailed descriptions of actual jungle battles and manhunts, vanishing rain forests and the ferocity of guerrilla war, *House of Jaguar* also reveals the CIA's role in both death squads and drug running, twin scourges of Central America." – *Newton Chronicle (UK)*

"Bond grips the reader from the very first page. An ideal thriller for the beach, but be prepared to be there when the sun goes down." – *Herald Express (UK)*

THE LAST SAVANNA

FIRST PRIZE FOR FICTION, 2016, *Los Angeles Book Festival*: "One of the best books yet on Africa, a stunning tale of love and loss amid a magnificent wilderness and its myriad animals, and a deadly manhunt through savage jungles, steep mountains and fierce deserts as an SAS commando tries to save the elephants, the woman he loves and the soul of Africa itself."

"A gripping thriller." – *Liverpool Daily Post (UK)*

"Dynamic, heart-breaking and timely to current events … a must-read." – *Yahoo Reviews*

"Sheer intensity, depicting the immense, arid land and never-ending scenes … but it's the volatile nature of nature itself that gives the story its greatest distinction." – *Kirkus*

"One of the most darkly beautiful books you will ever read." – *WordDreams*

"Exciting, action-packed … A nightmarish vision of Africa."
 – *Manchester Evening News (UK)*

"Unrelenting in its portrait of the modern African reality."
 – *Mystery File*

"A powerful love story set in the savage jungles and deserts of East Africa." – *Daily Examiner (UK)*

"The central figure is not human; it is the barren, terrifying landscape of Northern Kenya and the deadly creatures who inhabit it." – *Daily Telegraph (UK)*

"An entrancing, terrifying vision of Africa." – *BBC*

"From the opening page maintains an exhilarating pace until the closing line … A highly entertaining and gripping read."
 – *East African Wild Life Society*

TIBETAN CROSS

"Bond's deft thriller will reinforce your worst fears … A taut, tense tale of pursuit through exotic and unsavory locales."
 – *Publishers Weekly*

"Grips the reader from the very first chapter until the climactic ending." – *UPI*

"One of the most exciting in recent fiction … An astonishing thriller." – *San Francisco Examiner*

"A tautly written study of one man's descent into living hell … a mood of near claustrophobic intensity."
 – *Spokane Chronicle*

"It *is* a thriller … Incredible, but also believable."
 – *Associated Press*

"A thriller that everyone should go out and buy right away.
    The writing is wonderful throughout ... Bond working
    that fatalistic margin where life and death are one and
    the existential reality leaves one caring only to survive."
    – *Sunday Oregonian*

"Murderous intensity ... A tense and graphically written story."
    – *Richmond Times*

"The most jaundiced adventure fan will be held by
    Tibetan Cross." – *Sacramento Bee*

"Grips the reader from the opening chapter and never lets go."
    – *Miami Herald*

GOODBYE PARIS

ALSO BY MIKE BOND

NOVELS

Snow

Assassins

Holy War

House of Jaguar

The Last Savanna

Tibetan Cross

PONO HAWKINS THRILLERS

Saving Paradise

Killing Maine

POETRY

The Drum That Beats Within Us

GOODBYE PARIS

A PONO HAWKINS THRILLER

MIKE BOND

BIG CITY PRESS
NEW YORK

Big City Press, New York, NY 10014

Published in the United States by Big City Press

LIBRARY OF CONGRESS CATALOGING-IN-PUBLICATION DATA
Bond, Mike – author
Goodbye Paris / Mike Bond

ISBN paperback: 978-1-949751-02-4
ISBN ebook: 978-1-949751-03-1

Cover and book design by John Lotte
Author photo by © PF Bentley/PFPIX.com

www.MikeBondBooks.com

for Peggy

How many cities have we destroyed,
whose inhabitants lived in ease and plenty?

– THE KORAN

Silence in the face of evil is itself evil …
To not speak is to speak. To not act is to act.

– DIETRICH BONHOEFFER

We sleep safe in our beds because rough men
stand ready in the night to visit violence on those
who would do us harm.

– GEORGE ORWELL

If you want peace, prepare for war.

– PUBLIUS VEGETIUS

THE GREAT DEEP

IT ROSE FROM THE DEEP, a huge wall of roaring green that blotted out the sky and smashed me under, whacked my surfboard into my head and punched the air from my lungs.

I was going to die.

Cold water choked my throat. My surfboard pulled me deeper, tugged down by the undertow of this monstrous wave.

My lungs filled with water, my body screamed for air. I snatched at my board leash, trying to unhook it before it pulled me to the bottom.

After years of cheating death now it had me.

All your life *does* flash before you – a bullet in Afghanistan, an RPG in Iraq, a girl's naked thigh, Pa walking through the door in Hawaii with a banana clump on his shoulder, a schoolbook never read, Ma shaking a burnt hand before the stove, Mauna Kea's vast tree-thick slope, the billion stars, the frothing water taking me down down *down* ...

Not so bad, death. Silent. Alone. The bubbling depths not unfriendly, just uncaring.

The great deep. It doesn't matter if you're here or not, but now you're here you're going to stay.

End over end I spun in its succulent whirl, ever deeper, collided with sharp rocks at the bottom, ripped a knee spurting blood and my brief fear was sharks, *but why worry about sharks when I'm dying and who cares who eats me?*

My last air unfurled like a pearl necklace toward the surface so far above – you could barely see its light – what a joke this life, to pretend it's real when all that's real is death.

WAR ZONE

LIKE A LONG-DROWNED sailor I rose to the top. Must have unleashed the surfboard. Amazing to think this, that the brain still works when the body's dead.

A wave sloshed over my head and I went under again. Something hard yanked me up, punched my gut – shark?

A surfer, bearded and long-haired. Dragged me up on the beach. Salt-blurry faces peering down.

Blue sky. I was alive.

What did that mean?

FLASHING LIGHTS all over the place. People I didn't even know squeezing my hand. So lucky to be alive.

Plastic thing over my face. Trying to choke me. Silly, when they saved my life to now try to kill me.

I leaped up and tore off the oxygen mask. Surrounded by a wall of people. "I'm fine," my voice rasped. "Let me *be!*"

Guy in a white uniform with badges took me by both arms. "Look, bro, you not fine."

"I'm fine." I tried to get out of his grasp but he was a big guy, Tahitian, the linebacker type. I peered at the badge on his chest. Some kind of medic – for a moment I feared I was back in Afghanistan and got hit and Bucky had run through bullets to save me.

Roar of the ocean. No ocean in Afghanistan. "I'm fine." Whatever happened, and I had no idea what, I was okay. I checked the sun, huge, low and orange on the foam-flecked horizon. Time to go home for sunset drink. The time every day when I and the three women I lived with would all sit on the lanai, smoke a joint or two. Lexie and I would drink Tanqueray martinis, Erica Russian vodka, and Abigail some kind of Australian rosé the color of her fiery auburn hair.

"Gotta go," I said.

The huge Tahitian medic sat me down. The way you swat a fly. I realized I was not as tough as usual. Something had made my knees weak, and my right shoulder, once injured by a bullet in Afghanistan, kept slipping out of the socket.

"So who the fuck are you?" I said to the medic, trying to be nice.

"Hey, bro," he smiled, "you almos' drown." He pointed to where the bearded surfer stood bent over, hands on knees, vomiting on the sand. "That brother, he save you."

"Surfer dude," I said, my voice rough with salt water. As if no further explanation was necessary.

And it wasn't. Surfers, like my own Special Forces, or the Rangers, SEALS, Marines, 82nd Airborne, Foreign Legion, Spetsnaz, GIGN, Israeli Defense Forces, and all those other fine military clans, take care of their own.

As all we humans should do.

———————

THEY FINALLY let me go. The ambulance blared off; I waved at the other well-wishers apparently upset over my pending death and seemingly delighted, as I was, that I was alive.

I found my board, which someone had brought ashore, and my backpack, and had the good sense to call the house, as I couldn't find the damn rental van and couldn't remember if I had driven it there in the first place. Of course Erica answered. The most ferocious of the three, maybe because she's a lawyer and bills you for every second, one way or another. But they were all fearsome, each in her own way.

Erica showed up in the rental van I thought I'd had. "They just called us," she snapped, tossing my board on the roof and giving me a smack upside the head. "Who you think you are, taking on that wave?"

I struggled to figure out what she was talking about. "Oh yeah," I said. "*That* wave."

"Yeah," she growled, reaching across to click my seat belt. "*That* wave."

"I was out there," I protested. "It came out of nowhere. I had to try –"

"You dumb fuck," she said, driving off with more than necessary acceleration from the sandy parking lot of surfer vans, leaving a little rubber on the highway like she often does with her platinum 911.

But that was back in Maine. Another lifetime though just weeks ago. This was an aged white Toyota minivan full of diving gear, beach towels, and six-packs of Hinano beer. And laying rubber was not one of its strong points.

When we got to our beachfront bungalow, Lexie and Abigail were waiting on the lanai. Unfortunately neither looked any happier than Erica, and I had a sudden desire to head back to the beach.

"I'm out of here," Abigail announced. She'd been back to her old ways, hustling surfer dudes on the beach and turning most of them down.

"I'm so *glad* I have to start teaching again," Lexie said.

"You *want* to go back to that freezing place?" I queried, voice rough with salt, thinking how cold it was now in Maine but the surfing might be good. In a wet suit.

Lexie scowled at the other two. "I never would've come ..."

"Me neither," Erica added. "I thought you invited just me."

"I did, each of you, one by one. And one by one each of you said no. Then you all came," I protested, but nobody was listening. I stubbed my toe on the threshold going into the house, poured myself a tall glass of Tanqueray, discovered some ice cubes that weren't half-melted or covered in fish scales, found a half-smoked joint, and sat on the lanai watching the magnificent fiery sun sink into the miraculous orange sea. Thanking God or whoever, for this. And that I was still *alive*.

As regards my three bedmates, I'd always assumed that the best of all possible worlds would be to live with three brilliant, independent women.

It turned out different than I'd expected. And much more fatiguing. Maybe because I was over thirty, a little past my prime, with many broken bones to prove it.

And I'd already done several tours in Afghanistan and one in Iraq, so I hated war.

And here I was back in a war zone.

True, the erotic part was fabulous. It wasn't like those silly porn movies, one guy with three women where the women are doing it to each other too. No, these women weren't at all interested in that – in fact had come to actively dislike each other but had one common priority: to screw me to death.

When all I'd done was love them.

And all I'd wanted was to live a quiet life.

And surf every day.

"Oh by the way," Lexie said, yanking at her long blonde hair as if wanting to kill it, "you got a call from some guy in Paris."

"Paris?" That magical city on the other side of the world I loved so much.

"He said his name was Mack. Said you'd know."

Mack. One of the bravest, kindest, smartest Special Forces guys I'd ever served with, both in Afghanistan and Iraq. What could he want? What was he doing in Paris?

Already it wasn't right. That he'd leave a message on an open line.

B A D   N E W S

MACK NEVER MADE MISTAKES. Big and kindly but ruthlessly efficient, he could be hilarious and emotional, and was always reliable, truthful and generous. Never once did he abuse a prisoner or risk collaterals, yet we were safer with him than nearly anyone else.

An enigma. That this huge guy could be so disciplined and dangerous, yet full of kindness and courage, and absolute determination to make the world a better place even at the risk of his life. A life which he loved intensely, from French cafés to the stark mountains of Afghanistan. He loved the rough kindness of the Afghani people yet killed those who attacked us. Most of all he loved the girls we used to meet on R&R in places like Bangkok and Sydney, and whom he tried to bed, every one. Till he met Gisèle, a French medical worker in Waziristan, with whom he fell instantly in love. As if she were the only woman he'd ever known.

All of us Special Forces guys had learned what we could about combat medicine – to save each other's lives. But Mack tried to heal everyone – American or local – spoke good Afghani and some Arabic. And no matter how hot the situation, Mack was there too, risking whatever it took for his buddies.

As we did for him.

TAHITI IS 11 HOURS behind Paris, so seven-twenty in the evening here was six-twenty a.m. tomorrow in Paris.

I called a number that validated me then connected to another. I gave them Mack's name and ID and they patched me through.

His number rang and rang. Then he answered.

"So why," I asked, "you call in the middle of your night?"

"I don't sleep much these days," he answered in his rough, gruff voice, as if you're talking to a grizzly bear. And he looks like one too, except bigger and stronger. "What you doing in Tahiti?"

I told him about the Tahiti Tsunami, the world-famous invitational longboard contest I was competing in and also reporting on for *Surfer News*.

"Who's that woman answered your phone?"

"Lexie – you remember Bucky?"

"That shithead –"

"He saved my life."

"Then sent you to Leavenworth ..."

"Anyway, she used to be his wife. And before that she and I had a thing, between two of my tours."

"She didn't seem to care if you were living or dead."

That made me chuckle, which hurt my salt-abraded throat. "Damn near did die." I told him about the monster wave that had taken me down. "What's with Paris?"

"Anybody on board?"

I glanced around. The three women were out of sight, probably all sharpening knives in the kitchen. "Nope."

"I got good news and bad news."

"What's the good?" I said, knowing it would be, as always, outweighed by the bad.

"After we pulled out of Iraq, I switched to Home Office –"

After we left Iraq meant 2011-12, when Obama pulled the plug. *Home Office* is the CIA, loved and hated by nearly every SF guy. "That sucks," I said. My own relationship with the Agency had been less than amorous, due to a few "goatfucks" as we call them, the unhappy clash between intelligence and covert action.

"– and they assigned me here, DGSE liaison."

DGSE, *La Direction Générale de la Sécurité Extérieure*, is in many ways similar to the CIA, but smaller, and more focused. For years it's fought the spread of Muslim terrorism while also battling the interference and incompetence of most French politicians and the nutty politically correct media, all who make its existence almost impossible.

Its counterpart, DGSI, *La Direction Générale de la Sécurité Intérieure*, like the FBI is responsible for domestic security, as are many smaller overlapping agencies, including ATS, the Anti-Terrorist Section of the Paris Police. Like ours, French intelligence agencies fight over turf, data sharing, and other allegedly cooperative efforts, but they've learned to work together better as terrorist attacks continue to increase.

"You're a lucky guy," I told Mack, meaning anyone who works with DGSE and lives in France is lucky, even if they have to work for the CIA.

"Remember Thierry St. Croix?"

"Of course, God love him."

"Well, he's now my opposite at DGSE."

More good news. Thierry was a French officer Mack and I had worked with in Afghanistan, attached to the Lafayette Brigade stationed at FOB Nijrab in the high steep mountains near the Paki border. About five-ten, lean and muscular, a ragged face, a scar down the right cheek and another under the chin, a typical French soldier, tough and duty-driven, but with an off-hours joyous side that made me grin just to think of him.

I'd learned to love France early in life, having gone there the first time with Pa and Ma after high school freshman year. Pa had been invited to the military college at Saint-Cyr to talk about covert operations. Even though he'd been out of the SEALS nearly ten years by then, everybody wanted him to speak, all over the world. Afterward we spent a week in Paris and climbed the Eiffel Tower and stood stunned in the ethereal beauty of Notre Dame, and rode the Métro and ate tons of pastries and went to the Louvre and lots of other haughty places, to bars and cafés smelling of *pastis* and cigarettes, to strange restaurants with hauntingly beautiful odors.

Then my junior year my parents, fearing I was becoming a Hawaiian "surfer punk" as Pa kindly put it, sent me to a bilingual high school in Paris. I disliked the studies but loved France, skipping classes to hike the Alps, surf at Biarritz, and climb the perfect limestone cliffs of the Lubéron and Mont St. Victoire.

Given my French experiences, and as Thierry was also a climber, we soon established a deep rapport during the long winter months in our Forward Operating Base in those deadly mountains.

"And the bad news?" I added, taking my mind off Thierry.

"Mustafa al-Boudienne," Mack said.

"He's dead." I could still see the narrow, unshaven face, lean, hard, almost bronze-colored. The fanatic pitiless eyes smiling at me down the barrel of his gun. "The Foreign Legion got him. North of Mosul, you know where ..."

"He's alive and well, back in France. Planning to kill as many people as he can."

"Can't be." I had that feeling in the gut that comes from horrible news. "He's an explosives guy, can kill thousands."

"Ten days ago we caught two *jihadis* sneaking back from Syria. They said he's here. So we checked all the border cameras, found him coming through Strasbourg, six weeks ago."

I felt the sorrowed fear of facing a tidal wave with sand slipping from under my feet. "Why call me?"

"You and I were the only ones to survive him. You saw more of him than me. You're really the only one who can ID him."

"I wanted to kill him, back then. While we could."

"I asked our friends at DGSE. And got backing too from our side."

"No way. I won't do it."

"All your expenses plus a nice fee?"

"I don't *want* to –"

"Look, idiot, we know you're broke. And we need you in Paris. To help us find Mustafa."

Mustafa had killed thousands of people in Iraq, including many Americans. ISIS's top bomb-maker, he could tailor an IED so we couldn't detect it, and as a result many young Americans went home in pieces, if at all. And because Mack and I had been his prisoners we were the most likely to ID him. But as Mack was blindfolded during our execution sessions and I was not, I was the best person left in this universe to recognize him. Because he'd killed everyone else who possibly could.

But after multiple combat tours in Afghanistan and Iraq, a bullet-smashed shoulder, plus two undeserved jail terms and various other miseries, I had no desire to get tied up with the Agency, which with all its constipated rules and feckless paranoias is a prison of its own. "Hey, I'm free. Making a nice living in surfing contests and writing articles, living with three women, all that ..."

"Don't you want to get Mustafa? Before he kills again?"

It had been less than two months since the tragedy of Notre Dame, and the source of the fire was still unclear. True, part of the cathedral had been saved, but its mystical and magnificent core was gone, its spirit, gone after 850 years, gone forever.

Stepping into its vast magical aura, in the ancient odor of the stones, the hazy incensed air, the eight centuries of prayer, sorrow and joy, took us to another time, another way of life.

All destroyed now.

It was losing a loved one you thought would never die. And now they were dead you couldn't think of them alive again. Never again would there be that smoky, mystical connection, so that the people who had prayed here eight hundred years ago felt close to you. Were family.

You could create a copy of what was lost, but it would be Disneyland. No way to replace the huge oaks cut in 1190 for ceiling beams. They don't exist anymore. No way to reproduce the vast brilliant glass windows through which the light scintillated like the spirit itself.

No way to reproduce the skill, art and love of workers 850 years ago. Who would probably regard us, if they could, with astonishment and scorn.

The French government, having just lost the world's greatest architectural treasure through stupidity, arrogance, negligence, laziness, and bad faith, raced to cover its ass. Fearing the fire might be due to Islamic terrorism, it had instantly announced, while the flames were still raging and the cathedral's roof was collapsing, that the catastrophe wasn't due to terrorism, although Muslim terrorists had recently tried to burn the cathedral down. The tragedy was due, the government insisted – long before anyone could possibly know – to workers renovating the roof. And when the director of the roof work stated that none of his crews had been near there before the fire, he was quickly silenced.

Though I told myself I wasn't here to sorrow over the loss of the world's greatest architectural treasure, but to help protect Paris from a new danger, the ISIS bombmaker Mustafa.

But sorrows live inside us, and over time they can grow. And as you get older, if you're lucky enough to get there, they can take over your life. Ask my Pa. Who's dead now, so you can't. Ask any veteran with a scarred face, a limp, or who can't sleep at night.

BOAR PÂTÉ

"PARIS IS ALWAYS a good idea," Audrey Hepburn once said. Even from her movies you can tell she was a lovely person, and correct about many things, including Paris. So despite my sorrow at the loss of Notre Dame, and despite my previous miseries with the Agency I stuffed myself at 23:00 into a tiny cavity on Air Tahiti Nui, code-share Air France, to Los Angeles, an 8-hour and 15-minute Airbus ride. I soon fell asleep, as I'd medicated all my recent surfing injuries with my old friend Tanqueray, plus a large joint smoked before takeoff and whose benefits lasted most of the flight.

And I dreamed of Paris. Its memory had kept me alive during those lonely Leavenworth months. Because jail is the absolute deprivation of freedom and Paris its greatest incarnation.

Trying to stay sane at Leavenworth, I'd studied what I could get of French history, architecture, language, writers and wine. The medieval language of troubadours, the majesty of so many great minds like Villon, Montaigne, Hugo, and Zola to Giono,

Camus, St. Exupéry, Malraux, and Némirovsky. It was they, throughout those long cold months, who'd kept my soul alive.

Then a brilliant young lawyer and West Point grad took interest in my case, and thanks to her one cold November day six months later I stepped out the door of Deathtrap Leavenworth.

The sharp thin Kansas air dizzied me, the view of blue sky and distant prairie burned my eyes. I felt sorrow and desperation for all the friends I'd left inside. I grieved and wept and felt great joy all the way on the bus to the KC Airport, bought a one-way ticket to Paris and stayed there till my last dollar ran out. Then I was stuck doing covert jobs which raised my blood pressure, anguished my soul and made my stomach hurt. When I could, I wrote articles for *Surfer News* and whoever else would tolerate my grammar, but that barely paid the rent of my lovely shack high over the blue Pacific, to say nothing of gas for my ancient Karmann Ghia, rusty but undaunted.

The second time I got sprung, two years later, was from Hawaii's most soul-deadening place, Halawa Prison. I'd been sent there for delivering weed to a wounded and handicapped friend named Mitchell and to other injured vets who needed it to kill the pain and PTSD. The person who sprung me from Halawa was the cop who'd put me there, once she'd found out the real deal. My first night of freedom I was sitting on my Honolulu lanai, delirious in my sudden unexpected liberty and getting hammered on Tanqueray and weed when she showed up in a black leather skirt with nothing under and proceeded to fuck my brains out.

Not that I had a lot of them anyway.

But that's another story.

THE ONE GOOD THING I got out of Halawa Prison was my nickname, Pono. In Hawaiian it means the right, good and moral way to live. When I ended up in Halawa I realized my outside life was over – I'd be forty-two when I got out, providing the system didn't give me more time for some dreadful pointless reason. It was how I was going to live for a long time. At first I was crushed, hopeless. But after a few weeks I began to realize it was my fate and I had to make the best of it. And making the best means taking care of others, our *kuleana* – responsibility to the greater good. Though I was heartbroken, I tried to work with others, make their lives less heartbroken. And that's why my fellow prisoners named me that.

AT 10:12 WEST COAST TIME we landed at LAX, where I dozed for five hours at the gate, then muddled aboard the next Airbus, a 380 which carries more people than a cruise ship, or so it seemed.

In the belly of this monster I wandered like Jonah till I finally found my seat. Having lived two weeks with three energetic and sensual women, I still needed sleep, and the prospect of getting any in Paris was poor.

Beside me was a woman in her late twenties, crewcut, rectangular steel rims, a wide thin mouth. High hard cheekbones, a peremptory dissatisfied air. Her elbow covered the whole armrest between us; I managed to keep my shoulder from touching hers.

Flipping through yesterday's *Le Figaro*, I was reading that one of the ISIS-linked killers who had assassinated a police couple two years ago in their home in front of their 3-year-old son had been released after four months in prison, when the woman made a *tssk* sound.

I glanced at her. "It's garbage, that," she said in French.

"Yes, it's horrible …"

"They shouldn't print it."

"Why not?" I was beginning to wonder where she was coming from.

"It was a setup. Once the cops realized they had a marital murder-suicide on their hands they grabbed this poor Arab and killed him. And dragged the other poor Arab into it."

"It says here" – I held open the paper – "that the police shot him in their house, covered in their blood. This other guy's fingerprints were all over the family computer ..."

"All lies."

I scratched my head. "Terrorists are the *victims?*"

She made a frustrated motion with her hands. "It's the clash of an ancient religious culture with a capitalist European white male-driven hegemony."

"Islam isn't ancient. It began in 670 AD, many centuries after Judaism or Christianity ... I've spent years in Islamic countries, from Morocco to Afghanistan, and met many wonderful people. It's a fascinating, mystical culture, but ..."

"But?" She looked at me as one might an insect.

"Islam represses women. Total domination, burkhas, genital mutilation, child marriage, legalized rape, veils, hijabs, niqabs, abayas, beatings, imprisonment ... a woman can't do anything without a male's presence or approval ... Even in the United States a half million Muslim girls have been genitally mutilated ..."

She shrugged: *your country is evil anyway.*

"Instead of worrying about white male hegemony or whatever you call it, why not try to help the almost one billion severely repressed women in Muslim countries? They're much worse off than women in the West." I was pissed for a moment, then saw her face, hard, severe. Her voice like ground glass, edged with sorrow. I wondered what her life had been, maybe an abusive father, absent mother, unhappy siblings? How she'd grown up, the tragedies along the way ...

We should limit our opinions, I've concluded, to those situations where we have personal, direct experience. Thus no one who has not lived in a Muslim country can possibly know their reality – the police state of the mind and speech, the crushing enslavement of women, the absolute fanaticism of the religion, the total lack of democracy.

With this in mind I said, "In my own life, I've learned the hard way that what matters is to do as much good as we can, and cause as little pain."

"No," she snapped. "What counts in life is to destroy injustice."

"In whose eyes?" I answered.

"Would you two please shut up?" huffed an old man from the seat behind us.

SHE SEEMED NOT TO CARE that hundreds had died in recent Muslim attacks in France. A hundred and thirty singing and dancing young people in Paris, nearly another hundred in Nice, hundreds more handicapped for life, journalists assassinated, a priest decapitated, police officers murdered, young women with their throats cut for wearing dresses.

French politicians after years of "multiculturism" and "inclusion" could no longer deal with this growing catastrophe, so pretended it no longer existed. Large areas of France that tourists have never heard of and never go were now dominated by Sharia. And French media were still telling everyone that these multiple massacres "had nothing to do with Islam."

The growing frequency of Muslim attacks on Jews, some of which had been fatal, as well as the growing leftist antisemitism had led France's top rabbi to say recently, "Our children are leaving, because France, once a land of safety, has become a land of exile for the Jews."

And at the Bataclan, where nearly a hundred people were slaughtered by Islamic gunmen, the French government allowed a Muslim rapper to sing the glories of jihad and call for "the crucifixion of non-Muslims," while ISIS ordered all faithful

Muslims in France to "kill the dirty French by stoning, knives, cars, or strangling."

A former president, Nicolas Sarkozy, had been charged with taking $60 million dollars from Muslim sources to finance his last election campaign. What had he promised them in return?

And Sarkozy was a conservative – how much more money were the Socialists and ultra-left politicians – most who were pro-Muslim – getting from Islamic sources? And what did *they* do for it? And how to find out?

Thinking of such complicated things hurts my head, so I drifted off, half-dreaming of the last time I'd seen Thierry St. Croix.

Good people make me happy. And Thierry is a good man in love with his wife and family and country. He's France at its best – large-hearted, outgoing, big-handed, close to the earth and wine and food and nature, fighting his country's enemies to the death.

Last time I'd seen him was at our FOB up in the mountains. It was winter, so mail was rare. One day he got a package with a can of wild boar pâté from his parents in Cluny. I traded five pairs of new socks for a bottle of fabulous *Standart* Russian vodka and we drank it with the pâté and Afghani *naan* flatbread and tried to invent limericks in Franglais.

Now I couldn't wait to see him, to thank him again for the boar pâté. And see if he had any new limericks.

And I was going to find Mustafa al-Boudienne, the mass murderer now planning more slaughter in France. It had been eight years since he'd imprisoned Mack and me for weeks in Mosul and done every horror to us that he could. That had been my first tour in Iraq, after one in Afghanistan, with more in Afghanistan to come that would bring its own horrors.

This time when I found Mustafa, he wouldn't survive.

"READY TO DIE?" Mustafa jabbed his AK muzzle into my eye and sneered down the barrel. I tried not to flinch so he wouldn't do it again.

He was tall and thin, with a black keffiyeh around a dirty neck, a thick short beard and sharp mustache, frizzy hair and black empty eyes. He spoke French because he grew up in France and didn't speak Arabic, though we were in Mosul in Iraq, where most folks spoke the Maslawi dialect.

I couldn't stop trembling. Tried to stop because I didn't want to show fear. That would only make him worse. I was going to die, and wanted it to be easy. My gut twisted and burned. Sweat and spit filled my throat, making it hard to suck air into my empty lungs.

"Filthy American!" he smiled. "Shall I let you suffer a bit, no?"

This I feared. When they shoot you in the gut and leave you out in the heat for sepsis to set in. Forty-eight hours of agony, begging for death.

I wanted to say 'May Allah guide you' or something foolish like that. But whatever I said would just make my death worse.

Sorrow beyond belief. Yet millions of people had been shot just like this.

Get over it.

He snickered, scanned the sky. He stepped to my right side, angled the AK down at my ribs, so the bullet would cross my gut and smash my left pelvis and thigh. The perfect slow death. I stiffened, exhaled, faced the bloody earth and waited for the bullet to hit.

F A L S E   H O P E

AT 11:05 NEXT MORNING the Airbus landed at CDG and I grabbed a cab to the 7th Arrondissement and the one-bedroom safe house that DGSE had set aside for me.

It was on Passage Landrieu, a narrow, cobbled alley of ancient three- and four-story buildings, a vestige of real Paris but close enough to the tourist Disneyland of Rue Cler and the Eiffel Tower that the presence of another American wouldn't be noticed.

A fourth-story walkup, a main room with a kitchen to one side, a bedroom and bath, a scintillating view over a tree-lined courtyard and slate and gray metal roofs to the Tower, the smells of good food rising on the spring breeze from the kitchens below – what more do you need in May in Paris?

I put my few clothes away, took a quick cold shower to wash off the salt of Tahiti's blue Pacific and all the air miles in between, poured a tall glass of Côtes de Provence rosé from the bottle DGSE had kindly left in the reefer, sat down and called Mack's landline.

A woman answered, hoarse and urgent. "Gisèle?" I said, "that you?"

"Pono? You're too late!"

"Too late? I just got here."

"They took him."

"Mack? *Who* took him?"

"He's gone ..." She swallowed a sob. "They found his car. Empty. With blood on the seat."

"*Who? Who* found his car?"

"Mack left home at seven this morning, like always. He usually takes the Métro to the Port des Lilas Station near his office and walks from there. But today he had to go to Normandy later, so he drove to the office." She swallowed. "He never got there. They found his car an hour ago, on a side street off La République. Blood on the seat, the driver window." She took a breath, calmed herself. "How did they *know*? Was it because he called you?"

I snatched my coat and phone and stepped in front of an old lady to grab a cab to Mack and Gisèle's home on Boulevard de Beauséjour in the 16th.

I'd been looking forward to seeing Mack, and hunting down Mustafa together. Now he was missing, blood all over his car. And Gisèle trying not to choke up on the phone. As if the more calm and objective she could be, the more she could help Mack. When we both knew it might already be too late.

IT WAS A WIDE street of chestnut and plane trees in early leaf, stone four-story town homes with flowers in front and lots of Audis and Mercedes dozing at the curb.

Number 49 was a sculpted stone building behind a steel spike fence, a front garden with three cypresses and a Lebanese cedar on each side of the stone front stairs.

"Hi!" She turned aside when she opened the door so I wouldn't see her red eyes.

"Hey." I tried to hug her and stepped on her toe. "Damn!"

"It's okay." She hugged me back, her cheek wet. "Thanks for coming."

Her blonde, tangled hair had tumbled down her brow and she kept pushing it aside. Her cheeks were bone pale, her eyes shiny. It wrenched my heart – even in the deadly no-one's land of Waziristan between Afghanistan and Pakistan she'd always seemed fresh, energetic, and organized, despite the horror and tragedy she faced every day. But the horror and tragedy had never struck someone she loved with the focused and undivided passion they had for each other.

"We'll find him," I said stupidly, my arm round her shoulder walking into the living room that seemed too bright and pretty for this moment.

It was a big place, a double *séjour*, dining room, large kitchen, four bedrooms upstairs and assorted baths, well-furnished, lots of bookshelves, good paintings and a couple of nice tapestries on the walls.

"At first I hoped there might be some reason," she said. "That he'd hurt his head somehow, went to a hospital ... Hôpital Saint-Louis, it's only five minutes from there ... But he's not anywhere. No one's seen him."

"The car – no witnesses?"

"No one. As if it didn't happen. Suddenly his car is there, illegally parked in a delivery zone. It was the shopkeeper who called, wanted it towed."

"The blood on the seat," I said. "There's no proof it's his ..."

"Don't say that! You *know* it is. I *know* it is. Don't dredge up false hope."

I sat heavily in an antique chair. It squeaked. She sat across from me, open-faced, wrists on knees, hands dangling, her lovely face contorted with pain.

"Tell me the whole deal," I said. "Mack's last morning, his last week – phone calls, people on the street, things he might have said late at night while half asleep."

"I've already gone over all this," she exhaled. "With the Agency and the French."

"Do it again. This time don't leave anything out."

As she spoke I was stunned by her self-control. She was not going to cede to emotion because pure focus was essential to any hope of saving Mack. She sat there, knees locked, wet tissues in her clenched hands, speaking softly and clearly. "Mack watches everything. All the time. And if he sees or feels anything, he aborts. If we're together he tells me what he's seeing and I check it out too."

This was old news. One of the many troubles with covert life is it destroys your freedom. You never know if a person on the sidewalk behind you has a gun, if there's a bomb under your car or waiting for you on the street, if there's poison in something you breathe or eat, or if you're in the crosshairs of a sniper's rifle a quarter mile away. Never when you sleep can you be sure you'll be alive in the morning.

"If it's a tail I tail it," she went on as if she had to convince me. "A car, person, doesn't matter. And anything digital gets double-screened at the office ... but lately there's been nothing. No way these bastards could've even known Mack was on their trail."

"Why was he going to Normandy?"

"He didn't say ... I wasn't even supposed to know he was going ..."

"Someone didn't want him to go there?"

"Ask Thierry." She watched me. "But he'll want to know how you know."

"What about the COS?" This was the CIA's Paris Chief of Station.

"Harris? Maybe *he* doesn't know."

I sat back, eyes on the floor, tried to imagine how it might have happened. "No bullet hole in the driver side window?"

"No bullet hole anywhere. No brass, no powder."

"The window was up?"

"It's spring in Paris. Of course the window was up."

"So he got whacked."

"Whacked?"

"Sorry – I meant someone hit him on the head. So he's probably not dead."

"Probably not?"

"Probably a grab."

"That's what Harris thinks." She looked down, nodded. "Me too."

"Harris?"

"COS, like I said. Mack didn't tell you?"

"Never said his name."

So somebody named Harris was COS, but that probably wasn't the Harris I knew. In the midst of this awful dialogue I glanced out the ancient window at the afternoon sunlight cascading down the broad new leaves of a chestnut tree in the garden. It shimmered with life and meaning – a vision of something forever beyond us – innocent and true, the miracle of sunlight on the green magic of leaves, in this world of mysterious beauty we do not love or understand.

Gisèle's lips were moving but I hadn't heard. "Say again?"

"What are you, deaf?"

"Actually" – I banged a hand against my ear – "too much incoming."

"What are you going to *do*, Pono?" She stood over me, gripped my wrists in her strong fists, burrowed into me with those blood-red eyes. "If it's a grab, *how* are *you* going to *save* him?"

How could I save him? What had I learned from the magical sunlight on the leaves? "What's Harris's number?"

She told me and I memorized it. "When you talk to Thierry,"

she begged, "please let me know the latest? I've been calling him every ten minutes … can you, maybe you, you could find out if they know *anything*?"

"This COS, what's he say?"

"The French are in charge."

"It's their turf." I shrugged. "But …"

"He says it's their operation, their terrorists, their danger." She glanced around the room, seeming to see nothing. "I always knew this was coming. Even when we met, and then you guys went back to Afghanistan and I never expected you'd survive, either of you."

"But we did." I wanted to add that Mack too would keep surviving.

It never occurred to me, nor would I have cared, that I might not survive either.

T O O   L A T E

OUTSIDE HER HOUSE I called Thierry, left a message.

They'd be torturing Mack now. Trying to learn what he knew. It was a waste of time, but no doubt they were doing it mostly for fun.

How had they known where he was? Had they tracked him? When?

Like Gisèle said, was it because he'd called me? Was it me they were tracking?

That was nuts. I'd been far away in Tahiti with three wonderful women. Why would these homicidal nutcases be after me?

Thierry called right back. "How is she?"

"In control."

"Where are you?"

"Front of their place."

"We're hitting every angle. Nobody knows a thing."

"The blood in the car?"

"O Positive. Same as Mack's. We'll know for sure when the DNA comes back."

"Where's Mustafa?"

"Vanished since Fontainebleau."

"There's a connection?"

"Between this and Mustafa? Get over here."

I grabbed another cab and for cover gave the driver the address of a bar on Avenue Gambetta in the 20th Arrondissement, the Bistrot du Poinçonneur, which just happens to be around the block from 141 Boulevard Mortier, home of DGSE.

We travelled a cross-section of Paris in twenty minutes from the high-class park-side apartments of the 16th through fancy shopping districts and offices across the Champs Élysées and then the grittier neighborhoods of what used to be working-class Paris till you end up in the city's illegal immigration capital, the 20th Arrondissement. I tried to call Gisèle to tell her what Thierry'd said, but her land line was busy. I wished I'd asked for her cell.

MOST OF MY TROUBLES have been brought on by myself. Joining SF was the best thing I've ever done, but it led to tons of trouble. Like when I shot the dying Afghani girl who'd been burned alive, to put her out of her misery, and got sent to Leavenworth Army prison. Or got caught with a kilo of weed in Honolulu destined for injured Special Forces buddies who needed it to ease the pain, and got ten to fifteen in Halawa Prison, a circle of Hell even Dante couldn't have imagined.

Or when I bumped into a beautiful drowned woman off Waikiki and ended up hunted by her killers. Or when I went to Maine to save an SF buddy from a false murder charge and soon faced one myself.

I wouldn't change any of this, but it sure had made for a

crazy life. But that's how life is. You do what you think is best and pay the consequences.

Less than a month ago I'd left Maine for Tahiti with my three bedmates, promising myself I'd give up trying to improve the world.

I was going to surf and make love and care for hungry animals and injured buddies and let the world go to Hell all by itself.

But now I'd left Tahiti for a rainy May in Paris, on a well-paid but non-existent loan to the Agency I disliked. Not that for them I even existed. Which meant if I got in trouble they'd never heard of me. Or if I got too cumbersome they might just deal with me themselves.

There were three good reasons why I did this:

I wanted to kill Mustafa al-Boudienne.

I wanted to protect our country, our freedom, and our way of life. For which I've risked my own life so many times.

Most important: Mack asked me to.

AFTER 9/11 when I decided to drop marine biology and go into the Marines, my father, as a former SEAL, advised in his usual cogent manner against it. "Nah, don't be a bullet sponge in the Marines, go in Special Forces. Those guys have all the fun. And unlike the SEALS don't have to spend all their time in the damn ocean."

The first step to SF was Ranger training at Fort Benning – incredibly tough, exhausting and exhilarating exertion – marching and running with heavy packs, climbing vertical hills and jumping off tall walls into muddy rivers and nasty bush and every other unfavorable kind of terrain you could imagine.

I'd grown up on the Big Island barefoot and nearly naked, climbing trees and mountains, surfing and windsurfing monster waves, swimming and running everywhere, even to the top of

14,000-foot Mauna Kea, avoiding school as much as possible – the typical Hawaiian back-country kid.

Thus Ranger training wasn't a piece of cake but not that hard. Most of my fellow applicants were in good shape, but not nearly as tough as guys used to be – too much beer, TV, video games, and the misperception that watching football made them men. So while these guys were dying out there I was having fun.

But the fun ended at the Special Forces selection course at Fort Bragg – another twenty-four days of astoundingly unpleasant physical challenges, after which I was admitted as a Weapons Sergeant candidate to Special Forces Qualification Course, which made everything before it seem like kid's play.

Next thing I knew I was in Afghanistan.

And if you aren't crazy by the time you leave Afghanistan then you were crazy to begin with. Because you have to be crazy not to go crazy there.

"YOU'RE TOO LATE," Thierry said, when I'd walked the three minutes from the Bistrot du Poinçonneur to DGSE.

"Screw you." I hugged him. "I just got here!"

"Too late to find Mack." He looked the same but not. It had been a long time. Still slender and intense, he now stooped a bit, maybe due to the old shrapnel in his back. His face was less tanned and weathered than in Afghanistan, his now-silvery hair still cropped short.

His office was on the third floor of DGSE's central rectangle overlooking a square of greening branches and bright new grass. "What'd you find in Mack's car?" I said.

"PTS is checking prints, but I doubt there'll be anything." The PTS, he didn't need to tell me, is the Technical and Scientific section of the French police. "The blood, it's surely his –"

"Gisèle says there was no bullet ..."

"No trace of a bullet in the door or elsewhere. We think he was hit with something, a steel bar, a wood club ..." Thierry raised his hands, a furious expression of not knowing.

"Who hit him, and how did they get close?" No one surprised Mack; he was always alert; when he drove down a street he watched everything on both sides – the cars, the pedestrians, the building doorways, windows and rooftops – the way we all do ... We'd learned this long before Afghanistan, but being there had only made it deeper.

"We don't understand." Thierry shook his head. "We've towed the car to the lab, they're working on it now."

"Whoever did it had to be following him. Or waiting for him."

"Why wait till he was using a car? Why didn't they take him one day in the Métro?"

"It's too public. And covered with cameras. No angle not seen." Or maybe, I wondered but didn't say it, did Mack get grabbed to prevent him talking to me? How could that be? "My side, what do they say?"

Thierry glanced at his watch. "It's not even eight a.m. in Washington. We've called his people – *your* people –"

"Harris?"

"They're studying everything they got off the Embassy roof since yesterday. NSA's geared up, they're screening every internet connection to or from the Paris region ... we have new algorithms we've developed together ... all the information sharing agreements are in place, no worries there ... But on the physical side we're taking the lead."

The US Embassy roof, in fact the entire top floor, is one huge listening device that picks up every cell phone conversation in the greater Paris area. NSA covers Paris like a digital blanket, all of France ... all the world. How many trillion exchanges a second did NSA store away in Utah? Every single event in time? In them, could you find the truth?

"The cathedral?" I said. "What's the real deal?"

"The real deal is we don't know. It could be terrorists at the computer level, or somebody climbing up there with an untraceable fuse ... Not that we can find anything in what's left of the rubble."

"And Mustafa," I said. "What's new?"

"Mack was working with people here, tracking him since he came into France from Freiburg on March fifteen – we think –"

"And from Freiburg?"

"Mustafa was in a tan 2013 Volkswagen Passat with Austrian plates. Stolen in Torino. We put a drone on it but lost it in the Fontainebleau Forest, south of Paris."

"I know where Fontainebleau is." The former NATO HQ in Europe until General de Gaulle took France out of NATO in 1966, Fontainebleau is a beautiful town surrounded by huge oak forests, the private hunting grounds of King François in the 1500s, now one of the world's loveliest places to hike, rock climb, hunt deer and boar, and revel in the magnificence of the French countryside. And only forty minutes by road or train from Paris.

"You know there's lots of terrorist safe houses in the surrounding towns, Avon, Melun, with direct road and rail access to Paris ..."

Thierry needn't say more: now that French intelligence had intensified its search for terrorists in the many Islamic-ruled districts around Paris and other cities, their prey was shifting to the less-populous nearby regions. It was like hunting boar: when you focus on one area, the boar, who are smarter than most hunters, simply slide into a new location.

"And Fontainebleau is where you lost him."

"For the moment." Thierry leaned back, fingers linked behind his neck, his long legs stretched under his desk. "But we will find him, never fear."

"Fear is all I've got right now. Fear for Mack. For France. For all of us."

Thierry nodded, chin out. "We've faced Muslim invasions before. And won. Today the French media's so left-wing it thinks Israel, the only European democracy in the Middle East, is a fascist state and Saudi Arabia and Iran, which enslave women and execute many people per week, are the world capitals of *liberté*, *égalité* and *fraternité*." He raised his hands. "And our former education minister wanted to replace French history with Islamic Suras, and Muslim criminals get shorter jail sentences because *French culture made them do it?*"

"Fuck it, Thierry, this is old news ..."

He stood, as if affronted. "We've given you a broom closet for an office and a partner named Anne Ronsard. She's been working with Mack since Mustafa reappeared. Very bright and tough; she's been hunting terrorists for years. She's also a recent widow with two kids, so keep your hands off her."

"A widow? How?"

"I'll let her tell you about that. If she wants to."

A MATTER OF TIME

"**HOW MANY CAMERAS,**" I asked Thierry, "you got in Fontainebleau?"

"Anne's working on that. But we don't have a single image of Mustafa. That's where you come in."

"I don't keep any in my wallet."

"Stop joking. *Find* this bastard!"

I smiled. "I just remembered one night four of us SF guys stumbled into some firebase near the Paki border, exhausted and near-frozen. Hadn't found one bandit, but still scared by what could've happened ... we'd damn near got killed. I wanted so bad to get out of Afghanistan. Then I hear your voice, you're sitting at a table talking your crappy English –"

"It's better than your French –"

"– and I forgot how tired I was, just felt happy you were there."

"We took care of each other, *mon cher*."

"We all took care of all of us."

He grabbed his phone and punched in a number. "*Il est là. Tu viens le chercher?*"

A woman's voice on the other end said, *"D'accord."* Which even I knew means *okay.*

"I need to see Mack's car," I said.

"Anne will take you. She'll issue you a sidearm, phone and radio, all that shit."

"I want a Glock 19. And an AAC silencer –"

He stood. "That's up to Anne."

His five other lines were blinking. His phone sat companionably beside gold-framed photos of a beautiful woman and four tousle-haired kids, two boys and two girls. From our time in Afghanistan he'd told me about his wife, back then with only two kids. The great gift of life.

But he was not the Thierry I'd known. It was as if he'd just learned that someone he loved was dying. Like Notre Dame, that *everything* and *everyone* he loved was dying.

I shook his hand, pained by his fear of this war we might lose. Then he gave me a big-toothed grin. "One thing is not allowed."

"What's that?" In France, everything is allowed as long as you don't brag about it.

"Tu n'as pas le droit de le tuer." (You don't have the right to kill him.) He went on in English: "Not until we have talked to him all we want." Again the raised hands, the Gallic shrug meaning *then we'll see.*

Not that I gave a damn. For me, Mustafa al-Boudienne was dead meat, no matter how we got there.

THERE ARE MOMENTS THAT SCAR *the rest of your life. Usually they're when the rest of your life won't be very long: a few seconds maybe.*

I've been there not a few times. They stay with me. Especially at night.

This time Mack and I were knocking down doors in Mosul with the rest of the squad behind us, a normal street-clearing oper-

ation that, one way or another, had already killed so many of us. A narrow rotten alley jammed with two-story broken-stuccoed pale-painted buildings, electric wires hanging like nooses between them, ratty cars lurking along the sides.

You know the drill, one guy either side of the door, you kick it in and your buddy dashes inside right, you go left, ready to spray bullets at whoever is stupid or crazy enough to want to stop you.

Mack dashed right and me left into an empty room, low couch, yellow-orange afghan, three puffy pillows, polyester rug on a dirty concrete floor. Rough concrete walls, low ceiling, bare light from a single filthy window. A door to the left – my side – one to the right, Mack's.

We slid along the walls, one on each side. Mack motioned to my door. I nodded at the other door, showing my concern that we not leave his side unguarded. Mack tossed his head toward the street outside: Okay, so we wait for the other guys. A smattering of fire outside, a rattle of bullets along the far side of the street, and I worried should we go back to check on our guys but there was no need, plus the useless risk of going out the door when the shooters had seen us go in. Mack nodded his head again at my door: Let's check yours first.

He seemed to have a reason. I turned the handle. It opened. I backed against the wall and shoved the door wider, ducked my head around the jamb, saw a long dim corridor with two side doors off it and an open window at the end. Through it I saw a patch of hills and a few houses stacked against it like dice thrown at a wall.

I was breathing so hard it was rattling the comms in my ear. There was something wrong here but I couldn't figure what. Often you think that, only to find that no, there's nothing different, it's just the normal horror and constant misery of war.

We checked the two doorways in my corridor – a move that can easily lead to death. But no problem: two bedrooms with plastic sleeping mats on the floors, four mats in the first room, five in the second. Both rooms empty. I sidled up to the window at the corridor end and glanced down on a dusty courtyard maybe ten feet by fifteen, garbage, plastic bottles, rusty cans and a dead goat lying on its side as if sleeping – but it wasn't sleeping because it was raising an extensive colony of flies. The wind was blowing away from us but the smell was still terrible.

A flash of movement out the window to my right, a white sleeve or something that vanished. I nodded to Mack, pointed. Your side.

We went back and lined up on both sides of the other door. In the street outside, the firing had slowed; I could hear our guys calling up and down the street as they moved toward our building, others doing backup. I kicked the door open and dashed in.

No motion in the corridor, a window open at the end with the same view of the brown hill and crappy houses. The same two doors along one side, both closed. I tiptoed down the corridor and kicked open the first door: another empty room with sleeping mats on the floor and a pile of trash in one corner.

What was going on?

Whoever had flashed that white cloth must be in the second room. A truce flag? Someone wanting to surrender? Three guys in another squad had died that way last week.

We slid along the corridor walls. I kicked open the second door and we dashed in, Mack right, me left.

Kids. Lots of kids backed up against the far wall. Little ones in front, big ones behind. Wide-eyed and open-mouthed. Maybe fifty.

Taking shelter among the kids were four bearded bastards with AKs. Two had vests, what seemed the real deal. "You do anything, we blow you up," one said in shitty Arabic. "And all these kids."

If we tried to duck back out the door they'd shoot us both. If we tried to shoot them we'd blow up the kids.

I didn't want to die. I didn't want Mack to die. And I especially didn't want all these kids to die.

We'd had detailed training on how not to get captured. Because if we did they'd torture us interminably, then kill us.

I actually thought of outshooting them. Insane.

How silly that when you're going to die you'll do anything to postpone it, for even a few seconds.

I heard our guys in the street, their voices dim beyond the concrete walls.

The bearded bastards took our weapons, roped and gagged us and shoved us ahead of them down a ragged stairway at the back of the corridor, the kids following, sandals slapping on the stairs.

The stairway opened into a stinking tunnel with damp walls and urine puddles. They'd planned this, I realized: the kids, the dark corridors, the seeming innocence of the place. I was furious with myself, but there was nothing either Mack or I could do. Our buddies would soon discover the empty rooms, then the stairway. But by then we'd be long gone.

The tunnel ended in another stairway that climbed to a wide, low garage with a halal butcher truck to one side. The concrete floor of the garage was sticky with grease and desert dust and other things. They shoved us into the back of the halal truck, two bearded bastards with us.

"We could have shot you. But we didn't," one smiled. "We want to have fun with you."

My life as I'd known it was over. It was just a matter of time.

BLACK AND BLONDE

TOO STUNNING to be pretty, Anne Ronsard was in her late twenties maybe, not that you could tell. Slender and mid-height in a short black skirt and black cashmere sweater, black hair in a page boy across high-boned cheeks, flashing black eyes, a slender face with dimples, a sharp nose just a little too big, a tough smile in a wide, voluptuous mouth. A sense about her of adventure: someone who *loves*. And the stern glance of someone who's seen too much and therefore doesn't believe in much of anything.

Except protecting family and friends, and the country she loves. And with the strength, courage and power to do it.

"*Voilá!*" She moved aside in the corridor so I could see my "office." Like most intelligence folks, Thierry had misspoken: it was *smaller* than a broom closet. A desk with a phone and a bunch of buttons – "internal," Anne said. Four computers with keyboards in Arabic, French, Russian and English – "internal" also. A chair that had survived the 1870 German siege of Paris and howled like a burnt cat every time it moved. A second chair of the aluminum type and, as the French would say, *vastly degraded.*

"*On est bien ici,*" (This is great) I said sarcastically.

"*Oh oui,*" she replied enthusiastically. "*On a de la chance.*" (You're lucky)

"*Comment ça?*" I replied (How is that?).

Her chin rose: the icy look of a French woman about to admonish a dumb but dutiful servant. "You don't like?"

"Let's go see Mack's car."

She led me down corridors out the back to the garage and a gleaming red Indian Scout motorcycle, unhitched two helmets from the saddle and gave me one.

My heart sank. I'd been in three bad motorcycle wrecks and had sworn off bikes forever. Have a number of friends now dead or crippled for life from riding them. Every motorcycle, statistics show, will kill or badly injure at least one person in its lifetime.

I nodded at the Indian. "Not on that."

She buckled her helmet, tucking her black hair inside it. "Afraid?"

"You can ride that ugly thing if you want but I'm getting a car." (*Vous pouvez conduire cette chose moche si ça vous plaît. Mais moi, je vais prendre une voiture.*) I took a breath, rather pleased with myself for such a long harangue.

She slapped the back seat. "Get on!"

She was right; we didn't have time. I've jumped from airplanes, been shot at, climbed nasty cliffs and fell off a few, took on killer waves with sad results, and have done many other dangerous things and yet survived. So what was one more high-speed motorcycle crash?

She gunned the Indian, turned back to me. "By the way, on our team we don't *vouvoyer* each other. We're family, we use the family tense. You could say *Tu peux conduire cette chose moche*, but that's very ugly French. No one will listen to you if you talk like that."

We roared out the heavily guarded DGSE exit right on Boulevard Mortier and howled through ratty roads to the Périphérique, the high-speed four-lane highway that circles and chokes Paris, much of it along the old line of the city's castle walls.

Walls that do no good anymore because the attacker is already inside.

She accelerated fast, darting in and out among cars and down the narrow spaces between them, me holding on dearly around her trim waist, my forearms across her bare thighs where she'd tugged up her short skirt to wrap her legs around the hundred pulsing horses of the Indian's snarling screaming engine, and I leaned when she did and tried not to show that I was terrified and sure we were both going to die.

Nonetheless we didn't die, and after what seemed an eternity we pulled into the Préfecture of Police forensic garage, where technicians from the INPS, the National Institute of Scientific Police, were going over Mack's car.

A black BMW M240. 6-cylinder turbo, 335 Horsepower, a 6-speed stick and fast Pirellis. A demon car. A technician in white was leaning in the open driver door, another swabbing the back seat. When they saw Anne they stood up. "What you got?" she said.

"*Cherchez la femme,*" one grinned.

"It was a woman in the car," the other said. "Who hit him."

"Nuts!" Anne snapped.

"She left a hair. A long black hair dyed blonde."

"Maybe his wife?" the first said.

"She has short blonde hair. And doesn't dye it," Anne pointed out.

I could have told them that. And Gisèle has always worn her hair short, ever since I first knew her when she and Mack hooked up in Waziristan.

"This could've been some other time. Anybody."

"No, it's fresh. She took a shower this morning. *Le Petit Marseillais Shampoo with Shea Butter and Honey.* Made in France."

"*Merde*," Anne said very quietly. "You got this already?"

"We're not stupid."

"How you know she hit him?"

"When she reached across from the passenger seat and hit the back of his head, a few molecules of his blood spattered on her hair, *this* hair, that got caught in the seat belt and broke off when she pulled back." He shrugged. "That's how it seems."

"DNA?"

"Nothing yet."

"Prints?"

"Not yet."

Anne turned to me. "This makes no sense. Let's go see Gisèle."

"I'll call her," I said.

Gisèle's land line was still busy. "Maybe she's gone shopping," Anne said.

"When her husband's missing?"

We jumped on the Indian for another shorter but equally mind-blowing trip through raging traffic and smog on the Péréphérique, up Avenue Foch – named for one of France's many World War I generals under whose command 1.4 million young Frenchmen died – and around the Étoile's grand Arc de Triomphe, which in true Roman fashion celebrates Napoleon's victory at Austerlitz, in which many more thousands died. And all the Pyrrhic victories since.

We decelerated like a returning space shuttle to the 16th Arrondissement and Mack and Gisèle's house.

It didn't matter how many times we rang the bell or called the land line, Gisèle didn't answer. "You don't have her cell?" Anne said sharply.

"Just the land line."

"Where you from, the last century?"

She was getting irritated because things weren't looking good. "I'll call Thierry," she snapped. "He'll have her cell."

For an insidious moment I thought of a prison cell not a cellphone, and was back pacing a cell of my own, even the one in Beirut, worst of them all.

Five minutes later Thierry called with Gisèle's cell number, but it too didn't answer. *"Merde, merde et merde!"* Anne hissed, stalking back and forth, lit a cigarette, took one puff and tossed it in the gutter. She called Thierry again; even I could understand her angry slang, "This's truly screwed up."

He said something and she nodded at me. "We need to go in."

"Mack'll have tons of security on that door," I said. As if she wouldn't know.

"Thierry's sending someone."

I'd been barely five hours in France and already Mack was missing, injured and maybe dead, clobbered by a woman with dyed blonde hair. And now his wife was missing too.

She could be at a meeting. But the medical office where she worked as a spinal injury specialist said she hadn't been there all day.

Why wouldn't she answer?

I was dead tired. Grainy eyes, slumping shoulders, aching spine, the dizzy unreality after a long flight, when midnight is noon, and the bright Pacific becomes the rainy Paris smog.

I bent over hands on knees and took a breath. On Tahiti it'd be nearly sunrise now; soon Lexie would leave for her endless flight back to Maine, Abigail would be patrolling the beaches for some hunk she couldn't turn down, and Erica would be earning eight hundred bucks an hour lounging on the lanai drinking gin, smoking weed, and writing briefs for clients on the other side of the world.

Thierry's 'someone' arrived ten minutes later, a balding potbellied guy with a thin black mustache and mothy black sweater, in his mid-forties, a worn black jacket, beret and jeans, with a strange cellphone and a little toolkit he took from his pocket. Five minutes later we followed him into Mack and Gisèle's house, expecting to find her dead on the floor.

Room by room we checked, the *double séjour*, the dining room, the four bedrooms and assorted baths. On the kitchen counter lay the flashing phone, off the hook.

Dead or alive, Gisèle was not there.

THE HALAL TRUCK wandered the bumpy rutted streets of Mosul for maybe ten minutes. Away from the Coalition sector deep into the lawless labyrinth where our soldiers had not yet gone to conquer and die.

In the distance you heard the normal gunfire and explosions: just a regular afternoon in Mosul. Occasionally the jangle of Arab music, the rumble of vehicles or clatter of voices. "This's got to be the Shia quarter," I whispered to Mack, and a crushing pain thudded into my kidneys.

"Shut up," somebody said. "Or I kill."

Despair washed over me. No way we'd survive this. The pain in my kidneys from being kicked radiated out into my body and linked to my despair: the antithesis of life. Why had I come to this bedeviled, beleaguered country to fight these fanatics?

I'd ended up fighting the Taliban in the rough frigid mountains of Afghanistan, settling scores for what the Saudis had done to the World Trade Center, the Pentagon, and all the poor people on the United and American flights who died that day. I'd seen the pictures of people jumping to their deaths from the burning buildings. And I was going to avenge them.

Then GW Bush told Tommy Franks at CENTCOM to let Osama Bin Laden escape from Tora Bora. It took a while for us to figure out what had happened, that indeed we'd had Bin Laden pinned down and GW let him walk with a thousand Al Qaeda across the Paki border into the wilds of Waziristan. Because GW wanted Bin Laden alive so he could say that Saddam Hussein was sheltering him in Baghdad, and thus we had to attack Iraq. Then he lied, 264 times according to the record, about Iraq's so-called Weapons of Mass Destruction, and to prove he was a man, he and five-time draft-dodger Vice President Cheney, had sucked our combat effort dry in Afghanistan, and sent me and so many of my comrades into the endless pit of horror, danger and despair known as Iraq. A soldier can know a war is evil and wrong, but he doesn't get to choose whether or not he fights in it.

Now, rattling through the dusty, hot and fetid Mosul streets in the back of the halal truck – halal being the Muslim butchering process of hanging an animal upside down and cutting its throat so it bleeds to death – I realized how ironic it was.

They were going to cut our throats too.

ALLAH PROMISES

"MAYBE GISÈLE has a safe hole," Thierry said when I called. "Someplace she and Mack could've set up, outside *us*, that only they know? Maybe she didn't trust us to keep her safe."

"You *didn't* keep her safe."

"Maybe she went undercover?"

"She'd never do anything to complicate finding Mack." I glanced out the rain-streaked window of Mack's living room, umbrellas like bobbing pansies below, cars like scuttling bright-eyed mice.

Anne came from the dining room. "Gisèle got that last call at two-forty-seven."

I could see it from where I stood in the living room – the flashing phone on the kitchen counter. "The one she didn't hang up."

"And guess where from? A public phone in Molenbeek."

"Oh God." Molenbeek is another huge Muslim enclave like Seine St. Denis – this one in Brussels. From Molenbeek many of the major terrorist attacks in the last ten years had been launched. In 20 years it's projected that Muslims will be the majority in Brussels, the capital of Europe, then Molenbeek will be a shrine, the place where it all began.

If something big was going on, Molenbeek was part of it.

"WHY WAS MACK GOING TO NORMANDY?" I asked when we got back to Thierry's office.

He raised an eyebrow. "Normandy?"

"What are you saying?" Anne snapped.

"Gisèle said he was planning to go to Normandy the day he got grabbed."

Thierry sat back, hands behind his head. "Oh fuck."

Anne stared at me darkly. "We didn't know."

"Why was he going?" Thierry said.

"Gisèle didn't know."

Anne looked out the window, took a breath. "Jesus."

"Who was Mack running?" I said.

Thierry looked surprised. "No one."

"Not that we know," Anne added.

"Then what," I said, "*was* he doing?"

She turned to me. "He didn't tell you?"

"He said Mustafa had shown up and could I help track him down. He said my side would carry the costs but I'd be working with you. Why – what else is there?"

She glanced at Thierry, who took a breath, nodded.

"He didn't mention *Martel*?"

"What's that?"

Thierry leaned forward. "He *did* tell you we'd brought in a couple of *jihadis* fresh back from Syria, didn't he?"

I sensed Thierry knew exactly what Mack had said. "You tell me."

"It took time, but these two guys finally opened up. We'd shipped them to Morocco – so much better to discuss things in your own language – and eventually they both told us, independently, that 'a great man is coming. He has killed many unbelievers. He will unleash great sorrow on you.'"

"'What kind of sorrow?' we asked. They said this great man has come to direct an operation called Martel."

"Named derisively, of course," Anne said, "for Charles Martel, the king who chased the Muslims out of France in 732."

"I know that ..." I snapped.

"One action is to fly an Airbus into the Eiffel Tower. 'The infidels have already lost their ugly cathedral,' one of the *jihadis* said. 'Now they will lose their Tower.'"

An icy feeling shot down my spine. "Those Algerians tried it with an Air France plane in Marseille, way back in 1994 ... wasn't it?"

"December 24 to 26."

"And you guys killed them all."

"But we lost a man." This of course was not widely known. What was known was that a group of Algerians hijacked an Airbus 300 with 220 passengers in Algiers. They began to execute passengers and ordered the pilot to fly to Paris. Air France insisted the plane didn't have enough fuel to reach Paris. The Algerians agreed to a fuel stop in Marseille. There, after hours and hours of stalling, of fake press conferences and tense waiting, a team of the GIGN tactical intervention force assaulted the plane, killed the four hijackers, and freed the passengers.

Like the Israelis at Entebbe, one of the most amazing successes in the almost impossible craft of hostage recovery.

"But no way they can blow the Tower up," Thierry said. "Damn thing weighs over ten thousand tons, over a thousand feet tall. And unlike the World Trade towers it won't burn because it's all exposed steel –"

I scratched my head, trying to kick-start my brain. "One of these *jihadis* told you all this? About using a plane to take down the Tower?"

Thierry nodded.

"What was the other action?"

"The other strategy involves some kind of backpack nuke from Iran or Pakistan." He gave a weary puff.

"The Soviet nukes?" I turned to Anne. "They're long past their use-by date."

She actually snickered. "And you're the one who believed Mustafa was dead?"

"Guy *rises* from the dead," Thierry said, trying to soften the tension between her and me.

"There's more." Anne sat forward, hands clasped one on top of the other over one knee. She cocked her head at Thierry; he nodded. "There are sixty-seven nuclear launch sites in Pakistan, as best we can tell. And from what Indian intelligence tells us –"

"Indian intelligence," I huffed, "lies about Pakistan."

"Everybody," Thierry grinned, "lies about Pakistan."

"Pakistan's always ready to knife us in the back," I said. "They sheltered Bin Laden and wouldn't tell us, though they knew where he was ... And it's the Pakis," I added, "who gave the North Koreans nukes ..."

"Pakistan's a terrorist money conduit," Thierry said, "from Saudi, the Emirates, Qatar, Abu Dhabi, and all those other Salafist desert dictatorships to ISIS and other terrorists. We can't get them to stop."

"Even Hezbollah, the Iranians," Anne said, "the Pakis are working with them."

"And that," Thierry said, "could mean the damn backpacks."

Out of the corner of my eye I glanced at Anne, stark and severe in the short black skirt and black cashmere. "And now we, the French," she said, "are in bed with Iran."

"And you're the ones," I said, "who gave us Ayatollah Khomeini –"

"And *you're* the ones who made him inevitable," she said, referring to the American 1953 coup that removed the democratically elected Iranian president Mohammed Mosaddegh and turned power over to the Shah. "And the purpose of that coup" – she looked at me balefully – "was to give you guys and the Brits Iran's huge oil fields –"

"In any case," Thierry broke in, "*jihadi* number two tells us some of those Soviet backpack nukes made it to Iran, and now – *le bon Dieu* only knows how – Mustafa and his ISIS buddies have one that may work."

"Your new best friends in Teheran," I snapped at Anne, "what do they say?"

"They're looking into it."

"Since when?"

"Since we told them. Five days ago."

"They know."

"Of course they know," Thierry said. "But they're working fiendishly on their own nuclear weapons. They don't want inspectors or journalists or anyone else coming around."

"So –" I took a breath. "They won't help."

She half-smiled. "They're making every effort."

Not only was there a plan to take down the Eiffel Tower, maybe with an Airbus, there was another plan involving a small nuclear weapon to take down Paris. I exhaled like a man who's just been condemned to death. Now it wasn't just Mack and Gisèle in great danger. It was the Tower. And maybe Paris. Maybe the world.

I felt a bit nauseous. "Where's Mustafa now?"

"Our two *jihadis* said he's traveling in a tan Passat with Austrian plates. They saw him once, in the car, but recognized him. Then we backed up border cameras and caught him crossing at Strasbourg, got the license plate. He may have come through Stuttgart from Munich and down to Freiburg. Stolen in Torino a few days earlier."

"When was this, Strasbourg?"

"Six weeks ago. We found the car again on backed-up satel-

lite pix as it was entering Fontainebleau Forest, heading southwest. Sky clouded over and we lost it. Could never find it again."

"Shit!" I said uselessly. My mind screamed with tactics to
catch him, fears we'd lose him, the harm he'd do. "How you
know it's him?" I persevered, against hope.

"They'd seen him twice in Baghdad, in Abu Bakr al-Baghdadi's
HQ. They never broke, on that one."

I glanced at Anne. "He's still in Fontainebleau?"

She shrugged. "But we have no photo of him."

"And that," Thierry smiled at me, "is why *you're* here."

All this suddenly felt like a trap. One you willingly enter but
can never get out.

"As soon as we heard Mustafa was here," Thierry added,
"and about the Martel operation, we notified Harris."

"What's he got to do with it?"

"Well, as COS he's our contact under the intragovernmen-
tal information sharing agreements. And because you and Mack
are the only ones who have known Mustafa and survived, he
put Mack right on it. And Anne" – he nodded at her – "has been
working with Mack since."

The thought of Mack being there, alive, working with Anne,
with anyone, saddened me. I took a breath, tried to forget it.
Thought about Gisèle, tried to forget that too.

"Why'd Mack call me?"

"You'd seen more of Mustafa than he had. That's what he
said."

"So why," I said to Anne, "are *you* on it?"

"Why?" Thierry smiled at her. "Because she's the best we
have. *That's* why."

I looked at her lovely hard face. Beauty scarred by pain.
Which made it even more beautiful.

"So," Thierry added, "Anne wants to go to Fontainebleau,
see if we can ID Mustafa."

"ID him?" I laughed. "Fat chance."

"We'll send forensics to do Mack and Gisèle's." Thierry gave a weary cough. "Go to Fontainebleau with Anne. That's where Mustafa was last."

"I'd rather check out where Mack's car was found."

"We've got plenty of people doing that. Only you can *recognize* this guy."

DGSE'S DRONE had lost Mustafa al-Boudienne's stolen Passat in the middle of the Fontainebleau Forest. This could mean that Mustafa had either stopped there, or had gone on to any number of towns and cities beyond.

Anne took the A6 south, weaving the bike at high speed between the lines of slower cars. Once when I glanced across her shoulder the speedometer was jiggling so fast I couldn't read it but thought it said 185. Hell, I told myself, don't worry. That's barely a hundred twenty miles an hour.

"Slow down!" I finally yelled through the motorcycle's howl and wind wail.

"*Non, non,*" she yelled back. "*Le bon Dieu nous protège.*"

The good Lord protects us. Did she really think that?

It certainly wasn't true, as we would soon learn.

TERROR

PARIS'S SOUTHERN SUBURBS are so ugly you have to get almost to Fontainebleau before you're past their graffitied, polluted, dangerous, dirty, and sometimes lawless streets.

From my earlier years in France I remembered this drive south fifty minutes without traffic jams to Fontainebleau's forests and climbing rocks. Back then, once you left Paris you were quickly in orchards, vegetable farms, dairies, poultry farms and wheat fields. But that's all gone now, to welfare apartment towers and auto yards and trucking depots and little subdivisions hopping over each other like aberrant toads.

It was near dark when she geared the bike down at the crossroads deep in Fontainebleau Forest where DGSE's drone had lost Mustafa's Passat.

My ears were ringing and my body vibrating too hard to speak lucidly. "Aren't you afraid of getting caught for speeding?" I yelled, gesturing at the bike and batting my ear in the vain hope of hearing something.

"You crazy? I do what I want."

She racked the Indian back on its stand while I stood there with my balls rattling. On benumbed feet I hobbled along the road to where it snaked down into a little valley of gray lichened granite outcrops under a thick canopy of tall broad-limbed oaks. It was easy to see why the drone had lost the car, if it was visual only.

Anne came up. "They lost him right here." She showed me her phone with the drone video on it and the little red arrow showing where we were.

The clouds reflected the lights of Fontainebleau and shadowed the great trees. The air was redolent with new growth, green saplings, ferns and early flowers, the rain-watered dank soil.

"You can smell God," she said.

"You're Catholic?" I'd already assumed this since she was wearing a crucifix on a golden chain between her small lovely breasts, and she had the no-nonsense sexiness of so many Catholic women.

"I just love God."

I shrugged. There's no way I'd still be alive without the help of some power far more all-seeing than me. I just didn't know what that power was. Or how to reach it.

"Me too," I said.

She hitched up her skirt and headed for the woods. "Got to pee."

She came back a minute later, tipped the bike forward, leaned across the seat and kissed my cheek. "You see, my brave warrior, we've made it safely so far."

This was true, but offered no guarantee for the trip back.

"If *you* were Mustafa," she said. "Why would you be *here* and where would you be going?"

"Why would he have taken this back road through the Forest," I asked, still batting an ear, "if he was going beyond

Fontainebleau? Like to Nemours or Sens or somewhere with lots of Arabs to hide among? If he was going farther, wouldn't it have been faster and safer to bypass Fontainebleau and keep going?"

"That's what I think." She straddled the Indian. "Let's go into Fontainebleau and walk the sidewalks, check out the restaurants and bars?"

I was dizzy with fatigue, so any action sounded good. It was a clear evening; people would be out strolling or sitting in cafés. If Mustafa was here we might just see him.

I was trying to remember what Mustafa looked like, but that was from eight years ago. No way he'd look the same.

SHE CURBED THE INDIAN near Fontainebleau's public market, chained our helmets to it, and handed me a clear plastic earbud microphone like the ones we used in SF, similar to the US police CodeRED Watchman. The earpiece fits easily into the ear and the lapel mike is semi-invisible, with an easy button for transmission.

"We stroll down each side of Rue Grande," she said. "You're the one who has to ID him, and I'm nearby for interdiction and support. If you see him you tell me, and I'll call in backup and we wait for the right moment to take him down."

I nodded, but if I found Mustafa could I keep myself from killing him?

Did Mustafa know where Mack was? Gisèle too?

In hostage rescue it's the first few hours that count. Once they've hidden you in a squat somewhere among the growing Islamic areas of France – or elsewhere in Europe – the chances of finding you are zilch.

Nine hours already gone. I was getting nowhere.

RUE GRANDE is a large bright avenue bisecting Fontainebleau for a mile between low stone and stucco buildings, bars, restaurants, clothing stores and bakeries mixed in with small apartment buildings and a few homes, lit by the welcoming ambience of warm windows glistening on sidewalks full of young animated people, on passing cars, scooters and bikes, and bewitching with the fragrances of food from the cafés and the open bakery doors.

Mustafa was a little under six feet, as I remembered, a skinny rough guy with a tapering muscular trunk and runner's slim legs. The eyes dead like those of Germans in the old photos of them shooting Jewish children. A hard, rectangular face, wide thin lips cut halfway between sarcasm and scorn. Long thin nose. Frizzy black hair cut short, the sharp beard and mustache. A face in which torment was written. And much more torment wished on others.

If he had a different beard now, or none, could I recognize him? By the black unfeeling eyes? The stony cheekbones and cruel mouth? His voice? Was he even *here*, in Fontainebleau?

Why were we doing this instead of hunting for Mack in Paris? For Gisèle?

I wandered casually, hands in pockets, along the east side of Rue Grande, keeping time with Anne's progress on the other side. Checked each passing guy, the male faces in the flitting cars, the men clustered at the bars and in the early chairs and tables set out on the chilly sidewalk.

Then I saw him. A tall guy standing quickly and turning from a table as if he'd spotted me. Black beard, black coat with a furry collar, long dirty jeans, black boots.

I pressed my lapel button. "Got him."

"Wait for me!"

I slipped between two tables and around three chatting women and came up behind him as he ducked out the back door. I let the door swing back, pushed through it and tailed him down a narrow cobblestone alley half-lit by city lights off the clouds.

"Mustafa!" I hissed.

He ducked his head, started running. I leaped on his back and pressure-pointed his throat till his knees buckled and he fell backward on me. As I flipped him over he swung a knife that I knocked aside, wrenched his arm back under his shoulder and shoved him hard down on his face.

I flex-cuffed his right wrist to his left ankle and called Anne. "I'm in the alley behind the Café Splendide."

"You *have* him?"

I looked down into the terrified, hate-filled face. "No, but I've got another nasty one."

She came up tucking her Glock into her shoulder holster, glanced at him and scoffed. "They won't even arrest him."

"He pulled a knife –"

"Legitimate defense. You attacked him."

"Let's call the local *flics*. See if they have a file on him."

"They won't be able to stick him with anything."

"*Vous allez payer*," the guy mumbled. "The mother of all lawsuits."

"Your mother's a pig." I tucked his knife up under my sleeve and we walked away, leaving him cuffed ankle to wrist around a sewer pipe in the alley.

"THAT WAS STUPID," Anne huffed as we stood on the corner waiting for the *Walk* light so she could cross to the other side. "I thought you were smarter than that."

"He took off when he saw me."

She snatched my arm. "Listen, you, this isn't America! You can't just *grab* people –"

I felt angry, betrayed. "He had a knife."

"*Most* Arabs carry knives. Get over it." The *Walk* light flickered green and she stalked across Rue Grande like a woman deserting a lover.

I was nauseous with weariness and mad at myself. My stomach burned and my muscles felt weak. All I wanted was to go to the apartment in Passage Landrieu and sleep. But how could I, with Mack and Gisèle missing? And Mustafa festering among his evil friends, planning more suffering and death?

But once we got into the rhythm of hunting Mustafa in every Fontainebleau café, brasserie, restaurant and bar, in every car and passerby, a new energy filled me. Determination born of total urgency – Mack tortured, Gisèle too. And a mass murderer loose in France, organizing his next massacre.

AT THE FAR END of Rue Grande she and I switched sides and worked our way back up the street.

By 22:20, the crowds and traffic had thinned. I felt a savage mix of frustration and sorrow, when every minute counted and I hadn't done a thing except knock down the wrong guy.

How could I even recognize Mustafa after eight years?

Why were we down here chasing shadows when Mack and Gisèle were probably being held somewhere in Paris, 45 miles north?

When we got to the Indian she stepped away and spoke briefly on her phone, then came back. "That was Mamie," she said.

"Mamie?"

"My mother-in-law. She lives with me, takes care of the kids. Just telling her I'll be home soon."

She climbed on the Indian and gunned it. Buckling her helmet, she tossed me a sideways glance and slapped the saddle behind her. "You're going to be *okay*, baby. Just don't hold your breath."

WE ARRIVED BEFORE WE LEFT. That's what happens when you exceed the speed of light.

I got off the Indian with aching balls, wind-savaged cheeks and shuddering thighs, trying to remember where I'd put my keys (in my pocket, it turns out) and what floor my apartment was on (the fourth, apparently). Anne tugged back a sleeve to check her watch. "See you here, five-thirty?"

I nodded dumbly. It was now after midnight and it seemed five-thirty was due in about thirty minutes.

In the apartment I set my phone for 05:00 and toppled on the bed. Couldn't sleep. Tried not to think what was happening to Mack right now.

And probably Gisèle.

TERROR UP YOUR SPINE when you're going to die right now. The hot rifle muzzle nine inches from your eye, you're cuffed to a stake, you've just seen the three guys next to you shot in the head. And you're next.

Singe of cordite on the muzzle, trace of smoke snaking away. Bullet waiting in the chamber, hard steel backed by high explosive in a brass cartridge with a center-fire rim which when hit by the firing pin will explode from the pressure driving this wedge of steel at 2,900 feet per second through the skull between your eyes, crushing and shredding your brain and everything you've ever been and loved. And though the pain will be nearly instantaneous it will last forever.

Sometimes they shoot you in the eye. The three Iraqis before me they'd shot in the forehead, their brains blowing out the backs of their heads all over the posts they were tied to, pale bloody flecks floating away like gnats on the dry desert wind.

So maybe they won't shoot me in the eye. In the last instant of my life I don't want that.

TROUBLE WITH NUKES

IT HAD RAINED in the night and the gray roofs of Paris glistened in the dawn. I stood at the window transfixed as usual by the beauty of this place. Ineluctable, because it made no sense – who cares about another smoggy overpopulated city? But there *is* something about Paris I can't understand but that makes my heart happy every time I'm here – its beauty, the astounding proliferating architecture – the most exciting city on earth, fabulous food and wine and magnificent women – sometimes you pass ten to twenty stunning women in every block – they have no idea how beautiful they are with their long slender bodies and flimsy spring clothes – the statues, monuments and fountains everywhere. As if life were something to be celebrated and commemorated.

At least it had been, before the loss of Notre Dame. People seemed different now, sadder, less lighthearted. Dispirited.

Thinking of the latest plan to attack the Eiffel Tower, I detoured to it across the Champ de Mars to check its new security measures. Far above me the Tower gleamed in early morning light, a lance-head filigree of human genius against a bright blue sky. It seemed so huge, impossible that humans had built it.

"OUR JIHADIS coughed up a bit more," Thierry said when I got to DGSE. "The Iranian side of the puzzle. There actually may *be* a bomb, headed to Paris. An Iranian official of some kind. Will have it in his suitcase. Which doesn't go through security because he's a diplomat."

"Holy shit. They *said* this?"

"More or less."

"Stay on them. Make them spit it all out."

"Too late."

"Shit. And the Iranians?"

"Same as before. They know nothing."

I exhaled wearily, trying to think it all out. "Maybe they don't."

THE TROUBLE WITH NUKES is they make everything unsafe. Not only in today's nuthouse scenario of many nations – some of them stark raving mad – able to kill everything on earth 28 times over. But just having nukes puts you at far higher risk from your nuclear neighbors.

Like handguns – the more handguns exist the more likely people will be killed by them. The more nuclear weapons, the more likely people will be killed by them. Millions of people.

The backpack nuke is a perfect example. The more of these small portable devices get out there, the more likely one will go off. Law of averages and all that. Which of course will be then followed by many more in a fearful cascade. The technology is not that complicated; there are terrorist bombmakers out there working frantically right now to produce them.

Their greatest advantage is they don't have to be delivered by another weapons system such as a missile. They can be small and portable enough to be brought into a city in the back of a small truck. Or a large suitcase.

And they can take your city hostage. Hide and seek: *Try to Find My Warhead Now!*

Or destroy everyone any instant their owners want.

I could not imagine how to deal with this. None of my training prepared me for it. I was the guy who climbed the cliff to rescue a hostage or was usually first into a firefight – not because I wanted to but because I didn't want my buddies to risk it. Not the kind of guy to outthink a terrorist or an Iranian nutcase with a nuke.

Though all us SF guys who stay in the game get plenty of info from old buddies and up and down the channels. And we all keep abreast of shit: it's simple survival.

From what Thierry was saying, DGSE couldn't figure it either. Nor, apparently, could any of the folks on our side. Nor, supposedly, could their opposites in Iranian intelligence. But who, either honestly or dishonestly, professed no knowledge of it.

The Iranians, with testing of their own missile-based nuclear weapons only a year or two away, had no desire to get caught in a scheme like this. This is where the links between Sunni terrorism and Iranian-backed Hezbollah were so difficult to discern. And what in its medieval complexity the Iranian government wished, versus what the hardheads in their Revolutionary Guards, Hezbollah and Quds intended to do.

When most Iranians are just like us and want to live and love their families and friends in peace and quiet. With enough work and freedom to make a decent life.

But in Iran it doesn't matter what most people want.

Nor most other places either.

———

THE ANTI-TERRORIST SECTION of the French Police recently moved to the 17th Arrondissement, in one of those shiny glass monsters popping up along the Péréphérique. A stone's throw from the equally new and even more monstrous home of the Justice Department that sticks into the Paris sky like a stack of huge shiny cereal boxes.

There I sat in a half-lit room with my eyes closed, trying to remember exactly what Mustafa al-Boudienne looked like.

"Keep his face in the front of your mind," the technician named Antoine said. "We will slowly create this same face on the screen, but you must keep the real one in your mind and not let it slip away, not even for a moment." He leaned back, scratched his chin. It made a loud scraping noise in the silent, darkened room.

"Black frizzy hair," I said. "Five-eleven, maybe –"

He flashed steadily through hundreds of images. "That's one-eighty meters."

"Rectangular face, big jaw, small ears close to his head ... muscular but lean ..."

"We will make this –"

"And his eyes, you can't imagine – there was no life in them."

"I can imagine. I will show you."

"And the beard," I said, "it was cut short. But thick."

"Under normal conditions, we like to do a robot-portrait within hours of the crime, while the perpetrator's face is still fresh in the victim's mind. Though sometimes it's better from a distance, a day or two, after the victim's stress has diminished ..."

For two hours Antoine worked the computer's drawing pad with my every suggestion and correction, till slowly, awkwardly, the face of Mustafa al-Boudienne stared back at me.

As I remembered him, eight years ago.

But what did he look like now?

When he stood over me with the black muzzle of his AK an

inch from my forehead, Mustafa had a short thick beard and mustache that nearly hid a crimped, downturned mouth. It gave his face the look of a hive of hornets, and thick eyebrows from which his black dead eyes glittered with joy and hatred.

He jabbed the muzzle into my chest, dragged it down my ribs. I tried not to look but saw his finger on the trigger. Just relax and take it. Sweat poured down my chest onto the dirt. Just take this. He twisted the muzzle into my side. Giggled.

"**FORENSICS** has gone through Mack and Gisèle's house at the microscopic level and found nothing," Thierry added. "Except that they make love a lot."

"I could've told you that," I muttered.

"No matches with our database on the door handles, the phone, any of that ..."

He looked weary and nervous, angular, unkempt, in a wrinkled shirt with a coffee stain down the left side. *He's been here in the office all night,* I realized, and this worried me more. Thinking how we hunger for good news when there isn't any.

"And the DNA of the blonde-dyed black hair will be back soon," he continued. "Maybe, just maybe, somewhere in our database there's a match."

"Gisèle's not been heard of since Pono left the house yesterday at one forty-eight," Anne said. "Her cellphone still doesn't answer. It doesn't show up on the France Telecom locator nor ours, and her face hasn't hit a single surveillance camera in the Paris region – and we have thousands of them."

Thierry made more coffee while Anne and I summarized the Fontainebleau trip, the guy I'd grabbed. "Good try," Thierry said, and I gave Anne a quick sneer.

Thierry leaned forward on his desk, clasped his hands. "Yesterday afternoon we sent fourteen officers into the streets around Rue Beaurepaire, right off La République, where we found Mack's BMW. No one, *not one person*, noticed the car or anything happening in it."

"That's crazy," I said.

"Impossible!" Anne added.

"It could be Mack was attacked somewhere else and the car was then driven to where it was found."

"In which case there'll be somebody's else's DNA in it," she said.

"Hopefully. Or" – he gave his head a questioning tilt – "it happened there, where we found it."

"Hah!" she scoffed. "A million people would've seen."

"Didn't you have a transmitter," I said, "on that car?"

"Mack wouldn't allow it. Said anybody he was dealing with would be smart enough to pick it up, and that would be the end of the relationship."

"True," I said.

"When he left home we assume he drove down Avenue Victor Hugo to the Étoile then Friedland to Haussmann to La République and straight out Belleville toward DGSE."

This was logical, I realized, a big arc across the middle of the Right Bank, from the chic apartments of the 16th through the showy 8th then the dirty working districts of Paris and train stations to the illegal migrant sectors where DGSE was based.

"But he never got here," I said.

"And his car was back by La République, on Rue Beaurepaire," Anne said.

He steepled his fingers, took a long quiet breath. "The total distance by that route, from Mack's place to here, is 17.6 kilometers."

"If that's the way he went –"

"We checked the car's onboard computer. Mack drove 29.3 km that morning, enough to go from his house in the Sixteenth to DGSE and halfway back. Another four km beyond Rue Beaurepaire –"

I took a breath. The multitude of possibilities was stunning. We were talking about an area covering much of the right bank of Paris. How in all these vast neighborhoods of ancient stone and stucco and tall steel and glass, could we ask everyone who lived there about a black BMW gone astray?

"I'm asking for ten more agents to work this," Thierry said, "starting at La République."

"We need more people than that!" Anne snapped. "It'll take us weeks to cover it."

In Thierry's harrowed face I saw a sudden flash of how bureaucratic French intelligence could be – the need for signoffs, no one wanting the lead. "I'll find out who's running things on my side," I said. "Maybe we can double up?"

The CIA's Paris Station Chief, I reasoned, would have a few French "consultants" to hit the streets with us. Ex-military tough guys, Foreign Legion and Mali vets looking for a little extra fun and cash on the side. A joint deal; both sides stayed in touch and everybody came out ahead. We Americans owe a good part of our 1776 independence to the French under Lafayette. And they owe us for saving their ass in World Wars One and Two. Plus all the money we poured into France under the Marshall Fund. To keep France from turning Communist. As it was about to do.

Thierry gave me a quick grimace. "The person running your side is Cedric Harris. I'll give you his number."

"*Major* Cedric Harris?"

"That'd be the one."

"That little bastard's the one who put me away. The first time."

"*Ah!*" Thierry exhaled. "*He* was the one?" He turned to Anne. "I told you about this, when Pono went to Leavenworth Army Prison for shooting that Afghani girl who was burned and dying?"

"I remember. But then" – she gave me a bemused look – "idiot, you shot the husband too."

"He was the one who burned her!" Thierry said.

"Major Harris," I said, "was the Army prosecutor at my trial. He tried every nasty trick in the book to get me. He didn't give a damn if I was guilty or not. They needed to show that the good old USA doesn't tolerate war crimes."

"That wasn't a war crime," Thierry said. "It was an act of mercy."

"Not shooting the husband," Anne interjected.

"He poured kerosene on her," I said. "And lit her afire because he thought she'd glanced through her burkha at another man. She was fourteen. Her father, too, he was in on it. Family honor, the father said."

"You shoot him too?"

I shook my head.

"You should have," Thierry said.

"So why are you here?" she said. "And not in jail?"

"A fantastic lawyer. West Point grad. She got wind of my case and blew it apart. I was out in six months."

"But then," Anne went on, "you were in jail again? You like it there?"

"Ah, yes?" Thierry said.

"A lot of our injured vets end up in Hawaii. The weather doesn't aggravate their wounds, the medical care is excellent, and even if you have no legs there are ways to get around."

"That doesn't explain *your* going to jail there," Anne said.

"I was delivering weed to a buddy who had lost his legs in combat, when a cop pulled me over. He had a dog who smelled it." I shrugged. "It was a setup. I got ten to fifteen in Halawa Prison, the worst in Hawaii and one of the worst in the US."

"So why aren't you still there?" she persevered.

"An undercover cop I'd smoked weed with once, she set it up. Then when she met my buddy without legs – he came to prison to see me every day, lots of vets did – she realized what she'd done, vanished the evidence, convinced the cop who arrested me to change his story, put her brother, also a lawyer, on the case, and got me out."

"Wow," Anne said. "I would never get anyone I've arrested out of jail."

I smiled at her. "You're probably a lot nastier than she is."

Thierry raised a placating hand. "In the present situation, then, we have two separate crimes. The arrival in France of Mustafa al-Boudienne, and Mack's disappearance."

"No," I said, "we have three."

"Of course," he nodded. "But Gisèle is surely part of Mack's disappearance."

"There's nothing else," Anne said, "I can try. To find her." She turned to me. "What about Mack?"

"What about him?"

"Where is he in this?"

"In what?"

"Maybe I've been missing something." She leaned forward, musing. "In this tangled web with the black-haired blonde-dyed girl, with something in Normandy?"

Exasperated, I leaned back in my chair. "You got to understand, when you've been through what Mack and I did, he'd never let you down. He'd never get caught up in some tangled web ..."

"Sure," Anne said quietly.

"So," Thierry broke in, "let's get all those new agents out there. They have photos of Mack and Gisèle, and Pono's sketch of Mustafa."

"Sure," Anne repeated, subtly conveying the absolute impossibility that any of this might work.

Thierry glanced at his desk, a defeated man stumbling back into the ring for another round. No matter the cost.

No, I wanted to tell him. We haven't lost yet.

B E I R U T

"A PLANE HAS TO HIT the Tower straight on," Thierry said. "To knock it down."

"Like the Saudis did to the World Trade Center in 9/11."

"And just like it, the Tower's been a terrorist target for years. The most-visited and most-loved human structure on earth – what better way to make your name than knock it down?"

Thierry rubbed his neck wearily. "After the 1994 Algerian attempt things were quiet for a while as the terrorists went after easier targets – the Métro, or a concert of happy young people, families on a sidewalk, an office full of journalists, cops with their backs turned. But they've always come back for the Tower ... a 2014 attack with automatic rifles, could've killed hundreds of people – we caught them at the last moment ... Another one later that year, then in 2015 the ISIS press secretary, Mustafa Al-Adnani, released a video promising the Tower would soon be destroyed, so for months we had no end of young terrorists trying to find enough explosives to knock it down."

"So far so good?"

"You did know that in August 2017, two of the Muslim group that five days later killed 16 people and injured 126 in Spain had gone to Paris and taken pictures of the Tower from every angle, mostly of the security installations, the entrances and exits, and the lines of tourists waiting to get in?"

"It'd take a truck full of *plastique* just to take out one pillar."

"Like Beirut?" He meant the 1983 Iran-backed bombings of the US Embassy, the US Marines compound, and the French paratroopers' headquarters, all of which had killed nearly 400 people, and had driven the US out of Lebanon.

"Or Nairobi?" he added, referring to the truck bombings of the US embassies in Kenya and Tanzania that had killed over 220 people and injured 4,000 more.

"And with all the new security measures there's no way a truck can get near one of the Tower's four pillars. There's vehicle blocks, a ten-foot bulletproof glass wall, a tall picket fence. And we have hundreds of surveillance cameras covering every angle, every face tied to instantaneous facial recognition systems."

"I checked the Tower out this morning," I answered. "That kind of surveillance won't stop a truck. And that picket fence won't stop bullets. They can mow down hundreds of tourists. And they can get over those walls and fences in seconds ... There's the four operations entries and two exits, all easy to smash into ..."

He nodded. "It's the best we could get."

"What about drones?" I persisted.

"There we're okay. In the area around the four pillars we neutralize their controls. Knock out their signals. They have to land. And they can't carry enough explosives, anyway, to hurt the Tower. Just kill some innocent people ... And we're scrambling cellphone waves around it so no one can use their phone to set off a bomb ... We jam the frequency, so the phone picks up our transmission and nothing else ..."

This was more old news. Every cell phone transmits and receives radio waves to communicate at the speed of light – digitized voice or data in the form of oscillating electric and magnetic fields. The rate of oscillation is the frequency. You jam or scramble the frequency and the phone will pick up your message and nothing else. And can't set off a bomb.

That was the idea. But new technology can now unscramble jammers before they ever reach a phone. Meaning that a phone could still trigger a bomb ...

I wondered if Thierry was right.

That you could blow out a pillar and the Tower would still stand.

It hadn't worked in Beirut.

HER NAME WAS NISA, which in Arabic can also mean *woman*. A DGSE advisor, she had written three brilliant books on Islam and the West. Maybe five-ten with thick, curling dark hair down both sides of a long neck, a nose and lips slightly too big and eyebrows too wide, a fearful wondrous glance as if hoping for the good but expecting the bad. A look that said, *life is too short, we must not harm each other.* She was someone whose face told you all you needed to know: she wouldn't lie.

I liked that about her, as I'm used to people who rarely tell the truth. She had that clear, front-faced way of speaking to you that couldn't be mistaken. And the look in her eye of someone who's seen far too much and can't hide it.

She had a broken upper front tooth that had been well repaired but was still visible, and I wondered how she got it.

She had an undergrad in biology from Nantes and a doctorate in anthropology from the Sorbonne, Thierry had said, but that she knew her history and lit too. "Her background is straight-up Algerian," he'd said. "Grew up in Stains, a miserable Muslim ghetto north of Paris –"

"I know where Stains is."

"First generation, father a devout Muslim. Mother fully

veiled, never allowed to leave the house without a man. Her father never acknowledged her successes in school, she was not allowed to tell her mother. At eighteen, just having acquired somehow a copy of *Madame Bovary*, she revolted."

I grinned. *"Madame Bovary?"*

He nodded. "She saw it as a parable of herself. The change was subtle at first, she says, a disinterest in prayers – for which she initially felt guilty – then slowly a wonderment at what the world might be like for a young woman not saddled by Islam."

"She's married to a doctor," Anne said. "Cardiologist at La Pitié."

La Pitié-Salpétrière is Paris' largest hospital, a sprawling campus of buildings that is almost an entire arrondissement by itself. To be a cardiologist there is to be at the very top of one of European medicine's greatest centers. "From Algeria too?"

"Lebanese. He escaped Beirut during the 1990s, at the end of the civil war. It's quite a story ... Maybe she'll tell you sometime."

SHE HAD the instant effect of making you trust her. She, Anne, Thierry and I sat at his conference table, the sun low through the western smog over the rooftops and shining fully into her face.

Like many journalists, human rights advocates, and writers who have dared to criticize Islam, she and her family had to have full-time police protection. That she was a Muslim and a woman merited her an even greater level of danger.

"What do you make of all this?" Thierry asked. He had summarized what we knew about Mustafa's sudden appearance, then Mack's and Gisèle's disappearances and what the two *jihadis* had told us about Mustafa's return to France and the plan to attack the Eiffel Tower and maybe Paris with a backpack nuke.

She leaned forward, thinking, tugged a dress hem over one knee. "The first thing to understand about Islam is that it divides the world into the House of Islam and the House of War. And everything not Muslim is in the House of War, and needs to be taken over and Islamic law enforced."

"We know that," Anne said. "That's why we asked you here."

"This belief underpins what is now happening. Makes it inevitable." A phantom smile crossed her lips. "I have heard of this Mustafa. He has a large following among our young men."

"What's he selling?"

She leaned back, one wrist and hand still on the table. "An imaginary way out."

"Out of where?"

"A shattered family, rabid religion, no money, nothing at all, living in a Salafist den in one of the Lost Territories of France, where if you don't conform you don't survive ... That kind of thing."

"The Lost Territories?" I said.

"The parts of France run under Sharia," Thierry said. "The places most French never go, and tourists never hear about."

"The most dangerous," she added, "is all these young *jihadis* who grew up in France and are now coming back from Iraq and Syria, hating France for what we are, and my fear is that they're going to melt right back in and expand the war here."

"They already have," Anne said, "for years."

Nisa *tsskd*. "Not like the war that's coming."

"HOW MANY TIMES," Anne said, "could we have stopped World War Two before it started? If it hadn't been for politicians too craven to act? We could've stopped Hitler when he went into the Rhineland, when he was ready to retreat at the slightest response from us. And we did nothing. How many other times? And the First World War? Why are we *doing it again?* Why do we always wait until the danger is probably insurmountable before we do anything?"

"France today," Nisa said, "is where it was in the 1930s. The German 'soft' takeover before the Second World War – it's what Islam's doing now. Other writers say this but nobody listens ... The best-known Algerian writer, Boualem Sansal, warns in his latest book that Islam intends to conquer Europe, that it's a constant theme in Islamic politics and literature. But nobody listens. 'Europe is afraid of Islam, it's ready to give it whatever it wants,' he says. The greatest living French writer, Michel Houellebecq, says it in *Submission*, and Eric Zemmour in *Suicide Français*. More and more French writers are saying it – and thus living under 24-hour police protection –"

"And you are too," Anne added.

"True. Which is very difficult for Ali at the hospital, for our children at school. But it's not proper to criticize Islam, just as in 1936 in France, when to criticize Germany and Nazism was uncouth and politically incorrect."

"Thirty years ago," Thierry said, "we had a hundred mosques in France. Now there's two thousand, plus thousands of prayer cells and madrasahs, most funded by Saudi Arabia and other Middle Eastern Salafist hardliners. We have no idea what they're preaching in most of these mosques, let alone in the prayer cells. We can't wire them all, can't put agents in them all ..."

"But the ones you do track?" I said.

"The big, dangerous ones, we try to. But we can't shut down most of them, even when they're preaching war against us. The courts and media won't allow it."

"These Lost Territories," Anne said, "are not just the hundred or so regional ones, there's many hundreds of smaller neighborhoods we don't go into. We need to bring them back under French law, get them out of Sharia. We need to get the veil off the streets, out of women's lives. No more genital mutilation, home imprisonment, brutality and rape."

"Everything's so much harder now because of the EU," Thierry said. "It has lousy intelligence sharing, poor collaboration and no enforcement. With their inability to police Europe's borders they've put us in a very dangerous situation. While taking away all our tools to deal with it."

"It's getting like Beirut," Nisa said.

"That bad?" I said.

She turned to me. "You've been?"

"Many times."

"You liked?"

"I can imagine what it was."

"My husband is from East Beirut." This was the largely Muslim side of the city, and West Beirut more Christian, though many of the Christians have now left.

"His father was an accountant for the city water department, his mother was a teacher. They were religious but not fundamentalist. His mother could drive, wore the *abaya* over her hair but no *niqab*, no veil. She could go outside on her own without a man – they were living in the Paris of the Middle East, remember ..."

"When there was one." I'd heard from my Pa what Beirut had been like, before the civil war that killed 120,000, erased a good part of Lebanon and smashed this magnificent Phoenician-French-international city to ruins.

"Ali, my husband, was born in 1975, the year the civil war really started. By 1990," she said, "there'd been fifteen years of war. The city was destroyed. The ancient Phoenician quarters and the beautiful oceanfront hotels, the lovely nineteenth century buildings, all annihilated. A hundred twenty thousand dead – for what? All because of the Palestinians coming in from the south and the war between them and the Christians, then Iran's Hezbollah came in and everyone was trying to survive in basements as the city blew to pieces above them, thousands buried alive under falling buildings ..." She spread her hands, a gesture of appeasement. "Why do we do all this? It is the question that I try to understand every day ..."

"He got out, your husband?" Anne said.

"He got out, but no one else. His parents crushed by a falling building, one sister shot, the other blown up by a car bomb. He was fifteen, stowed away on a Norwegian ship out of Jounieh. When it docked in Genoa he walked to the French border – most Lebanese back then spoke good French – and then to Paris, to an uncle who took him in and sent him to school and gave him a family to love and protect him." Her eyes glistened. "He was a wonderful man, Uncle Sayeed."

"And now?"

She shrugged. "We do what we can do. Ali saves lives, I try to too." She looked at Anne. "Like you said, once it would have been easy to stop Hitler. But nobody had the courage."

"And nobody has the courage now?" I challenged.

Nisa looked at me hard. "We *can* contain it. We *can* stop it from growing. Can we reverse it? Probably not."

"Julie, my daughter," Anne said, "she's five now. Two years ago she nearly died of mononucleosis. An emergency doc at La Pitié saved her life. A Muslim ... Even before then I'd refused to make distinctions. But after that? When every day I thank that man?"

Nisa nodded. No one spoke.

"France is stronger," Anne said, "*because* of our Muslim and African communities. But we have to come together, stop hating each other."

"A lot of us don't hate each other," Thierry put in.

"True," Anne said. "But to go forward we must integrate the Muslims now in France. Not allow them to dominate. But we can't take any more. These people who say we have to be tolerant, open our gates to millions more? Let *them* do it. We've reached the limit. Or it will destroy us."

NO ONE ESCAPES

BARELY 24 HOURS ago I'd landed in Paris full of Tahiti surf power, hungry to see Mack and kill Mustafa. But Mack had already been snatched and Gisèle soon after, and now we were facing a tidal wave of terrorism that a day ago I couldn't have imagined.

On my way to see Cedric Harris I'd grabbed some chicken shawarma at a sidewalk stand near Concorde. Missing my beloved *souks* and *bazaars* and knowing somehow the worst for France was yet to come, I tried to recharge my jet-lagged brain and make sense of all this.

Mustafa had returned to life. He who I'd thought was dead, whom I should have killed when I might have had the chance. If I had, how many lives would have since been saved? Five hundred? A thousand? What do you do with all those lives on your hands?

Maybe like Dracula, Mustafa had to be revived before you could kill him. Had to be alive when you drove that final stake through his heart.

In the eight years since Mosul I'd never forgotten him. But I'd been at peace, thinking he was dead.

Now he was alive again. As much as I was hunting him, was he now hunting me?

JET-LAGGED, I wandered my way across the lovely Champ de Mars with the bronze-colored Tower at its end rising over the Seine and the world, past thousands of new pilgrims come this day to give it reverence and to email home pix of their nearest and dearest in front of it. Then down Avenue Rapp past lines of magnificent stone-cut buildings golden in afternoon sun to the Seine and its long tree-lined walkways upriver with the Petit Palais and Grand Palais and Le Louvre and so much of the world's greatest architecture facing you every step of the way ... And of course you haven't seen *anything* yet, not till you get around the bend and further upriver, toward the La Conciergerie and what was once Notre Dame.

To find Mustafa was why Mack had called me to Paris. And the CIA, who energetically disliked me for sometimes playing outside the rules in order to get things done, were paying me – *imagine that!* Via of course a Mexican roofing company in Fairfax, Virginia. Which no doubt didn't exist. So if this roof fell in, it'd be on my head.

Not that I gave a damn.

The CIA is annoyingly parsimonious, unless it's buying some minor dictator who'll plant a knife in their back five years later, when he mistakenly thinks he can do so safely.

Mustafa probably already had Mack. And maybe Gisèle? To trade her for me?

"No one," Mustafa had said eight years ago as he readied to kill us, *"ever escapes me."* Then almost benignly he'd added, *"Is it not written that infidels, unbelievers in the Koran, shall eternally suffer the fires of Hell? Can't you see Allah's will that awaits you?"*

But Mack and I *had* escaped him. And now he might have Mack again. And here I was within reach. How could I use this?

Though Mustafa had much bigger fish to fry. To destroy the Tower. To maybe incinerate Paris. Why care about me?

Because in his mind, brilliant as he was, this was the convergence of opportunities. Getting Mack *and* me while he took down infidel Paris and maybe the world was only one more proof of Allah's all-seeing will. Because it must work in every dimension.

"You will be broiled in Hell fire," he'd once intoned from the Koran. *"So many times that your skin shall be well-charred, and we shall give you new skins so that you may be burned again, for God is mighty and wise. Is this not written? Does it not promise you this?"*

I batted him out of my mind. *No worries, you asshole, I'll take care of you.*

Far more important was to get Mack and Gisèle back. Now.

Then kill Mustafa.

Together we could do this. Anne – upright, committed, and brilliant. I tried to imagine what her husband had been like. To love a woman like that. And be loved by her.

MAJOR CEDRIC HARRIS was a hard little man, barely five-eight. Thin pointed face, narrow blue-shadowed chin, sharp elbows, a slit mouth and thin-set brown eyes. He stood so straight he seemed to have rebar for a spine. His every word was chopped-off, precise. With no emotion.

For Major Harris, as I well remembered, duty was all. Never once that I saw – and I saw a lot of him – did he act naturally. As if each instant before he spoke he asked himself *What would a successful officer say here?*

During my Army trial at Fort Carson in Colorado for shooting the burned and dying Afghani girl, Major Harris was a true hound dog. He seized on every miniscule point however inane or false to build an image of me as a rogue killer who had to be put where he couldn't hurt people. Sometimes it was so hilarious I laughed, but each new false charge was another spike in my prison door.

Because of his ramrod posture my girlfriend Lexie – a stripper and school teacher who had most recently come with me to Tahiti along with Erica and Abigail, and who had earlier inadvisably married Bucky, the SF buddy who saved my life in an Afghanistan firefight then helped to send me to Leavenworth ... she who during my trial flew weekly from Honolulu to be at my side – called him "Major Hair-Ass," and soon we had my guards and even once the court recorder saying it too.

To no avail.

Now I'd left one of the traffic-clattery streets around La Concorde and entered a back door to an elevator to the third floor. I stood before him in his silent, elaborate office trying to keep down the bile in my throat and the hunger to kill.

"You're here." He gave a sharp nod across his flashy antique desk, didn't hold out a hand, which was too bad because I would've crushed it. "Let's see what you can do."

From the number of lines flashing on the console beside him I wondered if maybe Langley was already awake. I didn't salute, wanted him to know he was a useless asshole. But now he was our top guy in Paris, and to save Mack and Gisèle I might need him.

I sat in the rickety antique chair in front of his desk. "What's the latest?"

This seemed to rile him. But then, everything riled him. I'm sure he thought an orgasm, if he'd ever had one, was a duty. One you had to fulfill even if you didn't want to. "If you're referring to Mr. Rosenthal and his wife," he said, "it's in French hands. We're offering whatever technical help they want, but they're as technologically advanced as we are."

"Are you *telling* me" – I leaped up and leaned at him across his desk – "you don't *have* any French fucking networks? No guys on the street? Anybody who *knows* anything?" Like I've said, even while working with a close ally you need eyes on the street. But it had long been a fault in the Agency – they depend too much on cyber and satellite and often have no idea what's actually happening on the ground. I was furious that it was true even in Paris. And I wanted him to admit it.

He waved it aside. "You won't need access to any of that."

"Because it doesn't exist?" I sat and relaxed my fists on the armrests. Otherwise I might have killed him. "So why are you hiring me?"

"We're *not* hiring you." His lips crisped. "You don't even exist. I'm supposed to be nice to you so you'll work with us. Unfortunately, we need you."

"You *need* me? Bullshit."

You were the last to see Mustafa –"

"And live. So what?"

"We have no one since."

"That was eight years ago. When you were polishing your legalese elsewhere. So you could win a war crimes prosecution and further your career –"

He glanced at me bleakly through sad pale eyes. "You think that judgment *helped* me? When every single person in this man's Army was on *your* side?" He nodded his chin at his tapestried office with its wide damasked windows and ancient oak herringbone floors. "Now I'm stuck here." He slapped palms on his desk. "You think I *like* this place?"

If you don't love Paris, in my view, you're totally nuts. "I don't care if you like it. What I care about is you *knew* I was right to shoot that poor dying girl, and you prosecuted me anyway!"

"No." For an instant he was far away, elbows on the table, chin on clasped hands. "You shot her husband."

"He'd set her on fire!"

"Still." He shrugged as if I were a credulous fool. "It was illegal."

"I'd do it again." I wanted to strangle him. "You would too."

"No." He barely shook his head. "I would not."

"Enough!" I sighed. "Let's find Mack and Gisèle."

He sat up primly. "You'll liaison between DGSE and us –"

"You just told me you don't have anything. So what am I supposed to give them?"

"– and you will keep us apprised of every development in their investigation."

He went on and on. More bullshit how Mack had really still been SF on loan to him so Mack's kidnapping wasn't really his problem. Special Forces should take it.

"SF," I snapped, "has *zero* effectives in Paris. And doesn't know fuck-all about France or its Arabs!"

He grinned, the first emotion I'd ever seen him try to fake. We were both right: the French had the most advanced surveillance – sat, phone, internet and street camera, DNA physical reconstruction, odor identification, instantaneous facial recognition of thousands of potential terrorists, so that the moment a camera saw one the nearest law enforcement personnel knew. And of course the French had the only penetration, poor as it was – into Muslim areas. It *was* their fucking country, after all. At least it had been.

For all this us Yankees could be nothing but a poor cousin.

"So why was Mack going to Normandy?" I said.

"Normandy?" Harris sat back, a puzzled look on his craggy face. "When?"

"Afternoon of the morning he disappeared."

"No. He was on his way to DGSE when they grabbed him, not Normandy."

"No, in the afternoon he was *supposed* to go to Normandy. Why?"

"Beats me." He glanced up at me under bushy eyebrows. His hair was gray, he was almost bald, but his eyebrows were still thick and black. "Who says this?"

"Gisèle. Before *she* disappeared. Thierry says it's not part of this deal, hunting Mustafa."

"That's why Mack's working with them. *Was* working with them. Since Mustafa returned to Europe. Before that Mack was working on US-French terrorist links ... you know that."

"Mack never told you, about Normandy?"

"Not a word."

"You don't even overwatch your *own*? Who the fuck *are* you? You didn't *know* where Mack was, all the fucking *time*?"

Harris held up a cautionary palm. "Sooner or later the watcher is watched. Which has bad consequences."

"Only when *you* screw up."

"Remember, Mack was you guys. Special Forces. Not *us*. Whatever happens, buddy boy, you know the script ..."

"Call me that one more time I kill you."

"What, *buddy boy*?"

In an instant I was out of my seat and clenched my left hand around his neck. Between fingers and thumb I had half of it. He leaned back in his white leather chair and smiled. "Now you know," he whispered, "why I need you here."

I yanked back my hand, embarrassed. What I'd done was militarily unconscionable. I felt shame. But this man had sent me to prison on a lie.

"Why?" I managed.

He twisted his head, loosening his neck. "Because no one else can do it."

"You little shit, don't give me that."

He stood, six inches smaller than me but somehow larger. Patted me paternally on the arm. "Go forth, brave knight. The queen's love awaits you."

"You're fucking nuts," I fumed, and walked out.

EARLY IN THE GAME

MUST'VE WALKED a mile before I finally sat at a café near Pigalle, sweaty, thirsty, and hungry to understand.

Somebody was lying.

Maybe everybody was lying.

Had Harris really not known about Normandy? Was Mack not really working for him? Or for DGSE? More non-accountability? Who was telling the truth?

Simple spying, Harris wanted. You watch how DGSE operates and feed it back to the Agency, who apparently in this matter couldn't find their dick in a rainstorm.

Nothing new there.

I would no more betray the French, I'd silently told him, than my own beloved country.

I'D ORDERED a second Ricard when Anne called.

"What'd he say?" as sharply as ever.

"They're letting you guys take the lead."

"*What?*" Her voice went up an octave. "*What!*"

"Hey, be nice. They're offering tech support."

She spat. I heard traffic in the background, a big boulevard. "Where are you?" I said.

"La République."

"Nothing yet?"

"It's early in the game, Pono."

No it's not, I nearly said. "Nobody recognize anything?"

"Not Mack, not Gisèle, not the BMW."

I started walking toward the nearest Métro. "I'm going straight to Rue Beaurepaire, where the car was found."

"Our people have already interrogated everyone there. No one recognizes a damn thing. As if they're blind. How does that car suddenly get parked there, and nobody sees?"

"I'm going to try a different angle."

"*What* angle?"

I didn't know. "Tell you when I get there."

"*Tant pis*," she snapped. Which means anything from *too bad* to *tough shit*, often used sarcastically.

"I'll call if I find something."

"No." Her voice rose. "Call me when you *think* you find something."

I didn't know how to say *fat chance* in French so I just said, "*Tant pis*."

ON THE WAY I stopped in a bookstore for a copy of *Submission*. "You must read it," the woman behind the counter said. "Finally someone is speaking the truth."

"What is the truth?" I wondered aloud.

"The truth is we've had enough." She took my money and gave me change. "Everyone knows somebody who's been killed or handicapped by the terrorists. My cousin Barbara was on the Boulevard des Anglais when that Muslim killed eighty people with a truck and injured a hundred more. Both her legs are cut off above the thigh. She's twenty-nine, with a husband and three kids. She can't work as a teacher anymore, can't take care of her kids, can't be a wife to her husband ..."

I felt my guts congeal, didn't want to hear this. "She and her family were there," the woman went on, "celebrating July 14, our national holiday. The Boulevard was full of happy families, lots of kids running around ... lots of tourists who got killed too ..." For a moment she said nothing, then, "How could one man do this? How could he kill and injure all these people? Why?"

I shrugged. "Allah told him to."

She nodded. "Yeah, Allah told him to. And we have eight million Muslims now. At least half of whom do whatever they think Allah, or the Koran, tells them to."

I looked at her, a pretty face lined with strain, graying auburn hair. "Where do we go from here?"

She scoffed. "Most French people want the mosques closed, they want the imams and the terrorists sent home. But our government? They care more about their image in the eyes of the media than they care about the French people they're supposed to represent." She puffed, a mix of rage and discontent. "The government doesn't represent the people."

"Maybe they never have?" I had to add. "Few governments do."

"Things have to change," she said angrily. "One way or the other, things have to change."

"That's difficult," I said. "Under the circumstances."

"We've had revolutions before. Maybe it's time again."

LES QUATRE VENTS was the seventh café I got to. A block off la République, on Rue Beaurepaire, near where Mack's BMW had been found. It was a lovely name – *The Four Winds* – reminiscent of the days you read about in the 12th century troubadour stories, when the Four Winds of the Earth were a known fact. Pinned inelegantly between three streets, it was ancient, from long before Baron Haussmann destroyed Paris by trying to make it beautiful.

At five in the afternoon Les Quatre Vents had few clients – two Arab kids playing hooky at the foosball, an old black man caressing a half-glass of red, two hookers getting lit to start the evening, a gray-haired woman in a pink beret with two plastic grocery bags and a cognac.

The *patron* was a beefy guy in a red wool vest with lots of little coats of arms on it. He had big red-haired forearms, a red beard, curly red hair and a round scarred face with a broken front tooth. I asked for an *express* and a glass of *monbazillac*, a sweet Dordogne white wine served cold, often with *foie gras* but that's great by itself.

"*Non.*" He waved a negating finger, "I have a better one." He snatched a pale bottle from the reefer. "*Bergerac moelleux*. From last fall. Exquisite, the taste of *terroir* –"

"I'll take two."

Nodding surprise, he poured two tall thin cold glasses and set them side by side between his huge fists, waiting for me to taste it.

"One's for you," I said. "For the suggestion."

He laughed and tossed it off and wiped broad lips with the hairy back of a hand. "What you want?"

I tugged an envelope with pix of Mack, Gisèle, the BMW, and my reconstruction of Mustafa from my shirt and spread them out before him.

"Like I told the other cops," he said, "I don't recognize this couple. Never seen them." He turned to check the other tables inside and out, the busy street beyond the wide windows. "And that car got towed away before I came on shift. But" – he jabbed a red-knuckled finger at Mustafa – "this guy I've seen."

NOTHING SHORT OF TREASON

"WHEN?" I said, afraid he'd stop talking.

"Thirty-one years I been *here!*" The *patron* slapped huge palms on the counter. "This bar." He glanced around at the football banners and trophies and photos on the wood-paneled walls. "Sure, it's near La République. But it didn't use to be like this."

I tried to slow my pulse, nervously watching Mustafa's picture on the counter as if it might disappear, or the patron might change his mind and say *Never seen him*.

"This guy." I nodded at Mustafa.

"Let me explain ..." He glanced at the window, then back to Mustafa. "This whole neighborhood was one big family. When people came in I greeted them like family, cared for them like family. I didn't overcharge and everyone loved it here and it was always a warm place for companionship and a chat. We cared and watched out for each other. Now all the French people are gone, or dead."

"It's true in lots of places." I glanced at Mustafa. "This guy ..."

He held up a palm. "Now when my wife walks down the street she gets spit on for not covering her head. For going out without a man to watch over her." He swiped at the bar. "Like that famous writer said, Islam makes people unhappy. And now they want us all to be unhappy too."

I glanced out the dappled window at the old, tired façades, the walls of graffiti and dirt. "Can't you leave?"

"In this economy? Go back to St. Malo? What would I do?"

"There's no jobs in St. Malo?"

He laughed exasperatedly. "Go there, try to find one."

I nudged Mustafa's picture.

He snatched it in his rough red fingers, and I feared he'd crumple it. But he only stared at it more closely, from several angles.

An old man with a cane came in. The *patron* drew him a *pression* and came back. "He showed up" – he shrugged – "maybe six weeks ago. A top guy, the way these others kiss his ass. Another bigmouth lecturing a table of hairy acolytes about the moral depravity of France, and how true believers are going to punish us for our unveiled women in short skirts who drive everywhere as if they were men. Women rutting with men not their husbands."

"Sounds like fun," I said. Six weeks ago was just after Mustafa's Passat had vanished in Fontainebleau Forest.

"So what do these guys do instead?" He spread his hands wide, seeking explication. "They fuck *each other*."

"This guy," I said, trying to seem relaxed, elbows on the counter, "he comes here?"

A hard grimace and a glance round the bar. His red face

swung back to me. "My daughter grew up here, a lovely neighborhood back then. A star student. Now she's come back to teach fifth grade in the Nineteenth, but it's got so bad she can't even do her class. The Arab boys, they attack everything. They throw crap ... they don't show up for school, they beat up other kids because they're not Arab. The Jewish kids got attacked so many times the families all left, many gone to Israel. The Arab girls, they beat up any girl, Arab or not, who wears a skirt, shows her hair or listens to music."

He glanced away, back at me. I felt a rush of empathy. "One morning," he rasped, "my daughter comes in to teach her class and someone's shit on her desk." He rapped meaty knuckles on the bar. "Why would anyone *do* that? When all she's trying is to give them knowledge so they can get a job, a life that's not a mix of welfare and crime? *Why?*"

I shook my head. "I have no answer."

"It's happened so fast," he said. "In only thirty years. *How?*"

"This guy ..."

"These guys, the bad ones, they're always coming through. They walk down the sidewalk with a mattress on their shoulders and disappear into one of the squats that've taken over the neighborhood. How many squats?" He raised his hands. "Right here? Hundreds. If not more."

He poked Mustafa's picture with a hairy forefinger. "This guy came, like I said, about six weeks ago. Then not for a while, then this week twice, met with a group of local wiseguys for an hour or so, then left with one of them."

"With the same guys?"

"Yeah, the same."

"He have a beard?"

"No, clean-shaven. But I think it's him."

"When?"

"Last night, is why I remember. And two nights before. Like I said."

"What time?"

"Late, near midnight."

"These other guys, you see them often?"

"Once a week maybe. They like to come in and run the neighborhood from my bar. Gives them a sense of power."

I couldn't believe that Mustafa, who must have known we were hunting him, would show up in Paris. But perhaps he scorned us, thought he was safe. After all, we weren't far from the Islamic strongholds that French cops don't enter. "What's the second language in Paris?" goes the latest joke. The answer of course is "French."

I went outside and called Anne. *"Mon Dieu!"* she gasped. "We should've run all the interviews again, after we got your Mustafa picture. It's my fault –"

"Now maybe we can *get* him."

"You're an angel to have thought of this … *Okay,*" she said, thinking fast now, "we insert a team, set up a site … What's it like, this bar?"

I described Les Quatre Vents. "Okay," she repeated. I imagined her intently pacing, phone clamped to her face, a dead Gauloise between her fingers. "The basement – what's it like? Is there an upstairs? Mezzanine? The building, how many stories? Give me the address, I'll pull it up … *Mon Dieu* Pono this is the best news in days – *Merde!* – I'm on my way!"

"But no setup," I said. "You and I meet first, figure it out."

"Any minute Mustafa could come walking through those café doors. Or later tonight. We *have* to cover this!"

"We do a big team it'll spook him … He's got a sixth sense –"

"We don't spook people. We take them down."

"Right now, he's mine."

"No way. He's on our soil."

"Just get over here. I'm headed to a café on the corner of La République called The Pinnacle, where I can see both exits of Les Quatre Vents. If you can't find it call me back."

CARS AND TRUCKS CLATTERED past on La République, buses growled and vans rumbled. I sat at my café table in their racket and stink and tried to figure what to do.

If we brought in a team someone would know – most Muslim neighborhoods have excellent sentry networks – and Mustafa would vanish. If his guys came back to Les Quatre Vents, what could we learn? Unless we sent them to someplace empathetic like Morocco, it would take too long to find out.

Far better to tail Mustafa when he left the café, to where he was staying. To grab more folks. Maybe even Mack and Gisèle.

But DGSE wouldn't take the risk. The steel nerves to have a major terrorist in your net and let him go to see where he went. DGSE would want action. Anne's guys in the cellar. And on the little mezzanine with its red flowery wallpaper, its narrow wooden staircase and white piano in the corner beneath it. Her guys going in one at a time like café regulars, scruffy losers, who would be at my side if Mustafa came in. And if we did get contact, DGSI and GIGN would be out there to block the streets, commandos up and down the sidewalk and both sides of the back door.

Take them all down, then weed out the chaff.

Because France is already, thanks to Islam, a police state.

Anne pulled up another scratchy aluminum chair and sat beside me. She was puffing and her forehead was sweaty.

"Where's your damn Indian?" I said.

"I've got an undercover car." She coughed, puffed a bit more.

"You should quit smoking."

"Fuck you." She nodded her chin at Les Quatre Vents. "That's it?"

"That's it."

"Tell me everything about it."

I told her what I remembered. "Shit," she snapped, huddling forward. "That's all you *got*, from that place?"

"I was trying to get him to talk," I said defensively.

"You have to *see* better, Pono." She scanned me earnestly. "It could save your life. Mine too. Lots of people's lives."

"Goddammit *I'm* the one who found him."

"True. You did." She stood. "I'm going to wander in there. Back in ten."

I checked my phone. 16:17 already. Mack a prisoner 29 hours. Gisèle 25. And what was I doing about it?

Over the top of *Le Monde* I checked that no one was coming in or out of Les Quatre Vents. Then a line at the top of the page caught my eye: "Corsican gangs attack Muslims."

The article was about a gang of racist Corsicans that had demonstrated outside a welfare housing project of Muslim immigrants. You had to read all the way to the end of the article to learn the reason the Corsicans were protesting: a bunch of young North Africans from this project had set a pile of tires on fire in the middle of a street, ambushed the firefighters who arrived to put it out, tried to kill them with steel bars and bats and burned the fire trucks. And *that* was the cause of the "demonstration" by the "racist" Corsicans.

The media is getting just like the law: you have to read the fine print. Which most of the time ain't there.

ANNE SAUNTERED BACK. "Let's call Thierry."

"No way." I put down *Le Monde*. "If we bring in a team it'll spook Mustafa and we'll never see him again. And he'll keep killing people."

She waved at the waiter, ordered a beer. "You want something?"

I glanced at my empty *espresso*. "Yeah." I turned to the

waiter, a tall skinny West African in a frayed brown-and-red sweater vest. "You got Bergerac *moelleux?*"

"*Non, Monsieur.*" He pointed a skinny ebony forefinger at Les Quatre Vents. "You must cross the street to get that." He looked down at me. "A *sauterne,* instead?"

"A Ricard." I watched him leave then turned to her. "Let's you and I decide how to do this. *Then* we call Thierry."

"How to *do* this? We put people in the cellar and in the back of that mezzanine. Once you ID him we grab him. That's how we *do* this."

"I want to protect the *patron.*"

"Bruno? He's cool."

It annoyed me she already knew his name. "Where would you set up? All the apartments around here are crammed with people ... You think you won't be seen?"

"It's just you and me." She shrugged. "And my people in the cellar and up on the mezzanine."

"How many?"

"Three on the mezz. Maybe five in the cellar. A few others in cars outside. Same old same old."

"Way too many! We can't without somebody seeing!"

"It's what top management's going to want."

"Thierry doesn't *want* it –" I sat back exasperated. This was stupidly going south. "Okay, let's do *nothing!* Pretend it's a dream, that the guy who looks like Mustafa is really a high school soccer coach. We should bother the big guns for that?"

She eyed me. "What are you saying?"

"Let's be sure it's real. Before we call Thierry."

"No chance," she scoffed. "He'd have us shot. First *me.*"

This made me grin and like her even more as she leaned back in the skinny aluminum chair in her black leather jacket and black leather boots watching me and Les Quatre Vents at the same time, as well as everyone sitting on the terrace or walking or driving past, all the while looking innocent and bored as Hell.

She was unforeseeable – angry one moment and cheery the next. Her smile lit up a room; her scowl made me fear for my life. I'd left Tahiti happy to be free of three women: how was it that I suddenly cared about this one? When she clearly wanted little to do with me?

"And what do we do," she said, "about *your* folks?"

"Not yet," I said, returning to the present.

She sat forward jiggling the table. "*But?*"

"But *what?*"

She grimaced. "We're not *supposed* to shut them out."

I was sick of this. Dizzy and sick with weariness and time change. Scared I couldn't save Mack and Gisèle, disgusted at every instant wasted. That I'd lose Mustafa too. "We're just confirming hunches," I sighed. "Before we waste their time."

"Mother of Christ," she whispered.

I took this in, watching the frenetic pirouette of vehicles around the square, the determined faced-down passersby, the threadbare clientele of this bar in a place more Algiers or Dakar than Paris.

It couldn't have happened by accident, this tidal wave of poor hungry people shaking France to its foundations. This fast-growing minority that hates it. Somebody had wanted this, but who? What were they getting out of it? From whom?

Anne squeezed my hand, her own strong yet gentle. Like her, powerful but slim. "Are there possibly people," I said, "within the government, a political party ... behind all this?"

She looked around, at the immensity of it. "All *this?*" Shook her head. "Too big for us to deal with."

"But if it's the *cause* ..."

"Right now we're battling the consequences. Which are a catastrophe ... An avalanche of catastrophes, each bigger than the last ..." She shook her head, a rejection. "We don't have time to analyze *why* ..."

"But that's how you win."

"*Win?*" she snorted. "We're just trying not to lose."

It was getting dark and starting to rain, car headlights dancing foggily around the gray monument. "Even now, we can't keep up with the thousands of crazies we have to watch," she said, almost as an afterthought. "More than twenty thousand, to be precise. And lots more coming back ..."

"Twenty thousand what?"

"The S File. Twenty-two thousand Muslims with terrorist links, many who've gone to Syria or Iraq and returned. A lot of them we don't even know where they *are*."

"Like Mustafa."

"And we're already spread so thin we can't begin to cover them all. While the government keeps cutting our budgets." She nodded fiercely, as if she'd made a point. I followed her gaze through the misty evening toward the bedraggled statue and fountain of La République, thronged by bongo drummers, beggars, and illegal Africans selling weed and trinkets. I tried not to remember when I'd been here before, when the glorious statues of dolphins graced the elegant granite square. Now there were store windows advertising "Wall Street English." On the other side, cafés, banks, restaurants, sporting goods stores, a few meandering cars, Arabic graffiti sprawled across doors, walls, gates shutters and half the vehicles hunched along the dogshit curb.

"Who funded it?" I persevered. "Who got paid? To trash this once-beautiful place, to trash France?"

She gave me one of those dreary *you're a dreamer* look, as if to say that I might as well try to walk to the moon.

"Who won?" I said. "Who lost?"

"Pono." She squeezed my hand again. "Let's not get in over our heads."

But the only way to get things done, I've learned the hard way, is get *way* in over your head.

France had spent hundreds of years and millions of deaths

fighting Islam. Originating about 620 under Mohammed, Islam had conquered in its first 100 years most of the globe between China and the Atlantic – the largest, fastest territorial conquest in human history – from Pakistan and Afghanistan to Iran, across all the Middle East to Turkey and up into Central Europe, across North Africa to the Atlantic. An empire drenched in blood and fear that by 720 had spread to Spain and Portugal and north into France, raping, pillaging and burning its way toward the complete conquest of Europe. Till Charles Martel, Charles the Hammer, stopped it dead at Tours, only 125 miles from Paris, in 732. The battle that saved Western civilization.

And now to invite this danger back to undermine your own nation, the way of life of your people, your culture going back thousands of years, seemed nothing short of treason.

CATASTROPHE

HAD TO CALL Major Hair-Ass, so I left Anne at our sidewalk table and ducked into a stone doorway down the street.

He seemed less than elated to hear my voice.

"I've been checking around where Mack's car was found," I said.

"French already did that."

"They didn't get everyone."

"You're wasting time."

"There's a café here, the patron ID'd Mustafa."

"The one they lost in Fontainebleau? He may have nothing to do with Mack and Gisèle."

I stared at the phone with hatred, softened my voice. "Why do you think that?"

"Why do I think it?" I could feel his dislike. "Because I've been at it a Hell of a lot longer than you, buddy-boy. That's how I know."

I glanced at the doorway's ancient pitted limestone blocks and reminded myself how much I might need him to help save Mack and Gisèle. "So who's on this?"

"I told you already. Somebody has to go first. For this, it's the French."

I remembered heart-wrenching tapes I'd heard in SF training that were from way back in Vietnam, the voices of Marines in a firebase being overrun as they called in artillery and air strikes on their own position. Stoic, no screaming. Realizing they'd been abandoned and were about to die.

"What's with Mack and Gisèle?" I finally said.

"Not a damn new thing."

"You sent out word?"

A moment of silence. "Word?"

"To all the nutcase imams and mullahs and Islamic websites and all these other crazy fundamentalists in France and all across Europe! To the fucking terrorism funders in Kuwait, Saudi and all those places! *That we want Mack and Gisèle back!*"

"I told you: we don't have the resources."

I huffed. "You mean Mack was SF, not yours. Therefore he's not your problem –"

"No," Harris said tiredly, "not that. The 'truth' we're getting from the French *is no more bad news about Muslims.*"

"Which *French?*"

"All the way from the Imam-in-Chief."

I snickered. That was a joke, coming from Harris. "But you're letting the French run it all, *carry the ball,* as you'd probably say ... ?"

"I hate football analogies." Harris exhaled tentatively, as though his stomach hurt. "Particularly from guys who've never played the game."

"I *have.*" I tried to reach him across uncountable dimensions and technologies. "So why are we throwing *this* game?"

You could feel him stiffen, right down the digital wave. "You give us everything you can learn inside the French system. That's your job."

"*My* job is to help find Mack and Gisèle."

"Says who?"

"Me."

"*You?* We don't give a *shit* about *you!*" He stumbled for words, in frustration. "It's the big picture, you idiot! And you just don't *get* it. Just like you didn't *get* it before!"

"You mean when you crookedly sent me up?"

He laughed bellicosely, and I reminded myself, *Never stop hating him.* Not that I ever had.

He sighed like a patient father with a stupid, stubborn son. "You can be sure, if needed, we'll be there for you."

"Good to know." I rubbed my aching back against cold stone, watched the serpentine mist slink up the ancient streets and hide Les Quatre Vents behind a veil of foreboding, the few cars like scavenging sea creatures with darting yellow eyes.

"IT'S YOUR BALL," I told Anne amiably when I got back to the café.

"*C'est notre ballon? Qu'est-ce que ça veut dire?*" (What does *that* mean?)

I told her most of my call with Harris. "Shit," she said, then, "Okay, have it your way."

"It's not *my* way. It's Harris, Home Office." I looked across La République at Les Quatre Vents. "Too dark, too much fog, can't see it well. Have to go back."

She stood. "Me too."

I held her arm. "No chance. You'd stand out there like tits on a boar."

"What?" she cocked her head.

"*Comme des tetons sur un sanglier,*" I tried, but she'd stopped listening.

She yanked out her phone. I pointed at her. "You bring in a team and I'll shoot you, I swear. With a water pistol that fires yellow dye you can never wash off."

She gave me the finger, stood and walked away, turned back. "I'll be in the car."

I gave her back the finger, stepped out into La République and almost got hit by a woman on a bicycle with no light. "Asshole!" she yelled as she zipped past, her wet raincoat buckle slapping my face.

LES QUATRE VENTS was warm and cozy. Seven men at the bar, four Arabs and three old black guys. Somebody'd been recently smoking hash, and its odor on his clothes had sunk into the room.

Seven tables, four empty and three with guys sitting round them, all Arabs. Espresso cups with cigarette butts squashed into their dregs, empty pastis glasses, cigarette foil on the floor – even though inside French bars there's supposed to be no smoking.

I leaned against the counter. Bruno came over with a Bergerac *moelleux*. "Nobody here you care about."

"Who are *those* guys?"

He capped the bottle, glanced at the flyspecked clock on the flyspecked wall. "Come back ten-thirty. Before that you're wasting your time." He slapped huge palms on the counter, snatched my glass. "That'll be ninety centimes."

I put down a euro coin with a German eagle on it and walked out, sucking in the salty cold Paris night.

ANNE WAS WAITING around the corner in an old brown Opel too beat-up to look cop.

"Nobody yet," I said as I slid into the battered passenger seat. "I go back at 22:30."

She checked her watch. "Two hours and ten minutes …"

"You go grab something to eat, I'll keep watch. Then we reverse."

"I'm not hungry."

I scanned the street again. "Damn work rots your guts."

"Mack used to say that."

"We used to say it about Afghanistan." I watched the mist thicken on the windshield and listened to the silence between me and her. It was charged, this silence. Resolute. Not the silence of peace.

"Mack talked about you," she said.

"I hope you didn't believe him."

"Gisèle too. That twice you saved his life …"

I tried to remember when this was. "He exaggerates sometimes."

"Yeah?" she smiled, tugging a curl of dark hair under her chin. "And that lots of women have the hots for you …"

"More lies."

"No doubt. I'm glad I don't."

I grinned. "Me too."

She switched on her phone. "Now what?" I said.

"Calling the kids."

I tried not to listen but her voice with that incredible strong softness to it resonated in my ears and wouldn't be shut out. First with André about his math and that if this other kid was being nasty, just ask him *what have I done to offend you* … Then with Marie, *Listen, Chérie, La Fontaine is fun, you must try*, then a few words explaining why … *He has so many double meanings* … To both kids, *I'll be home soon, we'll have a long weekend* …

Then Mamie's fiery voice slicing through the wavelengths. Their two voices intertwining as I watched out the Opel's windows for danger and tried not to listen – this sharing and harmony among women so different than among men.

She killed the phone and sat up in her seat. "Damn, life is complicated."

I chuckled. "No shit."

No one was wandering the foggy streets. My body sensed

no danger. "In the last few weeks," I said after a while, "since Mustafa got ID'd coming into France and you started working with Mack, was there never any clue this might be coming?"

"I've gone over it a thousand times. We shared what we could, each staying within our borders. If there'd been something I would've known."

"How'd you work it?"

"Mack brought in all your international stuff, I did the local and national. We made a good team."

Already it hurt to think of Mack as if we'd lost him, this hulking generous guy I loved like the brother I'd never had. *If you weren't so fucking stupid*, he'd told me one time in a Hanoi hooker bar, *I'd think we were related.*

I smiled at that. "In danger he was good to work with."

"He was super-smart, wise, careful, caring." She faced me, sudden tears in her eyes. "You think it's not killing me, this?"

"You knew Gisèle?"

"I had dinner with them a couple times, lunch once just her and me."

"Do you think he was fucking this woman with the blonde-dyed black hair?"

"No way." Anne shook her head. "Mack and Gisèle had this intense erotic focus on each other ... No one was gonna break *that* up. You even got *near* it you got electrocuted. It heated up a room. And the funny thing was they didn't *know*. We'd sit there having couscous and I'd suddenly wonder why the room was so hot, looked up and there they were, Gisèle and Mack, staring at each other ..."

"So what was hardest, working with him?"

"Hardest? He had to work for Harris. That was the hardest."

"Why? He could've gone outside, made three times the money."

She tilted her head in agreement. "But he was like you, Mack was." She brushed away a tear. "So damn stupid he always did what he thought was right."

I smiled with love and sorrow.

We'd been using the past tense about Mack. I feared it was true.

"MAYBE MUSTAFA won't show." Anne flipped on the wipers to clear mist off the windshield. "It's like so much of this work ... for damn nothing ..."

"True." It was nice to have it in the open, this truth. "Then what drives *you* so hard?" I had to say it, tired of it hanging between us like a lead curtain.

She nodded, eyes on the street. "After Éric was killed I was ... useless. They gave me a month off, then I came back and was useless and they gave me another month. Every night, every day, every moment I was choked by this most barbarous sorrow ... While having to be there every minute for the kids, make it easier for them ..." She stopped to watch a single car waver its way toward us down Beaurepaire, rolled down her window and pulled out her Glock till the car passed.

"Then I realized" – she slid the Glock back in its holster – "that the only way I could survive was to find the ones who killed Éric. And kill them one by one."

This was the first I'd heard that her husband had been murdered. "Like the Israelis did to the Palestinians after Munich," I said.

"It was right, what they did."

"Dead killers never kill again."

She bit her lip, scanned the street. "After two months of sorrow I showed up at the office and said I can't leave this job. Not while the people who killed Éric are still out there."

"And the kids?" I said.

She sat back. "What about them?"

"How they doing?"

"Two years after their father's death? They miss him every day. Like I do."

Perhaps this was meant to make me keep my distance, but it only made me like her more. "You going to find another man?"

She scoffed. "You *are* a prick, aren't you?"

"Kids need a father. Not just a Mom."

"What do *you* know about kids?" She pushed back against her seat and clenched the steering wheel. I thought she was angry, then she turned and gave me a look of such kind affection that I leaned across and kissed her, softly, delightedly when she didn't pull back, just put her fingers to my cheek, ready to restrain me or simply an affectionate touch.

The taste of her lips, soft yet resistant, relenting and pushing back, the taste of her tongue, her saliva warm and welcoming, dissolving in mine, made me shiver, her silky hair caressing my cheek, her slender neck in the crook of my arm.

"You shouldn't have done that," she snapped, pulling back.

"Why not?" I said stupidly. "Kiss me again."

She sat facing forward, a hard look on her face. "We're here to hunt terrorists. Not to act like teenagers in Daddy's car on some dark street."

I took her hand. It was rough and clenched, a little chilled. "Since Éric died, have you made love with anyone?"

She gave me a nice crack alongside the head. "Who you think you are, asking such questions?"

"Have you?"

She sat there fuming. In the darkness I could barely make out her features, her profile with its high brow topped by curls, her sharp nose, her full lips and strong chin. She turned to me, dark eyes glistening. "Why do you ask such questions?"

"Look, Anne, the *deuil* is over."

"You! What do *you* know about grieving?"

I told her, of friends lost in firefights and a beloved father recently dead. She sat there, hands gripped in her lap. "We're all the walking wounded," she said finally.

"Have you?"

"What, fucked other guys? Of course. I'm not a nun."

"So make love with me."

She instantly shook her head. "With you it would be different."

"How so?"

"With them I didn't care. The relief of an orgasm so I could go back to hunting the ones who killed Éric."

I caressed her cheek. "I'll give you tons of orgasms ..."

She looked at me earnestly, shook her head. "With you it's different. First of all, we're working together ... not supposed to."

I took out my phone and starting punching numbers.

"What are you doing?" she said nervously.

"Calling Thierry, asking if it's okay."

She slapped my hand. "Stop that!"

I shut the phone, kissed her again. My whole body ached for her. "When you want to, I do too."

She flipped on the wipers, turned to face the street. "Watch that damn door. I want to get this bastard."

I felt a little foolish having let myself go like this. But I liked her too much to not speak. "Wonderful as you are, Anne, you can't be a mother and father too. Plus you're working thirteen, fifteen hours a day?"

"Just till I find the ones who killed Éric."

"That could take years."

"We'll get there."

"Then?"

"We're going to take a long vacation – Argentina, New Zealand, Bhutan, all those wonderful places humanity hasn't yet destroyed."

"Don't wait too long."

She snickered, that French half-hiss that conveys more meaning than some dictionaries: disgust at human "progress," or at my comment, or at time itself which will not stop until it kills us all.

KISS HIM GOODBYE

SHE GOT OUT of the car, pacing and making calls, tossed the butt in the gutter and climbed back in.

"You stink," I said.

"Fuck you." She nodded at Les Quatre Vents. "Maybe I'll go in now."

"Shit no!" I sat up in the Opel's creaking seat, rolled my shoulders, stretched a weary neck. "You'll stand out ..."

"Like tits on a boar, I know." She grinned white teeth, half-shadowed in the streetlight through the windshield. "We're already in ... See that third-floor apartment over Rue Thomas? That's us. And we already have two guys in Bruno's basement. And a guy up in the mezz ..."

I turned away. "You're going to ruin everything."

"See that green taxi with tinted windows, over my left shoulder, forty meters? We have five guys in there ready to go. What you worried about?"

I shook my head, weary in every molecule. "Kiss him goodbye."

AT 22:30 I left her in the Opel, returned to Les Quatre Vents and stayed till it shut at 01:25. I watched for any of Anne's people but saw no one on the mezzanine and no one looked out of place.

Mustafa never showed. Nor any of his buddies.

I told Bruno goodnight and stepped into the rainy cold darkness. The fires of the rioters on La République smoldered and stank on the wet wind. Riots all the time now in Paris. Why don't the cops, I wondered, clear them out? Who tells the cops not to? Why?

I got into the Opel. "You assholes chased him off."

She shook her head. "He just didn't show, that's all."

"It was a stupid move." I was angry but there was no way to prove he'd been scared off.

"We may have tracked down the hair."

"What hair?"

"The woman who hit Mack. The lab says she dyed it blonde but it was black. And we have a possible DNA match: Yasmina Noureff. Born in Reims of illegal Algerian immigrants, twenty-two ... used to live in Seine St. Denis. It's where many of the 2015 terrorists lived, a huge Islamic stronghold north of Paris –"

"I know about Seine St. Denis," I said irritably.

"We originally got her DNA off the side of the toilet in an apartment she lived in for a while. And where two cousins of one of the *Charlie Hebdo* killers spent time."

"Where's she now?"

"I wish we knew."

"What might be the connection?"

"Connection?"

"Her and Mustafa?"

She puffed, rejecting it. I felt dazed, wondered how long since I'd slept. Tonight's possible failure and my fury at DGSE's quick setup for maybe blowing a chance at Mustafa choked me; I felt betrayed, that Anne had somehow betrayed me too.

"You guys have *totally* screwed up," I said.

"What?" In the half-darkness her face showed veiled astonishment. "*We're* the ones screwing up?"

I faced her. "Four reasons."

She gave me the finger. "Go ahead."

"*First*, instead of following Mack and Gisèle's trail when it was hot, why did you insist on a sidewalk sweep in Fontainebleau? Just because you'd lost Mustafa there?"

"That was part of it, yes." She leaned toward me, her face nasty and sharp. "But mostly I sent us down to Fontainebleau because that was my *gut*. I *work* on my gut. Usually I'm right. Mustafa *was* there that night. I'm sure."

"I doubt it. *Second*, why did I find the Mustafa connection easily at Les Quatre Vents? And *you*, DGSE, with your billions of euros, didn't?"

"Like I said!" She pounded the steering wheel. "When we interrogated every café near where Mack's BMW was found, including – *three times* – Les Quatre Vents, that was *before* you did Mustafa's visual. We had no likeness of him, weren't sure of a link ... And at that point we were frantically trying to find witnesses to what happened – the BMW, Mack, the blonde-dyed woman, the whole mystery ... And you haven't helped."

"And *three*, why did you *specifically* tell me not to bother going there? When Mack had vanished while investigating Mustafa?"

"I told you not to bother because we'd done it three times already! And I wanted you out looking for Mustafa. Because *you*" – she jabbed a finger at me – "are the *only* one we have. To find him."

"*And four* – why did you put a team on *Les Quatre Vents* when I *specifically* asked you *not* to, or to at least tell me if you were *going* to?"

"That was over my head. Happened too fast. I told them *not* to, but the bastards at the top want clean, fast arrests and no news. France does *not* have a Muslim problem – remember?"

"*What* bastards at the top?"

"Shut up."

The more I thought about it the angrier I got. We'd had a chance to maybe grab Mustafa, thus maybe save Mack and Gisèle, and we'd blown it. She and DGSE, and somebody at the top, had blown it. I stared furiously at the Opel's ratty dashboard, unlocked the passenger door. "I'm walking home."

"I should drive you but I'm damned if I'll bother."

I grinned, aching to take her in my arms, this lovely woman with the hard, pained face. But I was too angry. "This sounds like the basis of a long relationship."

"You ignorant *bastard!*" Tears gleamed in her eyes. "How could you *know* what's going on? How could *you* know?"

Maybe I'd misread her. Misread everything. I held my head in my hands as if it would break. "Why, Anne? Why do they *do* this? *Why?*"

"It's part of the catastrophe." She bit her lip. "The catastrophe that's happening to France."

My fury about the setup washed back over me. I shoved open the passenger door. She gave my cheek a friendly pat. "See you at seven."

I slammed the door and walked up the alley away from her. She backed up a moment after me then stopped. When I reached the corner she was gone.

NOTHING WRONG

I TOOK A DEEP breath; my injured shoulder relaxed; energy pulsed through me. *Free.* Why did she make me feel like I couldn't breathe? Or was I just paranoid?

Paranoia in ancient Greek means *outside the mind*. Isn't this what all these Buddhists and other meditation types are telling us to do? To widen our understanding?

So paranoia can be good. Tells us to watch out even when we see nothing wrong.

If our ancestors hadn't been very paranoid all the time we wouldn't be here.

And paranoia was telling me something was hidden in the French response to Mack's and Gisèle's kidnappings. And something in Anne I couldn't read, that evaded the information-sharing agreements we had at all but personal levels.

What did she know that she or they didn't want me to know?

Why had Major Harris wanted me here? Why had he agreed that Mack should ask me? Had he now asked Thierry to run me up a dead alley? No, Thierry would never do that without telling me. Or was there somebody higher up, in France, who didn't want me in this?

How would they even *know* about me?

Were *they* who ordered the setup on Les Quatre Vents, and blew our chance to grab Mustafa?

What was in it for them?

I crossed the Boulevard Saint-Martin barely ducking traffic and turned down Rue de Turbigo toward the Seine, seeing only the dirty sidewalk, cigarette butts, candy wrappers and pigeon shit, the leaning mildewed buildings and sleeping cars, furious and unable to understand what had happened.

Ahead on the old tired street of ancient stone buildings was the 15th century tower famous in military lore, where the Duke of Burgundy, Fearless John, murdered his cousin, the Duke of Orleans, who had taken refuge there.

You can't hide forever from people who want to kill you, the tower said. The better solution is *Get them first.*

Rain washed my face and soaked my clothes. I turned back toward Sébastopol and downhill toward the Seine, crossed the magical square in front of the Hôtel de Ville and crossed the Pont d'Arcole over the Seine to the grim remains of Notre Dame all bathed in darkness. For a while I stood at the barrier in front of the cathedral, lost in its majestic façade and the soaring intricate towers, tried to imagine its creation, each of the thousands of stone carvings, the scintillating windows all celebrating the beauty of the spirit.

This enormous work of art that people built eight hundred fifty years ago – could we recreate it now?

No way.

ALONG THE SEINE the underpasses were clogged with miserable people trying to stay out of the rain under blue tarps and cardboard. One was holding out his hand to passing cars; I kept going, stopped and went back.

He didn't speak French but a little English. I gave him ten euros and the others began to cluster around me. I gave them a bit more till my money ran out.

"Where you from?" I said to him.

"Congo."

"How did you get here?"

"My family save money. To come in a boat across the water. To England."

"Why England?"

"No hope at home. No food. Just hunger."

The others stood around us, watchful, expectant, as if I could deliver them somehow. "You English?" one said. "You take us there?"

"No." I watched their eyes drop. "I live here," I lied.

"We go England," another said.

England can't take you, I wanted to say. *They can't take any more.* "In a few years," Nisa had told me, "there will be two and a half billion Africans, another billion in the Middle East. Most of them starving. There's too many people and will never be enough food. They all want to come to Europe."

"In most of these places," Thierry had added, "they refuse the idea of birth control. For the men, many children is proof of manhood."

"Yes," she'd nodded. "No matter how many of them die."

The misery of overpopulation, I thought miserably. With no solution. I found an ATM on the next corner, went back and divided two hundred euros among them. "Go home," I wanted to say. But couldn't.

I turned and walked on.

My phone vibrated, a non-traceable number, hopefully Anne.

"Just checking in," a gravelly voice. Major Hair-Ass.

"Christ," I sighed, "it's two-twenty ..."

"If you're up," he chuckled, "why shouldn't I be?"

"Go to sleep," I huffed. "I'll call you at 08:00."

"Anything new?"

"Not a thing."

"You doing okay?"

This checked me. "Working the same deal. Headed home."

"He didn't show." It wasn't a question.

"I don't know why. The French, they screwed it up."

"That's what we're going to tell them. But it isn't true."

"We can find out."

"Go home. Get some sleep."

How could he know I hadn't been at home? I hadn't spoken to him since yesterday afternoon. "No need for you to be up," I said, pushing back.

"Of course I'm up. Just like you."

"Why?" I wanted to ask him, *What are you afraid I might find out?* But I shut down instead.

I grabbed a cab at St. Michel. Harris had to have a bug on me somewhere, to know so much. Son of a bitch, I was going to ditch it.

The cab driver was playing Arab rap on the CD, mouthing something about *Hang the whites* and *Death to the Jews*. "Is that about Israel, that song?" I said.

"What?" He turned it down, faced back at me.

"Is that song about Israel? Death to the Jews?"

"It's about Notre Dame. The Jews destroyed it. Everybody knows that."

"That's not true –"

"It is true. Predicted in the Koran."

"I'm a journalist from Ireland and I'd like to know what you think of France today, *la Situation?*"

He eyed me in the mirror. "What you ask?"

I repeated the question. "You work for the government?" he said.

"Of course not. I'm Irish."

He stared at me again. "You write what I say?"

"I can't guarantee, but I'll try."

His lips tightened. *Such guarantees should be easy.* "We are not all terrorists, but we get blamed for everything. Some people" – he raised his hand – "they think all Arabs are terrorists."

"The terrorists – do you agree with what they do?"

He inclined his head to say, *That is the question.* "We understand *why* they do this ..."

"Why do they do this?"

"Look at the evil, how these French live." He opened the window, spat. "You are from far away – do *your* people act like this? Half-naked women walking free in the street like dogs in heat, as if they were as good as men, laughter and drinking, no prayer, no love of God ..."

"Where are you from?"

"Blida, in Algeria."

I know where Blida is, I wanted to say. "But these people whom you call evil, they have let you come here and live in their home."

"It was stupid of them."

"And that song about the Jews?"

"The Jews are an offense against Islam. Everyone knows this. Even in our French mosques the imams teach us the famous line from the Hadiths, *The Muslims will always fight and kill the Jews. Not a single Jew will hide behind a tree but the tree will call out, "You, Muslim, God's servant, there's a Jew hiding behind me, come kill him ..."* He smiled back to me. "Is not true?"

"But terrorists kill everyone, not just Jews –"

"To the terrorists they are all infidels, who do not live the right way. The world will be better when everyone is Muslim."

"But you fight each other all the time."

"Only because of the infidels –"

"Look out!" I yelled as we headed for a crosswalk with three drunks stumbling through it against the light.

He stopped six inches from the last drunk, who yanked out his member and pissed in our direction. Sadly, the wind was against him. With a snort my driver spun around him, turned back to me. "You see, I would have passed in front of them."

"What about Israel? Does *Israel* have a right to exist?"

He pulled over, twisted to face me. "You are a Jew?"

I felt compromised, at a crossroads. "If I am?"

He glanced forward angrily. "Get out."

"Fuck you. Take me where I'm going."

"*Get* out!"

I shot a few nice pix of his badge and face and license before he spun off in an unpaid huff. And I stood on the corner in front of the Église Saint-Sulpice feeling free again.

The last time I'd felt free – was it before that big Tahiti wave?

Does freedom always try to kill you?

I couldn't answer such questions.

It was a quiet walk the last two miles to Passage Landrieu through the windswept foggy stone-cold Paris night. I was in the zone, exhausted, intense with fear for Mack and Gisèle and the impossibility of stopping what might happen. Just another penitent along these damp lonely streets with their centuries of lies and takeovers, the death of virtue on all sides.

Hair-Ass had to have a tracer on me. Where?

He and Mack had discussed me, and it was Hair-Ass who had sent me a ticket and a nice advance.

But why would he want me here when he knew I hated him? When he didn't like me?

Was there some other reason he brought me here, something I didn't know about?

In the apartment in Passage Landrieu I assiduously checked

all my clothes but didn't find a thing. It then occurred to my lizard brain that the tracer might not be *on* me but in this apartment. That would be why Hair-Ass knew when I was home. Supposedly both DGSE and Harris's teams had swept the place, but what did that really mean? The last sweepers could have easily installed something. Or, as it was a safe house it probably was hooked up all the time.

Normally I use a signal detector to check a place the moment I enter. I have an old Spy Hawk that works great. But I'd come straight from a surfing contest in Tahiti and my wearying bacchanal with three brilliant women, where the last thing in my mind had been bugging devices. I'd left my Spy Hawk in Hawaii along with my lovely cheap and dilapidated house overlooking the magnificent blue Pacific, my surfboards, my ancient rusting Karmann Ghia, my good buddy Mitchell, and all my other friends and fellow veterans and beloved animals. I'd intended to pick up a detector from DGSE or from our own team, but everything had gone to Hell so fast when I hit Paris I hadn't done it yet.

So I started with the easy stuff.

I called an 888 number that gives me hyper signal detection on my iPhone, and holding it to my ear I wandered the apartment from bedroom to bath to living room to tiny kitchen. Naturally it was the bedroom where the most powerful device was located. Maybe it's just salacious voyeurism, but the bedroom's where most of the truth gets told. As well as the best lies.

I crawled around on hands and knees with my iPhone till I found where the scratchy interference was loudest. It was under the bedframe up in the Philips screw hole that bolted the left headboard post to the frame. I left it alone and squirmed around under the bed trying not to breathe dust bunnies but could find no other bugs. As I moved away from that single device the hissing scramble in my iPhone got weaker.

In the living room was another bug where no idiot should

put one – in the middle of a two-circuit electric outlet behind the couch. It was a working camera as well as audio, but why had they placed it right behind the couch, where no camera could see a thing?

Or had somebody moved the couch?

I shut off the lights, waited for my night vision to return, and checked every room for the minuscule flicker of an LED. Rolling my right fist into a tube I scanned every ceiling and wall for the glint of a pinhole camera.

The best bet for a camera was the bedroom. Every spymaster I've ever known loves a good show.

Again I left it as it was.

Another camera was on the icemaker control of the refrigerator, the usual one on the toaster, another in the Wi-Fi adapter stuck in a living room wall, and of course one in the microwave's display panel. None in the smoke detectors, the stereo, the clock radio in the bedroom, or in any other weird place like the toothbrush holder in the bathroom.

I had a moment's concern for the national debt of both nations that they should spend so much on such a silly process. Then I got tired of looking for more, pretended I'd seen nothing, and went to bed.

Lying there, I worried why Hair-Ass had first tried to chase me off but now was urging me on? Why the fake empathy? When the only feeling for which the smarmy little lifer could be accused was sadistic ecstasy over another person's heartbreak?

03:44 AND STILL couldn't sleep. Imagining how an Iranian backpack nuke might make it to Paris. Or were Thierry's *jihadis* bullshitting? We knew they weren't lying about Mustafa – he *was* here and may have grabbed Mack and Gisèle. Nothing compared to the trail of sorrow he'd left numerous times in Iraq.

And far worse even than destroying the Eiffel Tower was the

little evil box that would blow Paris apart. And maybe start a chain reaction till everyplace on earth was tattered and charred.

I tossed off the covers, got cold and squirmed under them again. Wandered into the kitchen for a glass of milk and stubbed my toe. Glanced out the window at the half-lit cobbled alley, the trash bins hunched like sleeping bums, the pale drained façades with the telephone wires across them like jailyard chains. Listened to the silence and wondered why would Mack have a 22-year-old dyed-blonde Algerian woman in his car?

A hooker? Would he do that? My mind said no.

A girlfriend? No.

How then did she get in his car? How did she get close enough to hit him?

Mack was not a guy you surprised; even asleep he was dangerous. Why had he let down his guard? How hadn't he seen it coming?

Was she a *source*? His? Whose?

I stood looking in the bathroom mirror not seeing myself, not seeing the dirty sink edge and tarnished faucet, the despair of it all. Wanting to launch myself into an abyss of forgetfulness. *That* was the weariness of it, the grinding down with no respite.

I wanted to call Anne but remembered I was mad at her and at this whole French goatfuck that had maybe lost us a chance at Mustafa.

Too late to call her anyway. I took a leak and scratched my itchy back against the doorjamb.

Suddenly I felt alive, aware, energized, didn't want sleep.

Ready for war.

Wanted to call her and make up somehow. *She's asleep,* I reminded myself.

Out my window the Tower loomed over the half-lit city like a great dark angel in its sacred cradle of night. *This is who we are, we humans. This is what we can do.*

Nothing was totally lost, while it stood.

L I O N H E A R T

THOUSANDS of Paris street cameras had grabbed countless algorithmic matches for our Mustafa image. Faces picked out of Métro crowds, intersections, bus lines, sidewalks, stores, and public buildings that sort of matched the image Antoine and I had created yesterday.

So here I was on a stool in a dark room scanning all these matches for a face I barely remembered. The trouble with GaussianFace and all the traditional FRAs, Face Recognition Algorithms, is they miss the human factor. I've learned that recognition is more than what you see. Each person has an individual essence, a separate aura, something our body and brain recognize before our rational mind does. Or we have that delayed sensation of "I *know* that person ..."

In my first hour of scanning I found Mustafa nineteen times, the next hour five, and by noon another seventy-nine. You never knew for sure, had to check out every possible face, and all the positives got put on the master file and then we would try to trace each one.

Did the FRA provide a possible name? An address or driver's

license? Did he take the Métro? What exit did he use? Where did his trip begin? End? Who did he know?

Was he carrying anything?

What did he do during the ride?

Was he alone?

Then we went back and scanned the crowd around him – did anyone arrive or leave with him? Follow him to another train? For each and every instant of film, we did this. For all the possible Mustafa's. Over and over, to make sure we hadn't missed him.

What did he look like, anyway? Could I even remember?

Or was he really even *in* Paris?

Yes, because Bruno at Les Quatre Vents had recognized him. Or had he only identified my pictorial memory of a man last seen more than seven years ago? Who bore no resemblance to the man who might be now wandering France with a small nuclear weapon?

Had Mustafa been staying in Fontainebleau but going to Paris for meetings? What meetings? What were they planning?

My eyes burned. I was staring through a wall of melting glass that divided me from the world. A sense of failure overwhelmed me.

Gisèle. Right now they might be raping her. Tying her down on a table somewhere and raping her one after the other. In front of Mack.

"BUT WHY," I repeated, "was Mack going to Normandy?" We were back in Thierry's office bolting down a quick lunch of pâté sandwiches, chips, and Orangina.

He leaned across his desk as if protecting it. "I wish I knew."

"He never gave you a hint? Nothing?"

"Let's say it's not covered by our intra-governmental agreements on information sharing."

"Mack was on some *other* deal? Is that what you're saying?

For *you*? While he was hunting Mustafa with Anne and Home Office and all your friends?"

"The Normandy thing was for that afternoon. He got grabbed in the morning while on his way to work. Normandy's not relevant."

"We can't assume that."

Thierry gave me a bleak look. "As I just said ... We don't know why he was going to Normandy. Nobody does."

"You know *where* in Normandy?"

"Les Andelys, maybe, according to the car's computer from the last trip," Anne put in. She was acting friendly, as if we hadn't had a nasty fight last night. "A village on the Seine, with a town a mile inland from it. Hour and a half drive down the Seine from Paris."

"But why there?"

She shook her head.

"We don't even know," Thierry said.

A new thought stunned me. "I've been stupid," I said. "Stupid all along. Whoever kidnapped Mack left the BMW where it was as a joke. They're making fun of us."

"Don't be silly!" Anne snapped.

"What is Max and Gisèle's address?" I shot back.

Thierry shuffled in his papers, grabbed his phone, checked it.

"49 Boulevard de Beau*séjour* in the 16th," Anne said.

"And whoever snatched him left the BMW on Rue Beau*repaire* in the 10th."

Thierry looked at us; his eyebrows rose. "They're saying they took him from his *lovely home* to their *home territory*? Taunting us to find them?"

"You're snatching at spiderwebs," Anne said.

"I don't think –" I started to say.

She cut me off – "Or it's coincidence."

"The two addresses," Thierry put in, "I'm inclined to think are not coincidence."

"They're just fucking with our heads," I said.

"Mustafa's got bigger fish to fry," Anne said.

"No, no, no." Thierry shook a finger. "Mustafa's probably behind Mack and Gisèle's grab."

"And the Eiffel Tower attack."

"And the Air France Airbus."

"And the bomb."

"And Notre Dame?" Thierry clenched his fists. "And Normandy?"

THE EIFFEL TOWER high above us buckled, lurched, twisted, its huge steel beams screaming and wrenching apart as it toppled down on us with a gigantic howl. Then the camera view changed and from a distance you saw the Tower smash down on the Pont d'Iéna and into the Seine.

"Assholes," I said.

"You have to admit it looks real," Anne said. We were sitting around a screen at DGSE, she, Nisa, Thierry and I, watching an ISIS Twitter video of the Tower collapsing from a terrorist attack, linked to photos of an Air France Airbus. Then a terrorist's face, speaking French into the camera. "Things are going to happen, worse than 9/11."

Then a second Twitter video, this one promising to blow up France.

"Probably made in Qatar," Nisa said, "or some other Salafist place, the Emirates, Saudi ..."

"So many Middle Eastern airlines landing now in Paris," Anne said. "All it takes is one pilot –"

"Like the Air Egypt flight out of New York," Thierry said morosely, "where the pilot dove the plane into the sea shouting Allahu Akhbar?"

"Or the Malaysian," Tomàs added, "reciting Allahu Akhbar as he practiced the crash of Flight 370 on his flight simulator ..."

"For Muslims," Nisa said, "the Tower is an insult. An offense."

"It's beautiful," I countered. "What's offensive about that?"

"Look at its shape."

"Yeah, it's what the French were saying, back in 1887: we have the world's biggest dick."

Anne raised a finger. "There *was* a study done on that. Koreans have the smallest, and French *do* have the biggest."

"I doubt that," I said patriotically.

"There's a study on everything," Thierry said placatingly.

It irritated me, his efforts to minimize the hostility between Anne and me.

"Look what the Saudis knocked down in 9/11," he added. "The World Trade Center, the two most powerful pricks on the planet."

"For many fundamentalists," Nisa said, "the Tower is the apogee of evil. Why, they say, are we so poor and backward, while these infidels are given all these gifts by God? It is an evil that must be corrected."

"Technologies are evolving so fast we can't keep up," Thierry said. "Weapons we can't see, explosives we can't find, tactics to take over an airliner in flight that five years ago we couldn't have imagined."

I thought of the Eiffel Tower, its solidity. "Never happen," I said, feeling good for being so positive.

THE RAIN had started again – springtime in Paris. Anne stood next to me in the DGSE elevator rattling keys. "We're not taking that goddamn bike," I said.

"We're taking your car."

I knew she was hyper-stressed, but now she was losing it. "I don't *have* a car."

"You do now."

This worried me. French police drive mostly tinny little

Renault Kangoos and Peugeot Experts, frail, underpowered, and self-destructive.

Even worse, their car radios date from 1990, almost useless today, comms often dropped, easily hacked.

She walked me to the back of the garage where a few wrecks teetered on ancient tires. In the corner lurked a dirty Peugeot 406 that once had been blue. At least a decade old, battered, scarred and faded. She handed me the keys. *"You* drive."

I sneered down at it. "This's all you've got?"

"Wait and see."

It started fast and even, a smooth throaty rumble that belied its grungy appearance. I got out and popped the hood.

Anne stood beside me staring down like a new mother at the throbbing monster under the hood. "A Peugeot V6 racing engine. Fuel injection, five-speed, all that." She squeezed my arm. "We only have a few ..."

"It's a beast," I said happily.

"You should call it that," she said. "Every car needs a name."

We eased out of the garage right then left, then onto the Péréphérique. I tapped the pedal and it howled up through the gears to 180, nearly three times the speed limit. The acceleration so quick you feared your eyeballs would get stuck to the back of your skull.

It snarled in frustration when I eased off to 120 then down to 70. "Nowhere near as fast," Anne scoffed, "as my Indian."

"Fuck your Indian. It's too dangerous. And the way you drive it ..."

"That bike will *never* kill me."

"*Christ!"* I yelled. "Don't *say* that!"

She grinned and sat there smiling inside herself. This made me angry, and even angrier that it made me angry.

We quit the Péréphérique for the A13 west through the deep oak forests of Marly and St. Germain-en-Laye, then rolling orchards to Mantes-la-Jolie, *Mantes-the-Beautiful*, once a medieval jewel, now another dangerous ghetto of drug deals, halal butchers, constant prayers and black-gowned, veiled women.

Where the second language is French.

After Mantes the highway left the Seine and climbed through gentle hills of forest and wheat fields, the windshield wipers slapping lazily at the gray drizzle, the odors of freshly plowed earth and damp leaves through the window.

"We need to know," I said, "why was Mack going to Les Andelys? It's just a medieval village on the bank of the river where Richard the Lionheart built his castle, in 1198."

She turned toward me. "You *know* that?"

"In Special Forces we studied all the great war strategists. Richard was brilliant and courageous. A great tactician and a great warrior – he got his name for his ferocity in battle. The European side of my ancestors came from England and Normandy, joined him on the Third Crusade."

"Wow," she said. "My ancestors went with him too."

"Astounding. Maybe we're related."

"Yes, good we're not lovers."

I smiled, a little stunned, and tried not to look at her, prim and straight in her seat, feet and legs together like a schoolgirl's, that mysterious evanescent sad look on her face as she watched the river pass below us, as if I weren't there.

Her husband dead two years now.

I drove on silently, the Beast rumbling softly under its rusty hood, up through hills and forests down to the Seine again at the old town of Vernon, and past the ruins of the 12th century stone bridge across the Seine bombarded by mistake by American planes in 1944, then along the north bank through miles of forests and wheat fields, antique villages of gray stone, rambling castles and dappled meadows to the soaring bend in the river of white limestone cliffs with a huge white castle towering over a vertical outcrop high above the village of Les Andelys.

"One of the masterworks of castle construction," she said. "Built in one year, by six thousand laborers. Then Richard got killed, and we French took the castle, and for hundreds of years tried to tear it down."

Leaving the Beast by the Seine we followed a path along a wide grassy bank with a row of very old stone and oak-beam houses with steep slate roofs facing the water. One block up its narrow stone-paved alleys was a stunning church built, she said, in six months in 1197 by Richard and his workers.

"Why would Mack be out here?" I said. "What was he trying to find?"

She nodded at the rippling silvery river. "In the Third Crusade, Richard had nearly beaten Saladin. At the same time the Mongol hordes of Genghis Khan were attacking Saladin from the north. If Richard had been able to finish the war, that probably would've meant the collapse of Islam. But Richard was so sick, been sick for weeks, dysentery probably, he could fight no more. They agreed on a truce that kept Jerusalem in Islamic hands, along with North Africa and the Middle East, and has led to all the tragedies since ..."

She pointed to a narrow island of jutting trees with a single jagged roofline. "In the middle of the river, there, was Richard's personal castle ... In those days the whole place was high stone walls from behind and around the castle all the way down to the river, and pickets across the river – no one could go upriver unless Richard allowed it." She nodded her chin across the roiling silvery water toward the dark banks and jagged trees on the other side and the wide plain behind it. "More men have died in battle out there, on that plain, historians say, than on any other single place on earth. Over many thousands of years."

We came to an ancient arched stone bridge over a freshet. "For six hundred thousand years," she said, looking through the tangled dark brush of the creek to pools of dying sunlight, "we humans have fought for this place."

The wind down the creek bed was cold and scented with mossy leaf rot and pine. "In the 1930s," she said, almost as if seeing it now, "a couple lived on that island, very rich art collectors. One of them was French, the other American. I forget who was who." Anne started walking back toward the car. "When the Germans invaded, Hermann Goering came personally to the island to take their paintings. They died in Auschwitz ..."

From a bend in the Seine we looked upriver to Richard's castle gleaming in the afterglow of the sun. Tall on its stony peak, coppery gold against the dark forested hills behind it.

"Give me a minute," she said. "To call Mamie and the kids."

She stood aside in the shadows and I went down through the dew-wet grass to the river edge where the water roiled and eddied. Ducks sitting along the shore began to move into the water so I headed back up to Anne.

She shut her phone. "Why," I asked, "are we here? *Why?*"

She snatched my arm, fingernails biting in. "Let's go to the car and I'll show you. But first I wanted you to *see* these beautiful old homes, this great castle, this magical place called France that we're fighting for." She glared at me. "Come on, dammit. I'll show you *why!*"

We drove away from the Seine up a broad avenue lined with chestnut trees about two klicks to Le Grand Andely, a larger town of gray concrete buildings – once a magnificent medieval village, she said, firebombed in 1940 by the Germans as part of a plan to destroy all the towns along the Seine.

At the top end of town stood a small Gothic cathedral of perfect proportions. "The Germans damaged it, but it survives ... There were Roman villas here, Neanderthal clans –"

I scanned the darkening hills on both sides, their jagged teeth of concrete housing towers in the last orange rays of the sun. "Turn *there*," she said, pointing to a narrow, battered alley between two of them.

MORE THAN YOU KNOW

NIGHT HAD FALLEN, a few dirty stars poking through the haze. I parked the Beast in a far corner of the sandy parking lot between two welfare towers, in front of *Batiment* 2C. "Now what?"

"Two things," she said quietly. "*First:* if I ever call or message you the words *take tomorrow off,* that means come here *at once,* park right *here,* and a man will come out wearing an OGC Nice soccer shirt. You will take him *immediately* to DGSE. You will be *totally* responsible for his security till he gets there. Got it? Repeat it."

I did, twice.

"*Second:* We all know Mack had something going here. We've geo-located him to this building last month. But couldn't see in."

"No links?"

"We did a rundown on every resident and find no connection with our lists of fundamentalists or sympathizers."

"A building this size, has to be some."

"Not even one. We've picked up a lot of DNA, done some good listening. So far no hits."

"Thierry knows all this?"

"Of course."

I exhaled slowly. "Why didn't you guys tell me?"

"We had to be sure."

"Of *what*?"

"What side you were on."

"I'm on both, US and France."

"We're not the same."

"Who says?"

"We can't be ... What about Harris?"

"Says he doesn't know." I watched her. "Did Gisèle?"

She shook her head, eyes on the graffiti writhing across the pale concrete walls. "You're the one who said she didn't."

"You're saying *no* one knows," I insisted, "what Mack was doing here?"

"I planned to ask him, the day he disappeared. He was you, not us, but we were staying straight with each other. At least that was the deal ..."

"You haven't stayed straight with me."

"I have." She looked at me out of those dark oval eyes. "More than you know."

"Then tell me what I *don't* know."

She unclipped her seat belt. "First we check out this place."

It was the kind of building you see by the thousands in France, concrete towers for people the government keeps letting in but has no jobs for, places where the wattage is low, there's blood on the stairs and drug wars in the courtyards. Hallways smelling of urine and rodents, many doors broken and fixed with steel plates. The carpet sticky with old grit.

Where even the younger girls are veiled. Most of the graffiti is in Arabic except the promises to kill the French.

We climbed to the eighth floor, Anne behind me with a scarf

around her hair and face, showing only her dark eyes. At the top two steel doors squealed open onto a pallid hallway. "They could be here anywhere," she said.

"Who?"

"Mack's connection."

"You saying it was drugs?"

"In Islam it's good to sell drugs to the infidels. To fund the *jihad* … The stuff comes in on trucks. And goes out in little plastic packets."

"All this," I sighed, "has nothing to do with Mack."

"Imagine he was trying to find his way into a group that might be linked to Mustafa, what better way than to be some yokel American looking for hash?"

I looked at the scarred, graffitied walls. "We're not just playing cops and robbers here … what are *we* up to?"

"Hopefully." She knocked on a battered door. "We'll soon figure that out."

IT TOOK THREE HOURS. We knocked on every door and some of them answered. Anne showed them Mack's photo and asked if they'd ever seen him. Said he was her boyfriend and he'd gone away and she wondered if he'd gone with someone from here. And I was his brother from America and we would pay a thousand euros to anyone who could help us find him. Said it first in French then in Arabic, for those who didn't know French.

Her photo of Mack was the same I'd shown Bruno, Mack sitting on the Indian, big and muscled in a black AC/DC T-shirt, a sunny smile full of white teeth. A broad, deeply tanned face, bright black eyes. A woman's hand over his shoulder but that part of the photo had been cut away.

"Is that you?" I pointed to where the photo had been cut.

"That's Gisèle, on the back of my bike."

"I know it's your bike."

"Then what'd you ask for?"

Behind the first door a man with a bushy beard in a sleeveless undershirt would not let us in. He peered at Mack's photo a moment, biting a lower lip with a lone, twisted tooth.

From the room behind him came TV whisper, a child's complaint and a woman's soft murmur. He shook his head and shut the door.

The next door did not answer. The third was a gaggle of five children, no adults. No, the kids said, never we see this man.

They were all the same. On the fifth floor a woman with a bruised face looked at us in an instant of hope and faced away. Many apartments had children but no adults. Hashish smell lay heavy on the chilled moldy air, and scents of North African and Senegalese cooking. And in the whole bare building a kind of hollow acceptance that this, like these sordid gray mildewed walls, is what life *is*.

And no one had ever seen anyone who looked like Mack.

WERE THEY DEAD, Mack and Gisèle? Or were Anne and I chasing phantoms in Normandy while they were still alive but undergoing what?

What was I not *seeing*?

We took the A13 back, exiting the St. Cloud tunnel with Paris spread before us like a million chandeliers. And towering over them the pinnacle of France, the world's most-beloved structure blazing its message of beauty and freedom to everyone.

What if I had to give up Mack and Gisèle to save the Tower? And how many lives?

In the end, would that be the deal?

We grabbed a quick meal on the Champs Élysées, Anne halting me on the broad sidewalk under the young trees to look up and down the world's most beautiful avenue, the Louvre at one end and the Arc de Triomphe at the other, with the Défense Tower beyond, they and the vast city around and beyond them all glowing with the brilliance of human life.

We do all this and so much more. We could be gods.

AFTER MIDNIGHT I pulled up the Beast in front of Anne's place on a side street off the Rue du Temple in the 3rd. She checked her watch. "Early for us."

"Yeah." I rubbed tired eyes, dry numbed skin.

"I keep running it through my head," she said, "everything Mack and I did, everything he said, but can't find a connection. I'm *so* exhausted ..."

I looked at her, magnificent in all her weariness and pain. "You need sleep. More than anything, sleep."

"This is what I was trained to do." She looked at me pleadingly. "And I can't find a clue. No witnesses, no data trail, no pix, nothing. What am I doing *wrong*?"

I scanned the Beast's beat-up blue dashboard. "You're not doing anything wrong." *It's like a wound*, I wanted to add, *how it takes over your every instant with its howling demand.* But no, the wounded don't need to tell each other how bad they hurt.

She glanced at me, at her front door. "You don't need to drive all the way home."

I smiled, took her hand. "What a wonderful idea ..."

"But," she whispered, "we *have* to be quiet ..."

Through a coded doorway up half a flight to the elevator cage. A tiny elevator where it was hard not to rub against each other.

A third-floor tiled landing and four large bolted doors. She unlocked the left into a red-painted hallway then a wide living room and dining room across from it, kitchen to one side, and two doors at the end of the hall.

"Mamie sleeps in there," she whispered, pointing to one door. "And André and Julie in the other." She opened a convertible couch in the living room with a narrow bony mattress on coiled springs. "You sleep here."

"Where are you sleeping?"

"With one of the kids."

I took her hand. "No you aren't."

She looked at me, startled. "We have to be up in three hours."

I held her hand. "I'm lying down with my clothes on. You too."

She shrugged, turned toward the bathroom. "Have to pee."

She came back and stretched out on the bed and arranged a pillow under her head. I took the other pillow and lay beside her, bedsprings squeaking, and held her in my arms. She didn't protest and quickly fell asleep, breathing softly, her body warm against me. I kissed her nose, breathing in the rough fragrant essence of her, and lay with my right arm across her slender waist despite the pain it caused my bullet-damaged shoulder. I couldn't sleep, didn't want to, couldn't understand why being there with her made me so happy.

FROM A DEEP SLEEP she shook me, a lean breast against my ribs. Outside still dark, the streets silent. "I just had a dream," she whispered. "Have to tell you ... before I forget ... Mustafa's staying in a squat not far from République, or that Mack and Gisèle are ... or ..."

"Anne!" I whispered, "say it!"

She was asleep. Mustafa in a squat not far from République. Mack and Gisèle ...

I watched her as she snored softly beside me, something so holy in her aura of sleeping woman and mother that I was overwhelmed. As by the tasks before us.

Morning came too early, naked, cold and dark. The springs wailed as she climbed out of bed. A toilet flushed, a brief rush of shower and then the smell of coffee and she came back and kicked me. "Out of bed. Or I fold you up in it."

That sounded like a fine idea. But I sat up slowly, tugged on my shoes and realized they were on the wrong feet so I tried again. There came a whack upside my head that made my brain ring, but it was just Anne – "Hurry! I don't want my kids coming out and you there still half-asleep!"

I found the *WC* and fell asleep on the seat till she banged on the door.

With her razor I managed a quick scrape of my face, tucked a salvo of her Nivea under each arm, brushed my teeth with the nearest washcloth and was ready to go.

Her son André was seven, I remembered, and Julie five. André was slender but solid, with truculent black eyes under a black mop, a chiseled face like a Roman statue, a muscular soft tread. Julie came out moments later, slim and athletic with a cameo face, blonde hair, and a shy, fearful air.

"This is my friend Pono," Anne said. "He's a surfer."

"Oh yeah?" André offered, a little more interested.

"From Hawaii," Anne added.

"I want to go there," Julie said.

"Right now you're going to school, remember?"

We sat at a wobbly wooden table as the first orange clouds began to glow beyond the rooftops. Anne had made strong Italian coffee with steamed milk to pour on top and we toasted last night's leftover baguettes covered with butter and Bonne Maman wild cherry jam. Anne's hair was all tangled and when she turned from the kids to smile at me it lit up the room.

The second bedroom door clanked open and a gray-haired woman in a black robe slippered down the hall. She too was slender, tall as Anne, a paler, wrinkled face. "Mamie!" Anne said. "You should sleep."

"The coffee smelled too good." Mamie went to the counter and poured herself a cup, then turned on me. "And you are?"

"This is Pono," Anne said. "He works with me."

"I see."

Anne stood. "Julie, André, finish up! Pono and I will take you to the Métro."

"*I'll* take them," Mamie said, "to the Métro."

"We can go our*selves*," Julie said.

"I'll be dead first," Mamie said.

"Don't *say* that!" Anne snapped.

Mamie scowled at Anne and me. "Out!"

"*Mon Dieu!*" Anne sighed in the elevator, fluffing her hair over her jacket collar and settling her pistol holster under her arm.

"She doesn't like me, Mamie."

"She doesn't want me with any man. Afraid I'll fall in love again and make more babies then my new husband will be killed like Éric. She's Manichean, Mamie."

"But she helps take care of the kids –"

"Without her I couldn't do this. After Éric was killed they wanted to give me more time to be with the kids, get past the horror of it. Mamie said no, I'll come and live with you and take care of the kids till you find the ones who killed Éric."

"She was pretty fierce about taking the kids to school ..."

"She lost her father in the Algerian War and her husband in Iraq One, and now we've lost her son Éric too ... She has a very dim view of safety."

DO YOU PRAY?

WE WOKE THE BEAST and drove to 36 Rue du Bastion and the new home of the Criminal Brigade and Anti-Terrorist Section, the "ATS" of the Paris *Police Judicière*.

The *PJ*, as it's called, had lived for many years on Île de la Cité, a stone's throw from Notre Dame. Its historic edifice at 36 Quai des Orfèvres is famous in thousands of court cases, in movies and TV, and as home to Simenon's renowned series of Inspector Maigret.

In a new location, argued its proponents, we can group all our various divisions, have an inside shooting range, good holding cells, enough room for everyone. Quai des Orfèvres is way too ancient, cold in winter, boiling in summer, full of roaches and rodents, lousy tech facilities, overcrowded …

It now soared up in shiny newness at 36 Rue du Bastion, which got its name from a fortified tower that stood here centuries ago in the stone wall defending Paris. The new HQ is dizzying to look at: a great shiny serpentine slithering monster in a snake's new skin punching up into the sky over what had recently been railroad yards and before that the fortified wall, then pasture, and two thousand years ago a forest of oaks so tall and thick they blotted out the sky.

The new edifice still has that interior strangeness where things are jammed semi-temporarily, don't yet fit, yet there's still too much emptiness. Glossy crammed hallways, wide dark rooms of glowing screens, scowling faces pinned to bulletin boards. Business suits and Kevlar, computers and guns. Echoes, quiet conversations, a sense of intense purpose.

In one of the most secret sections of the French police, DGSI has built a database of the more than 22,000 S-List Muslims in France – those known to be involved in either planning or supporting potential terrorist attacks. In it is every detail they can find – vehicle plates, driver's licenses, telephone numbers, camera sightings, criminal history, networks of contacts, and any other information that can be gleaned from the nearly infinite megabytes of data screaming every instant across their screens.

"Though the real number of probable terrorists is much higher," said the ATS deputy chief, Tomàs Cribari. "And it's not just the young men any longer; it's often kids 14 to 18, who under the 1905 French law on the protection of minors can't be held or punished for their crimes. And now young women too – crazy as it seems, given their jail-like existence – they're the foot soldiers in some of these attacks."

Tomàs looked at Anne. "Just like you guys, and DGSI too, we face increasing dangers with increasingly insufficient resources. The avalanche of trained terrorists returning to France from Iraq, Syria and Turkey is doubling every six months. And the home-grown radicals are increasing even faster ... and you can't even talk to them because all they do is recite passages from the Koran and tell you you'll be tortured in Hell forever."

I grinned and got a quick smile from Tomàs in return. All this, too, was old news.

Below medium height, dark-rimmed thick glasses half-way down his nose, Tomàs was a bit too soft and roundish to be French. According to Anne he was the son of a Czech coal miner who emigrated to France after the Soviets crushed the 1968 spring uprising. He was fluent in several North African Arabic dialects, and led teams that had tracked and broken five major terrorist networks.

He pushed his glasses up his nose; they slid back down again. "And you, big old America, you have these problems?"

"We don't really have many home-grown terrorist networks," I said, "though we've had lots of attacks. But our Muslim population is growing very fast, gone from 2.5 million to 4 million in the last ten years. According to surveys thirty percent of American Muslims believe terrorism is justified ... But that's still over a million people who believe that terrorist attacks, even in our own country, are legitimate."

Tomàs nodded. "It's over fifty percent here. Yet we have Europe's largest prison population. Our jails are so overcrowded we're letting out nasty people because we can't keep them all. Not terrorists, but lots of killers, rapists and other felons who go right out and do it again."

"I'm headed back to the office," Anne said. "Call me if you find anything." Halted at the door. "*Anything.*"

She walked away, elegant and slim, beyond reach. With that funny knack of making you miss her even when you're mad at her, as I had been several times before last night.

"We've taken your computer portrait of Mustafa," Tomàs said, breaking the strain, "and matched it against faces that show up on our algorithms from cameras all across Paris."

"How many?" I asked, not wanting to know.

"Only about thirty-five hundred." Tomàs rubbed his palms felicitously. "So it won't take long."

For hours I sat in front of that softly illuminated screen. When my eyes stung too badly or got too blurred, I stumbled around the darkened room tripping over chair legs and cords till my vision came back.

It was afternoon. I stood, waited for the dizziness to stop, stretched, touched palms to toes, arched my back, and twisted my head from side to side to lessen the ache in my neck. In the WC, I took a leak and washed my face in cold water and dribbled some of it down my back. Sat at the damn screen again and took another hit of the ATS's bag-in-the-box Côtes du Rhône.

And there he was.

It wasn't just *seeing* him, it was the *feel* of him. He wasn't exactly what I'd expected, but close. Every person has a unique aura that we sense in each other. In him it was the innate swagger, the self-deification. A man for whom the rest of us are ants. A person so completely dehumanized he dehumanizes us too.

Anne returned and together we leaned over the screen, she, Tomàs and I, bumping shoulders and biting back the elation of a possible hit.

It *was* him: the retreating, lightless eyes and high bony cheeks, the grim lips, the steady sneer, how he swung his broad shoulders against the crowd, the way his feet toed outwards carving him space, his lock-kneed stride.

He wore a thin black leather coat with a collar up to his ears. His frizzy hair was short, well-trimmed. No beard, just the hard angularity and sullen mouth that had stared down the AK barrel at me seven years ago, as he did so often in the weeks after Mack and I were captured and frequently dragged out to be shot or have our throats cut, only be "spared" again and sent back to our cells.

I felt again the cold regret I hadn't killed him when I'd maybe had the chance, and that now I could. Kneeling bound and cuffed before him, I'd flinched at every nuance in his speech, every tightening of his finger on the trigger. Now, however, it wasn't a bullet in the back of my head, it was Mack and Gisèle, the Eiffel Tower. Paris. The future.

In this 7.2 seconds of video Mustafa was bobbing at a steady pace along a crowded sidewalk with a busy boulevard beside it. There were store signs and parked cars and cafés and a Crédit Agricole bank. "Where?" I said.

"Boulevard de Magenta, two blocks from La République. Yesterday, 4:17 pm."

"That sidewalk," Anne blurted. "That's where I saw him!"

"*Saw* him?" I said.

"In my dream."

"DO YOU PRAY?" *Mustafa said. "You're an infidel, not a person – we all know that – do even you pray? Here, now, with my rifle muzzle ten centimeters from your left eye – and yes, you can keep staring straight ahead but it will not save you – do you pray?"*

All was terror of that horrible piece of steel smashing through my head. "When I know I am dying it makes me love peace. That we could avoid all this."

He moved back, readying to shoot.

Does the brain have time to feel, when the bullet smashes through it?

"Do you pray?" he repeated. Insistent now.

Is this how I'm going to get it? For the wrong answer? "Of course I pray. Fear makes us pray. We can't help ourselves." I could have told him I'd do this whole Iraq thing again, die again, to stop him, but it wasn't true.

All I wanted was to live.

I CAME BACK to the *now*, this darkened room at the new ATS HQ.

From the far corner of his cave Mustafa smiled white teeth. "Don't fear, I'll be back."

"With this video," Tomàs was saying, "we can create good

images of him, much better than your portrait. Question is, do we spread out and show it to people in that area, see if anyone's seen him?"

"Then, like before," Anne said, "we scare him off."

Just the reminder infuriated me, and that she was now admitting they'd fucked things up. "No," I said. "Let's take the best images you create and run them through all your street camera footage again. There should be greater precision, we might turn out more positives, places he's been."

"We are already doing that, of course."

"And tying in the cell tower hits on his phone …"

"That too."

"This is the best news we've had in days," Anne said.

From the back of his cave Mustafa smiled mockingly. *"Inshallah."*

THE TIPPING POINT

"**EVERY EVENT** is rooted," Nisa said, "in what happened before. We can't understand today without knowing the past. Like Anne said about Hitler: we could have stopped him early, but no one had the courage. French politicians were all for appeasement, some were even being paid off by the Germans, like they are by Islam today."

"Yes, that is true," Thierry admitted.

It was late afternoon and we were back in his office with the orange sun melting into the room. "The catastrophe that happened," Nisa went on, "the sixty million deaths, the destruction of much of the world, did not need to happen. And for instance" – she leaned forward, jiggling her bracelets – "if no World War Two, no murder of six million Jews, so no need to create Israel, perhaps less war in the Middle East, no?"

Thierry laughed. "Remember what Yasser Arafat said? *'As long as Israel exists there will always be war in the Middle East. And even without Israel there will always be war in the Middle East.'*"

"So where," Anne said sharply, "do we go from here?"

"France has absorbed an enormous number of migrants in a very short time," Nisa said. "It needs years, decades, to integrate what it has taken in. Who was it, some Prime Minister, said *'France cannot take in all the misery of the world'?*"

"If you are concerned about the spread of Islam in France," I said to Nisa, "why are you still a Muslim?"

She turned toward me, her face half-lit by the window, dark-hued, fine features full of recognition and sorrow, awareness and fatality. Slender, strong hands, a topaz ring on the right finger. Nothing on the left.

"I grew up in a normal Muslim home. It wasn't Salafist but it was strict. Starting at age ten I had to wear the *hijab* – the head and hair cover – and the *abaya* – a long cloak covering the body to the feet – at thirteen. The *niqab* – the face veil covering all but the eyes – I wore from the day I began high school."

"You had no choice, about this?" Anne said.

"There was no choice. In the projects from the age ten or so it was always understood, wear the *niqab* or be raped. 'You weren't wearing a veil,' the rapists said. 'It's your fault – you provoked my desire.'"

"So," I repeated, "why are you still a Muslim?"

"Most Muslims in France, all they want is peace and to be left alone."

"Left alone?"

"By other fundamentalists trying to radicalize them. By the mosques and Salafist brotherhoods and the charities and all that ... And there's more and more pressure to conform, to observe the holidays, come to the mosque, to radicalize. And those who don't, well, bad things happen to them."

Thierry smiled, tapping his pencil eraser. "What's the point?"

"The Tipping Point, *that* is the point," Nisa said. "Once you reach that point it's too late to go back. Like when a dam, it breaks?"

Thierry nodded gloomily. "Are we there?"

"Not yet. But close."

"How would this dam break?" Anne said.

"Think of these Lost Territories of France. No matter what you try, they keep getting bigger. And more separate from France, more aggressive toward it. True?"

"We've had double the attacks this year," Thierry said, "that we had last year. And four times two years ago."

"But there's no single brain, or group, organizing all this," Anne said. "Is there?"

"From the Salafist viewpoint it's God's will. But ... it's organized from the Middle East. The Salafist charities, the *hawala* donations, all of this is coming together at a very high level. There *is* a plan. Not as Westerners might think, but a long-term strategic understanding among *immensely* powerful people, both the religious side and the fantastically wealthy ruling families, both whose only goal, like all religions and ruling families, is to stay in power. And many of them deeply believe in Islam, that it *must* take over the world." She raised her hands, dropped them. "And this huge success in expanding Islam worldwide creates the belief of being God-chosen. Which leads to more expansion, a combination of soft and hard conquest ..."

"How," I said, "has this happened, in France?"

"France?" she exclaimed. "France is, what you call it, the poster child of Islamic expansion? First you have enormous immigration over a short time, before people can react, then everything gets built – mosques, madrasahs, other schools, prayer cells – all funded by the Middle East. And once this is rooted you begin influencing politicians and media, to convince everyone that this enormous invasion is not a threat. That it's the duty of every French citizen to help these poor Muslims as they plan to take over your country."

"There is no middle way?" I said. "French Muslims who don't want to take over?"

"Read the latest polls. Half of French Muslims want France to turn Muslim."

"That's half of over eight million people," Anne said.

"Are there no moderate leaders?"

Nisa raised her hands, questioning. "There are media darlings like Rachid Raqmi, who everyone believes is working for peace –"

"Him," Thierry said disparagingly.

"Officially, he's an official voice for moderation. For inclusion, that violence is not the answer."

"President of the Muslim Anti-Discrimination Society," Thierry put in.

"MADS?" I smiled at the acronym.

"The usual fish soup," Nisa said. "Socialists, anti-Semites, Islamic groups, anarchists, urban crazies, political celebrities and far-out intellectuals. Funded by Salafists in Saudi, Dubai, the Emirates, Kuwait, places like that. They protest what they call anti-Islamic information in the media, in the government. Because no one is supposed to say these killers are Muslims. Or that the murderers at Bataclan were spouting the Koran as they blew kids' brains apart. That looks bad for Islam, so they don't want it out there."

"They go on TV," Thierry said, "and complain about anti-Muslim bias while Muslims are killing hundreds of our people, and everyone feels sorry for the poor Muslims and not for their victims. They control the vote in Muslim areas and no one can get elected there without them. They're tied in with the Socialists and that's why we can't pass anti-terrorism laws ..."

"That's all true," she said. "But if we can use him?"

"How?"

"The media loves him. They think he's trying to make positive change, diminish the influence of Salafism and terrorism ..."

"Solutions to what?" he countered. "This is a guy who talks

about Muslim poverty but lives in a magnificent townhouse in the Seventh and has a country home in Fontainebleau Forest. He says he's a devout Muslim but screws infidel women, drinks heavily when no one's looking ..."

"Most Muslims do," I said dismissively, and turned to Nisa. "You don't sound very optimistic either."

She raised her hands. "I *am* optimistic. I believe what we are doing *now*, right *here*, can make a difference. Look, I am a Muslim. A Muslim *woman*. I have certain cherished ideals. I want to nourish the *good* side of Islam – it can be a majestic and beautiful religion. It reminds me, always, to be grateful to God for this minute, this day, this life. To hear God's teachings and obey them, not because it's good for God but because it's good for *us*. To follow the good things Mohammed said, to take care of children, protect women –"

"Mohammed's last wife he 'married,'" I had to say, "when she was seven."

"It was the custom then."

"At least he waited till she was ten before he screwed her. According to the Koran."

She shook her head, said nothing.

"It's fine," I added, "to have multiple cultures. Look at the United States, multiple cultures make us strong. But when one culture, in this case the Salafist ideology, where if you don't believe in the Koran the sentence is death, grows strong enough ..."

She shrugged. "Am I not the one who keeps telling you?" She looked at Anne and Thierry. "Islam in France today is not my Islam. This new Islam is *not* multicultural. It does not respect other religions or cultures. French Islam scorns France. It wants to *destroy* France and replace it with Islam."

"Never happen," I said, wondering if this were really true.

———

OUR BEST HOPE was still Les Quatre Vents. Mustafa might even show up. Or one of his apostles. Someone we could take down silently and – let's be honest – torture chemically, psychologically and physically till he spoke the truth. Then kill him.

Wouldn't you? Don't tell me you'd turn the other cheek. He'd just plunge a knife in that one too.

But you hope turning the other cheek will at least put you on good terms with God?

God laughs, scratches his balls. *Damn fools*, he chuckles. *Give them another thousand years of Hell.*

SO BACK I went to Les Quatre Vents with Mustafa's updated pix. But Bruno wasn't there. Instead a heavy-set dark-haired woman in black. The place was empty.

"He's dead, Monsieur Rigard." She batted away a tear. "Last night."

I almost fell, grabbed the edge of the bar. "How?"

"He was going home after closing up this place. Like he always does ... They found him in the Canal St. Martin."

"Did he drown?" I asked, open-mouthed.

"He was stabbed and beaten. Yes, those were the words they used, the Police. Beaten and stabbed to death."

I tried to think. "He goes the same way, every night?"

"It's our old quarter, he refused to give it up."

I stared at her, disbelieving. "Who are you?"

"His wife."

I stood there wavering. She stared at me. "You okay?"

"I was just leaving." I wandered out onto the sidewalk, traffic snarling past.

If I hadn't come around asking questions, wouldn't he still be alive?

And now we'd lost the trail, and a major witness. A good man.

I sat at a café under an umbrella in the early evening rain and called Anne. A waiter came and I remembered how to say, *"Un express."*

"Oh Jesus," she said.

"We've been in the wrong dimension. This's bigger, worse."

"Shit yes."

"We're going to stop it."

She sighed. "Okay."

"No, we are. We have Mustafa's video. Sooner or later he's going to show on face recon and hopefully we'll have folks nearby to bring him down."

"Hopefully ..."

"Oh shit, you're so negative."

"And you? So what the fuck are *you*?" With a click she was gone.

I stared at the rainy street, rain in my eyes. Even now, if they'd been watching Les Quatre Vents, they could take me down. Two quick bursts from a passing motorcycle.

For many years I've wondered what it felt like, that stitch of bullets across your chest. Plenty of times it had nearly happened.

Forget that, concentrate on Mustafa. Because now we have 7.2 precious seconds of him walking along Boulevard de Magenta, two blocks from La République.

So close I could almost smell him.

Then I could see him, crystal-clear in my mind's eye. He smiled down at me. The bullet was about to smash through my face. *"Shall I shoot you in the right eye? Or the left?"*

P S Y C H O P A T H

ANNE was powerful, brilliant and exciting but I didn't trust her. And she worked for Thierry, who despite our years as comrades was hiding something I needed to know.

Was someone above him interfering in our investigation? Or someone like this Raqmi guy, France's latest media darling?

Meanwhile, Harris was either stupid or pretending to be.

And Mustafa was steadily advancing on his goal to destroy Paris. While Mack and Gisèle were suffering or maybe dead. And Bruno had been killed.

Back in Passage Landrieu I downed a last glass of Russian vodka, finished a container of wild cherry ice cream, stared at the blue-flashing Eiffel Tower and let my subconscious take over.

I must have been very subconscious because when I brushed my teeth I mistakenly used boxing liniment instead of toothpaste. It had a stinging bitter taste plus many unattractive additives, all of which set my tongue afire and banished any further rational thought.

BUT NO SOONER had I crawled bone-tired and tongue-seared into bed than *Highway to Hell*, the ringtone on my phone, went off. *02:08*, Anne, so I had to answer. "Don't you ever sleep?" I mumbled, trying not to use my tongue.

"We found her."

"Gisèle?" I struggled awake.

"Yasmina Noureff. Her with the blonde-dyed bloody hair in Mack's car."

"Maybe the gods *are* with us."

"She in a fourth-floor apartment of a five-story walkup in St. Denis, 23 *bis* Rue Fontaine. We're going in in 42 minutes."

"*No! You can't!*"

"It's not up to me –"

"That's crazy! What if Mack's there? Gisèle? You have audio? Infrared?"

"You're the one who doesn't like setups." She spoke closer to the phone, as if sharing this: "We don't have anything, just her location."

"You should *wait!* See what she *does* –"

"About Mack and Gisèle? We grab her, make her talk."

"That'll take days ..."

"I'll be at Rue Fontaine just around the corner from Boulevard Carnot in St. Denis. Look for the Indian." She puffed a cigarette. "Unless you and Harris want out."

02:16. I leaped into the Beast banging my head on the armored sun visor and tore across the Alma Bridge up Avenue Marceau past all the beautiful carved stone buildings bathed in somber light, to the Arc de Triomphe then Wagram – more lovely buildings, tree-lined sidewalks and closed cafés to the Péréphérique, holding my phone against the steering wheel trying to follow the little red line to St. Denis, sacred burial ground of the kings of France, now a Muslim ghetto. And where the woman lived whose blonde-dyed black hair had been spattered with Mack's blood.

02:31. The Indian stood nose-in at the curb, just another nasty bike in a dangerous neighborhood. I parked at the hydrant across the street.

Anne came out of the shadows. "You're just an observer."

"Fuck that. She's mine."

"Not if *we* take her down."

"Screw you. I'm calling Harris."

She snorted. "He wouldn't even have toilet paper if we didn't send it to him."

I felt a flame of patriotic rage. "Not true."

A complicit, low-eyed smile. "You know it *is.*"

"You'll ruin everything –"

"There's been an emergency gas leak. Two guys in Gaz de France uniforms are checking every kitchen on that stairwell."

"At two-forty a.m.? She'll see through that –"

"No matter. While she's dealing with them we have eight guys on the roof ready to come down the lightwell through her bedroom window."

I scrambled to think of something, to avert this. "Call Nisa."

"Call Nisa?"

"Let's see what she says. How can we get in there without hurting this Yasmina?"

She looked at me with incredulity. "Are you fucking nuts?"

I called Thierry. "Nisa's already on," he said. "I'll patch her in."

"Okay, Nisa," I said. "What do we do?"

There was silence. I feared the connection had dropped. "Pono," she said in Arabic, "do you speak this?"

"Not the Algerian dialect," I answered in my accented Arabic. "Mine's Iraqi."

"Speak French," Thierry broke in.

"They're talking bullshit," Anne said.

"Thierry," Nisa said in French, "Why not let Pono talk to her? He's trying to find out about his friend – it's personal, not political, not religious – Pono, you can remind her that the protection of friendship is very important in the Koran … mention the old one, *Your friend is he who mentions Allah to you in your presence and you to Allah in your absence.*"

I was so wired my hand was shaking. "I will mention her not to Allah, but to GIGN. So *they* don't kill her."

"Thierry!" Nisa's voice rose. "You *must* let Pono talk to her. To save this girl. Look, Pono," she added quickly in Arabic, "she's just a *girl*. She doesn't *know* what she's doing."

This just wired me more. "I'm going in." I looked at the wall of police and the Special Forces guys in black. "No matter what these guys think."

"*Save* her, Pono."

"He can't –" Thierry said.

"Thierry!" Nisa snapped, "you *must* convince them. These police."

"I don't have a choice here," Thierry said.

"Yes you *do.*"

"Don't go there," he said sharply.

"Pono," Nisa said, "you *save* this girl."

I turned to Anne. "Let me talk to Yasmina."

She faced me. "What about?"

"About the rest of her life in prison. As opposed to leveling with us. About maybe saving Mack and Gisèle, if she knows where –"

"She won't talk to you. Or she'll kill you."

"That's when you come in. With all your boys down the lightwell. The flashbangs and stun guns and all the live shit that will tear everything to pieces."

"When?"

I thought of Mack and Gisèle. "After Yasmina's killed me."

02:47, three minutes to go. "Let's hold off," Anne said. "Nisa wants someone to talk to Yasmina. Pono wants to try."

"He'll get killed." Thierry's voice on the other end, hard-edged.

"Here!" She held out her phone to me. "*You* talk to him."

"I'm going to knock on her door," I told Thierry, "and tell her I'm American, a friend of Mack's. That I just want to know where he is. And if she helps me I'll make sure you guys go easy on her ..."

"She'll kill you then come after us."

"You afraid of that?"

He scoffed. "Of her killing you, yes."

"But if she dies you'll never find Mack and Gisèle." I felt a rush of inspiration. "If I can bring her out alive, and we learn about Mack and Gisèle? And maybe Mustafa?"

"Let me think about it," he said as I walked down the empty cordoned street toward 23 *bis*.

The first line of cops clearly meant business. The kind who'd shoot you if you walked away. They were all big and very tough and had nasty weapons they clearly wanted to use. "*DGSE!*" I snapped, trying to sound French and showing the ID card Thierry had so unwisely provided me.

The second line of cops was of course CRS, the national riot police, and if you thought the regular police were tough and nasty you don't want to meet these folks. I swear they must have all been from Corsica or Alsace – a mix of brute strength and cagy wisdom that wasn't going to let any asshole through without a 21-carat ID and a bulletproof reason to be there. One of them laughed when he saw my DGSE card. "What, you want to give out parking tickets?"

"Let us through." It was Anne, a step behind me, her ID in their faces. "And get out of our way."

The final line was simply two GIGN guys in black Kevlar.

She locked her arm in mine as we neared them. "Yasmina's a *jihadi*," she whispered. "Doesn't care if she dies. Wants to."

I thought of Mack and Gisèle. "Lots of things are worse than death."

"Do as I say." She gave my biceps a little squeeze; it was like being caught in a forklift. "Or you'll find yourself back at the Farm with your dick in your ear before you remember leaving here. Or you'll be dead."

That reminded me of motorcycle rides with her, I started to say, but she was already shaking hands with the two GIGN guys. "Why are we standing down?" one said.

"This guy," she poked me, "he's going to talk to Yasmina." She looked at them. "A lot of lives can be saved."

"Hold on." He punched his phone.

She held his wrist. "I'm calling Thierry. It's his game, and he says it's okay."

"It's not his game. It's ours."

She grinned and handed him her phone. "Don't even *dream* that."

"How you been?" the other said, his voice sepulchral behind his mask. Proprietorial, someone who *knew* her. I caught myself in an instant's silly jealousy.

"I'm fine," she said tiredly. "How's your Ma?"

"Better. I'll tell her you asked."

I could hear Thierry's voice on her phone, patient and weary. "Yeah," the first GIGN guy said, "she's right here." He gave Anne back her phone. "He's on his way. Says let this guy go in. But *you* don't. He gets ten minutes. The instant anything triggers we all go in."

"I'm good with that," she said steadily, looked at me.

We walked arm in arm to the empty dark sidewalk smelling of rats and piss, to 23 *bis* and up the four crumbling concrete steps to the door. "Please come back." She squeezed my wrist. "*Please* come back."

I looked at her, trying to take all of her in, *everything*. Fearing I *wouldn't* come back. My heart thudded, my wrists were slick with sweat. What's said about your life passing before you, in a sense it was true: in her eyes was the reflection of my whole life, a moment's infinite cameo.

The door hung half-open, the lock and jamb smashed long ago. Inside the dark hallway smelled of Moroccan spices, burnt meat, spilt sewage and decaying garbage. The stairs were grungy. I halted at the fourth floor, scared and doubting myself, expecting a bullet any moment.

The light down the stairwell was faint, almost hazy.

I knocked.

No answer.

"Yasmina!" I called in French. "My name's Pono. I'm a friend of Mack's. I'm alone and not armed. I just want to find out what happened to Mack."

So silent I heard water dripping from a pipe. A distant siren on the Péréphérique, an Airbus descending for CDG, the throaty rattle of Arabic radio through a skinny wall. "Yasmina!" I knocked again, almost whispered. "I'm Mack's friend, just want to know what happened to him. And his wife – she seems a lot like you –"

"I'm here." A woman's voice behind me, a faint North African echo. "Take off your coat. Show you have no weapons."

The voice came from up the stairs behind me but no one was there. A pinhole camera in a wall. Micro-speakers, at least three.

"Why are you waiting?" Her voice soft, sedulous, authoritarian. "Take off your coat."

I did as I was told.

"Take off the shirt and the one under it."

Again I complied.

"Pull down your pants. To your ankles." This was obvious: to check I wasn't carrying a gun. I don't wear underwear, but she made no comment.

"That knife," she said, referring to the Kabar sheathed on my calf. "Keep your hands away from it."

"Enough of this," I said. "I'm clean. You can shoot me and check my body if you want. But I'd like to talk to you first."

"You piece of garbage. Why should I talk to *you*?"

"Not only for Mack and Gisèle. For you, too."

"To Hell with Mack," she spat. "He's betrayed me." Her intensity made her seem more valid, more in the right.

But she's not, I reminded myself.

She's a psychopathic killer.

And wants to kill you.

"How did he betray you?"

"Hah! If not, how are you here?"

How easily we fall into situations like this. Infused with super-courage to protect loved ones, friends, a clan or nation. Embracing our own often-painful deaths as we charge the enemy, snarling and screaming and dying for the chance to kill them.

"Take off all your clothes and leave them in the hallway. Unsheathe that knife and leave it there too."

I did.

Two double bolts snapped back and the door cracked open.

FARTHER FROM THE TRUTH

"HANDS ON YOUR HEAD."

It was silly but I did it.

"Get in. Shut the door."

She wore faded jeans with torn knees and a Mickey Mouse T-shirt with a homemade C-4 vest strapped around it. And held what seemed to be a detonator in her left hand and a Sig Sauer 9mm in her right. Her hands were long and thin-fingered and her face very white. She had long dyed blonde hair showing along the edges of her black headscarf, black eyes and the pale beauty of someone who has just died.

"Thank you," I said. "I would like to do as much for you as you do for me."

"Too late for that."

"You so sure?"

"You're the one who has this place surrounded."

"Not me. I didn't want this."

She false-smiled, as if the joke were on me. "I trusted him, you know? I *trusted* him."

"Mack?"

"Who else?"

"What happened, Yasmina? Where is he?"

She shook her head. "No matter how many of us you kill, you're still going to lose. You know that, don't you? We're invading you and *we* will win."

"Of course you won't. That's why you're cornered in a rathole in Saint-Denis while Paris goes on around you – people happily making love and eating and drinking wine and dancing and taking care of each other and their families and friends and this beautiful nation known as France ... All the things you hate ..."

"You'd hate them too, if you knew –"

"Knew what?" I said, but she didn't answer. "Even many Muslims," I added, "are doing these things – eating and drinking and making love and loving their families and France."

"*They,*" she hissed, trying to find the right word, "*they* are not true believers."

"But they are happy, hard-working, loving people! What's wrong with that?"

"*Everything!*" she snarled. Her hatred had the same effect as moments earlier, of somehow authenticating her: *She must be right, to be so angry.*

I let my hands drop to my sides. "Why are we here?"

She giggled. "So I can kill you?"

"Where's Mack? Gisèle?"

She raised the Sig. Despite myself I laughed. "One more score to get you in the door of Paradise? You know it doesn't exist, don't you, Paradise?" There was a chill in my body from knowing I had a good chance of being killed and couldn't change it.

Yasmina looked at me with the condescending condolence of someone about to die. "Paradise is for Muslims. Not kaffir shit."

"Enough of this, Yasmina – Mack's been my friend for ten years – is he dead?"

An almost invisible shake of head. "I can't say."

"Gisèle?"

Again the nearly imperceptible head shake, a flick of her eyes toward a corner of the wall and ceiling behind me.

Was it cameras? I didn't look. "Yasmina – why did you hit him?"

"Maybe I didn't. Did you ever wonder if they hit me too?" She raised the edge of her headscarf to show a black-and-blue gash above her temple.

"Why, Yasmina, *who?*"

She leaned against me an instant, shoved away. "If I knew, you think I'd be talking to *you?*"

"Why were you in the car, with Mack?"

She gave me the look one gives well-intentioned idiots. "Mack didn't tell you about me? In that phone call?"

"What call?"

"When you were in Samoa, Tahiti, someplace like that."

"You're with Mustafa? It won't work, Yasmina. You can't destroy France."

"Mustafa?" She looked at me venomously. "If you think that, go tell them what I say. Before I kill you."

"If you're not with Mustafa, then who?" I had a moment's inspiration. "Rachid?"

"Rachid Raqmi?" she spat. "He who loves infidels?"

I felt no fear, only a strange sibling link with her. As if we were one blood, could be straight with each other, share this moment, two people caught in the same twist of fate.

Maybe it was this stupid idea that saved me: "You haven't told me, what to tell who."

"That we're willing to discuss things. We have a terrible weapon we can decommission if you meet us halfway. We are not any more violent than you have been, in fact far less. What we require, simply, is Arabic language and Islamic religious teaching in all schools beginning at kindergarten, funding to triple the number of mosques so we can provide for our faithful.

And no impediments to immigration. This has to be all agreed," she added, "in the next two days."

"Not possible," I gasped. "The Fifth Republic –"

She glanced at my privates, somewhat shriveled by cold and fear. "Is that," she snickered, "all you've got?"

"What have you got that's better?"

"Sharia – don't *you* get it? Don't you *see*, it's inevitable *the whole world will be Muslim*? Are you *that* blind?"

"And you, have you been cut?" I said, referring to the Islamic practice of cutting off the clitoris and parts of the labia so that women have no enjoyment in sex and are thus less likely to stray from their always-fearful menfolk.

She grinned, and for an instant I saw her as she might have been, if she'd grown up free. A pretty college grad, boyfriends, a car. Very smart, maybe a young executive, a doctor ... Someone who would give back to the human race.

"Yasmina." I faced her thinking of what Nisa had said. "You're brilliant and perceptive, and you have a great kindness for others – please don't destroy yourself, please don't *deprive* us of you ..." I had to slow my words ... "We *need you* to make a better world ..." I stared at her. "You can have a good life, Yasmina. You can make the world a better place –"

"You tell them." She nodded at the door. "We'll give them a list what we want. In return for Mack and Gisèle ... And to save Paris?" She gave me a sideways grin, a cute high-schooler at an apple-dunking contest. "And the world? One *never* knows ..."

I backed toward the door. "They're still alive?"

She flashed her eyes, mischievous again. "Why do *you* care? We'll *all* soon be dead."

"You didn't answer me." I reached out a hand that she slapped away.

She waved the Sig. "Go tell them what I said. And that they're to move out of our *quartier*, leave us alone." A gypsy smile. "And don't forget your trousers on the way out."

I shoved on my clothes in the hall, dashed downstairs into the street's arc-lit night, my hands over my head, fearing all the guns waiting to shred me into a bleeding pile of dog meat.

"Hold off!" I yelled. "She wants to talk!"

A huge blast smashed me to the sidewalk grinding my face through broken glass and grit, a howling thunder that blew windows into the street and set off a wail of car alarms, a scream of broken pipes and the clatter of roof tiles, one that smashed my right hand and another that punched me so hard in the back I feared I'd die.

There was a terrible pain deep inside each howling ear; I was choking on blood because I hadn't expected the explosion and hadn't opened my mouth to keep from biting my tongue. *Bitch* how it hurt. I kept spitting blood that widened to a black puddle against my cheek on the dirty concrete.

The GIGN guys had come down the wall. And Yasmina had blown herself up.

NO GIGN CASUALTIES – they have a knack for staying alive in the most lethal circumstances – but pieces of Yasmina were broadly distributed over the neighborhood – her trachea wrapped around a light pole, a chunk of her left pelvis on the indented roof of a parked Renault Espace, her teeth buried in the wall of the apartment building across the street.

My forearms stung from my slide across the street when Yasmina's bomb went off. I had a lump over my right eye that only hurt bad when I pressed it. My ears howled like they always do after an explosion.

Most of all I felt bitter and saddened by the possibility that Yasmina had been a good soul caught in some web we couldn't unravel, and now we'd lost her.

This beautiful young woman and the best lead we'd had in Mack's disappearance, the *only* lead. Fury surged like bile up my throat – at Anne and DGSE and ATS – I had *begged* her, begged *them*, not to go in on Yasmina.

Just like they'd frightened off Mustafa, barely a day ago.

What was I missing?

I sat on the cold limestone steps of the building next door while Anne paced and swore, her heels clattering on the uneven bricks. The street now broadly lit by searchlights where cops and lab people in white gowns stepped carefully. Other cops were going through the nearby apartments with dogs, looking for guns amid loud protestations in Arabic and the sibilant howl of women.

More cops were sweeping the roofs, hunting the back alleys and scanning the windows. Amid the din of sirens, yelled commands and vehicles, I could hear the chatter of Arab radio from nearby apartments, called-in Emergency requests and Twitter feeds about tragedy, outrage, this latest attack on Islam …

Bad as the worst part of Cairo.

The deeper I got into it, I realized, the farther I'd be from the truth.

And the more in danger.

"WHAT'S YOUR EXCUSE?" I snarled at Anne as she paced past.

She yanked her phone from her ear and stared fiercely at me. "You could've had a whole lot of our guys killed –"

"I *told* you hold off!"

"You didn't say she was wearing C-4!"

"How the Hell could I? I didn't have time. You bastards went in too soon."

"It wasn't," she grimaced, "*us*."

"What?" I yelled again. "Then who?"

"You have a lot to learn." She snatched at my elbow. "Let's go."

"I'm not going anywhere with you," I seethed. "You and your friends have screwed up and I want to know why!"

Eyes flashing, teeth bright, she looked like a cornered wolf. "That's the last thing you *want* to know."

"First you frightened off Mustafa," I hissed, "now you've killed the only person who could help us find Mack and Gisèle!"

She snatched at my sleeve. "We're tired. Let's go home." It seemed so enticing, to lie there talking it through, finding the meanings. To come down from this night of terror and adrenaline. "No," I snapped. "I'm not going anywhere with you till you explain."

She cocked her head, almost whimsical. As if I had to be taught my own lesson. "All right then. See you at eight."

04:22. I'd get nearly an extra half-hour's sleep if I went with her instead of all the way back to Passage Landrieu. But when I looked up she was already small in the distance, then gone in the darkness.

I wandered back to the Beast, slid into its frigid seat, hung my cop radio on the rearview mirror and slowly trundled westward through late-night Paris. That once had been a place of great joy and beauty, and now felt raw with danger, hatred and loss.

The cold made me shiver and I thought of lying on my surfboard in the rolling cool green waves under a warm Tahitian sun.

Surf for hours and never think of anything but where *you are right now.*

I'd turned off the Péréphérique onto Porte d'Auteuil when the radio call came through. "Officer down, north side of traffic circle, Porte de la Chapelle. We need ambulance, homicide and forensics. We've blocked off the intersection, so come up Boulevard Ney."

I pulled over fast banging into a new black Mercedes whose alarm began to yowl. "Identify the officer," I yelled.

"Undercover. Female. Red motorcycle. Over."

SILENT AND DEADLY

SHE LAY TWISTED under the bike in a pool of blood behind a yellow tape barrier under the psychotropic flashing red and blue emergency lights of police cars and ambulances. Face-down, legs crumpled, feet sideways, jacket bloodied from the bullet hole in her spine and from another in the back of her helmet through the middle of her brain.

If I'd been with you, this never would have happened.

"Two guys on a big black bike," a cop said when I showed him my DGSE badge. "Black jackets, black helmets. Came up behind her." He nodded at the sidelines. "We've got a witness."

"She always checks her mirrors," I said. "Nobody comes up behind her."

He nodded at her body. "These guys did."

I stepped over the yellow tape and knelt to her, hands and knees in her blood, horrified by her smashed bloody face. Her cheek had crushed against the gritty paving stone, her mouth of shattered teeth draining blood.

If I'd been with you, this never would have happened.

It wasn't Anne.

I looked again, stunned, horrified, beyond joy. "Don't touch her!" the cop yelled. I yanked back my hand, bent to the rear of the bike to check the plate.

75 – Paris. Anne's.

I knelt to the dead woman again. She wore the shocked expression of not knowing what had happened.

"C'mon, buddy, back off," the cop said.

"This is my partner's bike and helmet. But it's not her." I felt suddenly sorry for this dark-haired girl with the smashed face. And so happy it wasn't Anne I was trying not to cry.

I stood dizzily, streetlights dancing in my eyes, remembered to breathe, tried to wipe the dead woman's blood from my hands onto my jeans. Stupidly realized I could call Anne. Because she wasn't dead.

She answered right away.

"Where the Hell are you?" I almost screamed.

"Somebody stole my damn bike. I'm so pissed! Thierry's giving me a ride home."

"You were dead ..." I couldn't stop choking. "You were dead ... fifteen minutes ago. You just came back to life ..."

"What the *fuck* are you talking about?"

"The girl who stole your bike? She was wearing your helmet, too, when somebody shot her in the back of the head ten minutes ago, Porte de la Chapelle."

"*My God!*" Anne caught her breath. "They thought she was me."

I tried to wipe the woman's blood from my knee. "They thought she was you."

"Oh God, the poor girl ..."

"When they find they killed the wrong person they're coming back for you."

"Fine with me."

"As bait? No way."

"Anybody comes after me, they die."

I WAITED on the sidewalk outside her place till Thierry dropped her off then I hustled her inside. We rode the clanking elevator to the third floor holding each other, her damp hair against my chin.

"I thought you were dead," I whispered.

She burrowed her face into my shoulder. "For how long?"

"Twenty minutes, maybe. Till I saw her face."

"I'm sorry." She gripped me tighter. "I'm sorry."

"Sorry? For what?"

The elevator opened. Anne unlocked her door. "We have to be quiet."

In the apartment she unfolded the sofa bed and briefly smiled at me out of the darkness, big white teeth and wide generous mouth, black eyes sparkling with the distant glow of a single streetlight. She who had died and come back to life, I who had lost her and found her again.

Her odor, the *heat* of her, was like fire. Taking off her clothes, she was the first woman I'd ever known, the *best*, the one different from the rest. She eased out of her blouse and slid down her skirt, smiling and kissing me, kicked her skirt aside and stood back in pink see-through underpants that showed her dark crotch.

We kissed standing there, again and again, my palms inside her underpants gripping her ass as she shoved her hips against me and her tongue against mine and her breasts into my chest, my cock hard in the cleft of her thighs.

She lay back on the bed and I kissed between her thighs through the underpants, licking them wet, the insides of her thighs, her lovely hairy crotch. She bent up her knees for me to pull the panties off, then twisted her shoulders for me to take off her bra. I kissed her breasts and nipples and her lovely soft skin all over, kissed the lovely tiny fuzz of her belly button and down into her lovely crotch, rubbing my lips softly and licking as she eased, moaned, sighed and rocked her hips to my tongue, then finally arched back and gasped, sighed, spread her legs and softly relaxed. We snuggled and caught our breath and then she slid down and took me in her mouth, the most indescribably delicious feeling, then we rolled around a while taking turns and ended up fucking like the pastor and his wife, me on top, while the couch squeaked and howled like boiling monkeys. "We'll wake Mamie," she gasped. "Let's get on the floor."

Down on the oriental carpet atop the rattly ancient herringbone parquet. Being totally exhausted made it even deeper – we were too fatigued to fight it, and it took us down a hot red tunnel of total abandonment and bliss. Plus the first time with someone new is *always* hot. You come out of it burningly alive, fiercely awake, totally released.

Silly as it sounds, at the end we came at the same time.

What joy.

"YOU HAVE TO CHANGE everything," I said. "You have to start a new life." It was still night and we were holding each other under the down coverlet on the bumpy mattress. The awareness of how miraculously she'd escaped death, of the skill and determination of her killers, and the risks she now faced were beginning to sink into both of us.

"When I got back to where I'd parked the bike," she said, "it was gone. I walked up and down the street, wondering if my memory was bad ..."

"Your memory's never bad."

"Then I realized in that neighborhood things get stolen all the time ... I was so angry, after losing Yasmina, all that ... I called Thierry, he had arrived at the scene, he came right over ..."

"The two guys in black, they must have followed her, that girl, as she took off on your bike."

Anne shook her head sadly. "Poor thing."

"Did they want to kill you because of our investigation? Did they know it was you?"

She nodded. "Seems so."

"Or was it because of your husband, fear you'd track down his killers?"

"That had nothing to do with Mustafa ... Éric had identified a Chechnyan gang in the Pyrenees, they were selling heroin from Spain, pushing terrorism and burning synagogues, had killed a couple of policemen ..."

"And they killed him?"

She didn't answer, then, "I'll send Mamie and the kids to Normandy," she whispered, lips against my shoulder. "*Chez Cousine Claudine.* Nobody will find them there."

"And you?" I wanted to ask her more about her husband, but now wasn't the time.

"I'm staying here, let them come to me ..."

"No. They'll get you." I kissed her forehead, gentle skin over hard bone, imagined her pulsing brain beneath. "We have to find another place. And I'm not leaving you. Not for one moment."

"You want more sex, that's all."

"I'd be crazy not to."

She laced an arm between my ribs and shoulder. "My job hasn't changed. Nor has yours."

She was right, as usual. But no matter, I wasn't leaving her alone.

She soon was breathing softly, the fatigue lines of her face easing in the first glimmer of dawn. *05:29* ... another hour then get up. I nestled against her, breathed in and out with her till our heartbeats came together, inhaled the different fragrances of her hair and the glossy scents of her skin. And feared this was all fantasy due to shock and horror, and any instant I'd wake up to the real Anne twisted in a pool of blood beneath the bike.

Reborn. I prayed thanks for Anne's life and sorrowed for the other girl.

TWO HOURS LATER I stomped into Thierry's office, Anne unwillingly behind me. Nisa was standing by the window looking angry. "Why'd you guys hit Yasmina's?" I almost yelled. "When I was trying to talk with her?"

He gave me a curious look, as if *how stupid can you be?* "We were told to."

Anger surged from my skin, my bones, the grimace on my face. "By who?"

Nisa said nothing. Thierry eased back in his chair, as if to gain time. "France isn't one country." As if he were telling me something personal and deep, a divorce in the family. "France is not France. Not anymore."

I was too ravaged by Anne's near-death, Yasmina's death and the missed chance to get Mustafa, to follow such circumlocutions. "I don't care."

He gave me a bleak look. "Use your head, for something besides knocking down doors."

Too angry to sit, I stood by Nisa peering out the stained, streaked window at the courtyard where rain spattered puddles and ran rivulets down the curb. "I'm telling Harris everything."

Thierry laughed. "That won't matter. And he won't believe you."

He was right: I was a man without a country. Nowhere would anyone believe me.

"Listen to him, Pono." Nisa's voice had that element of bad news that must be given gently. "We've been arguing about the same thing, but Thierry's right."

I was still furious. "Right about *what*?"

"For years the ultra-left has run France," she said. "Under the surface they still do. They hate what France is – a world power, intellectual, scientific, cultured, financial, military, driven largely by white men and women. Instead they want inclusion, multicultural diversity, no borders, no nations, no capitalism, the forced merging of all peoples into one world. But this new Islam doesn't *want* to merge, they want to *dominate*. This new Islam's not a religion, it's a conquering ideology, a culture and law that feels itself superior, wants to crush all others."

I shrugged. "It's always been that."

"But now nearly fifteen *percent* of France is Muslim. Far more than the government admits. Over eight million. Of whom at least one in four are Salafists who believe every non-Muslim is a worthless infidel who should die. Recent surveys tell us that *over half* of young French Muslims think this."

I finally sat, exhausted by it all. "Most Muslims in France are honorable and hard-working, happy to be here."

She nodded, as if at an old riddle. "It doesn't matter who's the majority. Nor who's most accommodating. It matters who has the media behind them."

"Back in the late seventies and early eighties," Thierry said, "when the Socialists realized they were out of step with the French people and would soon be out of office, they opened the gates and brought in all the North Africans they could, as the Arabs in gratitude would vote almost exclusively Socialist. In a national campaign with several candidates, two percent of the votes can be a huge margin, and having millions of Islamic voters can win the presidency though you barely get thirty per-cent of the total. It's the only thing that's kept the Socialists in power during many of these years," he added with a wry smile.

I returned to my question: "So you let Yasmina be killed, with her own explosives."

He spread his hands a few inches: "The official statement from this office will be that her death was of minor consequence. And we will determine there is no link between her and any terrorist group ... And no one to blame. That she was alone, a deranged woman ... This has nothing," he smiled, "to do with Islam."

He was sarcastically quoting the oft-repeated political mantra that the slaughter of hundreds of French citizens by Koran-chanting terrorists had nothing to do with Islam.

Even the present administration hadn't changed this tune. *If we're nice to them*, they kept saying, *hopefully they'll be nice back ...*

"They set up Yasmina to die," I said. "Didn't they?"

Thierry sat back. "Who?"

"Someone higher up than you."

"That's ridiculous."

I was so angry I couldn't stop shaking. "That way there was no trail, no way to investigate links between her and the government's Islamic friends."

"You're overstepping here, Pono."

I kept seeing Yasmina in her silly Micky Mouse T-shirt and explosives vest, how close she'd been to giving in. To surviving. Had we not surrounded her. "That's the only way to win."

"She didn't have the only trigger on the bomb vest ..."

"Who?"

"We think someone else in the building had the trigger. They told her she had it, but it was a dummy. The real trigger was downstairs, next door – we're working on it, but with everything blown to bits it's hard to tell."

"They didn't want her to spill," Nisa said. "Was it Mustafa?"

Thierry sighed with fatigue, nodded. "Or somebody higher up."

I took a slow breath. "And you're *letting* it happen?"

"According to the government Mustafa doesn't exist. People's memories are short, we don't need to bring him back, don't need another homicidal Muslim taking up the front pages. Our rulers, that's how they think."

"So again, it was RAID who did the backup on Mustafa at Les Quatre Vents?" The elite unit of the national police – as opposed to GIGN, the anti-terror unit of the national gendarmerie – not that I gave a damn who was who. "It was them who blew our cover, spooked Mustafa?"

"We're not sure Mustafa was even going there that night. Maybe he was in Fontainebleau, and it was somebody else?"

I walked out. There was nothing else to do. It was all so depressing, this tired old notion of politics more important than human life. I had seen this game played too many times in the military, where it had cost my friends' lives.

The rain had worsened. I crossed Boulevard Mortier and down the tacky back streets of the 20th Arrondissement. The *halal* butchers and hooded women with downcast fearful eyes, their thick tent-like garments falling all the way to their feet, the cheap grocery stores of jingling music, the streaks of urine down old stone walls, the smell of fried meat and roach spray, the sharp-eyed men with long knives in their pockets watching from doorways, the old cars hunched by the curb like beaten dogs, it was all so alien, unlike France.

Never in my life, even in Afghanistan or in the horror of Mosul, have I felt so close to the truth. To what really goes on beneath the masks of life. That happiness is a temporary illusion and only pain and sorrow real. That we stand on air, on nothing. We think we're alive but it's illusion too, we think we're important but that's a farce. And death comes when it wants.

We've always known this, hated it, feared it, tried not to think about it. But like a friendly serpent it slithers back, poisons and enwraps us. While our hunger for happiness lures us along the tattered path of life like the mechanical bunny that dogs chase around a track.

But I've also learned in times of great challenge to turn the horror aside, rise above failure, the impossibility of victory. To laugh at fate, disown and refuse it.

Just because everything was going wrong that didn't mean we couldn't win.

We just had to think smarter. Move faster. Be more silent and deadly.

S A B O T A G E

"THE DEAD GIRL," Thierry spread photos across his desk of scattered coffee stains and papers, "is Rolinda Rastes, 27, a Romanian immigrant without a passport or any other ID."

"How you know?"

"Prints. She already had a long file. Pickpocketing, grabbing money off restaurant tables, graduated last year to breaking and entering and jewelry theft, stole a Vespa and did three hours in jail. No doubt intended to sell Anne's motorcycle ... The judges keep letting her go. One of thousands we keep sending home who come right back."

I looked sadly at the heart-shaped stolid face, the dark brows, lashes, hair and eyes. Part of the Romanian crime mafia that has expanded throughout Europe since the EU. "And look where it got her."

"I feel very sad for her," Anne said. "Like she was my sister – isn't that crazy?"

Thierry nodded. "Your death sister."

"And the next thought I have is, they think they've killed me. How do we use this against them?"

"The existential question." Thierry stood by the window watching the gray rain. "There's several options. One, we announce this poor girl was shot by persons unknown. She was a bit player in the Romanian crime mafia, on a bike she'd stolen, we think it's some gang rivalry, we're asking for witnesses ..."

Anne shrugged. "Or we say I *was* shot and you're working intensely on finding the killers."

"Or you disappear," Thierry said. "As if it *was* you who got shot, and we won't admit it?"

"Or you announce I was killed but call it an accident. Killed when my bike hit a tree or a parked truck –"

"Not that," Thierry said. "Then we'd need an inquiry ... who was the truck's owner? We'd have to identify them." He smiled. "We don't have to identify a tree ..."

"Say you're still trying to ID the victim. What you'd say if it *was* me."

"I think it's best we release no information at all. It's the best way to protect you. I don't want to use you as bait. Let the bastards think you're dead."

She shook her head. "You're throwing away a chance to get them."

He sighed, looked out the window. "In that case we need to disguise you, different hairstyle, different clothes, a new apartment."

She reached unconsciously for her hair. "I like my hair like it is."

"In any case, this will soon go away."

"Unless," I said, "the Romanians report her missing."

He shook his head. "They won't say a word."

With my knife I tried to scrape the dead girl's dried blood from under my thumbnail but some remained. It was brown now, nearly black. Caky and half-dry. Sticky lifeblood. In it the DNA of an alive young woman who hadn't known she was about to die.

"The best reason for the killers to think you dead," I said to Anne, "is they stop trying to kill you."

"My way's better," she said. "We let them know I'm still alive. And set a trap for them when they come."

It made pure tactical sense. But I didn't want it. "We let them *think* it's you. But it will be me."

"No way." She glared at me. "I fight my own wars."

HARRIS ANSWERED on the first ring. "That was close," he said, his voice rough. "She's an amazing woman."

How would you know? I started to say, a stupid question. After I'd briefed him on last night and what DGSE, Anne and I were planning, I added, "I have to report also, I have an emotional relationship with her."

"I know."

"But we're swimming upstream, and the French keep fucking up."

"Maybe they're not."

"Not what? Fucking up?"

"Yeah, maybe they're right on and you just haven't picked it up?"

This pissed me off. "I doubt that."

"French intelligence is handcuffed by judges, media and politicians." He cleared his throat. "They're in a terrible position. The police are even worse off ... It's not surprising you think they're fucking up."

"Where next, then?"

"We have a senior operative and his wife missing. And because the French are still our allies, we need to help them find

Mustafa. The two issues may or may not be connected. And," he added, "we need to find who tried to kill your girlfriend."

Again I thought of our lack of street knowledge, of local assets. "How?"

"Get over here," he harrumphed like a disagreeable uncle. "We need to talk."

THE SUN WAS halfway up the east when I got there. He was his usual abrupt self, shook my hand, sat in a leather chair by the coffee table, pointed to another. "Hell of a shock, when it came in, that she was down."

"You heard it?"

"I was on that frequency, because of Yasmina, that whole deal. Trying to figure where you were. Then came the *Officer Down*, and the moment it was a woman on motorcycle ..."

I didn't answer. "Twenty minutes later," he said, "you came on, saying she was alive." He shook his head. "Horrible twenty minutes." He glanced at the sideboard. "Get yourself some coffee, you want."

I glanced at the tired drip machine on the sideboard. "Maybe."

It felt like we were back at my trial, before I was found guilty and sentenced to twenty years. Because of him. It roiled my stomach. I beat it down. What did he remember, care about, of that time?

The coffee was rich and strong, Italian. Not like I'd expected. "It's good," I said.

He looked pleased I liked it, or maybe this was bullshit too. "You've really made a difference, since you got here."

This surprised me. "Things have gone to Hell ..."

"Well, you gave them the first decent portrait of Mustafa. So that led to the other real-time pix they got of him, including the last one in La République." He nodded, reflectively. "And you checked that café again, with the face photo. That was well done."

"Yeah, and got the patron killed."

"Could've been something else. We're checking that out."

"How?"

"Amazing what we can pick up." He pointed at the roof.

This made me smile: the Agency's preoccupied dependence on listening to everyone. Them and NSA.

He drank some coffee, set down the cup. "You were right about Yasmina too."

"I was?"

"If you had brought her out alive she would've been a well of information. We could have taken good care of her, got her away from that mix of fanaticism, fear and repression."

"What are you going to do about it?"

This took him back an instant. "You want me to harass Thierry because he's not doing his job? You really think that?"

I thought about it. "He's just so impeded. Blocked at every turn."

"Imagine what it's like for him. Going home at night wondering what has he accomplished? Who is getting away to kill again? He's got a wife and four beautiful kids. What about them?"

"What about them?"

"You think they're not at risk too?"

"So that's why he's fucking things up?"

"Of course not." He leaned forward as if his back hurt. "Just keep thinking and watching your perimeters and assume Mustafa's after you, too. And Anne."

I got up to leave. "Shall do."

He motioned for me to sit. "I asked Mack to bring you here because you knew Mustafa. But also because you finish what you start. You don't miss things and you don't complain." He nodded. "I like that."

"I almost bailed when I learned it was you."

"That's fine. You must remember, though, that I got you sentenced, back then, not because you shot the girl. Because you shot her husband."

"I know you think that," I said.

"But I'm glad," he continued, "that lawyer got you out." This was the West Point grad who'd reopened my case; she'd literally saved my life. Because no one survives twenty years in Leavenworth military prison. Not in any way worth talking about.

He was saying *although I did right to put you in prison, I'm happy you got out*. Nuts. Let *him* do the time.

He leaned forward at me across the table. "I'm glad you've hooked up with Anne. Isn't that what it's called these days, 'hooking up'?"

I felt my neck go red. "It's not like that."

"Sorry, sorry. I'm a single old bear, no grace ..." He reached for a half-empty coffee cup. "She's a remarkable agent, apparently. Been involved in some serious things." He smiled at me like a cheery old uncle. "No one to take lightly."

"I'm aware of that."

"Lost her husband couple years ago."

"You know how?"

"Like her, he was working for DGSE. They'd tracked down a bunch of Chechnyans in Pau who were pushing Islam and heroin all over the Pyrenees. In the shootout one of them was killed, the rest captured. A month later Éric gets his head blown off in the Bois de Vincennes, where he's playing with his two kids and Anne beside a little lake. He's in the water with half his brains gone and Anne dives to the ground on top of the kids and then sprints them to cover."

This choked me. "How do you know all this?"

"Mack told me."

"And now *he's* gone. And Gisèle too. And Bruno killed, Anne nearly killed. Who's next?"

"You and Anne." He leaned forward at me across the table. "You're both at severe risk. You gotta move. We'll put you someplace nice."

"We're getting our own place."

"Not on my dime." He sat back, palms around a crossed knee. "And we'll have you covered before you even move in."

This was true, I despaired. Fuck it, you just had to pretend they weren't there.

"A Navy SEAL, your Dad," Harris said, seemingly out of the blue. "Came to your trial every day."

This angered me. Pa had died just three months ago and I missed him every minute. Why did Harris give a damn?

"We know things," Harris said, "that Thierry, DGSE, all of them – don't. I'm going to give you what you need. You use what you can." He leaned forward again, thin black eyes on mine. "But you don't say where you got it. Agreed? Not ever."

"But why're they goatfucking us?"

"DGSE?"

"Who else?"

He stood, arched his back, massaging it. "They're fatally torn, the French. Between those who want to maintain their national identity and those who hate it. A division so deep each will do whatever it takes to destroy the other. And to Hell with France.

"This means," he pointed a thumb at Paris out the window, "some powerful people are going to sabotage anything you, we, or your buddies in DGSE, ATS and the cops try to do."

I sat back, nodded. "Already true."

He sat, scratched his chin. "You got to understand, this is personal. Coming from me, not" – he gave a glance at the room, the ornate ceiling – "not here."

I wondered what this meant. "Okay."

He kind of growled and sat upright, reminding me of a fierce old baboon. Looked me in the eye. "What I mean, dammit, is that some of the people you think are on your side aren't. Mustafa wants you, no doubt about that. Somebody on your side is also on his."

That he might have any personal concern for my safety seemed outlandish. But we were allegedly on the same team, and perhaps he feared repercussions up the line if I were to die under his stewardship. Though such repercussions were unlikely, given that some of the folks up the line would probably be delighted at my demise, my very existence unrecorded and denied.

I'd known I was in danger from Mustafa. But I'd neglected to consider that someone on my side might also be on his.

"NO, NO, cannot be true," Anne huffed when I got to DGSE and told her. "Not possible!" For an instant she looked moody and difficult, almost angry, then nodded, "Yeah, yeah. Could be true." She gave me that harrowed look of hers. "If so, we have to find out who."

"Someone on your side who's trying to sink this –"

"You're the one who keeps saying we have to expect the impossible."

I never understood what she'd meant till afterward.

When it was too late.

C O N F E S S

AN ARMORED LIMO had taken Mamie and the kids to Cousine Claudine's farm in rural Normandy not far from Lyons-la-Forêt, to help raise chickens and goats, grow apples, and make *foie gras*, Calvados, and Camembert. While Mamie paced the fences, fierce and vengeful, an ancient shotgun in her hands.

On our own we took several evasive maneuvers from her place to my bugged one-bedroom at Passage Landrieu. Where we left some stuff we didn't need, locked up, took several taxis to the 15th, where we paid cash to rent a short-term furnished apartment overlooking the new-leafed chestnut trees of the Place du Commerce. Ignoring Harris's offer to find us a new place, as I didn't want another safe house: when your killers came for you, it would be the first place they'd look.

To Airbnb we were just another wandering couple looking for a short-term home. For a while there'd be no way our enemies could track us down. Before DGSE and Home Office found us. Then maybe Mustafa.

IT DID LITTLE GOOD to try to figure who might seem to be on our side but was betraying us. Thierry was high up in DGSE but there were others well above him of whom he might not be fully aware. In the Machiavellian machinations of intelligence there are many shadowy movers and shakers so well protected by their positions and so connected to unknown sources and powers that no one even knows they're there. I as an American could have little chance to penetrate this; even Anne, as grounded in the intelligence world as she was, would have great trouble piercing its veils.

No matter our experience and awareness we were foot soldiers in a vast war whose deepest secrets were unknown to us; we lived and died following our determination to make a better world, but sometimes achieving just the opposite.

How much did Thierry really know? How far above him was the enemy, if there was one? What dangers did he, or his family, face if he tried to unmask it?

OUR NEW HOME was lovely and sun-bright and had no bugs or hidden cameras that I could find. With a wide kitchen, living room and dining rooms facing the Place two stories below, a bedroom facing the interior court ... If you're going to die soon, why not spend the money? Plus it had a real shower, not just a hose in a tub.

We dropped our stuff, made love in the shower, and downed some baguette, Camembert and *Fleurie*. Our kitchen had lots of good things to cook with, the refrigerator hummed diligently, the traffic sounded distant through the double panes, and the sun set in crimson splendor over the slate rooftops to the west.

"HOW I GOT THIS?" We were in bed and Anne twisted sideways to point to the lightning tattoo down her left biceps. "I had a boyfriend in high school ..." She pulled back. "You really want to hear this?"

I nestled against her lovely tits. "I love hearing everything about you."

"This boyfriend, he told me when he came inside me it was like a lightning bolt up his spine right into his brain ..."

"He was right. That's exactly what it's like."

"Then he dumped me and I was so miserable and my best friend told me I was the ugliest girl in our class, so I was really unhappy. Then I said to myself *Get over it, nothing bad's happened to you*. And to remind myself what a great fuck I was I went out and got this tattoo."

I put my hand between her thighs. "I like this one too."

She rolled so I could kiss it. A white orchid just above her glorious black hair. "I like both of them," I said.

She said nothing and I had a sudden fear she didn't care. "What was he like, your husband?"

"Éric?" she lay back, swallowed. "He was loving. Strong, gentle ... funny as Hell. God he could make us laugh." She sniffed. "But you could trust him. To the end of time."

"I'm sorry," I said. "I'm so sorry."

She slid down against me, tickled my chin with a lock of her hair. "He was a lot like you."

I lay with her head on my shoulder, thinking of the joy and sorrow of it all. And if you try to duck the sorrow you lose the joy.

How wonderful life can be, how intense, profound, multidimensional, exciting, exhilarating, terrifying and moody – which makes the thought of losing it horrendous. When every sweet moment is done it's gone forever, a delusional memory.

I didn't want to die. I didn't want Anne to die. But we would very soon, unless we got Mustafa.

THEY CAME in the middle of the night clattering and banging the doors and smashed mine open. Yanked me up and twisted the cuffs off the metal ring on the floor, shoved my face against the wall kicking me behind the knees so I fell and they dragged me up again. I'd been lying in a sombrous pain and tried to wake up but couldn't tell what was nightmare and what real.

When they shoved and punched me down the corridor and out onto the slippery yard I realized it was the execution ground, and the slipperiness was blood. They tied my knees and ankles together as I tried to kick them but they whacked me on the head with a rifle butt till I began to pass out from the pain.

A cold wind made me shiver, or maybe it was just the knowledge of what was about to happen. They tied my cuffed hands to the rope around my ankles so I couldn't stand, my knees in old sticky blood, new warm blood running down my temple from where the rifle butt had hit.

Overhead the stars were sharp as broken glass. Despite the darkness I could see three other guys kneeling like me. One looked at me, his white eyes wide with fear, his mouth agape. There was an empty space beside me and I wondered who it was for. A bright white light seared on, blanking out the stars. A shape rustled past, a metal bar banging my shoulder. I feared they were going to beat us, then realized that would be better than what was really going to happen.

They shoved someone down beside me and I could see blood running down the side of his mouth, realized it was Mack. "Hey, buddy," I mumbled. "This is it."

A huge pain exploded the side of my head smashing it down against my shoulder. "No talk!" a voice hissed. A voice I recognized: Mustafa.

He slid between us, raised a huge glinting thing to the light. A cleaver, thick with blood. He spun and swung it past my ear. It made a whistling sound, a metal hiss. I tried not to flinch.

"Tonight is goodbye," Mustafa said, a kindly almost-curious voice. "You will confess to your infidel murders or I will kill him." He slapped the cleaver sideways down on Mack's head, knocking him backwards. "You will confess," he repeated. "Or I will kill him."

Mack gave a sigh of pain or disgust, I couldn't tell. I imagined the blade flashing down, cutting off his head, it rolling across the ground. Mine too.

Even in this moment of death I cared more for Mack's life than my own.

"Cameras!" Mustafa chortled. "Action!"

The red light in the camera flashed on. "We will start with this false Muslim," he said, striding to the man on the right, beyond Mack. "Who is the true descendant of the Prophet?" he asked in a mild, curious voice, as if wanting to know. The ancient hatred between Shia and Sunni over the lineage from the prophet Mohammed, equivalent to how many angels can fit on the tip of a pin, and which has since caused so many millions of deaths.

The man said something I couldn't understand. Mustafa gestured toward the camera. Two flunkies lifted the tripod and moved it in front of the man, who had raised his face to the now-hidden stars and was mumbling something with trembling lips.

It was beyond horrible, this. If there were a God how could this God allow it? Fear clenched my heart; I couldn't breathe. Knew I was next. Or Mack.

The cleaver whistled down and with a soggy clunk bit into the man's neck. It stuck on the spine; the man's head fell forward, half disconnected. Mustafa yanked it free, dragging the man sideways, raised it and swung down, thunking into the spine in a different place. Pain exploded in my head – the rifle butt again. "Look down!" snarled the man behind me.

From the side of my eyes I could see Mustafa wrenching the cleaver free and swinging it down again, and the head rolled free in a wide-spreading pool of blood that gurgled across the earth between our knees, hot and stinky, bringing out the odor of the older half-dried blood beneath.

"So!" Mustafa stood over me. "That was instructive, no?" He tipped up my chin with the bloody tip of the cleaver. "What did you learn?"

"That you are a coward," I wanted to say but didn't, knowing it would just make him draw my suffering out longer. "Go ahead," I choked. "Get it over with."

"Yes," he nodded. "Get it over with." He raised the cleaver high, halted, turned to the camera and said something about getting a different angle.

I took a breath.

"I love you, man," Mack said.

"I love you too," I answered, the only time I'd ever told a man I loved him other than my father. Then I saw Pa's face, his diligent hedonistic smile, his laughter at the world. "They will burn in Hell forever," Pa chuckled, "if only there were one."

I raised my head, determined to look death in the eye. The cleaver glinted as it flashed down, twisted between me and Mack and thudded into the ground.

"Oh, I am bad," Mustafa panted. "Can't even aim this weapon straight." He shuffled sideways to Mack, raised it again. "Confess," he said softly, bending down to peer into Mack's eyes. "Confess to your infidel sins, before the camera, and perhaps I will not kill him."

"You piece of pig shit," Mack said, braver than I.

"Oh my," Mustafa sighed, a patient teacher with a recalcitrant pupil. "Now I have to kill you." Again the raised cleaver glinted in the camera light, flashed down between us. "Ah, I am truly bad. Cannot kill a kaffir, you think?" He turned and waved at the camera, "Stop!" His empty eyes swung back to mine. "Perhaps tomorrow? Perhaps I do better tomorrow?"

I sat up, the bedsprings yowling. There was someone in the darkness beside me. "Who?"

Anne eased against me and my heartbeat slowed, my breathing softened, and I was at home again.

FROM THAT NIGHT Anne and I became a single unit focused on our prey. We still reported to Thierry, confided in Tomàs, kept Harris semi-informed, stayed in touch with Claudine and the kids, and tried to work 24 hours a day. But night and day we focused on Mustafa, Mack and Gisèle, the Tower, and the backpack nuclear bomb. And this new enemy, the insider who was trying to defeat every move we made.

After a few days we had to sleep. By two a.m. we'd been at work since seven the previous morning. We'd tumble on the bed and make love, then, sweaty and drained, fall asleep in each other's arms.

We'd fed Mustafa's real pix into the system and were getting complementary hits from other camera locations. The same ugly, evil Mustafa trudging a sidewalk, elbows and feet wide, half-hiding his scorn, slipping into a bank with a plastic portfolio under his arm, standing in the Porte de Clichy Métro at the crossing of the Pontoise and Courtilles lines, watching the young women in their flimsy miniskirts walk past.

SHOOT FIRST

"WE HAVE A HIT!" Thierry on the phone sounded casual, almost happy.

"What kind of hit?" It was after midnight and Anne and I were so exhausted we'd given up and were headed to bed.

"Where is she?"

"I'll get her." I went into the bathroom where she was brushing her teeth. "It's Thierry." I put the phone on speaker. "He has a hit."

"*Oogle*," she responded, took the toothbrush from her mouth and spat into the sink, wiped her mouth with the back of her hand. "A hit?"

Thierry waited a second, building suspense. "Mustafa's cell."

"*O Mon Dieu*," she snapped. "*Not possible!*"

"16:23 today he walks into the post office at 38 Boulevard de Strasbourg. We just now got the link. They got him first with the outside camera and then a close-up inside. He pulls out a phone, and receivers in the post office catch the call. To Abdelasalaam Al-Fatah, Moroccan, 28, unemployed, an S-List guy, address in St. Denis, goes to the Salafist Al Rawda Mosque in Stains."

"That got closed," Anne said, "for preaching terrorism."

"It's open again. He's been in and out of jail since age fifteen, multiple burglaries, suspect in several rapes, lots more stuff."

"And he's *out?*"

"He couldn't be judged on rape, the judge said, because in the Muslim culture rape is not a crime."

I scanned the dark rooftops, the sky. It was like hunting where everything you kill gets stolen from you, till you starve.

"The phone?" Anne said.

"A prepaid throwaway ... No history, just that one call."

"Bought when?" I said, trying to wake up and think.

"Last Tuesday, a camera shop at Orly. Cash."

"Since then?"

"Nothing till this call at 16:23. That was eight hours ago. We're listening for anything new. He's disabled the GPS, we can't locate him."

"If we do," Anne said, "we take him in?"

"That's, of course, the eternal question."

"Have you put anyone on the St. Denis place?" Anne said. "This Abdelasalaam?"

"That's part of the eternal question. If we locate him, do we grab him, work him over? Or do we watch, see where he takes us?"

"That's where I'm headed now," I said. "A quick look."

"We've got guys to do that," Thierry said. "Arabs."

"You can show your guys a thousand pictures of Mustafa," I said. "But I'm the one who knows him. I know his smell. His aura. How he walks and what his face does when he looks at people. If he shows up there, we decide what to do – bring him in fast, or follow him."

"If we follow him," Anne spat more toothpaste into the sink, "we might lose him."

"So back to this Abdelasalaam," Thierry countered. "We watch who he is, his connections ..."

"Or we send him south?" Anne persisted.

"Under the new rules," Thierry mumbled, "we now need Ministerial approval for sending guys to Casa."

Casa is of course Casablanca, near where Moroccan *Sécurité* has a nice little place for intimate discussions. Out in the desert, far from the roving eye, its only neighbors some sandblasted, forgotten Roman ruins.

"No need for Casa," I said. "I'll take this guy down to Fontainebleau Forest and he'll tell us all we need to know."

Thierry said nothing, then, "ATS has some good pix of him, I've sent them to you. As you'll see, he's tall and skinny with bad teeth and a pockmarked face."

"I think we should bring him in," Anne said.

"Not yet. You two, can you be there in an hour? Surveillance only? You'll have full ATS backup. In case Mustafa does show? Not that I think he will ..."

"We'll have to use the Peugeot," I said.

Thierry snickered. "It fits the neighborhood."

This riled me. "There isn't a car in Seine St. Denis that can keep up with it."

"So take good care of it. When you're done we want it back."

When we're done. I thought of Mack and Gisèle, the Tower. Paris.

"Be careful," Thierry added. "There's lots of guys with guns in that neighborhood. If you have to, shoot first."

THE STREET was pallid under the arc lights. Dirty façades, drab awnings. Graffiti in Arabic and French, miserable cars toed into the curb, hanging wires, a furtive rat, sticky grunge on your soles. Gutters of trash.

"Nirvana," Anne said. She was half-slouched in the passenger seat, head barely visible above the door, while I watched the oversized rearview mirror for anything coming the other way.

A few cars patrolled the neighborhood. Abdel's was a brick four-story building squeezed in between many others of its kind, with a front door that hung open over a broken stoop.

It was a dirty, deadly and deteriorating place like so many in the Lost Territories of France, and just being there infected me with a dim view of the future. Things get worse. That was the rule. Things always get worse.

That's what it seemed like. That most folks in this hellhole of misery, fanaticism, and fear were just doing what they could to get by and raise their children. When all they probably wanted was to move out. And couldn't. Or they were faithful, but didn't believe violence was the answer.

The answer to what? Maybe people like Rachid Raqmi might have one. Or Nisa?

We were four blocks from where Yasmina Noureff had blown herself to bits. Or someone with a trigger had blown her.

02:14 on the Peugeot's blue dash clock. "I could use a cigarette," Anne said.

"Not in here."

"Screw you."

"And you're not going to stand outside smoking. And blow our whole scene."

"Screw you," she repeated. I'd noticed that two things made her cranky: one, if she hadn't eaten meat for several hours, or, two, if she wanted a cigarette.

"*No damn cigarettes,*" I repeated.

Okay, maybe I was cranky too. It had been a long day. We were exhausted and getting on each other's nerves. I'd been dizzy with fatigue and dying for sleep when Thierry'd called about Mustafa's phone and this guy Abdel. Anne had been beyond weariness too, but in ten minutes we were in the Beast and on our way. Now, sitting in its soft seats in the cool darkness of this dilapidated ghetto where absolutely nothing was happening, we couldn't stop falling asleep, heads nodding and jerking up, grunts and face-rubbings.

"The only way I can stay awake," I said, "is if we fuck."

She giggled. "You think I'm nuts? That'd be a DA."

"DA?"

"Disciplinary Action."

"You're making that up."

She shook her head. "We're not supposed to fuck on the job."

"Says who?"

"Thierry, for one."

I took out my phone and hit the code for his cell. "What are you doing!" she hissed.

"Calling Thierry to ask if it's okay if we fuck while we're waiting."

She slapped my hand nearly destroying my phone. "Don't you dare."

"I'm serious. We go in the back seat and do it with you on my lap and I can keep looking up the street and you looking back toward Abdel's door … Otherwise I'm going to fall asleep."

She fumed at this for a few minutes, took out her Glock and cranked it. With a sudden twist she crawled between the front seats into the back, laid the Glock on the rear panel, in a spinning motion unbuttoned, unzipped and pulled down her jeans.

How exciting new love and desire and constant threat of death and the fear of losing friends can turn a fuck into a volcano of desire and release, a revelation, a hardening of the will … And you come out of it less fatigued, can go on, run another ten miles.

I sat in the back watching toward the front as she came down on top of me facing the rear, her soft fine hair tickling my cheek. As always it was delicious, exciting, beyond delightful. But not for an instant did I lessen my gaze on the street; I intensified it, just as the ferocious pleasure of rising up and down inside her intensified everything.

She leaped off me. "Tall guy in a hoodie just came out the door. He's got something in his right hand and he's coming this way."

I rolled up pulling my Glock. I'd seen nothing my way, turned to face rear. "Ten meters."

"I'm not blind." She raised her Glock and stretched out on the seat facing the sidewalk. He'd have to look in the car window to see us. But we couldn't see him unless he did.

All was softly quiet but for a distant hiss of tires on the Péréphérique. A tiny click as Anne slid off safety. I took a silent breath, gauging the odds he'd look in, that he'd yank a gun and fire and we'd somehow have to shoot him before he did. Tried to remember where the lift mechanism was in the car door that might deflect my bullet: best option was to shoot him through the glass.

But I didn't want to shoot him. Not yet.

I wanted him to take me to Mustafa.

Then I'd shoot him.

The whisper of soft footfalls on the sidewalk, a snuffle, a spit, its whack on concrete. A slap-slap of sneakers as he neared, his shadow flitting across the window when he passed. Keeping my weapon aimed at him, I counted five seconds and was readying to slide out of the car and follow him but Anne shoved me down. "He's coming back!"

On the floor, face up, bent backward over the bump of the transmission drive shaft, the Glock in both hands, I tried to see through the car window glazed with our breath. "Maybe he saw something," she whispered. "Coming back to check us out."

"How far?"

"Fifteen meters ... He's pulling something from his coat –"

"A gun?"

"Can't tell."

"If it's a gun we have to shoot him."

"Then we lose everything ..."

"How far?"

"Five meters."

I slid to a half-sitting position, still below the door window, Glock ready.

"It's a phone. He's got a phone in his right hand."

"Get down!"

Again the shadow flitted across us. It paused, backed up a step, went on.

"What'd he see?" I whispered. "What did he *see*?"

"Can't tell. He stopped a second, by the window, then went on ... He's crossing the street. Back toward the house. Still talking on the phone."

I rose up to look as he climbed the steps and entered the building. About twenty seconds later a second-floor window lit up, went dark.

"Gone to bed," I said, pulling myself against her.

"Mon Dieu, you're *still* hard."

"I lost it when we were going to shoot him. Just got it back."

She eased down, tucking her panties aside as I rose up into her again, long and slow and hot and slick, how amazing it feels sliding into someone you're falling in love with ... *"Don't* stop," she whispered. *"Don't* stop watching."

"I'm not." I stared through the windshield seeing everything out there, *every* thing, as we rocked harder, faster, softer, slower, in this delectable heaven.

"He's back!" She dove aside and I edged up to watch through the rear window.

"Every time I start to come," she snapped, "he kills it."

He stood on the stoop, glanced up and down the street, took out a cigarette and lit it.

Something flashed further down the street: a car had turned onto ours, a block away, its lights off.

"Get ready!" I rolled into the front.

Another vague glimmer as a second car turned up this street, a block behind the first. "They're going to do a driveby," I said. "Or one or both of them will pull over and they'll all pile out and rake us."

"It'll be AKs …"

"Probably."

"We're fucked."

She was right; there was no time to drive off, to run, we were trapped. Had Abdel known we were there? Had he set this up?

The first car eased to a stop at Abdel's door. He tossed the cigarette, hopped down the steps and got in the back. The car slid past us, then the second, as we took quick phone pix of both. At the corner they both flicked on their headlights and turned left toward Stains and the A1.

I leaped into the driver's seat, gave them a few seconds and started after them as Anne scrambled up beside me.

"That son of a bitch," she said. "I was just about to come."

"Sorry."

"Did you?"

"Twice."

"Liar!"

"Put on your seat belt. This could be a fast trip."

She put her Glock on safety, opened the glove box and took out two more clips. "*Inshallah.*"

D E C O Y

IT WAS DANGEROUS to drive with no headlights but otherwise the cars ahead would see us.

"Why did he walk past us?" Anne yelled over the Beast's engine as she scanned the dark streets. "Then came back, went into the house and came right out?"

I hit third gear at a hundred ten just to keep up with the two cars ahead. "He was checking the street? Didn't see us?"

"He had us." She snickered. "Dead to rights."

I shivered at the thought of it, the bullets blunted by metal and glass punching through our bodies at three times the speed of sound, smashing and wrenching and ripping and shattering out the other side of us, pieces of us flying after them ... It was so awful my body refused to think of it.

The two cars ahead of us were heading away from Charles de Gaulle Airport onto the A1 south toward Paris. The Renault Espace that had been in second place passed the white Mercedes with Abdel in it, turned west on the Péréphérique, took the

Porte Maillot exit and Avenue de la Grande Armée toward the Arc de Triomphe.

"This is crazy," I said. "They're taking us for a ride."

The two cars reached the Arc and barreled straight down Marceau toward the Seine. Anne kept taking pix but we were too far behind to be accurate, the Beast throbbing and swaying with speed and bumps and turns. We were halfway there when ahead of us above the dark stone skyline I saw the Tower's lights.

"Yeah," she nodded. "Trial run."

I wiped my hand against the mist on the inside of the windshield but that made it worse. The stop light ahead of us turned red but the two cars howled through it almost nailing a taxi and a trash truck that seconds later I missed by swerving at high speed onto the sidewalk knocking down three bicycle racks *whang whang-whang* with clattering steel and headlight glass flying, then the newly one-eyed Beast found the road again, narrowing the distance between it and Abdelasalaam and his friends.

"Damn!" I yelled, feeling bad for the car.

"You should let me drive," she yelled.

"Easing back now. Know where they're going –"

"Like I said. A trial run."

"What does this guy Abdelasalaam have to do with the Tower?"

She nodded her chin at the two cars as they swung off the Alma Bridge onto Quai Branly. "Nothing and everything."

The two cars passed the Tower and dove left onto Avenue du Suffren, a wide tree-lined boulevard and behind it a narrow street of beautiful carved stone apartments facing the Champ de Mars, in front of the Tower. "This is crap," I said.

"Shut up and drive."

I laughed. "That's from a movie somewhere."

"It's mine now. Because I said it ... *Hold it* – they're slowing, *pull back!*"

I parked the Beast at a convenient hydrant. Fifty yards ahead the two cars slid into a bus zone on Avenue Suffren. Two guys got out of each car. One slung a big backpack over his shoulders. They locked their cars so the lights flashed, ambled across Suffren against the light and trotted through the trees along the back streets toward the Tower. Anne took closeups of the license plates and we went after them.

We slipped through the shadowed plane trees along the Champ, trying to stay out of their sight but not lose them. The Tower's red searchlights cast an eerie red through the thick trunks and rubbled ground; the wind from the Seine was cold and uncaring: *We've seen this for thousands of years: man against man. We don't give a damn.*

The four guys crossed the circle at Avenue Bouvard where in the day the tour buses park.

Now even at four a.m. the cops were here, moving toward these guys, and at least five *Sentinelle* soldiers coming forward from the pillars.

This is how they get you, came into my mind. *Decoy.*

Decoy. What did they want to distract us from?

If you win, I realized, *it will be because you understand.*

"They're coming back," Anne whispered. "The cops are turning away."

They were coming straight at us. I pointed at a tree. "There!"

She leaned back against a plane tree moaning as I shoved my body up and down her – nobody could tell, in the dark.

The guys passed in a silent hustle, one snickering, sneaker steps dying out in the hiss of Seine wind through the plane boughs, a sole siren far away, the throbbing night hum of Paris.

We followed them back to the Arc de Triomphe and Seine St. Denis till they deposited our alleged Abdelasalaam at his doorstep and two ATS teams picked up the tail, and she and I drove to DGSE.

In the DGSE parking lot I draped my head on my arms over the steering wheel. It felt good. "I'm so fucking tired."

"*Tant pis.* We have a full day ahead."

"So why were they driving that fast, if it was just a trial run? Why risk being pulled over or caught on camera, and then your whole scene is blown?"

"Two possibilities –"

"With you it's always two possibilities –"

"Either they saw us and were trying to lose us ..."

"Or taking us for a ride ..."

"Or it was a trial run for speed, to see how fast they could make that distance, if they had to ... That's why it was after two a.m., when there's nothing to slow you down."

"When do we take them?"

"Thierry's eternal question." She raised her chin and shoved open the passenger door. "Let's go see him."

"WE'VE ID'd Abdel's three friends." Thierry looked at Anne. "Thanks to your pix."

"And?"

"They all went home. Three to St. Denis, one to Senlis."

"Senlis?" I almost laughed, dizzily exhausted. One more lovely French medieval town living around its grand cathedral.

"You'd be surprised," he said. "They run the place."

Where didn't they? I suddenly felt bowed down, helpless.

Yet we had their license plates. "Who are they?"

An amazing amount of information had already been collected by ATS. After barely five hours we had their prints, phone conversations, DNA, the works. Most of all, we could now look for them on encrypted Telegram sites, the true heart of Islam.

"Nothing yet. Normal arrest records. Used to attend the same Salafist mosque in Stains –"

"Al Rawda," Anne said.

"But both dropped out a year ago."

"Because it got closed –"

"No beards, occasional visits to other mosques. One guy now drinks pastis, the other a little red wine. Both screw Western women ..."

"*Taqiya*," I said.

"Most guys, when they drop fundamentalism, it's *taqiya*." This was the subterfuge taught in the Koran, that a believer can adopt infidel ways in order to dupe his enemies into thinking he poses no danger.

"You going to bring them in?"

"For speeding?" He leaned back, unwilling to bear bad news. "We have to *prove* guilt, Pono, before we grab someone."

"Fuck that," I said, too tired to think.

"Go home, you two," Thierry said. "Get some sleep. Be back by two. There'll be plenty to do."

"You," Anne nodded at him. "You ever sleep?"

He half-smiled. "I'll sleep when we get our people back. And stop Mustafa."

Already with so little sleep it was total confusion. You start with nothing and try to get somewhere. To narrow it down. To a kill.

Then you find everything you thought was right was wrong. And vice versa.

Maybe because your enemies *are* smarter than you are.

NOW WE HAD MUSTAFA'S PHONE we could track him. "Whenever a phone is on," Tomàs said, "it's constantly seeking the nearest and strongest tower antennas and establishing connections. The phone's serial number is tracked by the antennas, and that data allows us to triangulate someone within a meter or two, establish their movements, who they talk to, all that ..."

"Just like we do in the States." I didn't want him feeling superior about this.

"And like in the States, for some phones this only works if the person's calling or messaging. But with smartphones and 4G, we can ping them and get a location. Or when someone uses any of the apps ... If there's a crime we can check to see if a suspect was near the scene ... or we check the closest towers for all the phones near the scene at the time, and run them through our data base ... We don't know where somebody is? We send him a phantom message, one *he* never sees, and the towers nearest him locate him."

It was like that ancient evil goddess with infinite twirling arms who always knows where you are and can strike you down at any instant.

But that was okay with me as long as she stayed on our side.

H A W A L A

IT WAS 08:08 when we got to Commerce and hit the sack, but I couldn't sleep. Drank from the milk carton in the fridge and chased it with a swig of vodka but still couldn't sleep.

At times like this when I can't figure what to do, I sometimes call my buddy Mitchell. Whereas I can't find the button to start a computer, Mitchell can make the digital world sing for him, dance to his tune. And there is nothing out there he can't find.

Nominally, Mitchell is a consultant to a division of Naval Intelligence that doesn't exist. He spends his days and most of his nights in front of a bank of computers seeking our digital enemies: the rich Middle Easterners who fund Islamic terrorism, their money deals, their Facebook, Google, Twitter accounts and all those other media diseases that plague our modern brains.

And he tracks the thousands of hackers that assault our defense systems every day, picking the bad ones and hunting them down.

He can solve any IT problem you can imagine. He can find his way into anybody's life, use their phone while it's in their pocket or on their bedside table, take pictures with it, record what they say, and find out exactly where they were at every instant and what they were doing.

And if their computer's hooked to the internet he can wander around inside it and copy, destroy, or alter anything he wants. Even if it's not connected to the internet he can climb inside it using external radio waves, and hang out there, invisible. For the Navy, he patrols the borders of our virtual world, hunting interlopers, hackers, leakers and terrorists, the same way he and I once hunted al Qaeda in the nasty mountains of Afghanistan and Islamic *jihadis* in the gritty deathtraps of Mosul and Falluja.

He'd give anything to be like me, and I'd give anything not to be like him. Because in the northern Afghanistan hills he took the RPG meant for me, and on Oahu three years later I took the jail rap meant for him when I was caught with weed destined for him and other wounded buddies to ease their ongoing pain and PTSD. And thus, as mentioned, I ended up in Halawa Prison. But now I'm wandering free, surfing the oceans of the world and making love with lovely women, while Mitchell has no legs, no balls, and has to sit down to piss.

But that's another story. One that drives me crazy every day, and which he surmounts with a courage that is unimaginable.

"What you up to?" I said. It was 08:13 in Paris, so 20:13 in Honolulu – exactly 12 hours apart. That meant he'd had his usual dinner of steak, papayas and Russian vodka, and was back patrolling his carpeted "Situation Room" with its twelve computers tracking nasties all over the world.

"I just found this kid, she's thirteen, on her way back from Iraq to Brussels."

"They're all coming back."

"We have pix of this one training with a suicide belt around her waist ..."

"What are you doing about her?"

"Just sent it upriver and they're passing it to VSSE – Belgian intelligence."

"Mitchell, I *know* what VSSE is –"

"They'll detain her at Brussels Airport till some judge figures out what to do with her. Too bad, she's a pretty kid – but same history: father's devout and the mother can't make a phone call or go outside without a male family member watching over her, and if somehow despite all this she manages to alert the authorities her male kin have the right to kill her."

"I'm so sick of all this …"

"Oh, and the girl's pregnant. They married her to some *jihadi* who blew himself up …" He took a hit of vodka. "Where are *you*? Why are you wasting my time calling me?"

"You should be so lucky I call you. I'm in Paris. Mustafa al-Boudienne has shown up."

"No way. He's dead. The Legion got him …"

"That's what we thought."

"The Legion doesn't lie," Mitchell said.

"There wasn't much left of his face … Local guy who ID'd him made a mistake." I updated Mitchell about Mack and Gisèle, all the other horrible things that had come down. Perhaps I should have told him before, but our old rule, never say what you don't need to, got in my way.

"You shoulda told me sooner," he muttered.

"It's got bad real fast." It had barely been a week since I'd come to Paris but seemed like forever.

"What you need?"

"Two things. *One*, can ATS find other numbers that 'associate' with Mustafa's number that we do have, even if its GPS is switched off, and it's used only once?"

He thought about this. "Sometimes. Depends on provider, type of phone, all that stuff."

I gave him Mustafa's number, the one he'd used just once to call Abdel, and all its details. "I'll see what shows up," he said, getting impatient.

"One other question." I told him what Thierry and Harris

had said about the financial and other links between French politicians and media and Middle East interests.

"Middle East interests? The ones who financed Al Qaeda? ISIS?"

"The Saudis, Qataris, Bahrainis – all of them."

"If it started long ago, it's almost impossible to track now."

"You saying you can't do it?"

He thought a moment. "No, I ain't sayin that."

"So how *would* you do it?" I said, enticing him into this. "If you had the chance?"

"Well, like we do now, we track financial transfers. From one bank to another. Every financial transfer leaves a trace."

"Unless it's *hawala*." The Islamic money transfer process which leaves no trace, *hawala* involves middlemen who pay each other based on honor, and in which money is transferred but never actually moves. Originating perhaps in Biblical times, it was further developed by merchants along the Silk Road in the 8th century because of bandits pillaging their caravans.

"Even *hawala*," Mitchell said. "I've got my ways."

"What are you waiting for?"

"You think I sit around expecting you to call and hassle me with all your stupid provocations?"

"Mack and Gisèle could be dead now."

"I'll call you back," he said irritatedly, and rang off.

I sat there worrying maybe I shouldn't have bothered him with all this. But if the Saudis and other Wahhabis had been financing French politicians and media to assist in Islamic expansion in France, Mitchell would be the one to find out.

But how? And if we learned they had, what then?

The process of *hawala* is simple. Say, a banker in Riyadh tells a *hawala* broker there that he wishes to give ten million dollars for the growth of Islam in France. The broker then contacts another who has a colleague in Marseilles who contacts the destination accounts depending on passwords and other verbal agreements.

The *hawala* broker in France dispenses the proceeds less a small commission. The broker in Riyadh now owes him this amount, which may be erased by the next transaction.

Half the money may be for the construction of new mosques, a quarter for new madrassas and other Islamic schools, and a quarter to "protect the rights of Muslims in France," meaning the financing of terrorist actions against the French people.

And nobody along the chain knows both the source and final destination of the funds. And no paper or digital trail exists.

Hawala brokers settle the debts between them often not by money but by other services or goods, whether it be a commission on the purchase of jet fighters for the Saudi Air Force, rockets for Palestinians, architectural services in Abu Dhabi, an apartment in Paris or a Capri estate.

If Mitchell thought he could unravel any *hawala* connections between Islamic funding and French politicians, he'd have to look not at financial transfers but at *benefits accrued*, a much more difficult process ... A French senator introduces a bill allowing people from certain Islamic countries automatic French visas, and two years later he retires to a newly-bought castle in the Dordogne – how to find the link?

THE BELL of St. John the Baptist up the Rue du Commerce had just tolled 11:00. We'd had a good three hours' sleep and had finished a breakfast of *pain au chocolates* and lots of coffee. I cleared the crumbs off the wooden table and took out a pad of paper, wrote across the top, "What we know."

"That's a good start," she said.

"*Stop* being negative."

"Okay so *I'll* list for you what we know."

"Please do."

"We know Mustafa's in touch with Abdel who's doing something with the other three guys. That all four attended Al Rawda

Mosque in Stains when it was preaching hatred and working with ISIS heavies tied into Bataclan and other massacres ... All four seem to have adopted *taqiya* – we need more intel on them –"

"Tomàs is doing that."

She sighed, rubbed her face. "Too many unanswered questions."

I leaned forward, elbows on the table. "There's just seven unanswered questions:

"*What's* happened to Mack and Gisèle?

"*What* is Mustafa planning? What's his link with Abdel?

"*Who* killed Bruno at Les Quatre Vents? And why? Because he could ID Mustafa?

"*What* is the Yasmina-Mustafa connection? She'd implied there was none. Was she lying?

"*Who* came after you but instead killed the Romanian girl?"

"*What* about the Iranian nuke? If there was one? How is it getting to Paris?

"*Who* was paying whom? *Hawala?*

"And last, *why* are your people getting in our way? Who at the top is trying to protect Mustafa?"

Anne sighed and dropped her pencil. "Everybody's working on all of these, but we're getting nowhere."

"Not true. How long have we had this Mustafa-Abdel connection? A few hours. We have Mustafa's pics now, we didn't before –"

"And we're no closer to finding Mack and Gisèle."

"We will find them." I somehow found the strength to say it. "I promise we will."

In any investigation, the more you dig the more you turn up. I'd come to Paris to help get Mustafa. We didn't have Mustafa yet, but now we had film, a phone, several sightings, and a growing list of his friends.

MUSTAFA NEVER reappeared that day on any street or public camera. According to his ATS tails, Abdel slept the sleep of the just in his St. Denis digs (at least he stayed inside, unless he had a tunnel out the back). His three Stains Mosque buddies had quiet days as well, except for one erupting into the parking lot behind his building to beat a large, ugly, chained dog with a stick.

"Someday that guy," Tomàs said, "we feed him to that dog."

At 18:05 we were still in an ATS view room when he got the call. He turned to me, eyes wide, a huge grin. "We have a positive for Gisèle!"

It nearly knocked me off my feet. "Alive?"

"Today, 14:40, she went into a Crédit Agricole in Melun with two guys and cleared out her and Mack's account – twenty-seven thousand euros ..."

"Oh shit. Who were the guys?"

"Arabs, late twenties. Kept their faces from the cameras."

"Oh shit *oh shit!*" I walked in circles trying to think. "*Then what?*"

"She vanished off the outside camera with one Arab on each side of her."

"Your guys've talked to the tellers?"

"They say she seemed tired. Told them she and Mack were buying a sailboat from these guys, and they wanted cash ..."

"She's drugged. Or ..."

"We think one of them had a gun on her. From what we can see."

"No sign of Mack."

"None."

"They're using him to control her. They have him somewhere, cutting him apart in front of her ... She's trying to keep him alive."

FIVE SECONDS

WE WAITED TILL MIDNIGHT for another sighting but there was none, so Anne and I went home to Place de Commerce where I lay in bed thinking about Gisèle. How to be ready, if she was seen again. How to accelerate camera review, so there's not a four-hour lapse between the pix and the ID.

In the morning we could go to Melun, talk to the tellers. But what more to learn? And ATS had doubled up on camera coverages: focusing on Gisèle and her two captors, but so far nothing.

Melun was only 12 miles by car from Fontainebleau. The other side of the Forest. The bank was only 10 miles from where Mustafa's tan Passat with the Austrian plates had vanished.

ATS had also increased surveillance on Abdel and his three buddies, but there seemed no link. They were going about their usual business, Abdel selling opioids in St. Denis, calling his clients "brothers," the other three on their daily jobs as vacuum cleaner salesman, *halal* driver, and second grade teacher.

One more dead alley.

Not true, I told myself. Abdel had spoken with Mustafa. Then he'd gone with the three others in two cars on this mad race to the Tower and back. What had been in the bag he'd carried over his shoulder? Why had he walked past us when we hid in the car, ready to kill and die?

Had he pretended not to see us?

HIGHWAY TO HELL on my phone. I twisted around in bed trying to find it without waking Anne.

"Another hit!" Tomàs said.

I glanced out the window at the dark street, then at my phone. *02:18.* "Don't you ever sleep?"

Anne sat up. *"Merde!"*

"Four hours and ten minutes ago, Gisèle was a front seat passenger in a red 2014 Clio headed toward Fontainebleau on the A6."

"The two guys?"

"The driver beside her, the other guy behind her."

"Now they have the money, maybe don't need her anymore. Taking her somewhere to bury ..."

"We have a partial plate, 77."

"Where's that?"

"Fontainebleau."

"How much?"

"The 77 and maybe three digits before it. There's a hundred and thirty-eight red Clios in 77 that match that."

I looked out the window inhaling the cool Paris night. "When will you know?"

"Ten, fifteen minutes. We'll have a short list."

I glanced at Anne, who was stepping into her jeans. "We're headed to Fontainebleau."

"That's why I called."

I threw water on my face and rubbed it with a dirty towel, gulped down last night's cold coffee, holstered the Glock under my left arm and the Kabar on my right calf, and Anne and I tore in the Beast across the 15th to the A6 south toward Fontainebleau.

WE'D REACHED the forest above town when Thierry called. "Pono, we need you to ID Mustafa if he's there, nothing more. We take it from there."

"Promise me: you *don't* kill him. Not till we have Mack and Gisèle. Agreed?"

"Of course. Of course."

I didn't believe him. Pocketed my phone and stared at the passing wall of black trees. Easy out here to get killed.

Anne was her usual 3 a.m. crabby self. "Imagine," she said, "a few years ago we didn't have cameras everywhere tracking everything. So why are crime rates going way up?"

"You know the answer to that," I said.

The bud in my right ear came to life. "We're on them," Tomàs said. "Avon, four and a half hours ago. Turning into the parking of an HLM on the right off the traffic circle."

Avon is the ugly, poorer and more ancient sister of Fontainebleau. In the middle of the forest that was once the private hunting reserve of King François the First and for centuries before that a Gallic encampment on the hills above the Seine upriver of Paris. An old town of ancient stone houses and surrounded by welfare towers for all the folks the French economy carries on its back. Some of whom are even on the S-List. Nothing beats feeding and sheltering the people who want to kill you.

"One guy in front?" I asked.

"With her, and the other guy in the back."

"When?"

"Last night, 22:47."

"They park there?"

"Right by the elevator. We're trying to get updates from the building cameras, but it appears they took the stairs to the third floor, with Gisèle in the middle between the two guys. They turned left, went 22 meters and turned right into Apartment 49."

"You don't have newer pix? From the building?"

"Working on it."

I tried to breathe. "We can't kill her."

"If we make a mistake, they will."

"If we grab her, do they kill Mack?"

"If they haven't already."

"They're using what's left of him to run her."

"So?" He waited. "You on board with this?"

I took a breath. "How fast can you line it up?"

"We're already there."

"You check with Harris?"

"No time. They could be killing her. Right now."

"We have to get in fast. Make sure we don't kill her."

THEY SET IT UP the usual way. The TAC squad on both sides of the door with me and Anne behind. Four more guys who looked like wrestlers backing us, more down the corridor, more outside where you couldn't see them. It was a long thin hallway with worn welcome mats in front of some doors, waning lights with bulbs missing, the whole sad migrant welfare syndrome.

We flashbanged in and had the two guys cuffed and up against the wall spitting with fear.

We ran back and forth through the three rooms but no Gisèle.

"Where *is* she?" I screamed at one guy, slammed him by the chin up against a wall, spittles of his fear down my knuckles. "Where *is* she?"

I was so angry I wasn't giving him time to answer, my ears so numbed by the flashbangs I couldn't hear. Anne smashed the other guy face-first into the wall, spun him around and clamped a hand on his throat. *"Where is she?"*

I shoved the tip of my Kabar against my guy's left eye. I wanted to kill him so badly my wrist was shaking. "Where is she?" I said. "I give you five seconds."

"He's going to kill you!" Anne screamed at him. "If he doesn't *I* will!"

"Two seconds," I said.

Anne had the other guy on his knees pleading, "They take her, I don't know where, they didn't tell us –"

"Who didn't tell you?" she yelled.

The guy looked up, eyes wide. "The Brother didn't tell us." He twisted his chin one way then the other. "This place, we were told to come and keep her, nothing more."

"The Brother?" She wrenched his head sideways, an inch from breaking his neck. "Say it all. *Now!"*

"Please," my guy begged. "Is all we know."

Over her shoulder she pointed to my guy, the bedroom. "Take him in there and kill him."

"We're not supposed to –"

"Do it!" she yelled. *"Now!"* She gave her guy another wrench of his neck, handed him off to the TAC team and followed me as I crab-walked my guy into the bedroom, my knife at his throat. We tied him to the bed while he mumbled and begged till she yanked a wad of duct tape across his mouth and he devoted his attention to trying to breathe. She yanked down his pants and his tawdry underpants, yanked out his dick and scratched a line across it with her slim little razor knife as he screamed silently through the duct tape.

She shoved a pillow down over his mouth, waited till he stopped bucking and writhing, took it away. "If you don't talk I *will* cut it off." She pushed the pillow down tighter then released it. "Tell us where the man is and you live to stand trial."

He broke easily but his story didn't help. Nor did the other guy's. We interrogated them separately; both said they'd been asked by two "brothers" at one of the four mosques near Melun to do a favor. The mosque was Salafist so these guys didn't dare say no. The favor was to stay in this empty unit and watch over a person being brought from Paris. They'd waited since yesterday; about three hours ago the other two guys showed up with a woman whose face was covered and who was very quiet. After an hour one of her captors got a call that made him angry. He swore at the other one for a while then they left with the woman, one man going over the garden wall while the other wrestled Gisèle toward the Clio.

Gisèle was gone again, probably for good. And the two guys who had driven her from Paris in the red Clio were gone too, they who knew where she'd been and where she was now. And maybe where Mack was.

"WHAT was in that phone call," Anne asked as we sat benumbed in the Beast trying to figure out what had gone wrong, "that made the one guy so angry they took Gisèle away?"

"Had to be a tipoff. That it wasn't safe, that place. Or that we were coming."

"*How*, how did they *know*?"

"Picked up the transmission? Or it's somebody on our side?"

Whatever the reason, Gisèle and her two captors had come and gone. ATS was dusting the apartment for prints of the two guys who'd come with Gisèle, but that was a long shot.

And we'd gained nothing.

But her captors had gained a lot: now they knew how close we were. And they'd figure why. And wouldn't make that mistake again.

DON'T GET CAUGHT

WE'D COME SO CLOSE to grabbing Gisèle, then blew it because of the time lapse between when an image is picked up on one of the thousands of cameras in the Paris area and when it finally pops up in your in-box. Provided you have the right kind of in-box.

Plus the time it takes for you to get to where the action is.

But really, we'd blown it because Gisèle's keepers got a call that we were closing in on the Avon HLM. They decided to take her, not kill her. Why? Where were they now?

Where was our leak?

Not me. I'd been scanned multiple times by the best, and nothing was found. I had a new, clean phone. The Beast was clean, as far as modern technology could tell.

Anne? No way, same as me.

Thierry? An ancient comrade of many combats. My gut told me what I already knew: impossible. Though I had to admit I understood him less and less.

And how much was he under the government's thumb? Sworn to secrecy, unable to refuse?

Was it someone else at DGSE? In all the hidden back rooms and prohibited areas at DGSE, who was really pulling the strings? Did Thierry even know?

And how much did Harris really know?

"What we think," Tomàs said, "is maybe our phones are getting hit, or calls between you and us ..."

"Or ATS and you," Anne said.

"How can we work without phones?" Thierry answered. "Until we find which one ..."

Without our phones we'd be even more handicapped. Not only could we not find our enemies, we'd lost the tools to do so.

"MUSTAFA GOT A CALL from an unknown number," Tomàs said. "It seems in the Seventh Arrondissement, but we can't locate it."

I rubbed my eyes and tried to see if it was still dark outside. "When?"

"One-forty-eight this morning. Then he called Abdel."

"What'd they say?"

"Nothing. Ten seconds of silence, then hung up. Possibly a signal?"

"It was about when Gisèle's captors got that call ..."

"And then another four hours later –"

I took in a breath. "What are they doing now?"

"Abdel's been staying at home and his three buddies are too."

"Mustafa?"

"From the few hits we get he's mostly in the area around La République or out in St. Denis, but we don't know if those are false, or from a device someone else is using ..."

"We still don't know shit."

"Though we seem to be dropping further behind, we're getting some answers. Mustafa and Abdel, or their devices, are in contact again."

"Yeah, sure. And we just lost Gisèle ..."

09:49, A SUNNY Paris morning. I was half asleep, Anne beside me on her stomach in a red negligée writing on a piece of paper on the cover of a book about Paris Impressionists.

It was time, again, to list what we did and didn't know.

"So far ..." I spat a feather. "We've lost at every turn."

"No!" She shook her head angrily. "We have Mustafa's pix and phone –"

"A phone he's never used before. That's probably in the Seine now."

"No, because he just got a mystery call from the Seventh Arrondissement then called Abdel."

"We still have no proof. That he and Gisèle-Mack are connected."

"Yes we do, because Mack was tracking Mustafa before he was grabbed ..." She bit her lip. "What did it have to do with that welfare tower in Les Andelys where Mack went? Yet no one says they've seen him."

"Somebody's lying."

"I can't figure any connections. It's driving me nuts."

I sighed, lay back, exhausted. Stared with gritty eyes at the dirty white ceiling. We're alive such a short time, why torment each other? I imagined being a Jew in the Ukraine in 1943, or an Israeli today. When the prospect of a peaceful life was not in the picture.

I yawned, rubbed my eyes, thought of her slim body under the red negligée and wondered if I had the energy to make love.

"If what Thierry's two *jihadis* said is true," she said, "about Mustafa's *Martel* plan to attack the Tower, then his phone link with Abdel, followed by Abdel's high-speed trial run on the Tower, is a first-degree connection."

I slid my hand up the lithe muscles of her back and around her strong shoulder. *"You're* a first-degree connection ..."

"Mustafa and Abdel," she turned toward me, "plan to attack the Tower. Mack and Gisèle were grabbed while he was tracking Mustafa. Yasmina was connected to Mustafa and also knew where Mack and Gisèle were, before she blew herself up. And Bruno at Les Quatre Vents was killed because he identified Mustafa. Am I right?"

"Maybe. So who called Mustafa last night? Before Mustafa called Abdel? Before somebody snatched Gisèle out of the place in Avon, two hours before we raided it?"

"The gods," she sighed. "Maybe the gods know."

BY 11:05 that morning we were back at ATS finishing the latest *To Do* List. Most of it would be done by ATS with other police teams plus DGSI and Thierry's teams too.

1. Track down the two goons who killed the Romanian girl thinking she was Anne. Find out from them who ordered the hit.

2. Cover Abdel and friends. Check *their* networks. See where they lead us.

3. Keep looking for Mustafa. Scan faces everywhere he might be and hook them up instantaneously. As ATS refined its grid of locations where he'd been ID'd, they would deploy agents on the streets there, to grab him if he was ID'd again.

4. Keep looking for Gisèle and Mack on every camera, particularly in and out of Paris. Interrogate the bank tellers again, see if there's anything more they remember.

5. Keep interrogating the two guys we'd caught in the Avon welfare tower. So far they knew nothing, were low-level nobodies. The police had sampled their peckers however and both had recently had sex with the same woman. The cops expected the DNA would come back Gisèle's. For this they could do ten years. Or if they got a sympathetic judge, nothing.

6. Bruno's murder: Paris police were doing door-to-door around the St. Martin canal, but so far no one had seen or heard a thing.

7. Yasmina: A test would soon ID her explosives. ATS was digging into her past, her networks, and where did they cross Mustafa's or any of these others?

8. Mustafa's phone: As Tomàs had explained, they were getting hits from cell towers activated by Mustafa's phone, building a map that seemed centered in the area around La République. ATS was now checking other numbers that "associated" with the one we had.

9. Of these "associated" phone numbers was one Mustafa had called seven times, and that had called him five times, that we couldn't track. It appeared to be located in the Seventh Arrondissement of Paris, but was blocked and we could get no closer. "We find this number, and we'll know who's giving Mustafa directions," Tomàs said. "Or who he's telling what to do," I countered.

10. The police and the Army would increase security on the Tower, Air France, and incoming Middle East flights. Maybe that would slow things down.

11. As always, there were three worries: *One,* had our interviews at the Les Andelys welfare towers spooked Mack's contacts there? Who *were* they? *Two,* did our smash-

down in the Avon welfare tower warn the people holding Gisèle, and now we'd never find her? And *Three*, how badly could we fail?

"THIS INFORMATION'S out of control," Mitchell said. "The French are very good at encryption, their mathematics is superb, their cohesion and team spirit formidable, their penetration excellent. But think how complex their connections – places where France has high-level intelligence links. From Morocco and Algeria to Sub-Saharan Africa, the Middle East, Iran, Pakistan and China ... Russia, too, Russia more than most. Some of these connections France has to keep in the loop – at least partially – on lots of their own operations."

"The *Russians?*" I said. "You think that's it?"

"Nah. They've been very grateful for our recent CIA feeds. We warned them of a major massacre in Saint Pete before it happened. Saved probably hundreds of lives. Putin even publicly thanked us ..."

"As you know we have leaks too," he continued. "We share with the Brits and they share with some folks we don't want to share with and the shit comes down the line and we can't catch it all."

"I don't have the clearances, but is that what you're doing now?"

"Most of it. My little deck of cards gets hacked about every seven seconds. You know how few of us there are to man the walls."

"How much gets through?"

He sniffed. "Very little, actually." Thought a moment. "But every year's triple the previous year's hacks. Don't know how much longer we can keep up."

So instead of spending his time in the desert of digital death hunting down our adversaries, Mitchell was now fighting a defensive war against the growing thousands of hackers at our gates.

When once he and I, free as cave warriors, had hunted our enemies across the desperate frigid ridges of Afghanistan, now were we all battling a rearguard action, and the enemy already within the walls?

I could tell myself *no*, don't worry. But couldn't stop.

"YOUR ORDERS ARE to tell me where the Hell you are!" Harris, raspy and belligerent as ever, on my phone.

"I may work with you, but I don't take orders anymore. Not from you. Not anyone."

"You signed up for this!"

"I'm here to protect my country. My friends. Nothing else."

"What the Hell are you doing on the Place du Commerce?"

"Had to hide out somewhere. Decided to keep it to ourselves."

"Good luck with that ..."

"Remember what you've told me, sooner or later the watcher is watched."

"Your French pals had you wired in hours. Gave us a feed."

"That's reassuring."

I told him about the goatfuck of the Avon welfare tower smashdown, how we'd missed Gisèle, the leak some-where ... Bruno's murder, the camera hits on Mustafa near La République, Abdel and his buddies and our high-speed trip to the Tower.

And I got the impression he hardly cared, his mind was else-where. Or he already knew this.

And as I'd wondered before, maybe Harris had brought me to Paris as bait for Mustafa. Was I, as that old saying goes, "just a pawn in their game?"

Since the French had found our new place on the Place du Commerce, maybe Mustafa had too. Or had somebody passed it along to him?

It's dangerous when even your friends can be enemies. When even an ally might cut your throat.

SHE SLID THE CANDLE nearer to relight the pipe, leaning on her elbows, her silky hair tumbling down her shoulders like a midnight waterfall, breasts loose against the sheet. I stroked her back, up and down her vertebrae like little seashells, the soft lithe flesh, the muscles around the shoulder blades. The velvet strength of her. She took a hit from the pipe and passed it, rolled onto her side, eyes on mine. "This sucks," she whispered.

"The hash? It's good."

"That we have to limit fucking to a few moments here and there. Because what really matters is Mack and Gisèle. And catching Mustafa. And there's no time for even five minutes ... When all I want to do is make love with you."

"I thought that's what we *have* been doing."

She scratched fingernails lightly across my chest. "It's spooky, but when I saw Mustafa in my dream it was just like that video. I recognize even the trash on the sidewalk, the backs of other people. The *For Sale* sign in that dress store window ..."

I laid back on the dirty sheets, dizzy with exhaustion. "Do they go anywhere, these dreams?"

She chuckled. "I dreamt of fucking you. Before we ever did."

I snuggled my face into her lovely hair. "How was it?"

She reached between my legs, gave it a nice caress. "About like it is."

"As bad as that ..."

She laced a thigh around mine. "As bad as that ..."

"You should have another dream about Mustafa. See where he is now."

"Afterwards." She leaned forward, eyes in mine. "We go somewhere? Even just a few days?"

"Sure. Afterwards." I brushed her upper lip with mine; she was so enticing, the softness of her, her musk, the look in her eyes when she came down on top of me. But all these wonderful things seemed criminal, a sin, till we fixed what was wrong.

Never before in my life had I felt guilty making love.

S T R A N G E R

HE CAME IN through the bathroom window, as in the Beatles song. He was tall and rangy, his ears half-chewed off and his muzzle braided with scars. He even had scars on his chest, from which I deduced it must have been one Hell of a catfight. Or he beat up a Doberman.

He was that kind of cat. Long-legged, intensely affectionate. Would never eat without first purring and rubbing his muzzle against our faces, to thank us for the meal.

He was not even an alley cat. Far worse, he was a roof cat.

The kind who survives on the rooftops of Paris. Amid all this lovely scenery of haphazard tilting tile and slate mansards with the Eiffel Tower in the distance – the postcard you see in all the Paris gift shops – these roofs harbor thriving condominiums of rats, mice, pigeons and other deplorables, and a rooftop cat's job is to get rid of them.

This he does by scrambling after a wily long-tailed rat across rain-slippery gutter at two a.m., with a 200-foot drop at the edge, or up a near-vertical slate mansard with the same drop below. The kind of guy who leaps across lightwells between two buildings to snag an unwary pigeon. Who will cross a kilometer of rooftops, streets, and lightwells toward the fragrance of a female in heat.

And kill any other male who shows up. And defend his own rooftops to the death.

We called him Stranger. As in Camus' *L'Étranger*, whose protagonist is Meursault, *Leaps over Death*, which this cat did every day on the rooftops. And as in *Stranger in a Strange Land* – he who is king among the aliens.

Though like most males all he really wanted to do was make love, hunt, eat, wander, and sleep. That's what's known as the good life. What we lost in the Garden of Eden.

Normally he arrives about 02:00, just as Anne and I are falling asleep. Diffident and anxious not to intrude, he leaps down from the bathroom window onto the toilet lid, patters on soft feet along the hall to the bedroom and hops on the bed, arches his back and kneads his claws into the bedspread till she goes to the fridge and digs out some hamburger and milk and puts it on the floor.

Usually up before six, we were on the phone or video or out on the streets or at ATS or DGSE before seven. On these early risings Stranger lounged on the bedspread sleepily digging his claws. He'd yawn and rub his eyes with a forepaw as if to say *I can't believe you're really doing this*. And go back to sleep.

We gave him scraps of *foie gras* and duck *rillettes* and raw grass-fed beef.

And what he gave us was the gift of loving company when all seemed lost.

"THE RED CLIO," Tomàs said, "was stolen two days ago in Melun. We found it this morning in a side street."

It was 07:20. In his office, Anne and me, both so tired we could hardly sit straight.

It made me furious that Tomàs could go so long without sleep and we couldn't.

"They took her there and met another car," I said.

"And left the Clio," Anne added wearily.

"We're checking the whole neighborhood. So far no one saw a thing ..."

"Of course." She shook her head.

"Prints?" I said, trying to be upbeat.

"The usual mess, takes a while to sort out. Not likely much we can use. But we're checking all the DNA for matchups in our base ..."

"How long?"

"Could take a week, no matter how fast we go."

"SO HOW did France get overrun so fast?" I asked Harris in his office later that morning as a bright sun cleared the rooftops of Faubourg St. Honoré and literally poured in the window. I'd given him the latest on Gisèle and the smashdown of the Avon HLM.

"Overrun?"

"Thirty years ago there were hardly any Muslims in France, and now they're nearly fifteen percent of the population and growing fast. How did this happen?"

He shrugged, always a man of few words. "You know the usual answer. When France left Algeria in '62 it stranded millions of pro-French Algerians, all now at risk of being slaughtered by the new regime. So many were brought to France, a million maybe. Then the government decided to let in anyone from a former colony, and then succeeding governments allowed them to bring in their families, and every Arab is related, so they say ..."

"And what's *not* the usual answer?"

"Some folks wanted it to happen."

"I MAY HAVE SOMETHING." Mitchell, as usual very laid back, but you can always tell from that hesitation in his voice that he's onto something. Like how you ease out your breath when you're aiming at someone from 600 yards and trying for a head shot.

I've always wondered what it feels like, a head shot.

It was mid-morning in Paris, late evening in Honolulu.

"*What?*" I said quickly, not wanting to wait.

"Our friend Thierry?"

"Like I asked you –"

"When I first dug into it, via his phone, personal computer, bank accounts, I was blown away, it was so fucking obvious –"

"*What?*"

"He was taking twenty thousand euros a month in crypto-currencies from a bank in Qatar – right out in the open ... On his home computer he was hitting *jihadi* sites –"

"That's for his work."

"Nuh-uh. You look at the content and it's clear it's not in his job description. The way he quoted the Suras, stuff like that. Bad news."

I waited. This was all somehow explainable. "Even worse," Mitchell said, "Holy Christ, he had seven calls to a St. Denis number that had three calls last week to Abdel."

"No way," I said morosely.

"And one call to guess who?"

"Don't tell me."

"Your friend Mustafa. On that same damn phone he used in the post office, when you guys first got the link."

"I don't believe it." The idea that Thierry might have been sabotaging us was nuts. The Thierry I'd known in Afghanistan would always put his buddies first. Would never screw things up. Not ever.

Halfway around the world Mitchell snickered. "I didn't believe it either."

"What you mean?"

"It was a fraud. Somebody's been setting him up, but it's not well done."

"You're losing me, Mitchell."

"They hacked his bank accounts and made deposits at certain dates, then wired them to accounts in Pakistan and Dubai set up in his name. From there the usual to the Caribbean then European banks. To somewhere safe in Switzerland. They made your buddy Thierry look like a crooked millionaire."

"Why didn't *he* see this?"

"He got a different version. Only bank investigators can see it. That and the French government, if and when they decide to take him down."

"Why would they?"

"If he finds something inconvenient."

It was all so easy, I realized, these days. "It doesn't hold together ..."

"But looks good on the surface. Thierry doesn't even know."

"The phone?"

"They just hacked his history. My grandmother could do that –"

"Who's behind this?"

"I'm not there yet."

"You mean you've discovered this but don't know who's doing it?"

"That's what I just said."

So how to find whoever was spreading this rumor, Thierry's alleged hits on *jihadi* sites, the falsified bank accounts and phone connections? They were doing this to render him ineffective, to banish him.

"How do we use this?" I said. "And counter it?"

———

WHEN THIERRY AND I went through a DGSE neutral site to check his accounts, nothing was amiss. No illicit payments. His cellphone had never been cracked.

"There's nothing wrong here," Thierry said angrily.

"There was."

"You're chasing phantoms." He shook his head. "Keep your eye on the target."

"There was." I sat exasperatedly in front of his desk. "I swear it."

He leaned back. "You getting enough sleep?"

"No."

He stood, distanced, wanting me to leave. "Maybe you should."

This was not the Thierry I'd known. Again, my instinct told me he was hiding something from me. Why? This was totally unlike him. Comrades in combat become nearly brothers. Afterwards, they don't mislead or fool each other.

I hated being the bearer of bad news. Particularly when the bad news had vanished.

I WALKED OUT OF THIERRY'S OFFICE into a gray Paris afternoon. My phone throbbed. Mitchell once again.

"So what you got?"

"More background ... That ever since Mitterrand came to power in 1981 till Hollande and his nutty crew left in 2017, part of the government has *intentionally* sold France down the river. Because of the money they get from the Middle East."

"Yeah, yeah, that we know."

"And the media, led by *Le Monde* and public TV and radio, whose executives of course are appointed by the government, ran a vast campaign to convince the French that, *One*, millions of illegal migrants are good for the economy, which has turned out to be *very wrong*, and *Two*, that France's long tradition of human rights protection demands that it respond with open arms to everyone – which turned out to be absolutely *everyone*, and thus *disastrous*."

"Get to the point, bro."

"Because most French media have long been subsidized by the government, the media stays nice. But there was one outlet that wouldn't stay nice, that continued to speak the truth, however raw and unpleasant ..."

"*Charly Hebdo*." This too was old news.

"And it only cost them twelve lives when those Muslims came through the door and shot them one by one."

"What you're saying is?"

"Either do what you're told, or look out."

EVIL PERSONIFIED

THE INDIAN HAD BEEN RELEASED from motorcycle
hospital after being repaired from when the Romanian girl was
shot, so Anne took off for a day to see Mamie and the kids in
Normandy.

I watched her go with some trepidation, but knew the bike
was free of bugs and there was no possible way anyone could go
fast enough to follow her. And as usual she'd been immune to
any concerns of danger, snapped at me, "I do what I want," and
roared off.

I'd wanted to go with her, wanted to see the kids. Even
though I'd spent little time with them I felt a tug of attachment,
a desire to protect and nurture. That the kids were hers made all
the difference. Her blood, her DNA, her beautiful, complicated
soul.

Until now, children had always seemed to me an adjunct part
of life. My ex-SF buddies who'd had kids changed completely,
were rapturously preoccupied and harassed by these little

beings, had fallen out of shape and some were even working on dad bellies. That had seemed to me a terrifying prospect.

I'd also wanted to see the unconquerable Mamie and meet her wild cousin Claudine. I yearned for emotional contact, to be in the presence of love, children and hope for the future.

THE CAMERAS we'd put in Anne's place weren't getting any action. We'd set up a semblance of occupation, lights on and off, a DGSI agent who looked like her had come and gone several times, always with what we'd hoped was invisible backup; as of yet no bad guys had shown up.

But something kept me coming back to check out the place. It was the kind of intuitive stuff I usually ignore, unlike Anne and her dreams of Mustafa. As Nisa had warned me at one point, "Whoever tried to kill Anne will try again. In their world, when you've screwed up, your reputation's on the line. And probably your life: you have to make it right or die. Worse, it makes the whole organization more visible, more vulnerable. More angry."

I was pretty angered too, by everything that was happening and not happening in this investigation, and exhausted on top of that. Still I again made myself take the 8 Métro from Commerce to République and wandered down Rue du Temple to Anne's block.

It was getting dark, another of those lonely Paris nights. I took a table at the corner café. I was dressed in the traditional black Paris windbreaker, faded jeans and running shoes, unlikely to appear out of place in the *quartier*. I ordered a Monaco, a beer and grenadine concoction beloved by the French but which I detest – few foreigners ever drink it, thus it made good cover – and sat outside the café in a corner protected from the cold wind by a huge plastic Danon sign, reading another annoying tract called *Libération*.

The French are very enamored of this word, partially because of common myths about the 1789 Revolution, portraying it as far more wonderful than the horrendous slaughter it actually was. And partially because they can't ignore that the Americans and Brits liberated them twice from the Germans, taking ten times more casualties in World War Two than did the Résistance. While by comparison the French killed three times more Jews than they lost members of the Résistance.

But that's not how the myth-makers portray it.

A country's like a person: if you don't feel good about yourself, maybe a lie or two will make you feel better?

There I sat in a damp Paris wind, reading an interview about how wonderful it was that so many new mosques were opening in France and that there no longer would be pork in French school meals, that new immigrants should be encouraged to bring in as many family members as possible, and soon illegal immigrants could vote.

And here was a photo of the interviewee, the guy Nisa had mentioned, Rachid Raqmi, looking suave in a thousand-dollar suit, the well-trimmed beard, the eyes beaming friendship and innocence. Followed by many nice words about his work to unite all viewpoints into one inclusive, all-loving movement.

Perhaps if I'd known less about the soft conquest side of Islam I'd have been more convinced. But the trouble with experience is that it makes you trust very little.

And makes you annoyed that smart people can be so stupid.

A guy in a Denver Broncos cap stopped in front of her building, checked the doorbells, and backed into the street to glance up at the third floor. He was tall and gangly and had dark sideburns and a lithe, muscular stance.

He crossed the street, looked up at the third floor again, used his phone to take a picture and sent it somewhere. He walked slowly back and forth along the opposite sidewalk, stopped to stare in the window of a lingerie shop and punched the glass hard with his fist, startling the women inside. I got ready to move in on him when he got a call. He stood between two parked cars scanning Anne's building, nodding and answering questions. I risked walking past him once and caught his Arabic-accented voice, "She is not doing this," and then, "Two nights, in bed at the same time ... no, no, the *lights* go out at the same time ..."

I lingered before the lingerie shop but it was too far so I only got an occasional word, "trouble," "inside," "night ..."

It was extraordinary that they didn't know Anne had moved, that they'd fallen for such an elemental trap ... And that they didn't know she and I were together.

The guy pocketed his phone, crossed the street to her building and pressed three doorbells. After a few seconds one buzzed and he entered.

I called Thierry. "I'm outside Anne's place. Guy just went in."

"You armed?" he asked.

"No."

"If he's gone in, he's armed. You can't chance it. I have three cars on the way."

"Uniforms?"

"Hell no. I'm coming too, fast as I can ..."

The front door popped open and an old woman came out tugging a shopping caddy. She tried to yank the door shut but I got in before her.

"It's not allowed!" she squawked as I took the stairs silently three at a time, listening for the patter of his running shoes above me on the tin treads, watching his shadow dance up the stairway walls in the thin yellow light, hearing the huff of his breath, the whistle as he stopped at Anne's door.

His phone buzzed. It took him a moment to dig it out. I eased up three stairs so I could see him through the bannisters above. The reason he'd had trouble digging out his phone was that in the other hand he was holding what appeared to be a 9mm handgun.

"*What?*" he said in Arabic. Then, "You're sure? You saw him?" Another moment of silence, then, "If so, he is already here."

He'd clearly been planning to break in on Anne and kill her. And now he'd got a call that I was here. Did they know it was me? Or just that someone had followed him? "If he is not in this stairway, below me," the guy said softly, "then ..."

I cursed myself for not having a gun, only the Marine Kabar I always keep sheathed on my right calf. But he had that 9mm or whatever that could blow a hole in me the size of a grapefruit or take my head half off before I could get near him. I had to stay back yet follow him till Anne and everybody got here.

Surprisingly, he went up three more stories to the roof, the door hanging open when I got there. But if he was out there on that roof he'd shoot me before I got close.

I backed down the stairway below the door, called Thierry again. "Where are you?"

"Three streets away."

"He's up on the roof and I'm half a flight down. He's got a 9mm. Doesn't know I don't have a gun –"

I leaned out the door, saw nothing. Leaned the other way. Nothing. I sprinted onto the roof, did a quick roll and came up with the knife in my right hand. Saw no one. At a clunk of wood behind me I spun toward it, slashing with my knife but it was only wind through the open door.

Looking over the roof edge I saw a dark form descending toward a lower rooftop three stories below. Free-climbing down from window to window, using tiny ridges in the brick.

Street punk, where'd he learn to climb like that?

He was almost to the lower rooftop. I squeezed over the edge and hung there, toes scrabbling for a hold, my bullet-damaged shoulder slowly tugging apart.

This was the stuff I hated. I'd developed a strong fear of climbing after falling off a number of nasty cliffs, the first when

I was a kid, then the deadly peaks where SF sends you, then other cliffs elsewhere, unnamed Himalayan and Andes mountains, places etched by danger into my heart. Tied to a fraying rope off a Honolulu office tower, or inching up a raw frozen granite cliff with no handholds that somehow had to be climbed. Dreams every night of canyon walls and volcanic ridges I've nearly fallen from. Knowing that sooner or later my bad shoulder will betray me.

My fingers started sliding from the edge. The guy had spit on it to make it slippery. I pulled up and slid sideways for a better grip.

Took a breath. Made myself stop shivering. Told myself to ignore the shoulder pain.

No way to die.

The grooves between the bricks were a quarter inch deep, enough that with strong fingertips and a hard edge to your soles you can very carefully go down it. But one tiny slip of a fingertip or toe and you're hurtling backwards and smashing down on the lower roof, to lie there trying to make sense with a smashed body and a jellied brain.

Holding the inside of the ledge with my left hand I swung right and dug my fingers into a brick groove, then the side of my right foot in a groove below, then the other foot. Gripping the groove with my fingers as hard as I could, I slowly let go of the roof edge and eased my left hand to a groove and pinned my fingers in.

All I had to do now was steadily move down this wall, one pressure point at a time, keep ignoring the shoulder as the humerus slid in and out of the socket.

Holding extra tight to the finger grooves, I slid one foot down, trying not to breathe and knock myself off the wall, toe-scrabbled for a hold, found one, dug in. Then the other foot, but for a while there was no groove, the angle was wrong, and I hung there pinned against the wall.

The edge of my foot found a crease. Slowly I eased down on it. It held. I took a breath, waited, took another. My right wrist was trembling, my knees weak, the shoulder in agony.

One by one I moved each hand. This was dangerous because they were my only safety, and to release one was a great risk. But I had to move them down, one at a time, or stay pinned to the wall forever. I waited, gathered strength, and did it again.

In maybe five minutes I was low enough to jump. The guy had disappeared from the rooftop. I ran toward the hut in the center that was the stairway exit and yanked the handle. It was locked. I turned to the edge; it was flat, graveled, with no wall at all, the eerie sense of stepping into space, down into the street with its tiny headlights in the streets below.

I ran to the third side: straight down into nothingness.

I shoved the humerus back into the socket, went back to the hut and yanked the door handle. Bolted solid.

The guy had gone through an open door and locked it behind him.

I called Thierry. "We're in front," he said.

"He went out next door, to your left as you face the building."

"Nobody's come out ..."

I tried to slide my knife between the door and jamb to push back the bolt, but the gap was too narrow. Nor could the knife cut through the door's galvanized steel cover.

I went to the side, stripped away the tarpaper and with my knife dug the plaster out in chunks till I could smash through the interior lath, grabbed the door handle from the inside and shoved it open and sprinted down the darkened staircase.

It opened out onto a paved courtyard with a door at one end and that led to a cobbled alley, empty and dark but for the silhouette of a cat trotting across it.

He was long gone.

I had lost him but couldn't see anywhere I'd failed. He was that clever, that sharp. That lucky.

Evil personified.

But to him, so was I.

WHO WANTED to kill the whole damn investigation? Otherwise why try to discredit Thierry, as much as he denied it?

The answer was *Who was most threatened by it?*

If the investigation threatened them, it was onto something.

At 21:00 that night – 09:00 that morning in Honolulu – I was standing at the DGSE espresso machine when Mitchell called back.

"Look, I only got a minute," he said.

"You're the one called me –"

"I shouldn't even be taking the time ..."

"Mitchell! Spit it out."

"I may have found the people who falsified Thierry's accounts. It's out of a server in Ukraine through another in Chechnya. But far as I can tell it comes from a physical address in France, someplace called Avon."

"*Avon?* That's next to Fontainebleau, where Mustafa vanished, weeks ago. We just missed grabbing Gisèle there ..."

"Could be just a pass-through – they're maybe not even in it."

"How soon can you find out more?"

A pause as he considered. "Give me a day."

EARLY NEXT MORNING I planned to take the Métro to 69 Quai de Valmy, though I really didn't want to go there. Where a guy named Bruno Rigard had been found dead. Probably because of me.

In SF I'd studied the Battle of Valmy. After France's 1789 revolution, the kings of Germany, England and Austria in September 1792 attacked the new French revolutionary army, intending to restore the French monarchy. And lost.

A war, historians say, that saved the Revolution. And changed the course of history.

I thought of the Tower, Paris. The world.

How, today, do you change the course of history?

K E F F I Y E H

IT MUST HAVE BEEN LOVELY once, the cool waters of the St. Martin Canal flickering in bright sun, the tree-lined canal and cobblestone paths along its banks, the carved stone buildings on both sides. It made your heart sink, how it is now. Multicolored graffiti and tags in Arabic in broad swaths along façades of empty storefronts and apartments.

69 Quai de Valmy was a four-story building in front of where Bruno's body had bumped up against the side of the canal. Just around the corner from the Rue Beaurepaire, a straight line from La République and Les Quatre Vents. On Bruno's way home.

A cold wind came off the canal. Traffic in the streets, footprints hustling along the sidewalks. Lots of people hurrying somewhere. I thought of Bruno, big and thick-muscled, a redhaired Viking. Who had dared to mess with him?

I walked back up Rue Beaurepaire to Les Quatre Vents and back again to Quai de Valmy. It had been after one-thirty when he'd been killed; his wife had said, after closing the bar.

Had Mustafa shown up at the bar that night?

It started drizzling, people under umbrellas and plastic raingear leaning into the wind. Everyone looking down. I came out on Quai de Valmy in front of the pedestrian bridge where the detectives said he'd probably been killed. In the dark, alone, a quick attack with baseball bats and knives – no one would hear. Just Bruno dying and trying to understand.

But Bruno was far too smart to walk across a bridge at one-thirty in the morning with a bunch of young Arabs coming his way.

Was there a gun, a silencer? Out here under the cover of darkness, who'd know?

Like Mack's disappearance, this made no sense. You didn't sneak up on either guy.

Halfway across the bridge, checking for bullet marks, I leaned over the rail and saw a little flutter on the side of the bridge, just below my elbow. Small, maybe two inches square. Cloth, cotton maybe. A checkered white-black pattern.

I thought it was a piece of Bruno's shirt, torn off when his body was dumped over the rail. But the coroner's report would've mentioned that. Then I noticed a little ledge broad enough for your sideways feet, where one could crouch down and not be seen from the bridge. Just above the ledge the little square of cloth fluttered in the rainy wind, linked by a single thread, ready to cast off on its voyage down the Canal to the Seine and North Sea.

I leaned over and tucked it into a Ziploc. That's when I saw the smudges on the dirty ledge. As if two pairs of shoes had trampled on each other but pieces of sole pattern still clear. Leaning further over the rail I snapped pix from several angles, the new rain running up my back and turning the footprints to slime.

On the other side of the bridge another little ledge with more rain-smeared prints. They were growing muddy but I shot pix of them anyway. You could still tell there'd been another two pairs.

I stood there trying to imagine it. Bruno coming home at his fast steady pace, exhausted from a long day at the bar, anxious to crawl in bed with his wife.

And two guys hidden on each side of the rail, who leap up and knife and bludgeon him to death.

He must have struck back a few blows before he died. I reminded myself to have ATS check hospital and doctor admissions for broken bones, abrasions, that kind of thing. It was a long shot, but something made it feel right.

It began to rain harder. I tucked my iPhone deep in a pocket alongside the Ziploc with the square of cloth, and grabbed a cab for the ATS Lab. Both the cloth and the footprints were probably nothing. But you could never tell.

I stared through the cab's rain-streaked windows at the bumping lurching stinking traffic and everything feeling miserable and cold. And I suddenly realized Mustafa probably wasn't going to shoot me or have me killed like he had Bruno.

Mustafa had other plans for me. He had Mack now and wanted me too. Only then, when he had us both like he'd had us before, would he finish our execution. As promised.

Mustafa was a man of his word.

"KEFFIYEH." Tomàs took the Ziploc of cloth from me. "It's a piece of *keffiyeh*."

"That's what I thought. But it doesn't have the frill on the edge –"

"It's not Afghani ..."

I smiled tiredly, thinking of being with Thierry in those bare cold mountains. "But this guy's no Palestinian," Tomàs said. "He's some minor Paris scumbag wanting to look good ..."

"Unfortunately," I said, "you seem to have no lack of them."

The pattern on the cloth was that worn by Yasser Arafat, who won the Nobel Peace Prize for killing lots of people, but that's another story. The fact that the torn cotton came from a *keffiyeh*, the square Middle Eastern headscarf, was very informative. Based on an ancient fishnet pattern that may have originated in Mesopotamia, the *keffiyeh* has been worn for thousands of years for protection from the desert sun. Since the mid-1900s the black and white *keffiyeh* has also come to symbolize Palestinian terrorism. Most Palestinian *keffiyeh* were once made in the Middle East; in recent years the Chinese have undercut the market and now nearly all *keffiyeh* are made in China.

LATE AFTERNOON IN PARIS was nearly dawn in Hawaii. That's when Mitchell called. "Got them."

"Who?"

"The ones who tagged Thierry."

"You're unbe*lievable!*"

"A furniture moving company in Avon."

"A *moving* company?"

"Chérif Frères, 60 Avenue Franklin Roosevelt. I checked our sats and it's a three-story house with a one-bay garage in front."

I tried to remember where I'd parked the Beast. "Think I'll head down, have a look."

"For once in your life, be safe."

FROM DGSE the Beast and I took the Péréphérique to the A6 south to Fontainebleau.

I was wasting my time but couldn't sit still. It was either this or hang around Les Quatre Vents looking for Mustafa. But Les Quatre Vents was closed, as Mustafa would know. Since he'd probably ordered Bruno's death.

As I roared along the A6 south in early dusk among multiple

lanes of speeding, smoggy traffic I went back through my list of hunches:

- Hunch #1: Mustafa had had Bruno killed for what he might tell me. Or as punishment for speaking to me.

- #2: Mustafa had Mack and then Gisèle kidnapped after Mack contacted me.

- #3: Mustafa must have been behind moving Gisèle to Avon then took her away before we could strike. How did he know we were coming? Was it the mystery caller from the Seventh Arrondissement? Was this the insider Harris had warned me about?

- #4: Yasmina was involved in Mack's kidnapping. Had she been hit on the head like Mack? Why?

- #5: Since Mustafa seemed tied up in all this, what relation did it have to the *jihadis'* stories of his plan to destroy the Eiffel Tower, an Airbus, or Paris with a bomb?

Again I had the sense that no matter where I turned it was the wrong way.

Traffic was heavy going the other way, then lightened after Villejuif. On both sides a dirty sea of concrete ran to the horizon where not long ago had been apple and pear orchards. And I wondered once again how France could survive.

There were fewer cars after Villejuif and by the time when we turned off the A6 at the Fontainebleau exit we were nearly alone, a blue carapace scuttling down a dark asphalt trail, a scimitar moon riding up the east and casting the Forest in an ethereal silver glow, the tall bare trees contorting shadows across the whirring black pavement.

The Beast and I had no sooner entered the Forest when this ridiculous little police car comes gasping up behind us with flashing lights. I turned into the parking lot where the forest hookers service the long-distance truckers.

The cops came up, one on each side, a husky guy and a tough-looking young woman. I gave them my Hawaii driver's license. They laughed. The Beast was registered to a used car dealer in Trappes, one of the Lost Territories of France. They laughed about this too. They checked the license plates. The woman wrote up something and handed it through the window. "You've got a headlight out," she said.

I didn't want to mention that this was from running over a bunch of bicycle racks on a sidewalk in Paris. "I could've told you that," I almost said, but had the good sense not to.

I was now fifteen minutes later than I wanted to be.

6O AVENUE FRANKLIN ROOSEVELT was a stucco and red brick building on a side street next to the Forest. As Mitchell had said, it had a one-bay garage with a slide-down steel door, a single front door with a kitchen window beside it, lights on in the two second floor and third floor windows.

There was no name anywhere. Nothing on the front door but the rusty steel street number and a small sticker above the mail slot saying "No publicity mail please."

I backed off, crossed the street and circled the block, found the Beast a spot where I could see the front door, and called Tomàs. "Going to be here a while."

"You're wasting time. The action's up here."

"Explain."

"Like you asked, we screened hospital admissions the night Bruno was killed."

I barely remembered. "So?"

"A guy named Tariq showed up at three in the morning at Saint-Louis Hospital with a broken jaw and two broken teeth. It's the closest hospital to where Bruno was killed."

I thought of Bruno's brute shoulders, his strength when he

slapped the bar with his thick red-haired palms. "That was dumb of them."

"We're not dealing with nuclear physicists here."

"Who is he?"

"You know his brother better – Abdel."

"*He's* Abdel's brother?"

"That's what I said."

"This could be enough to bring him in."

"Not under French law. And it would blow everything."

"Everything we can do will blow everything."

ANNE HAD RETURNED from Cousine Claudine's, and on the phone seemed grouchy and distant. "What's wrong?" I said.

"Not a damn thing."

"Miss the kids?"

"Of course."

I felt guilty, didn't know why. "Mad at me?"

"Why the fuck would I be mad at you? I've hardly seen you."

"Yeah, I miss you too."

"Pono, why are we doing this?"

"Doing what, goddamnit?" It made my heart hurt, the sound of her voice.

"Fucking up our lives. This way."

I sighed, felt empty and hollow. "What else can we do?"

"That's what I said."

"Wait! *Wait!*"

"*What?*"

"Two guys just stepped out the front door ... What time is it?"

"Nine twenty-seven."

"Wearing running clothes and shoes, both with backpacks ..."

"Going for a jog? Pono you're wasting your time."

I slid out of the Beast. "Gonna follow them."

"They have guns?"

I locked the Beast and set after the two joggers. "Will keep you posted."

"Pono," she was saying as I shut off. "Be safe ..."

THEY JOGGED north one block, then swung right into the Forest on a narrow path that glimmered in the moonlight. I kept well enough behind in the shadows where I hoped I couldn't be seen.

They were fifty feet ahead, moving single file, steady and fast, not slowed by the packs on their backs. My phone was bouncing in my pocket; I buttoned it down as I ran.

The trail gave out and they vanished across a slant of moonlight into dark forest. I closed nearer, but not close enough to spook them for fear they'd shoot me.

A crackle and crash of brush just ahead made me dive to the ground fearing a bullet. With a *thud thud-thud* of hoofs a deer pounded away. I stood slowly, wincing.

Moving fast behind them in the darkness it was easy to trip on snaking roots, blackberry tendrils and sharp rocks, to skid on wet leaves as branches ripped at my eyes, trying not to gasp for breath and give myself away, hoping to see one of them in the darkness ahead where they appeared and disappeared like spirits. Trying always to make sure they were both still ahead of me, lest one come up behind me.

Something like a baseball bat hit me in the forehead and I fell back cracking my head on a rock and rolled up to fight, but it was only a low oak bough I'd run into. My eyes were full of blood and I leaned over, head spinning, trying to wipe it off.

They were gone.

I had to keep running the way I thought they'd gone. But silently, or one of them might shoot me.

By a great oak at the edge of a bog I halted, gasping, tried to listen. *Drip drop* of dew from leaves onto damp soil, the sudden *ooh-hoo-hoo* of an owl, soft wind sifting through the tall trees, thunder of blood in my ears, patter of my blood on the dead leaves. Odors of wet forest, dank soil, rot and new grass on a cool northern breeze.

Snap of brush ten yards to the right. Again I hit the ground expecting a bullet but none came. No other sound: had I spooked him?

A whisper of feet across leaves coming up ten yards behind me. How did he get there so fast? Not possible, where was the other one?

They were going to pin me down between them.

I rolled sideways silently and pulled out my Kabar. Again no bullet.

My knee cracked.

A light flicked on, sharp and bright. A headlamp. It spun right and left, over my head as I clung to the ferns at the edge of the bog.

In the back glow of the headlamp I could see a rifle in his hands.

Where the Hell did *that* come from?

I wanted desperately to creep away before I got shot. But my cover wasn't good, and it would be suicidal to run.

The light snapped back to my right, danced among the trees.

One of them was coming my way.

The other was circling behind.

Was this how it was going to end? After all the sorrow and joy?

I didn't want to die here. Out in the forest. Alone.

HEAD SHOT

I HUGGED THE GROUND expecting to be shot.

Suddenly he turned away from the bog and passed on the other side of the great oak.

I stepped out of his way, a twig snapping under my foot but he didn't notice. As he passed I smelled the wine, the sour livestock odor, saw his bulky overcoated form against moonlight on a tree. An older guy, drunk, stumbling through the forest with a rifle trying to poach a deer.

Now I'd lost the two joggers with backpacks. Failed at one of the simplest rules of the tradecraft we'd learned so well.

Rule One: *Never lose contact with your target.*

Rule Two: *Always obey Rule One.*

With a crackle of brush my poacher wandered on, his headlamp flitting among the trunks. I stood breathing silently, listening to the forest.

"French dickhead," said a voice ten feet in front of me. "I almost shot him."

"Aye," said the other. "Me too."

The first voice sounded vaguely familiar; I tried to remember when I'd heard it before.

Had they *seen* me? If they had, why hadn't they killed me? Had they thought the poacher was me?

Blood kept running into my eyes; I couldn't see, wasn't sure where they were. One made a long raucous snuffle and spat, coughed and spat again, and I hoped maybe he was sick.

If they both had guns I was not going to win a fight. So I had to stay unseen till they moved on. But if one of them discovered me I had to kill him fast then the other. Almost impossible. I couldn't even tell how far he was behind me, which way he was facing. And I had to keep the knife in my right hand so I could kill him if he shot me, before I died.

Unless it was a head shot. One that drops you right away.

"Sha' *tafh!*" the other sighed, in Arabic. *This is bullshit.*

"Speak French, asshole," the first said. The voice tantalizing now, nearly familiar. He turned to my left ... I tried to think *is he right-handed*; then he'd have his pistol in his right hand, on the far side of me.

To take him from behind I had to grab his gun hand with my right hand and stick the knife so deep into his throat he couldn't scream – though he'd surely try, in those last nanoseconds, and to yank the knife away as the blood spurted out and he writhed around to fire the pistol I'd been unable to grip.

But why kill him, when I didn't yet know what they were up to?

My heart was beating so hard and fast I was sure he'd hear it. Or feel the heat of my muscles, smell my sweat, anger and fear.

I eased nearer, switched the knife to my left hand, at the level of his larynx, blade inward.

He turned away, as if seeing in the darkness, his soles sucking at the wet ground. "We're late," he called. "Hurry!"

I thought I knew that voice now. The one who'd said, eight years ago, *You'll never escape me.*

Mustafa?

Fury surged through me. *Kill him.*

Why was he here? Where was he going?

I followed them, silent as I could. Waiting for a chance to strike.

THEY RAN on through the darkness in and out of clearings bathed in moonlight back to darkness again, always in that slow, easy stride.

If it *was* Mustafa. I kept reminding myself, *you can't kill him.*

A horrible stench blinded me, knocked my breath away.

Skunk. Gasping and rubbing my eyes I tumbled backwards, scrambled away, halted, trying not to breathe the choking smell. Why hadn't it sprayed *them*?

Through burning eyes I saw the little white and black bastard coming after me, still pissed off. Maybe it was a she and I'd bumped her nest or whatever they have. I stumbled away, fearing I'd be sprayed again or that that Mustafa and his buddy would shoot me.

My eyes were seared, I couldn't breathe. Glanced back, but the skunk hadn't followed.

I've been Maced a few times but it was never like this. Mustafa and the other guy had to have heard my gasps – why didn't they shoot?

I caught up to them again, their shadows flitting through the trees. They picked up a narrow path and I followed, keeping my distance, knife in my hand, aware of their guns. And that I couldn't get close, stinking of skunk.

Would they shoot at a skunk, to drive it away?

Or was it good camouflage? Like the Sioux hunters dressed in wolf skins to get near the buffalo, because buffalo were used to wolves wandering near them?

They ran out into a little low-grass clearing flanked by tall firs with a dirt road at the far side. I halted at the edge of the trees. Now maybe I could circle and get them.

Kill the other one, then take the one I thought was Mustafa down and torture him till he said where Mack and Gisèle were.

Then kill him. If it *was* Mustafa.

Two dark shapes slid out of the darkness toward them. "Seven minutes late!" one whispered angrily.

"Ran into a hunter. Slowed us down," the one I thought was Mustafa snapped.

"Except for that," the other gasped, "we were on pace."

"Not good enough." This voice was an older man's, authoritative. "Not good."

"That's why we do these trial runs, Abu," the Mustafa one panted. "To know for sure how much time it takes ..." He'd called the older man "Abu," a term of respect.

They turned toward the dirt road, still talking, voices rising and falling harshly.

Now there were four. Even if only two had guns, I couldn't get them all. Mack and Gisèle were beyond my reach again.

I circled ahead, staying in the trees. They were still talking, but I couldn't hear.

They headed for a glimmer of glass and metal that became a long, low silhouette which I thought was a black or dark blue sedan. They stored the backpacks in the trunk and got in.

I caught the plate number before they accelerated away, with a 77 for the *Seine et Marne Département*. Fontainebleau? Avon?

If it was Mustafa, what was he doing in Fontainebleau with another guy from the moving company that hacked Thierry's accounts? Why go jogging at night in Fontainebleau Forest and meet two guys in a car with local plates who berated them for being late? What was in the backpacks?

Were these people the group Mustafa was working with? Who was this "Abu," the older guy?

That they were doing this at ten-thirty at night meant whatever they were training for was probably going to happen at night. Like the mad ride following Abdel and his three companions from St. Denis to the Eiffel Tower.

Or was it just safer to practice at night, when few people would see?

But why *here*? When all the action was going to be in Paris?

Or was it?

Was it even Mustafa?

"MUSTAFA?" Anne nearly screamed when I called. "You think it was Mustafa? Holy *shit*, but you're not *sure?*"

"I think." I caught my breath. "But I've lost him."

"You got the damn plate."

She linked Tomàs and Thierry in. They were ecstatic. "You're a genius!" Thierry uncharacteristically exclaimed.

"I've just run the plate," Tomàs added. "It's coming up now ... Belongs to a TV publicity company ..."

"TV?" Anne said. "What the Hell?"

"New Hope Productions. Based in Avon."

"This is *fantastic*," Thierry said, though he didn't sound happy. "Why didn't you call in for backup?"

"In the middle of the fucking forest?"

"We could've got the bastard."

"If it was him," I reminded him.

"We've got the plate," Anne repeated.

"Pono," he said, "you must stop doing this shit alone."

"It's the only way you guys won't screw it up."

"Get up here, fast."

"I've got to get the Beast."

"The *what?*"

"My car. That's its name."

"I don't care what you call your damn car."

"It's DGSE's car, anyway," Anne cracked.

"Get it," Thierry said. "And get up here."

"JESUS YOU STINK!" Tomàs stepped back from his office door, away from me.

"So I've been told." I ducked inside, wrapping myself in the blanket they'd given me downstairs, more to hold in the skunk odor than keep warm.

"What happened to your head?"

"Ran into a tree."

Holding his breath, he came close to inspect my forehead. "You need to get it stitched."

"That's not all he needs to get stitched," Anne snapped.

"We'll do this fast," he said to her, "so he can go home and shower."

"I'm not sure I want him."

"2016 Maserati." Tomàs stayed behind his desk, as far from me as possible. Reluctantly he sat and plunked his elbows on the desk, clasped hands under his chin. "As you said, registered to New Hope Productions ... and, get this: which is run by Rachid Raqmi."

Thierry stared. "Rachid fucking Raqmi? The president of the Muslim Anti-Discrimination Society?"

Tomàs smiled. "The same."

I was exhausted, tried to think. "Let's bring him in."

"If we do, he'll deny he picked up anyone in Fontainebleau tonight." Thierry slapped palms on the desk. "Anyway, what if he did pick someone up – what's the law against that?"

"He met this guy I think was Mustafa!"

"It's your word against his."

"Maybe someone," Tomàs added, "was using his car? Or stole it?"

Anne squeezed my arm reassuringly. "There'll be a shitstorm in the media if we accuse Rachid of anything ..."

"We ask him," I answered, "why is he meeting up late at night with S-List guys?"

"We can't prove it was Mustafa," Thierry reminded me. "You said you're not sure."

"I couldn't make him out in the dark. And the voice, how can I be sure? After all these years?"

"If it is and if we alert him," Tomàs chimed in, "then the whole damn crowd will vanish, and the trail will go cold again."

It was the same ancient question: when to pull the trigger?

"However," Anne said, "this could be a major success –"

"Astounding," Thierry added.

"– so let's move carefully," she went on. "Not blow it by making it public too soon."

"This could explain," Tomàs said, "why Rachid is orchestrating the campaign to allow former ISIS fighters back into France."

"When they're known terrorists?" I fumed. "And killed hundreds of thousands in Syria and Iraq?"

"He says they've disavowed violence, want to work for peaceful solutions. It's the false face of the new Islam."

Dizzy with fatigue, I looked for an empty chair but there wasn't one. "He could maybe give us Mack and Gisèle? And you won't grab him?"

"We'd get nothing from him. And he's got tons of celebrity lawyers who will scream and clamor for our heads. The government won't allow it."

"We fly him to Casa. Maybe I can arrange it," I said, thinking how to convince Harris. But that was impossible.

It was the opposite of where we'd been before. All along I'd wanted to follow people, wait and see where they took us. But DGSI/ DGSE had instead assaulted Yasmina's place, and she blew herself up. They'd staked out *Les Quatre Vents* in Paris and spooked Mustafa.

And the next day Bruno got killed.

But would grabbing Rachid help save Mack and Gisèle, and get Mustafa?

Though now we thought there might be a Mustafa-Rachid connection. We just had to see where it took us. If, as I'd thought, the voice I'd heard was Mustafa.

"We'll set up a 24/7 on Rachid," Tomàs said, "get all his digital stuff, his phone. Then we decide."

"If Mack and Gisèle die," I said furiously, "and if we lose Mustafa, *now* will be the reason."

"And if Rachid's car was stolen?" Thierry reminded me. "If the guy you heard wasn't Mustafa? Just some guy out running at night with a buddy? Training for a goddamn triathlon, something like that?"

Tomàs checked his watch. "It's three-ten in the damn morning. Go home, both of you. Get some sleep."

Anne scowled at me. "*He's* sleeping in the shower."

TIME AND BLOOD

"I'VE BEEN HANGING out with your furniture moving company," Mitchell said. *"Chérif Frères?* From what I can tell, they rent that building from a charity that's also in Avon."

It was 06:05 here in Paris, the sun not up yet, so cocktail hour in Honolulu. But Anne and I had had a good two hours' sleep plus a quickie in the shower after I'd scrubbed off as much skunk as I could, so I felt ready to take on the world. "What fucking charity?"

"The Muslim Anti-something –" He flicked through screens.

"– Anti-Discrimination Society."

"How you know?"

I told him about chasing the guy I'd thought was Mustafa and the other one from the moving company, their meeting with people using Rachid's car. Or with Rachid himself. "How'd *you* find them?" I said.

"Tracked them backwards."

"And this Anti-Discrimination Society is linked to the people who hacked Thierry's bank accounts?"

"To make him look like a crook."

"When that's the last thing he is."

"Obviously, they want to stop this investigation."

"WHO the Hell is MADS?" I near-yelled at Thierry. "Why aren't we following them?"

"We are." It was 7 a.m. and Anne and I had just arrived at Thierry's office. He turned to Nisa, who stood by the window watching the rain. "We disagree about this."

"MADS?" She scowled. "According to them, if you criticize anything Muslim you're a fascist Islamophobe. You can be sued, fired, even jailed. So even when Muslims kill hundreds of French people in a few short months no one's allowed to criticize them, because that would be Islamophobe ... You can't even say these killers *are* Muslims. No, they're *terrorists*."

"Everyone sees through that," I said. "Or do they?"

"Perhaps *taqiya*," she said. "They are not what they appear."

"So where," I said, "is Rachid in all this? When it's now clear that he's tied to the group that was hacking Thierry's accounts?"

"This is the problem. Where is moderate Islam really at? Or is it, as people like you say" – she turned to Thierry – "just a front for the slow takeover?"

"In this world," he said consolingly, "it's hard to know. Like Anne mentioned the other day about World War Two, the German slow takeover of the French intellectuals. The enemy can seem to be your friend, to be rational and moderate. Till the fun begins."

"I suppose," Nisa added, "that just because someone like Rachid is saying what we want to hear doesn't mean his words are true or honest. It could be all for show. And, if it *is* all for show? If Rachid is manipulating the media? If he too is *taqiya*?"

"You asked who is MADS?" Thierry smiled at me. "*That's* who they are."

TAQIYA, the art of dissimulation, Nisa went on to say, is an ancient tactic most recently utilized by Al Qaeda, ISIS, and other Islamic groups. It allows the faithful to ignore Islam's prohibitions in order to infiltrate the infidels. They can drink, take drugs, sleep with infidel women and ignore Ramadan, all the better to melt into the enemy population unsuspected.

"Like the Saudis who flew our planes into the World Trade Center," she said. "They embraced *taqiya* when they entered pilot training and pretended they were in the US because they liked it."

Even before my SF team reached Afghanistan we'd learned about *taqiya* and many other aspects of Islamic life and religion. Once there we ended up sometimes on these silly outreach programs to build alleged ties with the locals, which usually entailed no gain but great risk. But for all this we had to know the Koran, the Hadiths. Had to understand how these people so close and warm could yet be so fanatic and dangerous. And why they hated us.

The *Art of War*, that ancient book of strategy, says it best: *He who knows neither the enemy nor himself will invariably be defeated.*

We couldn't claim we knew the enemy. I wasn't sure we knew ourselves.

MADS of course was just more *taqiya*. The cooperative, friendly façade of moderate Islam. Red wine and canapés, media coverage, limos, and lots of sex with Paris models.

If Mustafa had embraced *taqiya* that only made him harder to find. He'd be among the millions of semi-Muslims in France – they identify with the culture but do not often practice the religion. But the moment they feel this culture is threatened, of course they defend it. Lapsed Catholics are the same. We all are. The trouble is their culture, beyond a certain density, is destructive of ours. And whatever Mustafa was doing, he knew we were hunting him. And he was hunting me.

In Special Forces you're taught that when a problem seems insoluble find a little piece you do understand, and solve that. Then find another, and soon they lead you to a major thread, and pretty soon you've conquered it from the inside out.

Looking for threads, what did I really know?

I knew that Mustafa had come into France in a Passat with Austrian plates that had been stolen in Torino, if one were to believe the Italians.

According to the two *jihadis* DGSE had "interviewed," Mustafa was planning a major terrorist attack, either on the Eiffel Tower, an Airbus, or on Paris itself. Worse than what happened to Notre Dame. But guys will say anything under torture. Wouldn't we all?

And supposedly Mustafa was meeting with guys at Les Quatre Vents, who had vanished.

He was in contact with Abdel and his three buddies.

He may have had some relation to Yasmina.

Mack and Anne were hunting him since he reappeared, then Mack disappeared, then his wife too.

Mack had gone to Les Andelys, was going there again the day he disappeared. But no one seemed to know why.

Mustafa had known right away I was after him. How?

And now the person I'd thought was Mustafa had maybe met with Rachid Raqmi, or at least with someone using Rachid's Maserati. And Mustafa had been staying in the house in Avon where the moving company had set up false bribery accounts on Thierry, to render him powerless. And Rachid was pushing for an amnesty for ISIS terrorists returning from Iraq and Syria …

Find a thread and unravel it, I told myself.

There wasn't one.

Every single thread we'd tried to pull on had broken.

Thierry bent over a thirty-foot conference table spread with every clue and lead we had, or thought we had, with every sur-veillance photo and scrap of conversation ... He looked up, focusing for an instant on each of us. "We'll find a way."

"It always takes time," Anne said.

Thierry nodded. "Time and blood."

"WE HAVE DNA," Tomàs declared breathlessly on Thierry's speaker. "From the *keffiyeh*."

"Whose?"

"Nassim Faraz. Friend of Abdel. An S-List guy."

"So now we have him."

"Problem is," Thierry snorted, *"what* do we have?"

On the surface we might have enough to arrest Nassim and Tariq. When Homicide had fished Bruno out of St. Martin canal he'd had no torn clothes; and now the piece of checkered cloth had come back with Nassim's DNA. But who could say when the cotton had been torn off and stuck on the bridge? No way to prove when. Nassim would say he'd climbed over the edge for some other reason, as a dare perhaps, at a totally different time.

If we had Bruno's DNA also on the cloth that would show a link. But there was none. A good lawyer and a pro-Muslim judge would get the case thrown out in no time.

Nassim would be free in an hour without saying a thing. And we, once again, would have blown everything.

Like what happened with Yasmina.

Like Mustafa never returning to Les Quatre Vents.

Like Bruno getting killed because I'd talked to him.

If we arrested Tariq, Nassim and friends we'd end up with four nasty Arabs who would give us nothing, and Mustafa would change cover and keep advancing whatever he planned to do to the Tower. Or to Paris.

Because Abdel was connected to Mustafa, and Abdel's brother Tariq had been one of the four who killed Bruno, probably Mustafa was tied to Bruno's death. Probably ordered it. And because Mustafa seemed to be the cause of Mack's and Gisèle's kidnappings, Abdel, Nassim and Tariq were connected to that too.

But how, in France, could you prove it?

And where was Rachid in all this?

I downloaded some pix and went to see Bruno's wife.

THE LIFE HAD GONE out of Les Quatre Vents. Empty of clients, dust in the corners, two bulbs out on the Amstel Beer sign. The reek of rotting beer.

"I'm closing down." Bruno's wife stood in black behind the bar like an Easter Island statue, erect and alone. "The bank can have the place. There'll be a loss, so I can go on welfare ... Imagine, *me* – on welfare?"

"I have some pix I want to show you."

"Since I was fourteen, I've worked every day of my life ..."

"Just four guys, won't take a minute."

She slapped the bar. "Give 'em here."

No matter how many times she stared at each shot of Abdel and friends she shook her head. "These are ugly bastards. If I ever saw them I wouldn't forget. But I've never seen them."

Another wasted interview. Getting further and further behind.

God had left the stage and the lights were going out. And it came to me perhaps nearly everything I had done was wrong.

TWO HOURS LATER she called. "There is *something*."

I'd been studying lists of names and license plates and tried to shift gears. "Yeah?"

"The night before my husband was killed, when I got to the bar for dinner shift, he said a guy had come in, North-African, asking for work." She sounded a little breathless. "The guy asked if Bruno had security when he stayed open late. Bruno laughed, told him he'd been here thirty-one years, that's all the security he needed …"

I sat back, rubbed my eyes. Another clue that would go nowhere. Whoever this guy was, Bruno was the only person who could identify him, so we'd never find him now.

Though maybe if we sorted out some pix of other S-List guys with links to the same Stains mosque as Abdel and his three buddies? You never know.

"Can you come to ATS, that's a police department, tomorrow morning? They need to show you more photographs."

"I guess I could. Nobody would know, would they?"

"They'll send a car for you," I told her. "Unmarked. Nobody will know."

I closed my list of license plates, struck by the fear in her voice. Which gave me a surge of fear for Anne. The kids and Mamie.

How long would it take Mustafa and whoever he was working with to find them too?

"FROM GISÈLE." Thierry handed me a fax copy of a handwritten note:

Thierry,

I have been told to write this, to save Mack from more harm. The people who have us will release me in return for Pono Hawkins. I do not wish this but it is what I have been told to write, to avoid further pain … After a torn space it continued, *If Pono accepts, they will send him coordinates where he and I can be exchanged. He must come alone. The people who have us say that if he is followed or accompanied in any way they will kill him and Mack and me also. I do not think they are lying.*

I stared at him, stupefied. "Where's this from?"

"A fax. From fucking Bulgaria."

I hadn't known faxes still existed. "Let's trace it."

"We've hit a wall."

"Gisèle doesn't write with a backward slant like this ... It's not her."

"Yes it is. We checked: the slant is different but the letter formation, all that, is identical."

"By slanting backwards –"

"She's saying she's doing it against her will."

FREE THE GUILTY

"WE HAVE A WITNESS," Tomàs on Thierry's speaker, "to Bruno's murder."

"At two in the morning?" I said.

"She lives across the Canal from the bridge where he was killed and thrown off. She's eighty-eight and can't sleep and sits in her front room on the fourth floor overlooking the Canal and thinks about the old days when she was twenty-two and in love with her new husband who went to Vietnam and got a bullet through his hip and it took him ten years to die. And she thinks about what could have happened if they'd just missed one train, not answered one call."

"Okay, Tomàs," Thierry said. "Okay."

"What I'm saying is she heard a yell, a curse ..." Tomàs caught his breath. "And when she gets to the window she sees four shapes moving down the far side of the bridge, and one reaches out and hugs the other, and she thinks it must have been some small altercation, already worked out."

"It backs your theory about the guys on the bridge –" Thierry said.

"It's not a fucking theory, we *have* Nassim's DNA!"

"But you can't prove *when* it got there. You know how the courts are. Any chance to free the guilty ..."

"That's why we don't *arrest* them," I put in.

"Problem is" – Thierry scratched his head – "we have to arrest *some* of them. To get the others."

"But when we have Mustafa," I said softly, "the end of the string ..."

Thierry looked up, smiled. "We don't *need* to arrest him."

"Good." I nodded, wanting to formalize it.

"But sadly he's not the end of the string."

"Fuck that."

"So maybe if the gods are with us we get Mustafa?" Thierry reasoned. "What about Rachid? If he is in fact working with Mustafa, that means he's far more insidious and harder to combat – because he can manipulate the media and thus the politicians. And *they're* the ones who are going to stand in our way. We must get more proof on him."

"There's more," Tomàs said through the speaker. "Yasmina's explosives –"

It revolted me, to remember her body splattered over the neighborhood.

"– stolen last year from a quarry near Dusseldorf. Driven across the Belgian border to Molenbeek. From there through Tourcoing and Lille to Paris."

"Speaking of Tourcoing," Thierry said, "we got a funny intercept the other day. This Sorbonne prof, he's French but pretends to be half Arab, does a column sometimes in *Le Nouvel Observateur*. We have him talking to some imam in Tourcoing about France becoming a Muslim nation – 'the first in Europe' he says.

"'No, no,' the imam answers. 'The second. Belgium will be first.'

"'Ah, to the second, then,' the prof laughs. '*Vive la France!*'"

"*Vive la France,*" I said, morosely.

"You have to see it as comedy," Tomàs said. "Or you go crazy."

IT WAS GETTING HARD to see any comedy, to remember anything but this relentless hunt, the eye-burning fatigue and wearied shoulders, the dizziness, the sickened gut. A few minutes at a café in the stench and scream of vehicles, wondering if the network of interlocking beer glass rings atop the smutty table is a key to anything at all, while the room around us is full of joy and laughter and happy conversation, amid the divine fragrances of foods and wines as Anne and I each down a double *express* and stale croissant while Anne swears at her phone and I scan the evening traffic through the rain-hazed windows. And I realize that no one, not one of all these people laughing and talking, the others out there hunched impatiently over their steering wheels, the face-down pedestrians and soaked, unhappy bicyclers, has the faintest idea what the fuck is really going on and how dangerous it is.

That we could lose it all, the cars and restaurants and streets and Tower and people and pigeons and sewer rats. All gone in a flash.

No one had a clue.

I'd felt this way before, detached, in a kind of supernatural awareness, aware of dangers that no one else feels ... To be among civilians in the States, contented in our naïve, goodhearted way – *we're good people, why should anyone hate us?* When those of us who know worry all the time ...

One night in a screaming Afghanistan blizzard at ten thousand feet I suddenly wanted to take the longer and more rugged way around a steep cliff, not knowing why. But it was such a deep urge I couldn't ignore it despite my three buddies treating me to language unusual even in Special Forces. But I persevered, and at the trail junction we came up behind thirteen Taliban all dug in with a Russian PK machine gun, facing down the easier trail we had avoided. We divided them up: three each, and as team leader I got four.

My old mantra – you're never more in danger than when you think you're safe.

Other times in other wars in other places. Even in Hawaii and Maine, fighting politicians and other crooks. To be aware of things most folks aren't.

But never like this.

No, I told myself. *It won't ever happen.*

It felt better when I told myself that.

NO WAY I'd survive an exchange for Gisèle. The moment Mustafa had Mack *and* me, he'd kill us. And Gisèle too. And laugh his heart out.

And no way to go in there with a hidden weapon. They'd grab it and everyone would be even worse off.

I thought of Abdel and his three friends in two speeding cars on a trial run to the Tower. Mustafa and the other jogger from 60 Franklin Roosevelt had done a trial run, too, that was seven minutes late. Would Gisèle's captors do a trial run? Practice the exchange beforehand?

If so, they'd do it at the same place, the same time.

If we could catch the trial run, we'd know where the real exchange was going to be.

Maybe.

———

ANNE AND I HAD JUST returned to Commerce and I was sitting on the bed taking off my shoes, when Mitchell called. "This is just the beginning," he said. "And it's complicated."

I waited, saying nothing, knowing Mitchell's predilection to spin things out, leave you hanging on each word. "What in life isn't complicated?" I said finally.

"Let me start at the beginning."

I pulled off my socks and scratched between my toes. "Why not?"

"Every time the Socialists run France, unemployment goes way up."

"When you have laws that you can't fire anybody, of course no one dares hire anybody. What's new about that?"

"Thus the Socialists are always looking for overseas contracts, anything to bring work into the country. If they can get a big contract to sell Airbuses or helicopters, or fighter planes –"

"Rafales."

"Yeah, Rafales. They just sold a whole bunch to India, for instance. A huge contract that will allegedly create 40,000 more jobs. And they sell lots of weapons to Middle Eastern dictators, contracts they can't afford to lose."

"This doesn't explain the past forty years."

"The *goal* of Islam is to make the whole world Muslim. And any effort, any expense, to grow Islam in France will be rewarded in Heaven. The billions in Middle Eastern funding here for charities, mosques, schools, sports groups, cultural events, plus all the money we don't know about –"

"*Hawala.*"

"Yeah, and *hawala*. Lots of it."

"The House of War. The strategy of slow conquest."

"As always, paired with violence."

I yawned, watching Anne undress at the foot of the bed. "So what's new?"

"I looked at the last ten years of contracts between France

and Muslim countries. Not just the so-called *defense* contracts ... but all major purchases by these countries of French goods and services –" The phone screeched while Mitchell scratched his beard against it.

"*Mitchell!* Don't *do* that!"

"– I wanted to know if any major concessions, where France protected some nasty Middle East regime or took a very strong anti-Semitic stance on Israel, were followed by sizeable purchases of French goods and services by these nations ..."

I felt let down. "*Everybody* does that! Christ, Obama wouldn't release the 28 pages of proof that the Saudi government helped mastermind 9/11, and he tried to stop American citizens from suing the Saudis for doing it. In return Saudi, Kuwait and Qatar bought thirty billion in F15s, Super Hornets and other crap ..."

"You have the *brain* of a hornet," he said. "All you want to do is sting."

"What I want," I said, getting angry, "is proof that some French politicians took money from Muslim sources and did favors in return. *That's* what I want."

"Why?"

"Because maybe we can find a path that leads to the truth. To find out who's trying to mess with DGSE and ATS and us ... To find a link between Rachid and the French government, see who's giving him all that air time and for what purpose ... to save the fanatics from themselves, or help them carry out their plan to destroy us all ..."

"Well if *that's* all you need ..."

"Then get going."

"Fuck you. Speaking of which, you getting laid?"

I watched Anne unhook her bra and slide down her underpants. "None of your business."

"Ah, so you *are*, then. That's wonderful. Live it deep, dear friend. Live it irreproachably deep." He cleared his throat. "Nothing lasts ..."

Q U D S

"AN IRANIAN NUCLEAR scientist is due in three days in Paris." It was Thierry on the phone as usual at two a.m.

"What for?" I sat up, instantly awake.

"Some EdF conference." EdF is *Électricité de France*, the world's largest utility and the operator of the country's fifty-eight nuclear power plants, which supply 88% of the nation's electricity. EdF is also the world's largest exporter of nuclear energy. French nuclear plants have an astounding safety record and give France Europe's lowest-cost electricity plus Europe's lowest level of greenhouse gases. It made a perfect cover for an Iranian nuclear bomb maker to attend an EdF conference on clean nuclear energy.

"When you find out?" I said, flipping the call to speaker so Anne could hear.

"He just showed up on an Air France reservation."

"I'll call Harris."

"What time is it in Honolulu? Why not call your friend Mitchell?"

I'd briefly mentioned Mitchell to Thierry; they'd never met in Afghanistan. "I wish I'd known him," Thierry had said.

Mitchell would know of any Iranian scientist working in the nuclear field. His files would know the scientist's family, where he lived and exactly what he did, his bank account, sexual preferences and a lot of other stuff.

"I'll call him. What's happening your side?"

"Still mapping connections, background ... I'll talk to EdF in the morning."

"If he does come, make sure Air France security in Teheran searches his baggage."

"He's got a diplomatic passport. His baggage doesn't *get* searched."

"Tell them do it anyway."

"It will have locks that can't be decoded that quick."

"Deny him a visa."

"Upstairs says no."

"*No?* What the fuck *for? Who* upstairs?"

"Foreign Ministry. *And* Interior. All those invisible assholes who run us."

"I want names –"

"Even I don't know. So many of these things are trade-offs."

I climbed out of bed and headed for the kitchen. "I'll call Mitchell now. And Harris tomorrow. What's his name, this Iranian guy?"

"Dr. Ahmed Arawa, 52, undergrad Mosul University, PhD nuclear physics Université de Lyon, postdoc Geneva, went back to Iran in nuclear research, everything that could be classified peaceful, principally energy production."

At the sink I filled a glass with water and drank it, hating the chemical taste. "Must be a hundred guys like him. Send me his stuff and I'll pass it on."

"But I haven't told you the best part. Before he went to university he spent four years in Quds as an explosives specialist. After that he did all his studies in nuclear."

Quds (*Sepah-e quds* in Persian) is the Special Forces branch of the Iranian Revolutionary Guards. It has eight target areas, the first of which is Europe and North America, and another is Iraq, where they were responsible for the deaths of nearly a thousand US soldiers. They have been a major terrorist force in Syria and Lebanon, and responsible for numerous attacks on civilians in Israel.

Quds trains and provides weapons for Islamic terrorist forces in many countries, often brings them to Iran for intensive weapons and explosives work, then returns them to their home countries to do as much harm as possible.

When you joined Quds, as Dr. Arawa had, it was for life. You could go back to the world, but you always owed them. Whatever they wanted. Whenever they wanted.

A one-way street.

Headed our way.

"You're going to have to keep him off that plane."

"Not happening."

"Or intercept it."

"Yeah, right."

Or maybe Dr. Arawa was working to develop peaceful Iranian nuclear energy. But he was Quds, and his background was explosives. The link between Quds and Hezbollah is deep, between the Iranian military and terrorism. On the surface this guy was working on nuclear energy. But he was also a bombmaker.

"You want to know his Quds codename? Doctor Death."

So maybe the story Thierry's two *jihadis* had told about a bomb coming to Paris was true after all.

———

"DO WE ARREST Tariq?" Tomàs said at our 07:00 meeting that morning. "He showed up with a broken jaw a half mile from the murder site, and we know that Bruno fought back. And do we bring in Nassim, the guy with his DNA on the torn keffiyeh? For a proper interrogation?"

Despite myself I grinned at the absurdity of it. "Once you arrest these guys, you have to give them lawyers, an imam, a cell phone, copies of *Penthouse* to wank off with and all kinds of other goodies. And they don't have to talk for weeks. If ever."

"Sadly true ..." Thierry said.

"Plus we alert Mustafa and everyone else, Mack and Gisèle die, Mustafa accelerates his schedule and does a hit on the Tower or an Airbus before we can stop it ..."

I was silent a moment, took a breath. "What are the chances it would be an Airbus hit *on* the Tower? An actual hit?"

"Jesus, they keep trying ..."

When my phone buzzed I saw it was Mitchell and went into the corridor to take it. "Yeah?"

"You alone?"

I told him where I was.

"You'll want to tell *them* –"

"Tell them what?"

"Your Iranian nuclear scientist?"

"Dr. Arawa."

"Guess where he's just been?"

"Christ, Mitchell, get to the point!"

"Kahuta."

"Oh fuck."

"Oh fuck is right. The Khan Research labs."

"Where the Pakis make their nukes and long-distance missiles."

"And just like the Iranians were doing before we sabotaged theirs, Kahuta uses gas centrifuges to make HEU."

HEU is Highly Enriched Uranium, essential to the production of nuclear bombs. "And," I added, "those bastards gave the Taliban surface-to-air missiles to shoot down our guys in Afghanistan." I took a breath, nauseated by the memory. "He was *there?*"

"*Then* – get this – he spent a week in Rawalpindia. Stayed at the Pyramid 2 Guest House but spent night and day at the labs ..."

"I remember the Pyramid 2," I answered. Located just northeast of Rawalpindi's sprawl, and about 100 km south of Abbottabad, where the Pakis were hiding Osama Bin Laden till our SEALS killed him, Rawalpindia is the Pakistan Institute of Science and Technology's nuclear research center. They do everything from fuel cycle development to plutonium extraction. Everything you need to kill people.

And Dr. Arawa had just spent a week there.

Now he was coming to Paris.

FOREIGN INTELLIGENCE

"MY FRIEND," Peter Ivanov said on the phone, his voice near as if we were in our favorite Istanbul bar trying to hook up with magnificent Turkish women. "My friend –"

"*Moy droog,*" I said companionably back in Russian. We *had* been friends for years, though at a certain frozen distance, ever since Turkey and the search for a Russian drug lord who later turned up dead in an empty yacht off the Amalfi coast.

"So why," Peter growled, "are *you* being caught *up* in this Paris *mess*? When everybody *knows* is *mess*! Last I know you are *surfing.*"

"You hear what happened to Mack and his wife? All this stuff going down in France?"

"Is not my fault. I did not invite these bastards into France. Notice in Russia we don't have lots of Arabs trying to blow things up."

"You've got the bloody Chechnyans ..."

"Chechnya *is* Russia!"

"Yeah, I know. So is Madagascar, probably."

He laughed. "Don't want it."

I imagined him sitting there in Moscow SVR. This incredibly tough guy with a boxer's nose and an ardent love for Gorki, Shostakovich, Russian food and women and all the other good things of this world.

"So how are you, Peter? Does my heart good to hear your voice."

"And mine yours. What can us backward Slavs do for you today?"

"I'm here at DGSE with Thierry St. Croix and Anne Ronsard. And Cedric Harris is on the line."

"Hello, Thierry and Anne, nice to meet you. Hey, Cedric – how you *doing*?"

"Everything's fine," Harris grumped, and I almost laughed at how he hated being friendly with the Russians.

"Next time you're in Paris," Thierry said.

"Or you're in Russia ..." Peter answered.

"We're looking," I broke in, "for anything you guys have on a possible missing Paki backpack. Or a copy, something new, probably built at Khan Research ..."

"Nothing from the top of my head. But we'll look in it."

"And anything you have on Dr. Ahmed Arawa. I know you guys have been in bed with the Iranians lately but this guy might be really bad news. Quds bombmaker. His Quds codename is Doctor Death ... I'll send you what I have. He's just been to Khan Research *and* Rawalpindia ..."

"That doesn't sound good."

"And," I made this up, "he's in touch with people you don't like in Grozny."

"You must send us these."

"Shall do. But get us what you can right away. Dr. Arawa's due in Paris in three days, so we're moving fast. We've just got some nasty confirming data, this could be much bigger than what we just did for you guys in St. Pete ..."

"Every day we thank you guys for that."

"Make it even. Give us what you can. Fast."

"I'll send it up the line real fast. It will come back fast. I promise."

"You guys are so fucking *organized!*"

He snickered. "It is Russian, to be organized."

YOU NEVER KNEW these days with SVR, the Russian external intelligence agency for which Peter Ivanov was a top guy, how much they'd help. The former KGB First Chief Directorate, SVR has a different team now, lots of very smart young women and men bilingual in languages I've never heard of, who can run the forty in under five seconds and have advanced training in everything from personal combat to giving great sex and parachuting behind lines.

And who are smart and fun to be with. Good drinking buddies and lissome lovely women.

Long as you remember who you're really dealing with.

But at the top, the ones who decide everything, they're the real deal. Pure strategic intelligence. If anyone could help us with Doctor Death and the Paki nukes it would be SVR. I could've asked Peter for a contact in GRU, Russian military intelligence, but he would've said no. And he'd know anything they know anyway. Even though they're lots bigger than he is. And in a lot more trouble lately.

"THINK OF IT as a harvest," Thierry said after we got off the phone. He tried to lean back in his chair that creaked dangerously.

"You need to get rid of that thing," Anne snapped.

It howled as he swung forward. "… if you harvest too early, you get a few that are ripe but most are still green. If you harvest too late, everything's mushy. If we harvest *this* operation at the right time, we might get it all."

I looked at him, thinking of the lives that could be lost if we didn't do it at the right time.

"Religious terrorism's like cancer," Anne said. "It changes shape, targets, goes into areas it's never been and starts death there ... Death anywhere."

"Like this backpack bomb," I said tiredly. "Isn't our job to defeat dangers *before* they happen?"

"Go track an asteroid," Thierry snickered. "Before it hits us."

I felt unreasoning fury at him, the whole deal. Incredibly weary. As if I were the only one who really wanted to stop this.

"HAWALA'S hard to track," Mitchell said. "You can never get it all."

It was noon in Paris, thus midnight in Honolulu. Once again, I felt guilty I'd asked him to do this.

"But," he said theatrically, "I found a bit you might use ... Your friend Rachid – he whose IT folks screwed with Thierry's bank accounts – he may have hidden income from some of the arms, oil, and pharmaceutical deals he's helped arrange between France and Muslim countries. But it doesn't show on any bottom line."

The thought was abysmally fatiguing. "We don't have the time, the energy ..."

"You don't do it yourself," he said. "You ask your computer to do it. That's AI."

"AI?"

"Artificial intelligence, peasant."

"*All* intelligence is artificial."

"We're getting some hits."

"Hits?"

"There seems to be a whole network of people connected to Rachid who are on this money train. Money coming in from the Middle East, politicians getting wealthy by promoting Islam's expansion in France. And because they got wealthy they got more powerful too ..."

"Payoffs?" I muttered. "That's going to be harder to prove. With the courts against you."

"Why would they be against you?"

"Because they're part of the problem."

ATS DID EVERYTHING they could to triangulate Mustafa. But he kept this phone nearly always off. Then two good things happened.

First, ATS tracked down three other numbers "associated" with this, the phone they'd picked up in his post office visit. The three new numbers were ones either Mustafa also used, or which belonged to someone often physically near him. A bodyguard? Subordinate? One of his bearded acolytes?

Second, ATS got two delayed hits after they sent him phantoms. Delayed because he kept this phone off, so the phantom message just sat there waiting till he turned on the phone.

The first was from a cell tower antenna in the Seventh Arrondissement. The second hit was within a half-mile radius of the HLM apartments in Avon where we'd missed grabbing Gisèle.

And it was a half mile from 60 Franklin Roosevelt, owned by New Hope Productions, the TV company funded by MADS, the Muslim Anti-Discrimination Society, and thus by media darling Rachid Raqmi.

"So it probably was Mustafa that I saw, on that run in the forest."

"It's enough to bring them in," Anne said.

"But not to hold them," Thierry answered. "MADS would just say they're a charitable organization under French law, they don't check identities of all the people they give aid to."

"Yes," Thierry said. "That would hold up in court."

"Can't be," I said.

"Thierry's right," Anne said. "Forty years of socialism has filled the courts with judges who believe that criminal acts are due to social causes, and that punishment only makes it worse."

"And now we're letting people out because we have no more jail cells," Thierry said. "Already we have the most overpopulated prisons in Europe. And because jails cause crime, we're not going to build any more."

Nothing new there. But now we had more possible phones to track, could narrow Mustafa down every time he used one. Till we could go in for the kill.

I wouldn't miss him this time.

THE FIELD OF MARS

"BE READY," the new fax said, Gisèle's same unwilling backward script. *"Starting tomorrow Pono must be ready for the exchange at any time 24 hours a day. After he is contacted he should make no calls or messages or emails or other connections with anyone. My keepers will know if he disobeys and they will kill me. They will contact him by calling twice with one ring on his DGSE cell, then a third time twice. Then the fourth time he must answer. If that is not acceptable my keepers will kill me."*

"There's no trial run," I said. "If I don't show up they kill her, right there."

Thierry nodded. "Probably."

"Don't be so sure," Anne put in.

I wanted to snap at her, tell her *nothing's sure*, but we both already knew that. Like nothing's sure about what would happen if I made the exchange. Except we'd all be dead.

Had to be a way to rescue of Gisèle without everybody getting killed.

Had to be a way.

It depended where they wanted to do the exchange. It would

be whatever worked best for them. And what was most difficult for me.

Had to be a way.

"THE EXCHANGE will be near Mustafa," Thierry said. "So he can intervene, if necessary."

Anne turned to me. "He's going to want to personally ID you."

"At that point I'll have no weapons – I'll be screwed."

"In Fontainebleau," Thierry persisted. "Or Les Andelys."

"Or La République. Or Seine-St. Denis ..."

"For them that's the smartest," Anne said. "On every street there'd be a hundred guns aimed at us."

"We have to say no," Thierry sighed. "To whatever they offer. Till we get something we can work with."

Anne huffed. "Good luck."

"THE DEAD MAN'S WIFE," Tomàs said. "She came in and our guys showed her some pix."

"That was nice of them," I said stupidly, too tired to care.

"No one she knew except one guy," he said teasingly.

"Okay, okay ..."

"You've met him, I think. Sort of."

"C'mon, out with it."

"Our hero, the head of MADS."

"What?" I was suddenly awake. "Rachid?"

"She says maybe a month ago, he came in one night. Shook some hands, chattered a bit in Arabic and walked out."

"Chattered with who?"

"Bunch of guys. She couldn't identify any of them. Said it was like some kind of politician, visiting his public."

"Nothing we can use?"

"Nah. Just more background."

MY EXCHANGE for Gisèle would happen at any time starting tomorrow. When soon after I might be dead. What was important, in these last hours? The kids and Mamie.

We jumped on the Indian and tore out of Paris past St. Germain-en-Laye, then Mantes like a bad ghetto one can soon barely remember.

Lyons-la-Forêt is only 65 miles from Paris but another world. Viking land where thousands of years of war has created tough survivors. In the middle of Normandy, the Forest of Lyons was what remained of the ancient oak wilderness that once covered northern Europe with a canopy so tall and vast that when Julius Caesar and his legions trekked from Paris to the Rhine they did not see the sun for forty days.

Today Lyons la-Forêt has still a bit of that: beautiful glades in all directions over undulating hills and wide verdant valleys broken here and there by wheat fields green in the lustful spring sun.

Cousin Claudine's was a 350-acre goat farm of mixed fields and forests, an ancient, toppling stone barn and late medieval house with a Norman tower standing over it like a watchful timeworn knight.

Beside the barn a cage of snails ready for the saucepot, a vast chicken house, expansive goose and turkey pens, and behind it rolling pastures where goats grazed on spring grass.

The kitchen was at the back on the ground floor, yard-wide paving stones, a huge black woodstove. It smelled of oak smoke and fresh herbs. Everything was cavernous – the height of the gnarled oak beams, each ancient foot-worn stone, the spiral oak staircase ascending into darkness, the souls of all the humans who'd lived here nearly a thousand years. Every fear and sorrow, every joy and full stomach, every runny nose, sad death, and wonderful orgasm. All here, in these cold stone walls.

Till now I'd had little time with Julie and André, and then they'd seemed distant and shy. But now, perhaps due to their relative isolation (Anne had decided not to put them in the local school because Mustafa's people might somehow be able to trace it), they took my hand and showed me the farm, introducing me to goats, chickens, an old mare whose back they climbed on together, an irritable donkey and lots of gobbling turkeys.

As I looked down on Julie's glowing pigtails and André's short dark hair and felt the warmth of their small hands in mine, I realized I was beginning to care deeply about them. And fear for their safety.

We had dinner in the old kitchen, nettle soup then fresh raw goat cheese on lettuce that half an hour ago was in the ground, then lamb so tender and juicy it reminded me of what meat used to taste like, with beets, broccoli, and all that other funny green crap they grow here too.

Cousine Claudine I loved right away, as if we shared ancient roots. White hair clipped page-boy short, a wrinkled sunny broad face with sharp black eyes and a humorous twist to a wide mouth.

The food came in an avalanche, each course punctuated by the Norman *trou*, a shot of hundred-proof calvados that goes down like fire and reduces to ash anything you already ate.

The oak smoke, marjoram and rosemary, granite air and goat manure odor from the barn and the memory inherent in these ancient stones all told me that if we survive the Hell we're in we too can live like this.

Just love each other and be happy.

Anne was an angel from a 16th century Dutch painting sitting with her children on a wooden bench in the medieval stone kitchen – the slant of her head and tumbling mahogany hair against an ancient window's golden sunset – she *was* the Madonna, Priestess of Life, the eternal mother's transcendent love, her subconscious gift beneath that love like the subterranean rivers that feed a valley. How could I refuse the joy that soared through me just to see her sitting with one arm around each child? Most of all I wished her husband could be there, as they too wished. But knowing he could not, and that he would want me to love his wife because he wanted her to be happy, I felt happy too, and deeply wished I'd known him. Wished that I'd been their friend. Now, if I cared for his children? Tried to give them what he would?

That was enough for me.

How good to live like this, in the depth of love and understanding. Which made me even more determined to come out of this horror with everything we could.

HOUR AND A HALF LATER we were back at the Place du Commerce and half asleep when Stranger dropped in off the roof.

He checked the kitchen and hopped on the bed giving us an annoyed patient look. We'd come home late and not put out his dinner. But as a good friend he pretended not to mind. Sat licking his left front paw as if that's what he did every night at eleven-thirty. "Liar," I told him, and fell back asleep.

"I KNOW WHERE he is!" Anne sprang up in bed staring out the window at the Tower's half-lit skeleton.

"Who?" I sat up looking around.

"Mustafa. Just *saw* him. Dream." She slipped naked in the moonlight from the bed to the window.

I shook my head trying to wake up. *"Where?"*

"Champ de Mars. Walking up an alley of trees, staring up at the Tower."

We scrambled into our clothes, grabbed our guns and mikes, ran downstairs to the Beast and raced the wrong way up Rue du Commerce to La Motte-Picquet and pulled over on a side street right off the Champ de Mars.

"You want to call Thierry?" I said.

"Not for a dream," Anne huffed, looking nasty and pissed off in black leather, black sweats, black Kinvaras, a black Glock under her jacket and her black hair all tangled with sleep.

I glanced at the Tower, nearly invisible in fog but for its beacons like lost lighthouses. "Okay then. You right, me left."

We're almost the same height so we looked straight into each other's eyes. Hers were black and flashing; she exhaled a ferocious intensity that made me love her and fear for her. "You see something, you tell me," I said. "You don't *do* a fucking thing."

She gave me a feral grin. "If it's Mustafa?"

"Not without me."

She laughed and we slipped into the dark alleys of trees on each side of the Champ de Mars, the Tower rising like a dark steel god far overhead, the long grassy park naked in moonlight, pebbles on the path glowing like crystals. There were the usual drunks sleeping against the trees, hustlers doing hash deals in dark corners, a hooker arguing with four African guys, a few illegals pandering toy Towers to the last straggling tourists.

No Mustafa. Just the same sad travesty of this beautiful place where cops don't go at night. Stink of piss and stale beer, rotting leaves and rain, the Field of Mars, sacred to the God of War. And the Tower high above it all.

"Nothing," I said into my radio.

"Me neither," she said.

"In the dream, where'd you see him?"

"Over here by the pony rides."

"I'll circle to you."

Seven minutes later I came up to her. "I'm an idiot." She leaned against me.

"Let's go home."

"Yeah." She nestled against me. "We haven't fed Stranger."

"Imagine the trouble we'd be in, if we forgot his dinner ..."

BLOOD OF JERUSALEM

IT WAS 05:45 when Thierry called. *"Nous sommes les idiots bénis de Dieu,"* he said. We are the blessed idiots of God.

"How's that?" I mumbled, trying to wake up.

"We have an amazing match."

"We do?"

"You and her," he said. "Get in here."

IT'S EASY WHEN you've had only a couple of nights with no sleep to hang in there as if everything's fine and you're just a little fatigued. By the time it gets to four days with no sleep you're done. By the time it's two weeks, three weeks, you're living on borrowed life, unaware, a zombie crushed by time. But you keep going.

At 06:47 we were there. Thierry buzzed in a minion with coffees and croissants. "Those phones," he said when the minion left, *"associated* with Mustafa's?"

I tried to remember. "The three other phones physically close to his, like an aide, a wife …"

"One of them has had seven recent conversations with Rachid."

"You correlated dates?" Anne said.

"Of course. The first call from this phone was May 25."

"When Mack called me in Tahiti."

"That explains it," Thierry said. "They had Mack's phone …"

"That you guys were supposed to keep clean –"

"Mack had been tracking Mustafa. That's how they got him."

"Then that's how they got me." I was so furious my stomach came burning up my throat; I needed to walk out in the hall and punch someone.

"The second call's when you landed at CDG."

"Before they tailed me from the airport."

"To Passage Landrieu, then to Mack and Gisèle's."

"But they already knew where *that* was …"

"Third call," Thierry said, "was after Pono visited Les Quatre Vents."

"When Rachid warned Mustafa to stay away." I took a breath, trying to sort this out. "How'd he *know*?"

"That's what we *don't* know."

Of course the other four calls fit in perfectly: at 02:17 the night Bruno was killed. The next was two hours before we crashed the door at the Avon HLM where Gisèle had been held – the call the kidnappers had received that made them angry. The third was fifteen minutes after I'd chased the guy with the Broncos hat across the rooftops. The last was from Mustafa to Rachid, telling him his nephew was a faithful believer and not to worry.

That's how they speak of young men about to die in a suicide attack.

"You tracking the nephew?"

"He's skipped parole. We find him, we bring him in."

I imagined Mustafa hovering, smiling in the shadows, swinging his cleaver shiny with new blood.

I closed my eyes. "Rachid's phone. What else is on it?"

"Another throwaway. Four other calls …"

"Yeah?"

"Pizza."

Anne snickered. "Pizza's not *halal*."

"Neither is Rachid."

"He's an imam and he doesn't do *halal*?"

"*Taqiya*."

"The next call?" I said.

Thierry chuckled. "To his mistress. Normally, we're learning, he calls her on a different phone."

"He already has three wives …"

"Hey, give the guy a break."

"Who's this mistress?"

"Élysée Pétain."

"No!" Anne said.

"Yes."

"Damn! We're way out of our league. When was the last time you balled the top anchor on public TV?"

Thierry yawned. "Happens all the time."

Anne turned to me. "This fake peacemaker, this *taqiya* guy, he's fucking the biggest mouth on television."

"It's called oral sex, in case you didn't know," Thierry snickered.

"You have her?" I said.

"She's caviar ultra-left – that whole mix of far-left media, university fanatics, anti-Semites, anarchists and Socialists. They call for killing the police, protest what they call Islamophobia, organize demonstrations and attacks on the government, all that. They say young Arabs need to express their discontent by spraying graffiti over every wall, but don't you dare tag the lovely stone walls of their own high-class abodes."

"This is where politics, media, money and sex all come together," Anne said. "She's not only a talking head but politically well-connected ..." Anne thought a moment. "And she's got a huge viewer base – and the government doesn't want to mess with that."

I thought of the mysterious groups that had made it possible for Islam to so quickly conquer so much of France. "This is the best news we've had in a long time."

"What," Anne said, "that France has a suicidal left?"

"Let's follow these bastards." I exhaled happily. "Follow them all. They're going to lead us somewhere."

"Rachid's two other calls?" Anne said.

"First was the cleaning lady," Thierry said. "Rachid wanted her to come in early."

"The other?"

"A hooker. Last night."

"To crack his place we work the cleaning lady. Did you talk to the hooker?"

"Local Tunisian girl, goes by *Mimette*. Said he couldn't get it up, wanted anal but she said no. He offered her two hundred euros if he could burn her cunt with a cigarette. Said then he could get it up."

"She said no?"

"Apparently not."

"YOUR IRANIAN," Peter said from Moscow, "could be trouble."

"I told you ..."

"You guys being so backward and all, you probably don't know about Directional Control."

"Heavens, Peter, yes, I actually *do* know about Directional Control."

"We've caught it twice on people trying to board our regional airlines, once Kazan, once Ural. Somebody gets on with this little video game, and with a matching transponder on the ground he can take over control of the plane and drive it to that transponder ... There's nothing the pilots can do ... I'm sure you know of this –"

"Sadly, yes."

"This Iranian, you sent us his stuff ... In Teheran and Pakistan he has developed these tools."

"Directional Control?"

"Did I not just say that?"

"He could be on a plane and direct it somewhere."

"Is not what I said?"

WE GOT THE LATEST from Gisèle at 09:18 that morning, in the same backward hand:

This is being dictated to me. Since Pono seems to like Les Andelys we do the swap there. He must be there at ten to nine tonight. Or Mack and I die. We send a precise location when he reaches Les Andelys. If anyone besides Pono shows up, or if he's wired, these guys cut my throat in front of the church that Richard the Lionheart built with the blood of Jerusalem.

I tried to figure what this meant. For sure Mustafa had no intention to let Gisèle go. She'd been kept alive to lure me, or to trade for something else, and once that was done she was dead.

And the Richard the Lionheart jab was just to remind us how ancient this war was, and that they were going to win. Or had they overheard us somehow, the day that Anne and I first drove to Les Andelys?

Mustafa's attempt to lure me in could also mean that Mack was still alive, if Mustafa's plan was to execute us together.

But why not just kill each of us when he could? Maybe because we were a stain on his past, the two infidels that got away – horrible to think of all the poor people who hadn't. And we were Special Forces, whom he hated for the severe damage and casualties we'd done to his terrorist militia, till we'd finally driven them into the desert and a Foreign Legion ambush.

And somehow tied in his head to Allah's will, that much he'd said during one execution, grinning down on us with his sweaty finger on the trigger.

I had barely twelve hours to figure this out. A problem with no solution.

Mustafa didn't need Gisèle. He'd kill her once he had me.

Would I die for Gisèle? Of course, that's what soldiers do.

The difference was that my dying wouldn't keep her alive.

"WE *HAVE* TO SAY NO," Anne said. "We don't have time to set up. We can't cover you. You'll *both* be killed."

I saw Gisèle with her lovely grin and mischievous eyes, her gorgeous golden hair. She who cared for everyone.

How do you choose among your friends which of them should die?

If we did the swap Gisèle might live. But Mack and I would die.

Anne, I don't want to die. Because I'd lose you.

THE HOMICIDAL MIND

IN SPECIAL FORCES you automatically learn reverse thinking. It's not taught, it comes from experience. You identify a goal and imagine being there, then figure how you got there, going backward step by step.

As always, asking what can go wrong at each step, and what if they all go wrong together? As they usually do.

An exercise old as the first humans. The homicidal mind, working things out.

So now I tried to imagine Mustafa in a police van, manacled, in a jail cell, his hopeless face staring between the bars.

Even better: his dying eyes gazing into mine.

But I could find no way to envision it.

"ANOTHER MATCH!" Thierry charged out of his office, pulling me in.

I stumbled in, still stunned by Gisèle's latest message and by what Peter had just said.

"The red Clio" – Thierry jabbed a finger at his screen – "was a 2014 Handi Rental then got bought by a woman in Melun then got stolen …"

My chest felt crushed, still thinking of Gisèle's message and Peter's news; I couldn't breathe. "I don't *care* who owned it."

"… We ran lots of DNA. And found someone bumped their nose against the driver's side window. Anyone who knew what he's doing would've wiped it off. But this guy didn't."

I sat, watched him. "*Who?*"

"Tariq," Thierry smiled. "He of the broken jaw and two missing teeth."

I exhaled. "It's enough to bring him in –"

"But *do* we?"

I leaned at him. "We know Tariq was in on Bruno's killing. Now we know he was one of Gisèle's keepers."

"And he's Abdel's brother."

"Abdel who talks to Mustafa."

"Who talks to Rachid."

"Who talks to Élysée and all that crowd …"

It was beginning to tie together. Slowly we were drawing a net around Mustafa. But we didn't have time for *slowly*, not with the Iranian bombmaker circling closer, an attack coming on the Tower, and Mack and Gisèle on the knife edge.

Though for the first time I had a slight feeling of optimism: *We're closing in* … "Let's get him," I said.

Thierry leaned back in his chair. "Think it through."

I paced to the window and stared angrily at the rain-drenched courtyard, the sad Paris sky, the gray stone walls. "Two options."

"I'm all ears."

"*One*, we only bring in Tariq. We've got him on two deals, Gisèle and Bruno. Or *Two*, we also bring in Nassim for the keffi-yeh DNA, and Abdel as a potential co-conspirator."

"We still need an Abdel-Rachid link." Thierry stood beside me staring out the rain-slick window; I watched his half-reflection in the glass, his face bitter with fear of the losses to come.

"What the fuck," I sighed, "do we do?"

"Nothing."

I nodded, turned from the window. Anyone we grabbed would never give us Mack and Gisèle, nor Mustafa. Mack and Gisèle would die and Mustafa would back off to wait a while and hit us again. And none of these bastards would even do time.

"I DO LOVE YOU, my chicken …" It was a gravelly deep voice, recorded perfectly by ATS surveillance.

"What are you going to *do* to me," she said, "tomorrow night?"

"I won't tell you now. You'll have an orgasm even thinking about it."

"Dirty Arab."

"I love it when you say that."

"That's why I *say* it."

"Dear friend, I *do* have a small favor to ask –"

"How many times have I *told* you," she giggled. "I *won't* do anal."

"You," he chuckled. "You are funny." His voice softened. "Can you put out some more good news for us?"

"What do I get?"

"You already know, little chicken, what you get … Here it is: I'm hearing, through the grapevine of course, a big Islamic event is coming very soon. Even bigger than Notre Dame. A protest against all this discrimination against us …"

She sighed. "It's about time."

"You must remind everyone about *why* we're forced to do these things, because of the yoke on our necks. The police violence, the discrimination, the prisons, the refusal to ban pork or teach our language in their schools ..."

"Everything you do makes things better."

"You can't source me on this, remember. It may be bigger than you think."

"Good."

"I'll give you more background soon. But to highlight our grievances, all the terrible things French culture does to ours, how they're arresting our young men, they don't respect our religion ..."

"It's true ..."

"Can you send something out tomorrow?" His voice grew seductive. "Like what would happen if Paris got hit by a meteor? But no one knew why?"

"I'll send it out. But you better be here tomorrow night."

"I'll be there ten-thirty, maybe eleven."

"I'll wait up, you big rooster. I'm going to bang your brains out."

"*Inshallah!*"

"*Inshallah!*" The phone died.

"His voice," I said. "When I chased those two guys in the Forest. The guy with the Maserati."

"Rachid, last night," Tomàs smiled. "Speaking to his beloved Élysée Pétain."

"Does he say the same stuff," I said, "to his three wives?"

Tomàs made a sour face. "I can you show you pictures. They're fat."

I checked my phone: "So what's the big Islamic event that's coming soon? When would that be?"

"Like if a meteor hit Paris?" Thierry checked his phone. "According to Rachid, about eleven-thirty tonight."

———

IN MUSTAFA'S MOSUL PRISON Mack and I had had no way to escape. Amid intensive security in an extremely hostile environment, we were taken out to be killed almost daily, then taunted with death and returned to our cells.

It was, I think, the seventh day. That's what, in any case, the later investigation determined. For me and Mack until then was an unending time of sorrow and pain, one torture after another, a rain of hatred poured down on us.

In SF we'd been taught the usual E&E regimes, Escape and Evasion, but they were little help. We were in two different cells – cells are not the word, they were four-foot tall concrete coffins in which you couldn't sit, lie down or stand. You squatted with your chin on your knees and your arms crossed or hanging along your sides; after a while your knees began to hurt so bad you couldn't stand even if that option were available. They thought it was funny, our jailers, and when they took us out to use the hole in the back yard they would kick us in the knees to prove how funny it was.

I had no contact with Mack, no way to reach anyone but the bearded men guarding my door, and then of course Mustafa and his buddies when they took us out to cut our throats or shoot us.

There was a water leak down the side of my little coffin that made a steady plunk plunk plunk on the floor next to my left foot. It was comforting, that sound, almost friendly like a ticking clock. By comparing it to my pulse, which in resting situations is about forty-eight beats a minute, I figured it made about sixty drops a minute, or three thousand six hundred beats an hour. In this way I measured the passing time, tried to take my mind off the agony in my knees and the pounding headache from being hit by the rifle butt.

Not that I felt sorry for myself. We, the Americans, had invaded Iraq in 2003 without, as the textbooks have it, any pretext. There were no Weapons of Mass Destruction, anybody with any experience already knew that.

I'd had no conflict with this shitty, sad little nation. Not a nation anyway, just a bunch of competing territories cobbled together by British and American oil companies.

I'd joined up after 9/11 to fight Al Qaeda in Afghanistan, but after barely a year there, when we were starting to win, we'd all been hijacked to Iraq by the GW/Cheney/Powell/Hillary pro-war cabal, and once the Iraqis started killing my friends I'd gotten locked into the conflict. But basically what US troops were trying to do now, when Mack and I had been captured, was to enforce some kind of peace among the battered remnants of poor Iraq, and we had little patience for those fanatics who wished to widen and continue the conflict. And in truth, once you've scraped the remains of a good friend off a cratered street you no longer have the desire to be neutral.

It was late afternoon, from the cast of the sun on the opposite concrete walls, when Mack and I were led out to be killed again. It was our fifth "execution," and maybe this one would be real. I hadn't eaten in days, my stomach contorted with fear, hunger, and dysentery. No matter how tough you are, how you have prepared yourself for death, it is still terrifying. You think of all the things you didn't do, all the joys; you misremember the sorrows.

Just Mack and me, shoved down on our knees before the camera as if it were a red-eyed god. Mustafa prancing with a big kitchen cleaver, swearing at us and spitting on our heads and calling us "idolatrous monkeys" and "kaffirs" and shit like that.

My heart thundered in my chest, I had trouble breathing, my mouth full of saliva that choked me when I tried to swallow.

He stood over me. "Say how sorry you are!"

I said nothing.

He kicked me in the face; I kept my balance, head down, saying nothing. Blood was running down the inside of my mouth; I would not spit it out and show he'd hurt me.

"Say it!" he yelled again. "How sorry you are."

It's a terrible temptation, when you know you're going to get hurt, to say what they want; your body begs for it. "I am sorry," I said, "for nothing."

He didn't kick me, instead turned to Mack. "You! You say it!"

Mack hunched, waiting for the kick. Mustafa swung the cleaver down and stopped it just under Mack's chin. He rested the blade against Mack's throat, yanked it sideways.

"You!" he called to me, "you can watch this – how I'm going to cut his throat, little at a time, let him drown in his own blood, yes?"

Mack said nothing, facing down. In some silly Hollywood movie, maybe the hero would say, "whatever turns you on" or something "courageous" like that. But in real life, when the blade's really against your throat, you're so terrified and traumatized and fighting to keep control and not give your fear away, not give this assassin a reason to gloat or feel good about himself, that you are speechless. Focused in these last instants on the beauty of life and the infinite sorrow of its loss.

Whatever doesn't kill you makes you stronger, the saying goes. Or can traumatize you for life. Make you jump at every passing car or unexpected footstep. Fourth of July fireworks make you feel you're being shot at, bombarded ... You go to any length to avoid this cele-bration, hide in the north woods, go abroad, or sit in a cellar smok-ing grass and listening to AC/DC to remind yourself what we should love most in life is freedom, love and sex, and what we should hate most is fakery, domination, murder and lies.

Mustafa didn't seem happy with our lack of response. He and his henchmen clearly wanted us to give in, to say something he could promote on the terrorist networks run on Facebook and Twitter and all those fools.

I feared he might kill us out of disappointment or anger, but he seemed almost resigned. Maybe being a terrorist isn't all it's cracked up to be. In any case, he ordered his fetid acolytes to untie the ropes linking our wrists to our ankles so we could stand.

As they led us back to our concrete coffins, Mack, just behind me, turned as if to call something back to Mustafa, an apology in Arabic, and as he did he bumped against me and in a quick down-ward motion cut the rope tying my wrists with something pinched between his thumb and forefinger and in the same motion handed it to me.

It took a half-second for me to realize what he'd done, that he'd handed me a broken piece of glass, as slowly, very slowly, the realization traveled from my fingers to my brain. He slapped his roped wrists against my back to remind me that we didn't have all day here, and though slow on the uptake I did the same, managing also to take a nice slice out of his wrist.

There we were, shambling down this corridor of doom with our hands no longer roped behind our backs. There was one bastard in front of us and two behind; you could smell their bad breath and bad teeth and unwashed clothes the way you can smell shit in the hippo cage at the zoo.

Not that we smelled any better.

We reached my cell, with Mack's just beyond. It was dark here, confined. One of the two bastards behind Mack fumbled keys at the lock of my cell; there's always time, in microseconds, to worry is this the best moment, but I didn't, simply reached around his neck and cut his throat with the glass as Mack grabbed the guy behind him and quickly poked out both his eyes and crushed his chin in one fast jab of his palm while I attended to the guy with the keys. In less than four seconds my first guy and the guy with the keys were bleeding out through cut throats and choking as they tried to yell and Mack's guy had slumped down the wall toward the floor. I gave him the same throat treatment as the others. We grabbed the keys and their guns – how stupid can you be to let jailers have guns?

"Where the fuck are we?" Mack whispered.

"Don't know. Let's find Mustafa."

"We do and we never get out. We get him later."

"Let's get him now." I knew this was crazy but I had to do it.

"No!" Mack grabbed my arm. "Let's put on their clothes."

It astounded me I hadn't thought of this. We stripped two of the three dead guys, tugged on their black pajamas over our own clothes, *wiping off the blood as best we could, squeezed all three into my little coffin and locked the door.*

At the end of this insalubrious corridor was a stairway that led to a door bathed in sunlight, and a minute later we were on a back alley in the wilds of Mosul, two more ragged Arabs in the throng.

"Where'd you get the glass?" I whispered as we padded along in our Arab flipflops.

"Some poor bastard left it in my cell. He was using it to write goodbye on the wall."

Watching for pursuit we made our way west toward the coalition zone, where we were almost shot by a nasty bunch of SAS who then hugged us nearly to death, poured a bottle of Oban down our throats and conducted us through low-level fire to our own nearest and dearest CO, ruthless Major Larraty, actually in tears to see us.

Twenty-one minutes later we led a group of fourteen SF back exactly to that building where we'd escaped, only to find it empty. Even the three corpses we'd left were gone.

No blood.

No Mustafa either.

At that moment I hardly cared, I was so happy Mack and I were free and alive. Then two weeks later when we were told that Mustafa had been killed by the French Foreign Legion north of Mosul, we were relieved and gratified. We didn't know, then, that it was another guy the Legion had killed, and that Mustafa had lived to slaughter many more people in the years to come.

And now in France I'd lost him once again.

And Mack and Gisèle too.

SURE DEATH

"DOCTOR DEATH is not on the flight from Teheran anymore," Thierry said.

"He's changed flights," Anne said.

"Or he's under another name? I'm looking at the manifest now. There's a Marcus Sulla ... Italian businessman. Traveling from Teheran to Paris."

Sulla I remembered was a powerful and ruthless Roman general and politician. Marcus could be Marcus Aurelius, two centuries later Rome's greatest emperor. But lots of Italians use those names. "Keep looking."

AT 20:45 I hit Les Andelys. Alone, in the Beast as promised. No wires, no transmitter, just my Glock and Kabar clipped under the Beast's back fender, my iPhone, mike and earbud in my pocket so I'd be there for their call. Plus my normal smelly self. Sweating because I was so scared.

So many times I've risked death. You have to do it with a

certain confidence. But now I wasn't confident. I truly feared I wasn't going to survive. Or Gisèle either.

Anne and I had exchanged goodbyes in our usual tough way. *We've had a few nice fucks*, I'd said, *and now I'm going to die.*

I'll find you in the next life, she'd answered. *We'll live in peace then.*

The pain in her eyes was atrocious. I held her face in my hands – *how like the human heart our face is* – distilling into this last look all my love for her and for all of life, praying for her to be happy, live deeply, the kids too ...

I felt bad for sneaking out on Thierry, Tomàs and Harris. But they would've somehow wired me, tagged me, backed me up. And Mustafa's people would've known, particularly since they were tracking us. And everybody would've died.

On my left, the Seine was high and silvery under the nascent moon. The ancient stone houses along its banks glistened in the ancient yellow streetlamps. King Richard's island loomed huge and dark amid the roiling water. I thought of the couple who'd lived there in that beautiful solitude then died at Auschwitz, their paintings stolen by the Germans.

The world seemed a very dangerous, predatory place.

Highway to Hell on my phone. "It's me," Gisèle said.

"Holy shit it's you." I could barely speak. "Are you okay? Is Mack?"

"Drive on Avenue de Gaulle toward Grand Andely."

As I did a set of headlights swung in behind me, and then a motorcycle's single beam.

My heart was thundering, sweat running down my wrists. *You have to manage this fear*, I told myself. *Or it will kill you.*

It's very hard to manage fear. To stop shaking when you're terrified. The cold fire in your gut that keeps rising up your throat. Your knees so weak it's hard to push down the accelerator.

"Take the next road to the right."

This one I knew, it headed past the fountain blessed in 791 by Queen Clotilde, wife of Charlemagne, the grandson of Charles Martel who had defeated the Islamic invasion at Tours. The road turned up the hill east of the town. There were lots of lonely curves with a long drop on one side.

The headlights stayed behind me. I began to hope what would happen next, and yes, at the top of the hill Gisèle said, "Turn right past the soccer field."

Ahead there was only one place: King Richard's castle.

Chateau Gaillard.

Gaillard means tough, robust, often used for large, fearless men. It was Richard's most advanced castle, based on what he'd seen in the Holy Land and like the one where he'd been imprisoned at Dürnstein in Austria.

And now I was driving toward it with my high beams picking out the white blossoms of the cherry trees on both sides of the narrow road.

We entered the forest, dark and high, my headlights tunneled as if undersea. I feared this was a runaround, and now they'd send me somewhere else. The road turned left down a wide, open hill with Chateau Gaillard on the crest beyond it.

"Park in the lot below the castle," Gisèle said.

"I'm not walking into that. It's a trap."

"No one will bother you there. We have their word."

Instead I pulled the Beast off the road where a skinny path switchbacks up to the castle. "Where are you?"

"*Run!*" she screamed. A thump on flesh, hiss of a fallen phone.

"Where are you? Say it quick!"

"Stables!"

I leaped out, grabbed the Glock and Kabar from under the back fender and ran up the hill. It was very steep and open and anyone with a night vision scope could have hit me easily.

They didn't. For an instant I halted, gasping, to check my

back trail then dashed left uphill into the trees and sprinted to the ridge. The castle was now in front of and below me, huge and unassailable on its vertical promontory over the Seine. But a string of trees led down to its left side, the tall wall where over 800 years ago the French attackers had climbed to the privy holes at the top and squirmed through them, and so took this impenetrable castle from within.

The privy holes at the top of the wall hadn't been used in hundreds of years. The stone blocks of the wall varied between one- and four-foot rectangles, and over time had developed nice creases between them where the medieval mortar had eroded away.

After having downclimbed the wall of Anne's apartment building, chasing the guy who'd come to kill her, I was less uptight about heights. And here I had good finger grips and toe-holds and soon climbed the wall's 150 feet, wormed through a privy hole and hid in a dark corner of a *meurtrière* – the slot where you fire arrows down on unruly visitors below.

My phone vibrated: Gisèle. "They still want to do this," she half-sobbed. "Once you show yourself in the courtyard, they let me go. I can run down the hill and disappear into town. Then you will give yourself up to them."

"Agreed."

But I was already above them and they didn't know it. They'd expect me to come from below up the open hill toward the outside walls. But I'd already be in the stables, hunting them.

I crossed forty feet of open stone blocks to a parapet that circled the inner walls, and cautiously scanned the open land below down to the road. I saw no sign of anyone nor any cars in the lot.

The rough stone under my palm was cold and wet with Seine fog. The few yellow lights of the town below blinked in and out of the mist, the ancient stone façades appearing and vanishing as in a dream. Even at this distance you could hear the Seine rushing madly along its banks, making everything else more danger-ously silent.

I had to know how many of them there were. And where were the ones whose headlights had followed me?

In the best of all possible worlds you take each one silently so the others aren't warned. In a shootout usually everybody loses, and Gisèle would be the first.

If there were three of them it might be possible. Five would be too many. Sure death.

From where I stood a stone staircase dropped to the next level, a broad paved inner courtyard. Below that in a narrow stone trench were the stables. Eight hundred years ago they had been chiseled out of the solid rock beneath the courtyard, ten of them.

The trench of the stables had two staircases back up to the courtyard, one at each end. If I came down either I'd risk being seen. It was a twenty-foot drop from the courtyard to the stable floor, enough to risk an ankle that would screw up the whole deal.

It was another climbdown.

A cascade of ivy snaked up the corner of two walls. I didn't want that to hold on to; it's too frail and wouldn't carry a per-son's weight. But by descending the wall next to it I'd be more difficult to see.

Staying in the shadows I circled the courtyard to the wall of ivy. Below, at the far end of the stables, a dark form crossed the white limestone of a stable entrance. Wishing I'd brought night goggles, I slid along the wall to the ivy and climbed down beside it to the floor of the stable trench.

There were ten stable openings cut into the stone. I'd have to check each one, hoping to kill whoever was there one by one. In which was Gisèle?

The moon came from behind a cloud, splashing the trench with light. I ducked back against the wall till the clouds returned. With the Glock in my right hand and the Kabar in my left, I cleared the first three stables, nothing inside but rank stone, old straw and bad memories.

Three dark shapes crossed from the far stable to the stairs up to the courtyard, then up another level to the parapet, where they leaned out over the wall scanning the open slope below.

Within a minute they'd realize I wasn't coming up the hill and my chance of getting Gisèle would be gone. Ducking low I fast-checked the following two stables then heard a voice from the next, in Arabic, "Kill the dirty apostate," or something like that. "Yes," she answered in a bruised voice, "you do that."

"What, slut, you don't be*lieve* me?"

Then two other voices, from the further stable.

Gisèle was alone in this one with a nasty proselytizer. I slid to the door, dropped to the ground and glanced around the corner.

In the penumbra all I could see was a shape standing before another reclining form.

"It is written," the voice continued. "And *still* you don't believe?"

"Tell me." Her voice changed. "Come closer, teach me to believe."

I was across the floor in less than a second and drove my knife deep into his throat and pinned him to the floor till he bled out and stopped twitching and choking.

"I saw you, in the corner," she whispered. "That's why I said what I did."

I held her for an instant, gloriously happy. "How many others?"

"Three in the next room. Plus whoever's looking for you down below."

She was pinned spread-legged against the wall by barbed wire tying her wrists to two rusty steel rings in the walls. Two more coils of barbed wire from her ankles to steel pins in the stone floor.

I unwrapped her wrists and she pushed down her skirt and bent over to unwind one ankle while I did the other.

"Where's Mack?" I whispered.

"They had us together, I think Saint-Denis."

"How could you tell?"

"Cathedral bells. Maybe a mile. North north-east."

"Where's Mustafa?"

"Not here."

I pulled her up. "Wait!" She tore a strip off the dead man's shirt, grabbed two empty plastic water bottles off the floor.

"What the fuck?" I snapped.

"DNA."

We eased up the stairs to the courtyard and out a side gate to the exterior moat, where 800 years ago hundreds of people had starved to death in the French siege. On the open slope below four headlamps were dashing back and forth.

They'd be watching the Beast so we couldn't chance it. Instead we slipped and slid down through the sumacs and young oaks of the near-vertical slopes below the castle, and reached the main road out of town where I got Anne on the phone.

"You're alive!" she kept saying, "Oh Christ you're alive. And Gisèle too ... *Mon Dieu* ... Where's Mack?"

"Two days ago they had him in what Gisèle thinks is an industrial building maybe in Seine-St. Denis."

"Parameters?"

"She could hear cathedral bells. Half a mile maybe. North north-east."

"Lemme talk to her."

I handed Gisèle the phone. Anne's excited voice and Gisèle saying, "God bless you, thank you ... Yes, I think it was an industrial building ... No, nothing else I can think of ... Except ..."

I watched her, intense. Knew this was something.

"A bus went by. During the morning every seventeen minutes. I counted the time with my heartbeat. Then in the middle of the day thirty-five minutes. Late afternoon till maybe seven, every nine minutes ... Don't know if that helps."

Anne's voice was ecstatic. "Of course it helps!"

"Other people lived there too," Gisèle went on, "like it was a *squat*?"

"Tomàs'll find it," Anne said. "Then we move in."

"Go in fast and quiet," Gisèle said. "Don't let him die now."

"Remember," Anne asked me when Gisèle handed me back the phone, "when I said *Take tomorrow off*?"

"Of course."

"He's coming for you. A 2004 green Citroën Xsara. We'll let you know what we learn. If it's a takedown we'll do it fast, before they know what we know."

Seven minutes later *Take tomorrow off* arrived and we stepped out of the shadows by the municipal swimming pool. A seedy guy about thirty-five wearing the OGC Nice shirt, who didn't say a word the whole way. In the back I held Gisèle's hand but didn't dare say much in case the guy spoke English, she squeezing my fingers in affection and pain, tears trickling down her bruised cheeks.

Now all I could think about was stopping Mustafa before he killed Mack.

SMALL PLEASURE

"WE'RE MOVING FAST," Thierry said. "131 Rue Beaumont in Stains, two blocks from the Al Rawda mosque."

I turned to watch out the car window at our slow progress on the Autoroute. "They'll have a hundred assault rifles in that block. We go in hard we'll get shot to pieces."

He sighed agreement, a gravelly fatigue, trying to get it up for one last battle.

"Thierry," I said, "we have to *win* this one."

"Mustafa doesn't know we know about this. Thanks to Gisèle's amazing self-control and memory. So if Mack's there ..."

Thierry was the team-leader at exfils. When we had guys down or missing he took over, with his particular intensity and lack of fear. With Thierry we never lost an MIA.

Not once.

Now he had to do it again.

"We go in quick with flashbangs and everything else and hope to save him ..." His voice waned, or maybe it was just the traffic as our wordless driver left the Route Nationale for the A13 toll highway.

"Or?" I waited.

"Or we try this new technique. Put everyone to sleep. Then go in."

I hadn't heard of this. "Don't ask," Thierry said. "Let me decide."

"What you think?" I said to Anne.

She had to yell over the roar of the Indian. "We can't risk a big crowd. I'll go in first."

I realized she'd get killed, right when we were close to winning.

"Wait for me!" I snarled.

"I'll be there first!"

"Mustafa, suppose he's there?"

"He knows by now you escaped," she said. "And you're trying to find Mack …"

"But he doesn't know we *know* where Mack is –"

"So I go in fast."

"Pono, where are you?" Thierry said.

I looked out the window. "Mantes."

"Grab the A14 north of Paris to the A86 and we'll meet you in Stains."

"Ten minutes, we'll be there."

"Ten minutes," Anne said over the Indian's howl. "Me too."

"Don't go in by yourself," I said.

"Fuck you."

What if I not only didn't save Mack, but lost Anne? I pulled a dirty trick. "Julie and André, they going to like growing up alone?"

"Fuck you!" she repeated, and I could tell by her sharp voice she was driving too fast, trying to get there before me.

"Wait for us," Thierry snapped, but she'd signed off.

"I want you doing 180!" I yelled at our driver in French. "I want you there *in seven minutes!*"

———

AN OLD tattered warehouse from the 1950s, back when this area was part of France. We pulled in a block away. The streets ahead were dark.

23:20. It seemed the night had lasted forever and it wasn't even midnight. I called Anne. "Where are you?"

"Two blocks away. Parked the bike. Coming."

Lights in three warehouse windows. A smell of meat cooking over a fire, chatter of Arabic radio.

"They don't have a clue," I whispered.

"Who doesn't?" Gisèle said anxiously.

"We're on our way," Thierry answered. "Wait for us."

"Stay in the car. I'll send people to get you," I told Gisèle, got out and bent to the driver's window. "Stay with her."

Anne came up beside me, nodded at the warehouse. "Let's go in."

She was all in black Kevlar, Garand in her hand.

I felt intense, perfectly on target.

"Don't either of us die," she said.

There was no front door. We ducked inside and stepped carefully across a cavernous dark area littered with refuse to a dark metal stairway where the cooked meat smell and Arabic radio was coming from.

I had a feeling it might work, but that I might die. That it was out of our control.

I eased softly down the metal stairs, Anne ten feet behind me. She had the automatic rifle so she'd take care of crowds while I dealt with finding Mack and killing Mustafa.

It wasn't Arabic radio but two men arguing on a speakerphone with someone. In an open space that seemed in firelight to have hangar doors on the left and office doors on the right. "How do you know?" one yelled. "How do you *know* they *don't* know?"

The fire was of broken pallet wood in the middle of the floor, two other men holding chunks of mutton over it, a dead sheep half-disemboweled behind them.

The voice I'd just heard was familiar from the surveillance tapes. Abdel, Mustafa's buddy from St. Denis.

"Kill the one you have," the phone voice said. "Before things get worse."

"Mustafa, he wants the other American first ... What he always wanted. Now that we have this one ..."

"Tell him we don't always get everything we wish, even if we're good Muslims. Even if we do *jihad* and kill the infidel. Kill this one you have, and Allah will reward you." The voice on the phone I now recognized too: Rachid. "Since," he went on, "you let the wife get away."

"She was a slut," Abdel said. "Everyone fucked her."

"Did you?"

"Of course. In front of the husband. We all did."

"Thank Allah for that small pleasure. Kill the husband now and take the escape route we've given you. Tell Mustafa not to worry, he will kill the other American some other day. Allah will bring him to him."

I could make them out now, Abdel and another hunched over a cell phone in the chiaroscuro of firelight against concrete.

Plus two others at the fire.

"Let's kill him now," one of the voices at the fire called. "And get out of here."

Abdel and the other man with the phone were still arguing with Rachid so it was easy to come up on them. I shot them both in the head from twenty yards, Anne's automatic rifle picked up the two at the fire and tumbled them halfway across the room.

I sprinted to the first office door and kicked it down. Nothing.

The second. Nothing.

Mack lay in the third, on his side on the floor, wrists and ankles tied. I thought he was dead, till he spoke, voice harsh with pain.

"You asshole," he groaned. "Why'd it take you so long?"

P R E Y

"THE PLANE FROM TEHERAN," Tomàs said on the radio, "Doctor Death's not on it."

"Where is he?" Thierry said. He'd arrived just after we'd sent Mack and Gisèle in an unmarked ambulance to a safe-house clinic in Neuilly. We were huddled outside the warehouse in a kaleidoscope of flashing lights while the forensics and other folks went in and out taking pictures and samples and putting little yellow numbered cones by each spent cartridge.

"They don't know," Tomàs said.

"They?"

"Teheran. And I don't think they're lying."

"You believe them?" Harris's voice rattled the radio. We'd called him instantly to say Mack and Gisèle were safe. "Turn the plane back," he said.

"Our folks say no," Thierry countered. "Teheran cleared the passenger list. Asking the plane to turn back is a provocation. And with billions in oil and weapons deals in up in the air right now between France and Iran because of American boycotts – even Renault factories – our government sees their point."

"It's your damn Tower," Harris said. "Your damn city."

I imagined the plane descending over the Seine, past the blackened shell of Notre Dame, La Conciergerie, the Louvre, the Concorde, the Tower rising above straight ahead, the two pilots in the cockpit raging and desperate: nothing they could do would change anything.

"Can't you send up Rafales," I said, "to block it?"

"You want we shoot it down, with two hundred seventy people? And hundreds more on the ground? For maybe nothing?"

"If the bomb hits CDG, a small nuke won't do much damage to Paris," I said. "Won't take down the Tower."

"It'll wreck everything north of Paris for a thousand years, and kill a million people."

It was insane to compare likely deaths, to choose the fewest possible.

Thierry's phone rang. He listened a minute, said, "Okay," and hung up. He looked down at the phone a moment, then up at us. "Doctor Death *is* on that plane."

"How?" Anne stuttered. "What?"

"Turns out Marcus Sulla has a Quds file."

I felt furious we hadn't figured this out before. Tried to think of everything we had to do. "How long we got?"

"Ninety minutes. At most."

"You have to scramble interception!" I insisted.

"No." He seemed lost in thought, came back to us. "Government thinks we're crying wolf. That we're anti-Islamic, causing trouble and getting in the way of multiculturalism."

I sat on a wall looking through the treetops and smog to the clouds over Paris, all ablaze with city lights.

When my phone buzzed it was Tomàs again. "You know the latest?" I started to say.

"Forget that, we got the real deal. A camera on La Motte-Picquet caught a guy who looks like Mustafa. Headed toward the Tower with a big backpack."

Breathing deep, I tried to think. "How big a backpack?"

"Big enough for a small bomb. Or a transponder with a fold-out antenna."

Like the backpack Mustafa had been carrying when I followed him through Fontainebleau Forest. "See you there."

"Wait for me!" Anne yelled.

"Where's your damn bike?"

We roared from the warehouse across Seine St. Denis to the Seventh and Avenue Rapp three blocks from the Tower. "Maybe it's not him," she said, out of breath. "Just some tourist with a backpack."

I glanced up at the Tower brazen with lights. Turned my half-blinded eyes back to the Champ, a sea of pathways like a blurry black-and-white film. Mustafa could be anywhere out there. With his evil weapon ready to bring death down on the world.

Anne and I split up as we had the night before, one on each side of the Champ. "If you grab him," Thierry said on the radio, "and that backpack's live it'll blow us all to kingdom come."

"Is it a bomb, or a transponder to bring the plane in?" In my earbud I could hear Anne breathing, the rustle of her clothes, her quickening footsteps. And in the background Thierry's quiet inhalations, the scrape of cloth on leather.

"I've warned the Tower guards, the Army *Sentinelles,*" Thierry said. "Everyone's looking for him. Got three squads of RAID on the way."

"Where's the plane?"

"On its way."

The city hushed, darkened, the air damp and foul. The streets lonely and miserable, empty of promise. A cop car wailed, faraway; another answered.

I returned to La Motte-Picquet, named for the French admiral whose navy helped the new United States win the Revolutionary War.

TO HUNT A DANGEROUS PERSON is traumatic. Not only was I hunting someone who could kill me, *wanted* to kill me, could kill many people tonight, maybe this whole city, if we didn't stop him. I reassured myself that there were two hundred other very well-trained folks here who would probably be the ones to catch or kill him. But I felt somehow it was going to come down to me and him.

And it's traumatic because you're trying to kill someone. As in all battle moments – those most horrible of times – you fear instant death, or a gory one, and you hunger to kill to end this fear.

It takes years off your life. My Pa died of it. It's acid in the gut, a dry mouth and loss of breath, a savoring of every moment heightened by the deadly knowledge of how fast it could end.

From weeks of little sleep and frequent risk I was so tired it felt like death. A transcendent zone like an overdose of those pills the Army gives you to fight without sleep. Everything's in a white light and very clear and you can see danger on the other side of a wall – you *feel* it. Not just sight and sound and touch but you actually *feel* it.

High on the drug of danger, to oneself and the world. You walk a razor edge over an indefinable height, a grand canyon of death, your prey on the same razor edge.

At Avenue Duquesne I saw a tall guy with a backpack duck into the Café des Officiers opposite École Militaire. I dashed across Duquesne against the light getting nearly smacked by a rampant taxi.

I couldn't see the inside through the café's misted windows.

Two double glass doors faced the patio of empty tables and chairs. No way to get inside without being seen.

But no reason to call Thierry till I verified this. Because by the time everybody showed up my prey would be gone.

In my throat that sweet taste of danger and revenge. A savoring mixed with fear. I checked the Glock – ready. The knife – good.

I looked down the side alley, keeping my eye on the front. Three quarters of the way down was the vertical black block of a doorway. At the end of the alley a brick wall: anyone coming out that door would have to turn this way, toward the front.

Palm loosely over the Glock under my black jacket, I eased the glass door open and slipped into the room. It was large and well-lit, forty tables maybe, mostly four or six chairs, a few large booths in the back, and tables for two along the windows.

Three people at a booth, gray-haired, overweight. Tourists. A couple at a window table holding hands across a clutter of wine and brandy glasses. A black waiter in a white smock, fatigue on his face as he stood over a table of four while one of them punched a code into his card reader.

Where was my guy? The backpack? No one at the cash register. Voices in the back kitchen, dishwashing machines and clatter.

No backpack near the loving couple. None by the booth of three tourists. I stepped around a chair for a better look at the table of four. Nothing there.

"Restaurant is closed, Monsieur," the waiter said.

Could my guy have gone out the back that fast? I raced outside to the head of the alley: no one. Dashed back inside. "Monsieur," the waiter said. "The restaurant is closed."

"Looking for someone." I pushed through swinging doors into a kitchen awash with sudden light and stainless steel. Two guys at the sinks, another putting something in the refrigerator, all in kitchen hats.

I ran back to the main room. The waiter was at the register, raising his hands to chase me out.

"Where are you?" Thierry said into my earbud.

"Cop!" I told the waiter, showed my DGSE badge. "I'm at La Motte-Picquet and Duquesne," I said to Thierry. "Guy went into this café with a backpack. Vanished."

"Idiot, you should've called. I'll send some folks."

"I'm coming!" Anne broke in.

A door flashed open at the back of the room. Toilets. A tall dark young woman with black pigtails, carrying a backpack. A wandering tourist washing up for a night on a bench somewhere, under a blanket in a doorway, over a Métro grate.

"Which side of La Motte-Picquet?" Thierry barked.

"Negative," I said. "A hippie tourist." I blocked her, held out my DGSE card. "I'm a cop. I need to look in your bag."

She gave me a wild, blue-eyed stare, stepped back, crinkled her nose to peer at the badge, said something incomprehensible, possibly Scandinavian. I pointed at her backpack, that I had to look in it. "Terrorist Police!" I said in English.

"Why didn't you say so?" she snapped back in English, slung off the pack. Inside it a jumble of smelly clothes, boots, cheese, cookies, toothbrush, ham and a half-bottle of Grand Marnier. A few battered books, an unused bar of soap. A sleeping bag and pad slung underneath, wrapped in a blue poncho.

"Where you going tonight?" I had to ask. How quickly one becomes cop.

She shrugged.

"Go to the Préfecture on Rue Fabert. It's just on the other side of Les Invalides. They'll find you a place." I turned to hurry back to the sidewalk. "Paris isn't safe at night."

"What was that all about?" Anne said.

"False alarm."

"Keep your eyes on the target, Pono."

"So what have *you* come up with?" I said angrily.

"No one," Thierry answered, in his voice the resignation that prefaces a bad time to come.

"He's out there somewhere," I said.

"Really?" she said. "How do you know?"

I waited for the light to cross La Motte-Picquet and turned down La Bourdonnais toward the Seine, feeling Mustafa ahead of me, waiting to attack.

Thierry came back on. "The plane's now due at CDG in fifty-one minutes."

"What do you *mean*?" I yelled. "Dropped off what screen?"

"Not on the approach path ..."

"If it's heading for the Tower you have to shoot it down."

"If it goes down it'll kill thousands of people. And everyone on board. Including that murderous bastard Marcus Sulla." Thierry sounded almost astounded, or as if about to laugh. At the insane horror of it all, perhaps. That we could do nothing. It didn't matter that in fifty minutes we'd all die too.

If I saw Mustafa I'd grab him. If he blew us up, as Anne would say, *tant pis*. Plus there were undercover cops here as well as *Sentinelle* soldiers, with Anne backing me up and Thierry on the earbud sending in reinforcements. No way we wouldn't get him, if he was here.

My earbud kept slipping out and I shoved it back in. "So far," I said, "not a thing."

"Nothing," Anne said on the other side of the Champ.

I took an empty breath. Mustafa was near. I could *feel* him. This might soon be over.

I turned southwest along the same alley of trees where Anne and I had hunted him last night, back toward the École Militaire, its splendid stone façade gilded by spotlights.

The gravel path felt good underfoot. A soft wind angled across my cheek, smelling of rotten leaves, wet dirt, the city's effluents.

No one had come; I ran to the corner and down the stairs of the Métro *École Militaire* through the tunnel under Place Joffre and back up to La Bourdonnais, into a side street and down an alley onto Rue St. Dominique, and back to the Tower.

A few bums, late drunks and lovers. No one who looked like Mustafa or carried a backpack.

Keeping in the shadows I swung toward the Seine, then right on Rue Montessuy away from the Tower. I could feel Mustafa's presence even stronger, the way I've felt the presence of a dangerous snake in the darkness or of someone sneaking up behind me.

"No one." I glanced at the watchful cops, the dark steel soaring into the fractured night.

Weariness overwhelmed me, my knees weak, arms feeble. When I sucked in a breath it did nothing. The pavement hard, unforgiving. The few headlights burned my eyes.

Halfway down Rue Montessuy a guy was disappearing around the far sidewalk onto Avenue Rapp. Something furtive, not because of his gait, which was forward and fast. Not his posture, it was tall and hard, bent forward by a rectangular pack on his back.

It was like tasting death.

I sprinted to Rapp and trotted along it but couldn't see him anywhere – after misreading the girl with the backpack had I confused this too? Or chased him the wrong way?

Across Rapp a street split into three – three ways he could've gone, plus up or down Rapp made two more. You have one chance out of five.

"Maybe saw him," I said to Thierry. "He's gone around the corner of Montessuy up Rapp, something big on his back."

"I'll send folks."

I turned on Rue Genéral Camou back toward the Tower and there he was a block away loping across the La Bourdonnais away from me. I dashed to the corner, ducked a bus and sprinted across it. He turned, an instant of recognition and hate on his face and he was gone over a steel fence into the bushes around the Tower.

I leaped after him tugging my Glock from the holster.

The bushes were prickly and stank of hemlock, piss, rats and mud. I pushed through them where I'd thought he'd gone, found nothing, crossed back and forth but could see no fresh footprints. I holstered the Glock, crawled out of the bushes and stood in an alley facing the Tower and he was fifty yards away hopping over the Tower's steel fence.

I ran toward him; he saw me and sprinted for the Tower. I reached for the mike to tell Anne and Thierry but it wasn't there.

I'd lost it in the bushes. If I went back to find it, I'd lose Mustafa.

DESCEND AT ONCE

HE HURDLED THE LAST barrier and sprinted across the half-lit esplanade to the northwest pillar and scrambled up it.

I was fifty yards behind closing in fast as he reached the lower horizontal steel brace a hundred feet up.

I climbed fast, my shoulder dislocating. The pain was bad. Each new wrenching of the arm from the socket made it worse; I couldn't pull up on it, had to hang swinging wildly over the abyss till the other hand found a grip. The slippery cold steel stank of rain, mildew and rust, numbed my fingers and stung my jaw when it pressed against it.

Thierry and the police and soldiers down below looked tiny as they yelled and gestured up. Above me the Tower gleamed balefully in the dark shadows cast by the city lights, Mustafa's dark form escalading up it.

As I climbed looking for handholds, almost biting the steel to hang on, gritting my teeth against awful pain in my shoulder, I realized he would have to put the transponder beneath the first floor because the cops were already up there and he wouldn't get past them. Already I could see the flashing black of uniforms scaling down to meet us.

A searchlight caught him, white on black; he gleamed, almost incandescent. "Mustafa al-Boudienne," a megaphone intoned from below. "Descend at once. Or you will be shot."

He swung inside the near-vertical steel and kept scrambling upward. Despite the shoulder pain I'd gained on him, or was he slowing to turn on the transponder? Might the GIGN snipers below mistake me for him? I had no radio contact; did they think I was a second terrorist?

He stopped. I was ten feet below him. We were nearly vertical now, the steel like ice, slippery as wet glass. The ground so far below swum dizzily when I looked down, the people tiny. "You, the second climber!" a megaphone intoned. "Descend at once!"

"Mustafa!" I called. "Mack is safe. His wife too."

"No matter," he yelled. "We have poisoned their hearts." He tugged a pistol from his shirt. "They will die of it."

"You thought you'd kill Mack and me, but you won't."

"The plane is coming. You will die. All of you."

I ducked inside the girder as the bullet smashed off it; he swung inside to get another shot and I ducked outside, lost footing and fell, dangling on the dislocated shoulder and swinging my feet crazily back and forth for a hold as his bullets wailed past me.

My toe caught a grip, then my other foot and I swung toward the girder intending to jump and hoping to catch it. Each time the gun roared I flinched expecting to be hit, and flinching made me almost fall; one bullet seared my cheek and another knocked a piece off the girder by my foot.

"The second climber!" the megaphone snapped again. "*Descendez!*"

Mustafa slid outside to angle down a shot at me; I was already moving and couldn't stop and there was no way he'd miss. He took another shot and hugged the Tower to reload his gun. As I climbed toward him I could hear his harsh breathing and the clink of metal on steel.

With a huge whack a bullet caromed off the steel by my hand; another sparked above Mustafa's head. I swung out over the abyss to yell down, "Don't shoot, I'm DGSE" – a lie, but understandable in the circumstances.

With one arm gripped around a girder I aimed the Glock at his chest and fired. The bullet knocked him loose but he grabbed hold again and shot back; the bullet sucked past my ear. I fired again, his body jerked and he leaped down the Tower straight at me.

In the millisecond before he hit I considered my alternatives – there wasn't time to duck inside the girder – so I held on with all the power of numb hands and fingers, my body and face pressed to steel. When he hit me with the backpack first it was like a truck that knocked me off the Tower but for the injured arm dangling again by its ruined shoulder as for the third time the megaphone snarled, "You, the second climber! Descend at once *or you will be shot!*"

Expecting to die, I swung inward on the damaged arm and found footing, then dove for the pillar below, grabbed it and started down its intricate latticework as best I could, terrified of the height or that they'd shoot me before I got down, or that the backpack would activate before they could stop it.

I'd killed Mustafa and his body and the backpack were down there somewhere. Mack and Gisèle were alive. But all I could feel was sick and relieved and afraid of falling off this slippery cold steel.

AT A COUPLE hundred feet above the ground I called down and Thierry yelled, "We have you!" I slowed, watching holds and footholds carefully, for in my sad experience the closer you are to safety the more you're in danger.

"The plane?" I yelled when I hit the ground.

"Twenty minutes. Descended to eight hundred meters, coming straight for the Tower."

"The backpack?"

"A transponder ... We're trying to shut it off." He pointed and I ran to it.

Two RAID guys had yanked the backpack off Mustafa's body, had broken off the cover and were trying to follow wires by the light of their headlamps.

"Get back!" I yelled.

"Who the fuck are you?"

They jumped aside as I emptied the rest of my Glock into the transponder, hitting what seemed to be a timer, some connections, two round metal canisters. They knocked the Glock from my hand, making my shoulder scream with pain.

Thierry ran up yelling, "He's DGSE!" His headphone buzzed and he turned away. I bent over, the hand of my good arm gripping my right knee, the other arm dangling as I tried to breathe fast and survive the pain.

I looked down at Mustafa's lifeless, battered face and tried not to throw up.

It wasn't Mustafa.

THIERRY TURNED back to me. "That was Tomàs. The plane's still coming. Fifteen minutes."

I ran to an elevator and punched the button for the top of the Tower, scanning the girders all the way up, knowing I'd reached the end and failed.

At the top I tried to slow my breathing, forget the agony in my shoulder, remind myself we'd saved Mack and Gisèle and killed their captors.

But was the plane still coming. Or would it pull away, now that I'd destroyed the transponder?

Was there a bomb?

Or had all of this just been a farce? A gambit to distract us while they laid a trap elsewhere?

I was so weary I told myself I didn't care. Just to lie down. Even for a moment. I scanned the wide top floor, seeing nothing but cops and soldiers. Lots of guns. We humans so in love with guns. Can't live without them.

I wanted to lie down and sleep forever.

We got Mack and Gisèle back, I told myself. And might have killed the guys who killed Bruno.

But if the plane hit, everyone on the Tower would die.

Anne was down below, would probably die too. The domestic life. Love and children. What more is there?

Finding Mustafa.

It felt, irrationally, that he was already here. That he'd *been* here, watching us enact that comedy on the ground, the attempt to kill me, my shooting his acolyte with the transponder that I'd then shattered with five rounds from my Glock.

I grabbed the elevator for the trip down. A cop in a black face mask was already there, seemed surprised to see me. A yellow *Police* armband over his black jacket, Sig at the waist, the usual accoutrement of nightstick, radio, whistle, handcuffs and Mace. A big black plastic case at his feet, the kind for carrying battery-powered lights. The doors hissed shut and we started down.

The drop dizzied me. I felt asleep on my feet.

We lurched to a stop. I looked out expecting to see the second floor. But we were still above it, halfway down in a near-vertical chute.

Like in a dream I tried to wake up. The cop in the black mask had his Sig aimed at me.

He pulled down his mask. Mustafa.

"Even if Mack did get away," he hissed, "instead I have you."

All our efforts, I realized, had been in vain. Evil, in the long run, will always win. The plane would hit the Tower and Paris would blow. He'd shoot me before I could stop him. It was like being buried alive, six feet under, breathlessly scrabbling at the concrete wall of your casket.

The car's speaker crackled. "Pono?" Thierry's voice. "You there?"

"Unfortunately," I said, watching Mustafa.

"The plane's four minutes away. Still on a strike path."

"I'm in this elevator car with Mustafa. He's got a gun on me and he's got a transponder."

"What? Oh *Jesus*! How?"

"Doesn't matter. He's stopped the car. Bring cars from above and below to assault this one. Guys will have to climb outside, blow the doors off."

"No time." Mustafa smiled the way he'd always done in my nightmares, before signing off with *"Inshallah."*

"Cars on the way," Thierry said.

"How long till the plane hits?" I answered.

"Three minutes. No, two minutes forty-seven seconds."

"No time." Mustafa patted the black plastic case. "This little box will bring that plane right here. It can go nowhere else. It will smash us to atoms, evaporate this tower. *See*, it *is* God's will."

"You mean the bomb?"

"You are well informed. It's in the plane's baggage. Because the passenger is a diplomat it wasn't security checked."

"But he's traveling as Marcus Sulla. Not a diplomat."

Mustafa gave me a congratulatory wink. "But, you see, due to his prominence in Iran, Marcus Sulla is treated as a diplomat."

Every second I could delay him, the better my nonexistent chances. "So why Rachid? Is *he* running you?"

Mustafa snickered, looked at the speaker in the corner of the ceiling, said nothing.

"Wasn't it Rachid you called 'Abu' the other night in

Fontainebleau Forest?" I expected this to shock him – how could he imagine I knew? But he stared at me with immobile black eyes, as if really watching somewhere else.

"What were you guys carrying in those backpacks, that night in the forest?"

He turned back to me. "You truly don't know? You are that stupid? In a few moments it will blow, and then, for the tiniest second, you will know."

The north wind came up, squeaking the elevator car on its cable. "*You* are the stupid one," I said. "*I* fooled you, in Les Andelys. *I* saved Gisèle."

He did nothing. Just watched me.

"*We* tracked you down," I went on. "*We* have your photos, your cell phone calls, know where you were – that bar near La République – Les Quatre Vents – we were ready to tie you up like the fat little pig you are, the useless, stupid pig ..."

It seemed I couldn't anger him. "Why are you doing this?" I added, trying to think of anything to divert him. "To the country that fed and educated and raised you ..."

He shook his head. "You have no chance."

"Yeah." I took a breath, tried not to look at the black plastic case. "I have no chance."

"None of you do. Not one of you." He swung the Sig wide, as if to include us all – me, the soldiers and police down below, the sleeping city, the world. "None at all."

The wind shook the car again as he swung the pistol to the side and I took my only chance and leaped at him as his bullet ripped pain across my left shoulder, numbing my arm so I couldn't grab his wrist with my left hand but reached across with my right and broke his wrist knocking the Sig away then drove the side of my right hand deep into his throat, his eyes bulging while his fists clawed at my face, his jaw shut and opened then the light went out of his eyes.

I dropped him and ran to the backpack.

Another elevator car bumped into mine from below.

"Got him," I told Thierry. "It's a transponder. Trying to disable it."

"Leave it alone!" he yelled. "For sure it's armed. Send you to Hell and lock the plane on the location. We have someone coming up beneath. Bomb engineer."

"They're here." I started to pry open the doors as three people in black with climbing gear clambered like spiders across the side of my car. The first commando waved me away from the door and blew it with an entry charge. "This it?" he said, moving toward the backpack. He slipped off his face mask and kneeled down to it, flipped it on its front and scanned its interior with a headlamp.

"No shit," he said.

I leaned over him, trying to hear after the blast. "No shit what?"

"Not made in Pakistan. From Iran."

"I don't give a fuck where from. Kill it!"

He yanked a phone from his vest, pushed in a few buttons and set it beside the main power line in the transponder. "Leave it there twenty seconds," he said. "Scramble its brain."

He glanced round the car, the towering darkness outside, the lights of the city far below, then at me. "This isn't the easiest job."

I looked down at dead Mustafa, the scrambled transponder. "I'm tired of it."

He smiled into my eyes. A knowledge shared that no one else has. Most of the time I don't even know it's there. But it links us all in ways I can't deny.

Sometimes I think it's worth it just for that.

Dizzy, I took a breath, caught myself. "Never again," he said.

"Yeah," I said. "Maybe never again."

TELL THE GODS

ANNE GRABBED ME as I stepped off the elevator.

"Get him to a hospital," the cop said.

"The plane's climbing!" Thierry yelled. "Back on airport approach."

I looked up at the silvery dark clouds. There, rising over Paris, the beautiful white needle of an Airbus gaining altitude, heading north toward CDG.

"What about the nuke?" I said.

"Doctor Death has one small carryon. No luggage, no bomb."

The bomb was a feint, had always been. There had been the transponder to pull the plane off course and into the Tower. I put my head down, from weariness, sorrow, relief and joy.

Anne held me. In my whole life I wondered if I'd ever been so happy.

Thierry hugged us. "Thank God," he whispered. "Thank God."

"What about Doctor Death?" I said.

"There's fifty GIGN waiting for him at the airport."

"They should kill him."

He laughed. "Not till we learn everything."

"We need to get you to a hospital," Anne snapped. "Your shoulder's bleeding. And that arm –"

I looked at it. It dangled down like a broken bough. Then the pain really hit.

NISA CALLED as I arrived at Bichat Hospital right off the Péréphérique. They tore off my shirt and swabbed the bullet crease in my left shoulder. One orthopedist after another tried inserting the right arm back into the shoulder but nothing worked. I asked for vodka and morphine and though they didn't have the first they gave me a lot of the second.

"I can't believe," Nisa said on my phone, her voice hoarse, "that you survived."

"We've been lucky." The intravenous morphine was hitting and I was in less pain and in love with the world. Most of it anyway.

"And up on the Tower, you didn't die ..." She cleared her throat. "You know, Pono, we live here, my husband and I and our kids, we're immigrants. This is a free country. There are no free Muslim countries. Here there is freedom, and opportunity if you work hard and are honest and care for others. That's why we came, or our parents did. We feel very grateful to be here ... It's awful when people come and hate it."

"Yeah. Things need to change," I said stupidly.

She gave a soft, sad chuckle. "Isn't it funny that so many of us try so hard to make a better world and it never happens."

"Yes it does happen, Nisa. All the time. *You* make it happen."

We said our goodbyes. My brain, flooded with morphine and the ecstatic release from pain, filled with emotion. I felt grace and joy for my life, for Anne, her kids, Mack and Gisèle, Thierry,

Nisa, Tomàs, all of us in the merry-go-round of danger and fear we'd just been through. And Harris, too, in his own way.

Two of the orthopedists were conferring worriedly in the corridor. A very young woman, slender and barely five-two, came down the corridor and broke into the conversation. She looked so young I figured she was what in the States we call a Candy Striper – someone who volunteers at the hospital in hopes of making medicine her career.

She came up to me. She had blonde hair, freckles and very blue eyes. She took my arm. "I'm going to raise it to ninety degrees," she said.

Wait a minute, I started to say but she already had my arm at ninety. "This may hurt." She grasped my biceps hard in both hands and with a nasty twist wrenched it back into the socket.

I sat, almost knocked out by the pain. She looked down at me. "You need to stop doing this."

"Doing what?"

"Dislocating the damn thing." She turned to the orthopedists. "You have to give it that twist," she said, "as the head of the humerus meets the coracoid process. Usually with multiple dislocations like this guy, the humerus is abraded and will slip back out again."

I sat on the edge of the bed like I'd been visited by angels. Anne came up and gave me a gentle smack upside the head. "Get your eyes off her ass."

"Who the Hell *is* she?"

"She's the new trauma surgeon. Only been here a week."

They wanted to give me a room for the rest of the night but I demurred. A cindery dawn was paling across the eastern rooftops when Anne and I got home and fed Stranger, who was as usual annoyed at our erratic hours. We tumbled naked on the bed wanting to make love but fell asleep first, holding each other.

For the first time since I'd met her, Anne was safe. Julie and

André too. And I had to remember that Mack and Gisèle were alive and free. And Mustafa dead.

But Rachid and his millions of smarmy acolytes were still out there festering. Ready to pay us all back for our sins.

GISÈLE AND MACK were having none of this rescued hostage kid-glove treatment. By the time we got to the clinic the next day they'd tried to check out and Harris had had to intervene with threats of reducing Mack to a mail carrier in rural Nebraska ("God, that sounds wonderful," Mack had said). Before the unmarked car came to take them home, Anne and I sat with them holding hands and fighting back the tears.

They each had their own horror stories from the last two weeks. The day I'd arrived in Paris, barely two weeks ago, I'd gone right away to see Gisèle when she told me on the phone that Mack was gone. But after I'd left her at their apartment she'd gotten a call that DGSE was sending a technician to check her place for bugs. When he rang the bell she checked his badge through the safety eyehole and let him in. Another guy jumped in behind him and they pinned her down, taped her mouth, cuffed her and punched a needle into her that stung horribly for a few instants, then she was out in the universe somewhere, then in a dark room with no window and voices in Arabic through the walls.

At first Mack was there too. They'd tied him to a chair bolted to the floor while she was pinned on a table before him and raped by whoever wanted to. A man would come in and drop his pants and say to Mack, "Tell us who your contact is in Les Andelys and we won't fuck her anymore ... If we keep this up we're going to destroy her cunt ..."

Then Mack was taken away and she was alone, left to lie on the floor at night shivering, trying to stay warm.

They gave her different drugs and brought Mack back. "We are taking you away," said the young man she'd named Evil because of his pitiless eyes above his black keffiyeh. They tied Mack to the table where she'd been raped, and with a quick jerk of a knife Evil cut off Mack's right big toe. Mack gasped, tried not to cry out. "This is what we do to him, piece by piece," Evil said. "If you don't do exactly what we say."

It was then they took her to Melun to withdraw the funds, then to the HLM in Avon which, she had deduced, was to be a new safe house till suddenly they got a call and spirited her away.

We never found Evil.

MACK KNEW MORE than Gisèle. "Yasmina was coming over to us," he said. "I picked her up that morning at St. Lazare train station in Paris. I'd gotten her out of St. Denis and put her with a non-fundamentalist family in that building in Les Andelys, and now I was taking her to DGSE, because I was afraid the Les Andelys place was blown. But nobody knew this; I didn't tell Harris or anyone at DGSE because I knew we had a leak somewhere, and that she might be killed if anyone found out where she was."

"What was her link to Mustafa? To Rachid?"

"We'll never know. Rachid won't tell us and everyone else is dead. But she'd known about Rachid, of course. And that Mustafa was back."

"How'd she get into all this?"

"That?" Mack pursed his lips. "I don't know much, but she'd come from Reims, her parents moved to Seine St. Denis six years ago, the father deserted them, got 'married' by the Stains imam to this fourteen-year old girl – younger than Yasmina at the time … She got stuck in a squat with some guys who'd attacked a bank and also had killed some Jews but we couldn't pin anything on them ... That's how I found out about her ... She'd never taken part in any of it. I thought I could turn her."

"Did you?"

"Sort of. Like I said, she didn't like the violence, then the other mass killings by other Islamic groups ... I followed her one day in the Métro, convinced her to take shelter with this family in Les Andelys ... you know the rest."

"Did *she* hit you?"

"Hell no. They surrounded us in the St. Lazare parking lot, had guns on us, hit her then me. That's what I remember."

"That's why her blonde-dyed hair showed up on the back of your seat?"

"What? I didn't know that."

I saw Yasmina clearly in my mind, her pretty, intelligent face, her feminine toughness. It hurt. "Why did she hate us so much?"

"Maybe she realized she'd been compromised and was going to die? Felt we'd betrayed her ... by incompetence, if nothing else." He glanced down. "Which is true –"

"You ever see Mustafa, when you and Gisèle were held? Rachid?"

"Rachid never. Mustafa twice."

"What'd he do?"

"Said he was going to get you too, then we'd go to Hell together."

"Is that why he grabbed you? Because you'd once escaped? Then why Gisèle?"

"I don't know," he said tiredly. "To make me more cooperative? No. Maybe he was afraid I'd told her something."

"And the Airbus, the backpack nuke?"

"Never mentioned them."

My mind foundered in it. Had Mustafa feared Mack was closing in on him? That Yasmina might know too much?

Or was it someone on the political side, in the government? Like the insiders who alerted Gisèle's captors that we were descending on them in Avon? Who'd nailed the Mack/Yasmina hookup at Gare St. Lazare? And maybe even the hit on Anne that killed the Romanian girl. And Bruno's murder?

If so, was it a message to Thierry? *Keep your soldier's hands out of this. Think of your future. Your family. The truth doesn't matter – get over it. Either join the future or die with the past.*

It would take time to pick up the pieces. One by one, in stupid, repetitive, mind-numbing detail.

Why Anne and I had been led on such a merry car chase by Abdel and the other three, we learned it had been indeed a dry run, to measure the shortest time from St. Denis to the Tower.

Mustafa was dead and thus difficult to interrogate, but we decided he'd been on a training run with the backpack when I'd followed him and his buddy through the forest to meet with Rachid. Maybe if they'd had a backpack nuke, Fontainebleau was where they'd have hid it. And maybe if we dragged Rachid back in we could learn more. Though the chances were slim.

IT HAD BEEN Rachid's voice I'd heard on the phone in the St. Denis warehouse, talking with Abdel and the other guy I'd shot, who turned out to be one of the ones Anne and I had chased in the Beast during the crazy late-night race to the Eiffel Tower. It took Tomàs no time to line up the phone calls; Rachid had stupidly used one of the phones we'd already traced.

When GIGN rooted him out of bed at 4 a.m. Rachid had been furious and profane; as a leader of moderate Muslims in France he was being victimized by France's Islamophobic government. By eleven that morning, when Anne and I crawled out of bed after a refreshing three-hour nap, he had already lined up four celebrity lawyers, all who'd offered to take his case for free.

By noon a "Justice for Rachid Raqmi Committee" had been

formed, led by several media darlings and representatives from the literary elite, as well as the usual gaggle of Socialists, anarchists, anti-Semites, university types, other "progressive" Islamic leaders and imams. Including, of course, Élysée Pétain and her fourth husband, the Senator Honoré de Montgonad.

When Élysée was asked by a courageous journalist if she thought there was any possible truth to the charges brought against Rachid, she huffed that the whole thing was a poorly organized campaign of false attacks and racist smearing by the Islamophobic police.

"It's going to be hard to prosecute him," Thierry said. "His lawyers will challenge everything ..."

"But he was on the phone with Abdel telling him to kill Mack. We heard it. He may have ordered the murder of Bruno, he'd been the brains behind Mustafa's attack on the Tower, all this other stuff ..."

"Tell it to the gods."

BY 18:00 RACHID had been released and had addressed a cheering crowd denouncing "French police fascism and criminal acts against Muslims" and various other atrocities. Filmed live by Élysée herself.

According to the government, Mustafa had never shown up in France, and it was to be announced weeks later that he'd died in one of the last ISIS battles in Syria. After I'd killed him in the elevator car and the GIGN guy had shut down the transponder, we stopped at the second floor where his body was removed.

As for the guy I'd shot on the Tower, the police had tried to save a mentally ill man who had climbed to beneath the first floor then leaped off. So far he had not been identified. None of us had ever seen him.

He'd been a very good climber, fast and fearless, physically and emotionally very strong. In a way it almost made me feel connected – not only because I'd killed him, but because he was a little bit like me.

One more of many things I didn't want to think about.

There was a feverish fuss in the media that Rachid never would have been arrested if he hadn't been a Muslim and a public figure for moderate Islam. Donations to his legal fund tripled as did condemnations of police fascism and racism.

As Tomàs had once said, "You have to see it as comedy. Or you go crazy."

Soon, though, I'd come back for Rachid. I knew just the swamp in Fontainebleau Forest to put him in. Though I'd have to watch out for the skunk.

THREE WOMEN AGAIN

"YOU'RE PISSED OFF, I know," Harris said. "You're exhausted and you've been through Hell and come out the other side saving two of the best people on this planet and killing the worst one. And saving the Tower and a plane full of people, by the way. But it should only take you a day or two to get over that."

I breathed out slowly. Even the tiger can smell the pit. "Where Anne and I are going, I'll send you pix."

"She's going to want to come back." His voice grew softer, confiding. "To hunt the men who killed her husband ... I expect you'll help her find them. And I expect you might find out if those men had a link with Rachid Raqmi."

"Do you think that?" I had to ask.

"Who's to know? There's so many S-List terrorists in France ... Though we all know the real number of potential terrorists is at least *twice* that ... They're dispersed, there's no head of the Hydra, they're not all connected – how do you find the top?"

"You saying it's insoluble?"

He sighed, looked out his window. "That's what Cazeneuve

says." Cazeneuve was the Minister of the Interior, France's "top cop", who'd recently quit the president's cabinet over frustration with its pro-Islamic approach. "He says we have five, maybe six years before it will completely overwhelm France –"

"Then what?" I had to ask.

"Get a boat and start rowing."

"For England?" I laughed. "A Muslim mayor in London? Thousands of mosques sprouting up everywhere? They're already fucked."

"For the other side of the pond."

I almost laughed again. "Rachid isn't the top."

"The French don't even know where the top is. How can you cut off a head" – he raised his hands – "if you can't find it?"

This was too much theory. "So what do *you* want?"

"Remember the shit you gave me that we don't have a good network in France?"

"You don't."

"When you come back, why not do it? For our country? Build me a network I can rely on. Good people, brave, tough ... You know the kind."

"Not without the French."

"Huh?"

"I don't do anything behind their back. And make sure they stay straight with us."

"Of course, of course. That's in the fabric of the thing ..." He gave me a conspiratorial grin, or as close as he could fake it. "I was wrong, early on, thinking there was no link between Mustafa and the grab of Mack and Gisèle ... If we'd had better folks on the street, maybe I would've known?"

I smiled, thinking of the climb I was going to do up Mount Pélé in Martinique with Julie and André. This huge green volcano in hailing rain. Because it always rains up there. How to climb it, one muddy and wind-ripped step at a time.

Easier than dealing with Harris.

I had tried to forgive him for sending me to Leavenworth but couldn't. His argument that my crime was killing the Afghani girl's husband didn't hold water: the husband had burned her alive and deserved to die. And if it hadn't been for that brilliant West Point grad who got me out, I'd be in Leavenworth still.

But Harris was my country, that I loved and had risked my life for so many years. And he was trying, like Thierry, Tomàs, Anne, and thousands of others, to defend our way of life from what the Czech Prime Minister had recently termed "an anti-civilization that stretches from North Africa to Indonesia, the greatest danger in modern times." How could I not want to keep fighting that?

"What were you going to tell me," I said, "that DGSE didn't know?"

"Ah." He leaned back, hands clasped behind his head. "They don't know who's screwing them over ..."

"Thierry knows. He just won't say."

"He won't say because he doesn't want to lose his job or his life, or his loved ones."

"Who is it?"

"Tell him to look at the previous president's cabinet. Politics, whether in the US or France, is based on compromise. There are people who were in power before but who still have direct influence on DGSE and top levels of government. There's more than one. Let Thierry find them. It will be good for France."

When I met with Thierry an hour later I told him what Harris had said. "The previous governments?" He smiled. "Which one? Just like before World War Two, there were lots of top politicians openly working with the Germans, people who then became leaders in Vichy and sent seventy-five thousand Jews to their deaths. It does no good to name them."

"Then you know?"

He shrugged. "Stay tuned."

MITCHELL OF COURSE was elated that we'd rescued Mack and Gisèle. "Don't ever forget what you accomplished," he said. "That your sticking with it was what saved them."

"We *all* stuck with it," I answered. "Anne, Thierry, you, all of us. We never gave up."

He exhaled quietly, and I knew he was wishing he'd been here to help. "This Anne," he said, "what can she possibly see in you?"

"Beats me."

"Beats me too ..."

Mack and Gisèle were back in their lovely house in the Sixteenth when Anne and I visited, Mack in the living room with his damaged foot up on the edge of the couch. "I'm going nuts with this," he complained. "The docs won't let me go back to work, and I want to tie up loose ends with these bastards."

"Rachid's been released," I said.

"I heard."

I told Mack about my plan for Rachid in the Fontainebleau swamp. "We'll get him," he grunted. "We always do."

"Nearly always," I said.

"Yeah. Nearly always."

"So why," I said, "did Yasmina come over to us?"

He looked out the window and the blazing green leaves of the plane trees. At the bucolic blue sky. He nodded, as if deciding something inside himself. "All the recent terrorist attacks, they shocked her. To kill so many innocent people – this was a *religious* act? What the Koran said, that unbelievers will go to Hell – what if it *wasn't* true? The last straw in her slow divorce from Islam. She reread the Koran, realized most of it's about killing people. Asked herself questions, breaking herself free. It's hard, you know, when you've been so ... indoctrinated?"

I saw where his head was going. "Don't you dare blame yourself she's dead."

He gave me that steely black look. "More this shit comes down, more I can't figure out why ..."

"It's our fate." I shrugged. "Fuck it, can't change it."

He looked out the window at the new leaves scintillating in the spring wind, turned back to me, and grinned. "Why would we?"

Gisèle brought us Côtes de Provence rosé, crackers and Rocamadour, and for a few moments we sat quietly as if none of this had ever happened.

"How are you?" Anne said, breaking the silence. "Really?"

"We're so lucky to be alive," Gisèle answered. "Strange, but that's mostly what I think of."

"She goes for a hike every day," Mac said. "Bois de Boulogne. Wants to get back to the clinic."

"Doctors say next week."

"She says there's too many hurting people out there," Mack grunted. "That she can't take more time off ..."

"Oh Mack," she scoffed. "You make me sound like a fake."

I smiled at them, at Anne. The world seemed split between the majority who work hard and care for others, and the minority who don't.

I wouldn't want to be in their camp.

ANNE AND I had reserved two bungalows on Martinique's east shore, one with three beds for Mamie and the kids, the other for Anne and me. Each dawn to go barefooting soft green lawns down to the glass-clear sea to swim out into the sunrise. The world's best Caribbean cuisine with rum so good it makes the gods weep. Vertical emerald mountains and an ocean brighter than light.

The surf in Martinique's lousy in some places – go to Le

Grand Macabou if you want fabulous, dangerous surf – but what joy to ride a windsurfer beyond the break and cavort in soaring, spinning flights across huge white-flecked crests and howling winds.

BEFORE WE LEFT PARIS I had a long talk with Stranger. Explained the virtues of retirement, that he'd paid his dues and didn't have to be a roof cat anymore. That he could live out his golden years in rural Normandy with Cousine Claudine. Be a house cat, a barn cat, whatever he chose.

"When you getting back from Martinique?" I thought I heard him say.

"Couple weeks."

He gave a quick glance around the apartment. "With the kids and Mamie you can't possibly live here."

"We found a dynamite place in the Seventh," I said. "A whole new set of roofs, older, not so steep. Lots of rats and pigeons."

He winked a yellow eye. "I'll hang out here for two weeks. There's a new hatch of mice in a building down the street. When you return come get me."

THE FIRST NIGHT in Martinique Anne and I were too weary to sleep, tossing on our big bed in the cool breeze, the soft waves susurrating against the velvet sand beyond the window. The moon threw silvery stripes across our naked flesh. I felt completeness, almost free, all spent, all action done, danger quelled, enemies dead.

"It's not so easy, for these Muslim guys," I said. "Can you imagine life with several different women telling you what to do?"

"You try that," Anne whispered, her hand down my ribs, "and see what happens."

"I'll have three. If I live with you."

"*You* would have another woman?" She dug her nails into my ribs. "*Two* other women?"

"Of course."

She readied for the kill. "You *think?*"

"Of course," I repeated. "*You* first of all. And then Mamie and Julie. Between the three of you, I don't stand a chance."

"For once in your life." She caressed my shoulder, snuggled against me and fell asleep.

I LAY THERE THINKING of what had happened and what it was really about. We had won, saved the Eiffel Tower and a plane full of people. Dr. Death was cooling his heels in a French cell till his Iranian masters traded the French some oil to let him out. Mustafa was dead, and others in Rachid's evil clan were either dead or headed for whatever minimal jail terms the French courts might give them.

But a much bigger villain, Rachid Raqmi, had walked away for now, even stronger than before. More beloved by his coterie, more praised by the media.

And he was not the only one. Islam's attack on the west had many perpetrators, not linked but separate. Like the ones who'd killed Anne's husband – how were she and I going to find them? In addition to the 22,000 known terrorists in France, how many others that hadn't been identified? We could cut off one head but that wouldn't harm the many others.

The war with Islam would go on, perhaps Islam would win. We were naïve and lazy, and believed ourselves to be good-intentioned. And they were smart, very driven, and ruthless.

It would be lovely for all of us to coexist. No religion should attempt domination but most do. And religious domination is the end of freedom. The end of human progress and evolution. The end of the individual.

If there's a solution it's love. The best of all possible worlds.

THE NEXT MORNING Anne and I swam out beyond the coral sands brilliant in rising sun, past myriad fish flashing and exploding round us, past a sleepy tarpon lazing across the bottom, out a mile to the edge of the vertical wall where the sandy bottom thirty feet below comes to a cliff that drops straight into the depths.

I dove maybe forty or fifty feet till the surface above was hazy pale green like an old glass float. The cliff wall was thick with coral and vegetation and alive with fish of all colors and sizes darting and feeding and looking for love. Drifting down there I thought of the great wave in Tahiti less than three weeks ago that had nearly killed me, that maybe I'd been saved so I could help save Mack and Gisèle. And meet Anne.

I rose slowly to the surface, clasped her close then sank to kiss her between the thighs till she tugged off her bikini bottom and we made love in the warm dawn with golden sands below us on one side and the dark abyss on the other.

THE END

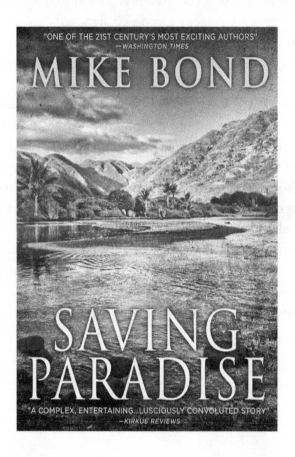

"ONE OF THE 21ST CENTURY'S MOST EXCITING AUTHORS"
—*WASHINGTON TIMES*

MIKE BOND

SAVING PARADISE

"A COMPLEX, ENTERTAINING...LUSCIOUSLY CONVOLUTED STORY"
—*KIRKUS REVIEWS*

SAVING PARADISE

When Special Forces veteran and Hawaiian surfer Pono Hawkins finds a beautiful journalist drowned off Waikiki he is quickly caught in a web of murder and political corruption. Trying to track down her killers, he soon finds them hunting him, and blamed for her death. A relentless thriller of politics, sex, lies, and remorseless murder, *Saving Paradise* is "an action-packed, must read novel ... taking readers behind the alluring façade of Hawaii's pristine beaches and tourist traps into a festering underworld of murder, intrigue and corruption." – *Washington Times*

EXCERPT FROM *SAVING PARADISE*

LOVELY, COLD AND DEAD

IT WAS ANOTHER MAGNIFICENT DAWN on Oahu, the sea soft and rumpled and the sun blazing up from the horizon, an offshore breeze scattering plumeria fragrance across the frothy waves. Flying fish darting over the crests, dolphins chasing them, a mother whale and calf spouting as they rolled northwards. A morning when you already know the waves will be good and it will be a day to remember.

I waded out with my surfboard looking for the best entry and she bumped my knee. A woman long and slim in near-transparent red underwear, face down in the surf. Her features sharp and beautiful, her short chestnut hair plastered to her cold skull.

I dropped my board and held her in my arms, stunned by her beauty and death. If I could keep holding her maybe she wouldn't really be dead. I was already caught by her high cheekbones and thin purposeful lips, the subtle arch of her brow, her long slender neck in my hands. And so overwhelmed I would have died to protect her.

When I carried her ashore her long legs dragged in the surf as if the ocean didn't want to let her go, this sylphlike mermaid beauty. Sorrow overwhelmed me – how could I get her back, this lovely person?

Already cars were racing up and down Ala Moana Boulevard.

When you're holding a corpse in your arms how bizarre seems the human race – where were all these people hurrying to in this horrible moment with this beautiful young woman dead?

I did the usual. Being known to the Honolulu cops I had to call them. I'd done time and didn't want to do more. Don't believe for a second what anyone tells you – being Inside is a *huge* disincentive. Jail tattoos not just your skin; it nails your soul. No matter what you do, no matter what you want, you don't want to go back there. Not ever.

So Benny Olivera shows up with his flashers flashing. If you want a sorry cop Benny will fill your bill. Damn cruiser the size of a humpback whale with lights going on and off all over the place, could've been a nuclear reaction – by the way, why would anyone want a family that's *nuclear?* Life's dangerous enough.

I explain Benny what happened. He's hapa pilipino – half Filipino – and doesn't completely trust us hapa haoles, part white and part Hawaiian. To a kanaka maoli, a native Hawaiian, or to someone whose ancestors were indentured here like the Japanese or in Benny's case Filipinos, there's still mistrust. Didn't the haoles steal the whole archipelago for a handful of beads?

Didn't they bring diseases that cut the Hawaiian population by ninety percent? And then shipped hundreds of the survivors to leprosy colonies on Molokai? While descendants of the original missionaries took over most of the land and became huge corporations that turned the Hawaiians, Filipinos, Japanese and others into serfs? These corporations that now own most of Hawaii, its mainline media, banks and politicians?

I'm holding this lissome young woman cold as a fish in my arms and Benny says lie her down on the hard sidewalk and the ambulance comes – more flashing lights – and she's gone under a yellow tarp and I never saw her again.

Couldn't surf. Went home and brewed a triple espresso and my heart was down in my feet. Sat on the lanai and tried to figure out life and death and what had happened to this beautiful woman. Mojo the dachshund huffed up on the chair beside me, annoyed I hadn't taken him surfing. Puma the cat curled on my lap but I didn't scratch her so she went and sat in the sun.

I'd seen plenty of death but this one got to me. She'd been young, pretty and athletic. Somehow the strong classic lines of her face denoted brains, determination and hard work. How did she end up drowned in Kewalo Basin?

Benny's bosses at the cop shop would no doubt soon provide the answer.

AS MENTIONED, I've seen lots of dead people. A tour or two in Afghanistan will do that for you. I sat there with my feet up on the bamboo table and tried to forget all this. Mojo kept whining at the door wanting to hit the beach but I didn't. Once the sun moved past her spot Puma jumped back in my lap and began kneading her claws into my stomach.

By afternoon the surf was looking good, and when you're under that thunderous curl you don't even think about Afghanistan. Or about Sylvia Gordon, age 27, KPOI reported, a journalist for *The Honolulu Post,* dead in the surf this morning near Ala Moana Beach.

But I had a raunchy feeling in my stomach like when you eat bad sushi so I quit surfing and went down to the cop shop on South Beretania to see Benny and his friends. Benny was out cruising in his nuclear Chrysler but Leon Oversdorf (I *swear* that's his name), Second Lieutenant Homicide, wanted to see me.

"Look, Lieutenant," I said, "I been cool. I don't drink or smoke weed or indulge in premarital sex or habituate shady premises –"

"So how the fuck you find her?" Leon says by way of opening.

I explained him. How it happened. All the time he's looking at me under these gargantuan eyebrows and I can tell no matter what I say he won't believe me. Just because I been Inside. I could tell him Calvin Coolidge is president and even then he wouldn't believe me.

"So she drowned," I said after a while, looking to leave.

Leon watched me with his tiny sad eyes. Him that helped put me Inside. "No," he said.

And what he said next changed my life. "She *was* drowned."

"I didn't do it," I said right away.

Leon leaned forward, meaty palms on his desk. "Pono," he chuckled, "you think we don't *know* that?"

"Know what?" I said, covering my bases.

"She was dead six hours before of when you found her."

The thought pained me horribly. This lovely person floating in the cold uncaring sea. When I could've held her, kept her warm.

"She was dead," Leon said matter-of-factly, "from being held underwater till her lungs filled up with good old H_2O."

"How do you know she was held?" I risked. "Even if she just normally drowned there'd be water in her lungs –"

Leon scanned me the way the guy with the broadaxe smiles down at you when you lay your head on the block. "This water in her lungs ain't ocean, it's fresh."

"Fresh?"

"Like from a swimming pool or something. You get it?"

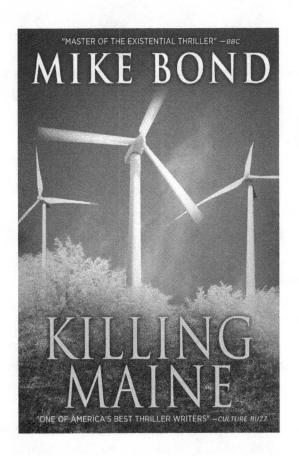

K I L L I N G   M A I N E

First Prize, New England Book Festival, 2016: Surfer and Special Forces veteran Pono Hawkins leaves Hawaii for Maine's brutal winter to help a former comrade falsely accused of murder. Pono learns first-hand about Maine's rampant political corruption, seeing huge energy companies pillage the State's magnificent mountains and purchase its politicians at bargain prices. Pono is hunted, shot at, betrayed, and stalked by knife-wielding assassins as he tries to find the real murderer. Nothing is certain, no one can be trusted, no place is safe, while Pono is the target of every cop in several states.

Second in the Pono Hawkins series after the critically-acclaimed bestseller *Saving Paradise*, *Killing Maine* is an insider's view of Maine politics and industrial crime, the state's magical and fast-disappearing natural beauty, how a lone commando hunts down those who hunt him against overwhelming odds.

EXCERPT FROM *KILLING MAINE*

DEAD OF WINTER

A COYOTE BARKED downhill. As I stopped to listen a bullet cracked past my ear and smacked into the maple tree beside me. I dove off the trail skidding down the icy slope toward the cliff. *Whack* another bullet smashed into a trunk as I tumbled past, couldn't stop sliding, couldn't pull off my snowshoes, the cliff edge coming up fast as a shot whistled past my eyes, another by my neck.

My head hit a boulder and I spun jamming a snowshoe in brush. Another bullet spat past my ear and splintered a root. I tore loose from both snowshoes and leaped off the cliff down into a cluster of young hemlocks and deep drifts and came up gasping for air, bleeding and alive.

The shooter was above the cliff I'd just fallen off and had no angle of fire till I moved away from the bottom of the cliff. Unless he descended to the clifftop. Then he could shoot straight down on me.

I was going to die. The cliff of snow-dusted raw ice and stone seemed weirdly primeval, as if I'd been here before. Below me descended the bouldery rubble of what had once been part of this cliff, with another cliff below that, and all down the slope tall frozen hardwoods where if you got pinned down you were safe till the shooter got your angle and then there were not enough trees to protect you.

I'd lost my right boot pulling out of its snowshoe. The sock, ragged and soaked, left a smear of blood on the snow. Was that footsteps near the clifftop, crunching crust? I was breathing so hard I couldn't tell. If I ran and he was already there he'd shoot me easily in the back.

There was a terrible pain in my left hand. I stared at it stupefied. The ring finger was splayed ninety degrees sideways, dislocated. Once I saw it, it began to really hurt.

Trying to catch my breath and listening for the shooter, I pulled the finger straight but it would not drop back into the joint.

A shadow fell high up across a birch trunk: my shooter was above the cliff.

Like a wounded deer I darted downhill, running and dodging between tree trunks, slipping, skidding and tumbling ahead of the shots. The rifle sound so terrifying, the loud *crack* that crushes your ears, the physical *whack* of it, and if that bullet didn't get you the next one will.

He stopped firing, maybe couldn't see me through the trees. I slid, stumbled and ran a half mile further down the slope then circled back uphill above my trail, found a blowdown oak and broke off a hard limb like a baseball bat. I climbed higher and hid above my trail in a hemlock clump where I could see uphill but not be seen. If he followed my trail down the steep slope I had a chance of getting him with my oak limb as he walked past and before he could raise his gun.

My foot was freezing and very painful as was the dislocated finger. The pain was making me lightheaded, likely to make mistakes. I couldn't move till dark, when I'd be harder to see and harder to shoot. Though I didn't think my foot could wait that long without turning to ice.

And I still didn't know where the shooter was.

Then came the snarl of a snowmobile on the ridge. Maybe it was him, leaving.

Or someone else going while he waited in the gathering dusk for me to return for my snowshoes and boot.

I sat cross-legged in the powdery snow watching my upslope trail, clasping my cold sodden foot, trying to set my finger back in its joint, shuddering, teeth clattering. The sun had quit the ridge and a deeper cold was sifting downhill. It was maybe minus twenty-five but going to get much colder. If I stayed out all night the shooter wouldn't need to come back.

When facing death you sometimes get flashes of awareness, tragic epiphanies of what led to this fatal moment. As you gasp for breath and duck side to side running and falling and dashing on, expecting a bullet to smash your chest, you know how easy it would have been to avoid this.

It didn't matter that three days ago I'd been surfing in sunny Hawaii. And now to help a buddy I couldn't stand but to whom I owed my life, I was freezing to death in somebody's gunsights on a snow-deep mountain in the backwoods of Maine.

MIKE BOND

A critically acclaimed poet, best-selling novelist, ecologist, and war and human rights journalist, Mike Bond has worked in many dangerous and war-torn regions of the world. Based on his own experiences, his novels portray the innate hunger of the human heart for good, the intense joys of love, the terror and fury of battle, the sinister conspiracies of dictators, corporations and politicians, and the beauty of the vanishing natural world.

CPSIA information can be obtained
at www.ICGtesting.com
Printed in the USA
BVHW041204160723
667310BV00004B/16